BY VICTORIA HOLT

Daughter of Deceit
Snare of Serpents
The Captive
The India Fan
The Silk Vendetta
Secret for a Nightingale
The Road to Paradise Island
The Landower Legacy
The Time of the Hunter's Moon
The Demon Lover
The Judas Kiss
The Mask of the Enchantress
The Spring of the Tiger
My Enemy the Queen
The Devil on Horseback
The Pride of the Peacock
Lord of the Far Island
The House of a Thousand Lanterns
The Curse of the Kings
On the Night of the Seventh Moon
The Shadow of the Lynx
The Secret Woman
The Shivering Sands
The Queen's Confession
The King of the Castle
Menfreya in the Morning
The Legend of the Seventh Virgin
Bride of Pendorric
Kirkland Revels
Mistress of Mellyn

DAUGHTER OF DECEIT

DAUGHTER *of* DECEIT

Victoria Holt

DOUBLEDAY
LARGE PRINT EDITION

New York London Toronto Sydney Auckland

PUBLISHED BY DOUBLEDAY
a division of Bantam Doubleday Dell Publishing Group, Inc.
666 Fifth Avenue, New York, New York 10103

DOUBLEDAY and the portrayal of an anchor with a dolphin
are trademarks of Doubleday,
a division of Bantam Doubleday Dell Publishing Group, Inc.

Book Design by Liney Li

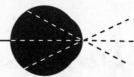

**This Large Print Book carries the
Seal of Approval of N.A.V.H.**

CIP Data applied for

ISBN 0-385-41965-1

Printed in the United States of America

September 1991

Large Print Edition

Contents

LONDON

Désirée

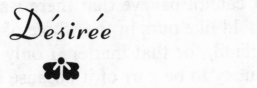

I often wonder how different my life might have been if Lisa Fennell had not made her dramatic entry into it; and I marvel that if people had not been in a certain place at the same moment they might never have been aware of each other's existence and their lives would have taken an entirely different course.

. . .

I cannot believe that there was another household like ours in the whole of London—or England, for that matter. I only knew that I was lucky to be part of it because it was dominated by the lighthearted, wildly unconventional, inimitable and altogether adorable Désirée.

At that time social status was held to be of the greatest importance in all classes of society and protocol in the servants' quarters was as rigidly adhered to as it ever was in higher circles. Not so by Désirée. Carrie, the tweeny, was given the same treatment as Mrs. Crimp, the housekeeper. Not always with Mrs. Crimp's approval. But Désirée ignored that.

"Hello, Carrie, how goes it with you today, love?" she would ask when she met Carrie about the house. Everyone was "love" or "dear" to Désirée. Carrie would squirm with delight.

"I'm all right, Miss Daisy Ray," she would say. "And how's yourself?"

"Bearing up. Bearing up," Désirée would say with a grin; and if she was aware of Mrs. Crimp's disapproving look, she gave no sign.

Everyone in the household loved Désirée—apart from two of the governesses who had come when I was five years old to teach me the rudiments of education. One left after a few months, because there were always late-night comings and goings to and from the house and she needed her rest; the other went off to teach an earl's daughter, which was more suited to what she had been brought up to expect.

But most people, once they had accepted that this household was like no other, succumbed to Désirée's charm—Martha Gee with a sort of exasperated tenderness; Mrs. Crimp with a few tut-tuts and a certain twist of the lips and a muttered "What next? I wonder"; Jane, the parlourmaid, with the utmost eagerness, because in her dreams she hoped to be another Désirée; and Carrie with unadulterated delight, because she had never known anyone who made her feel important before; while Thomas, the coachman, was loyally devoted, in the belief that anyone as famous as Désirée might act a little strangely if she felt like it.

As for myself, she was the very centre of my life.

I remember one occasion when I was about four years old. It was night and I awoke, probably aroused by the sounds of laughter coming from below. I sat up in bed listening. The door which connected my room with the nanny's was kept open. I crept to it, saw that she was sleeping deeply, put on my dressing gown and slippers, and descended the staircase. The laughter was coming from the drawing room. I reached it and stood outside listening.

Then I turned the handle and looked in.

Désirée, in a long flowing gown of lavender-coloured silk, was seated on the sofa; her golden hair was piled high on her head; there was a black velvet band round it in which stones glittered. Every time I saw her I was struck by her beauty. She was like the heroine of one of the fairy stories which I loved, but chiefly I thought of her as Cinderella after she had gone to the ball and found her prince—only Désirée had found several.

A man sat on either side of her and another was standing up, leaning over her, laughing. Their black jackets and white shirtfronts made a pleasant contrast to the lavender silk. They were silent as I entered and they all looked at me. It was like a tableau.

"Is this a party?" I asked, implying that if it was I wanted to be part of it.

Désirée held out her arms and I ran into her sweet-smelling embrace.

She presented me to the company. I had become aware by this time that there were others in the room besides the three men and herself.

She said: "This is my treasure, Noelle, because she was born on Christmas Day—the best Christmas present I ever had."

I had already heard it. She had told me: "You were born on Christmas Day, so you were called Noelle, which means birthday . . . Christmas birthday." She added that I was specially honoured because I shared my birthday with Jesus.

What concerned me at the moment was that it was a party and I had joined it.

I remember sitting on Désirée's lap while she, with mock seriousness, introduced me to certain members of the company.

"This is Charlie Claverham, and this is Monsieur Robert Bouchère . . . and this is Dolly."

They were the three I had noticed gathered about her when I entered the room. I studied them—in particular Dolly, because it seemed such a strange name for a man to have. He was rather square in shape, with fair whiskers—slightly gingerish—and a strong aroma which, when I became experienced in such matters, I recognized as a mingling of expensive cigars and whisky. I also learned that he was Donald Dollington, actor-manager, known irreverently in theatrical circles as Dolly.

They all made much of me, asking questions and seeming amused at the answers, which made me feel that it was a wonderful party until I fell asleep and was vaguely aware that Désirée was carrying me back to my bed. I remember being disappointed when I woke up next morning to find that the party was over.

•

The house was near Drury Lane, handy for the theatre, which was essential. It seemed enormous to me when I was very young—an exciting place with stairs leading down to the basement and then from the ground floor up to the fourth. There was always something exciting to be seen from the nursery windows, over which Désirée had had bars put, lest I fall out.

There were people selling things from wheelbarrows or from trays on straps round their necks—hot pies, lavender, fruit, flowers, pins and ribbons; then there were carriages and hackney cabs taking people to and from the theatres. I loved to watch them.

When I was six years old, Miss Mathilda Grey came to teach me. This was after the other two governesses had left to find more suitable employment. She must have been a little bewildered when she first came, and might have gone the way of the other two but for the fact that she wanted to become an actress. "Not like your mother," she pointed out. "Not just singing and dancing in light comedies, but a real actress."

I studied Mathilda Grey. She had scarcely the physique for a dancer. My mother was rather tall and she had what they called an hourglass figure. Miss Grey was short and dumpy and all she could manage to do was warble a little out of tune. But Lady Macbeth and Portia were not called upon to sing and dance. However, her ambitions, misguided though they might have been, prompted her to stay in a post which brought her a little nearer

to the theatrical world than she could otherwise have hoped for.

But after a while she became reconciled
and, I think, enjoyed being part of the household.

The most important one was Martha Gee,
my mother's dresser—but more than that; and
she took charge of us all as well as of my
mother. She was a large woman with keen dark
eyes which missed little and brown hair drawn
severely back into a large knob; she was always
dressed in black. She was fond of reminding us
that, having been born within the sound of Bow
Bells, she was without doubt a cockney. She
was sharp, shrewd, taking, as she said, "nothing from nobody" and always "giving as good
as she got . . . and a little bit more."

She had known my mother when she had
been a member of the chorus, and if Martha
Gee could not spot talent when she saw it, she
did not know who could. She had decided to
take my mother under her wing and guide her
where she should go; and it seemed that this
was exactly what she had done. Martha was
about forty years of age. She knew her way
around and had seen a bit of life. She told us
often that she belonged to the theatre and knew
all the tricks that some of them got up to,
which offers to be wary of and which you
seized with both hands. She bullied my mother
as she did all of us, but she made us feel that it

was for our own good and that Martha knew best. She treated my mother as though she were a wayward child. My mother liked it and used to say, "What would I do without Martha?"

Another one she could not have done without was Dolly. He was a frequent visitor to our house.

It was a very extraordinary childhood. There was nothing normal about it. There was always something exciting going on, and I was never shut out of it. When I saw other children walking sedately in the park with their nannies, I felt very sorry for them. Their lives were very different from mine. They were just children to be seen and not heard. I was a member of the most exciting family that ever was. My mother was the famous Désirée, whom people looked at when we went out together; and some came up and said how much they had enjoyed her in some play, and they produced programmes for her to sign. She always smiled and chatted with them and they were overcome with wonder, while I would stand by, smirking with pride because I shared her glory.

I used to keep awake so that I could hear her come in. If she and Martha were alone I used to go down and join them. They would sit in the kitchen and eat sandwiches, or drink ale or hot milk as the fancy took them, and there was a lot of laughter about some mishap on the stage, or the old gentleman in the audience who, as Martha would say, "took a shine to your ladyship!"

Mathilda Grey did not approve of my joining them but shrugged her shoulders and accepted it; it was one of the milestones on the road to becoming Lady Macbeth.

Sometimes my mother would be very late, and then I knew it was no use waiting. She would be having supper with Charlie Claverham or Monsieur Robert Bouchère or some other admirer. I was disappointed at such times, because that would mean she would sleep late the next morning and I would have very little time with her before she left for the theatre.

Dolly was a frequent visitor to the house and there would be long conferences. He and my mother quarrelled a lot, which used to frighten me at first, until I learned that they were not serious quarrels.

They called each other abusive names, which might have been alarming if I had not heard it all before. Sometimes Dolly marched out of the drawing room, slamming the door and striding out of the house.

We would be in the kitchen, listening. We could hardly help hearing had we wanted not to—which, of course, we did not.

"Sounds bad this time," Mrs. Crimp would say. "But he'll be back, mark my words."

And she was always right. He would come

back. There would be a reconciliation and we would hear my mother's strong clear voice trying out some song in the new musical comedy he had found for her. There would be frequent visits, more songs to be sung, perhaps a few arguments on the way, but nothing vital. Then there would be rehearsals and more arguments and finally the dress rehearsal and the first night.

Mrs. Crimp revelled in it. She was highly critical of much, but then one of her greatest pleasures was criticizing everyone who did not conform to her ways. There was my mother's name, for instance. "Désirée!" she announced derisively. "What a name to go to bed with!" Jane said she reckoned there were some . . . and more than one . . . who didn't mind going to bed with such a name.

"That's not the sort of talk I'll have in my kitchen," said Mrs. Crimp severely. "And particularly . . ." followed by a significant nod in my direction.

I knew, of course, to what they referred. I did not mind. Everything my mother did was perfect in my eyes, and it was not her fault that so many people fell in love with her.

Mrs. Crimp had a way with names. She pronounced them as, in her opinion, they ought to be pronounced. My mother was "Daisy Ray," and Robert Bouchère, the elegant

Frenchman who was such a frequent visitor, was "Monsewer Robber."

I myself was a little puzzled about my mother's name until I asked her and she explained it to me.

"Désirée is my stage name," she said. "It wasn't given to me in church or anything like that. I gave it to myself. People have a right to a name of their choice, and if they don't get the one they like to start off with, why shouldn't they change it? Don't you agree, pet?"

I nodded vigorously. I always agreed with everything she said.

"Well, you've got to know one day . . . seeing you're a part of it all . . . so listen, love, and I'll tell you how it all came about."

We were lying on her bed. She was wearing a pale blue negligee. I was fully dressed, for it was half past ten in the morning. I had been up for several hours; she had not yet risen. It was at this time of day when she was most communicative. I think it was because she was not entirely awake.

"What's your real name?" I asked.

"Can you keep a secret?"

"Oh yes," I assured her with delight. "I love secrets."

"Well, it was Daisy. Mrs. Crimp hit on the right one as far as the Daisy is concerned. I didn't think it suited me, love. Do I look like a Daisy?"

"Well, you could. It's a nice flower."

She wrinkled her nose. "Daisy Tremaston."

"I think it sounds rather nice, and when people knew it was yours, it would sound even better."

She kissed the tip of my nose. "You say nice things, love. And what's particularly nice about them is that you mean them. No. I thought for the stage I'd need a special name . . . a name that would stick in people's memories. That's important. It's the package that's important. Always remember that. You could be a real genius on the stage . . . you could be a knockout . . . but if the package isn't right, well then, it's going to be a lot harder. I can tell you, love, to get on in my business, you need all you can lay your hands on . . . talent . . . staying power . . . a push here and there in the right direction at the right time by the right people."

"And package?" I reminded her.

"That's it." She laughed with appreciation. That was another of her gifts: she made people feel that their most ordinary remarks were very clever.

"Désirée. It's got something, hasn't it, love? It means 'Desired.' It's a hint to everyone who hears it. Here, this lady is special. Tell them you're desired and they'll be halfway to believing it, and with a bit of talent you're halfway there, and with a bit of luck you can clinch it.

So I was Désirée for the stage and I kept to it.
Well, you have to go all out for it. Otherwise
there's a muddle!"

"So you're not Daisy anymore."

"It's all shut away in the realms of yesterday. That was the title of one of my first songs.
Rather good, eh?" She started to sing. I loved
to hear her sing.

When the song about memories being shut
away in the realms of yesterday was over, I
guided the conversation to where I wanted it to
go.

"Did Dolly help you choose Désirée?"

"Dolly! Not him! He'd be against it. He
thinks it's not quite good class. That's Dolly all
over. I don't always go along with him, though
I must say he has a good eye for spotting the
winner. No. This was before Dolly's day. This
was in my struggling days. I could tell you
some stories."

I nestled down to hear them, but there were
none forthcoming. It was just a figure of
speech. Something happened to her when she
talked of the past. I could feel the shutters coming down in her mind. She did tell me once that
she had begun life in a Cornish village.

"Tell me about Cornwall," I had demanded.

I waited breathlessly, for when I broached
the subject she seemed inclined to talk of something else.

"Oh," she said in rather a dreaming voice. "It wasn't right for me. I used to dream of coming to London even when I was a little one. I liked it when people came to the inn in the village. It was an out-of-the-way place, but now and then someone would come down from the big cities. There was one man from London. I used to get him to talk about the theatres. I knew then that one day I was going to London. I was going to be in the theatre."

She was silent, and I was afraid that she would start to talk of something else.

"It was all shut in," she said slowly. "That's how I felt . . . shut in. All Sunday-go-to-meetings . . . if you know what I mean."

"Yes, yes, I know."

"Too many gossiping old women . . . men, too. There was nothing else to do but look for sin. It was the only excitement they had. You wouldn't believe how much sin they found in that little old village by the moor."

"The moor must have been lovely."

"It was bleak and you should have heard how the wind could blow across those moors. It was lonely . . . no people about. I was tired of all that by the time I was six. And then when I started to know what I wanted, there was no holding me back. I hated the cottage . . . cramped and dark. Prayers morning, noon and night, and church twice on a Sunday. I liked the singing, though. Specially the carols. 'Away in a Manger,' 'Hark! the Herald Angels Sing.' I discovered I had a voice. Gran'fer said I'd have to watch. I was vainglorious. I had to remember all gifts came from God. They were to tempt you to vanity . . . and look out for yourself when Judgement Day came if you gave way to it. It was no credit to you."

It was the first time I had heard of Gran'fer and I wanted to hear more.

"Did he live with you?"

"He'd say I lived with him. They looked after me when my mother died."

I said rather tentatively: "And your father, too?"

I waited uneasily. I sensed that the subject of fathers was one I had to approach cautiously. I had never been able to discover anything about mine except that he was a fine man —a father I could be proud of.

"Oh, he wasn't around," she said lightly. "You should have seen that cottage—windows that let in hardly any light—cob walls—that's a sort of clay. If you've seen one you've seen the lot. Two rooms up, two down. You're lucky, Noelle, to live in a house like this in the heart of London. What wouldn't I have given for that when I was your age!"

"But you got it later."

"Ah yes. I got it, didn't I? And you, my angel, I got you."

"This is better than Gran'fer's old cottage. Why did you call him Gran'fer?"

"It's their way of talking down there. He was always Gran'fer, like all the other grandfathers. That way of talking was no good for the London stage. I can tell you, I had to get away, love. If you'd been there you would have seen why."

It was as though she were making excuses for herself.

"I used to go out to the moor. There were a lot of old stones there . . . prehistoric, they said they were. I used to dance round them and sing at the top of my voice. It sounded wonderful, and there was a lovely feeling of freedom. What I loved at school was singing. It was all hymns and carols. But there were other songs I picked up as well. 'Come to the Fair,' 'Early One Morning' and 'Barbara Allen.' If I heard a new song I had to sing it. How I loved to dance, too! I had to be careful about that. Singing—if it was psalms and carols—was all right, but dancing was wicked . . . unless it was country dancing. When they danced the furry dance, which is an old Cornish dance—a custom, so they couldn't say that was sinful—I'd be in the town dancing all through the day. I loved to dance on the moors, though. Particularly round the stones. In some lights they looked like young girls. The story was they'd been turned to stone. Someone like my

Gran'fer must have seen to that. Dancing on the Sabbath, most likely. They had Sabbaths in those days. Yes, I was always dancing. People said I was pisky-mazed."

"What's that?"

"Piskies are the little people. They get up to all sorts of tricks in that part of the country. They're a sort of fairy . . . not very good ones. They drive people mad and make them do all sorts of odd things. That's what they call being pisky-mazed. I went to the old witch in the woods once. People down there are very superstitious. They believe things you'd never hear of in London. They were always looking out for white hares, which mean something disastrous, of course, and knackers in the mines who did evil deeds to warn those who had offended of worse to come."

"It sounds a fascinating place. I'd love to see it."

"Some places are fascinating to talk of but uncomfortable to be in. There was one thing I had to do. To get away from it."

"Tell me about the witch in the woods."

"She came from a Pillar family. People of Pillar families have special gifts because one of their ancestors once helped a mermaid who was stranded ashore to get back into the sea, and for ever after members of the family had the power to see into the future. There are lots of other wise people down there. There are seventh sons of seventh sons. They can see what's coming. Then there are footlings, which means they were born feet first. And all these people are supposed to pass the gifts bestowed on them down through the family. So there are no shortage of these wiseacres."

"It does sound exciting."

She shrugged that off. "My Pillar told me that I could have a brilliant future. It would be my choice. There were two paths. How it comes back! I can hear her now. 'There be two paths open to 'ee, me dear. Take one and it leads to fame and fortune. Take the other and you'll have a good quiet life . . . but if you do you'll never be at peace. You'll always be telling yourself, that's what I *should* have done.' "

"And you took the road to fame and fortune. Wasn't that marvellous, and how clever of the Pillar to know it."

"Well, love, it wasn't all that profound. There was I, singing and dancing all over the place. Everyone knows what everybody else is doing down there. You can't keep secrets. I expect I talked. 'I'm going to London. I'm going to sing and dance on the stage.' That sort of thing gets round. But that is what she said, and then I knew it had to be."

"What did Gran'fer say when you went away?"

"I wasn't there to hear, love." She laughed. "I just have to imagine. Gone to Satan, I reckon, who was heating up the fires to make my arrival in hell especially hot."

"You're not frightened, are you?"

She burst out laughing. "What, me? Don't you believe it! I reckon we're out here to enjoy ourselves. We're the ones who'll get to heaven, you see . . . not those who go around making people's lives a misery."

"How did you get to London?"

"I got lifts. I worked on the way . . . mostly in inns. I got together a bit of money . . . and there I was, on to the next part of the journey. I was working in a coffee shop not far from here. People used to come in from the theatre. There was one man . . . a regular . . . who took an interest in me. I told him I wanted to go on the stage. He said he would see what he could do. I used to walk round in my spare time and look at the theatres . . . seeing the people's names up there and saying, 'I'll be up there one day.' "

"And you were."

"And I was. Took a bit of time, though. This man introduced me to an agent, who didn't look all that excited to see me and was only obliging a friend. I sang for him, and although he pretended not to be impressed, I could see the change in him. Then he looked at my legs and I did a few dances. He said he'd let me know. The result was a place at the back of the chorus. I remember it well. *Mary, Quite*

Contrary. Awful show, but a start. I was told to get dancing lessons. I did. It wasn't much but it was a start."

"And that was when you met Martha."

"That was a good day. She said, 'You can do better than that.' Didn't I know it! They didn't like my name. Too much of a mouthful, Daisy Tremaston. The agent suggested Daisy Ray. It always makes me laugh when Mrs. Crimp and the girls call me that. See how close it is, Daisy Ray? Well, it's all right. It sort of slips off the tongue. But is it a name people remember? Then it came in a flash. Daisy Ray . . . Désirée. Just that. You can get away with things like that in the profession. So I became Désirée."

"And you took the road to fame and fortune."

"Here! What are you doing, keeping me here talking? It is time I was up! Dolly will be here in a minute."

I was regretful. The session was over, but I learned a little more from each one, although I was aware that a curtain could come down if I was too curious; and what I wanted most was to hear about my father.

•

I was sixteen and quite mature for my age. I had learned a good deal about theatrical life and a little of the world. There were always people coming in and out of the house; they talked continuously and if I was there I listened. Charlie Claverham and Robert Bouchère were constant visitors. They both had houses in London, and Charlie had a home in Kent, Robert one in France. They came to London on business and were devoted to my mother. She had other admirers who came and went but those two remained.

There came a day when Dolly called at the house in that certain frame of mind which I now knew meant that he had found what he called an excellent "vehicle" for Désirée. It often happened that what he considered excellent was in her opinion plain rubbish, and then we were prepared for trouble.

It came.

I sat on the stairs near the drawing room, listening. Not that that presented any strain. Their raised voices reached most parts of the house.

"The lyrics are awful." That was my mother. "I'd be ashamed to sing them."

"They're delightful and will please your public."

"Then you must have a poor opinion of my public."

"I know all there is to know about your public."

"And in your opinion they are only worth rubbish."

"You must get this notion right out of your little head."

"If your opinion of me is as low as that, then I think we have come to the parting of the ways."

"My opinion of you is that you are a good musical comedy actress and many like you have come to grief by fancying themselves too good for their public."

"Dolly, I hate you."

"Désirée, I love you, but you are an idiot and I can tell you this. You'd still be in the back row of the chorus if you had not had me to look after you. Now, be a good girl and have another look at *Maud.*"

"I hate *Maud,* and those lyrics embarrass me."

"You, embarrassed! You've never been embarrassed in your life! Why, *Maud* is grand opera compared with *Follow Your Leader!*"

"I don't agree."

"A good title, too. *Countess Maud.* They'll love it. They'll all want to see the Countess."

"I hate it. I hate it. I hate it."

"Well then, there's only one thing for me to do. I shall get Lottie Langdon to do it. You'll be green with envy when you see what she makes of it."

"Lottie Langdon!"

"Why not? She'd fit the part well."

"Her top notes are shaky."

"That has a special appeal to some people. They'll love the story. The shopgirl who is really the daughter of the Earl of Somewhere. It's just what they like. Well, I'll be off . . . to see Lottie."

There was silence.

"All right," said Dolly at length. "I'll give you till tomorrow morning. Then I want a straight answer. Yes or no."

He came out of the room. I watched him go and then I went up to my room. I felt certain that soon my mother would be plunging into rehearsals for *Countess Maud.*

•

I was right. Dolly was paying frequent visits to the house. George Garland, the pianist who always worked with my mother, was in constant attendance, and the household was humming tunes from *Countess Maud.*

Dolly appeared every day with new ideas which had to be fought out; Martha was dashing round finding patterns and buying what would be needed. It was that period with which we were all familiar, and we should all be relieved when the alarms that flared up during it were over and the first night's misgivings were proved to have no foundations and we were settled for a long run.

We were getting near opening night and my mother was in a state of nervous tension. She had always been uneasy about *Countess Maud,* she declared; she wasn't sure of the lyrics and she thought she should be wearing blue, not pink, for the opening scene. She was sure her gown would clash with the costumes of the chorus; she was getting a little husky. What if she should have a sore throat on the opening night?

I said to her: "You are thinking of every calamity which could befall you. You always do and they never have. The audience will love you and *Countess Maud* is going to be one of your greatest successes."

"Thank you, pet. You are a comfort to me. There's something I've just remembered. I can't possibly dine with Charlie tonight."

"Is he in London?"

"He will be. He's coming up today. I've got a rehearsal this afternoon and I'm not satisfied with the dance routine with Sir Garnet in the last scene, when he sings: 'I'd love you if you were a shopgirl still.' "

"What's wrong with it?"

"I think he ought to come on from the other side . . . and I've got to make sure I don't drop my feather boa when I do that quick twirl at the end. But the point is, I've got to let Charlie know. Take a note to him for me, will you, darling?"

"Of course. Where is he?"

It suddenly struck me as odd that, close

friends as we were with Charlie, I did not know his London address. When he was in London he was constantly visiting us. In fact, sometimes it seemed as though he lived with us. My mother might have visited him, but I never had. The same applied to Robert Bouchère . . . though, of course, his home was really in France.

All the same, there was a vague mystery about these two men. They came and went. I often wondered what they were doing when they were not with us.

However, this was an opportunity to see where Charlie had his London residence, and I seized upon it.

I found the house. It was close to Hyde Park. It was small but typically eighteenth century in origin, with an Adam doorway and spiderweb fanlight.

I rang the bell and a neatly dressed parlourmaid opened the door. I asked if I might see Mr. Claverham.

"Would that be Mr. Charles Claverham, miss, or Mr. Roderick?"

"Oh, Mr. Charles, please."

She took me into a drawing room where the furnishings matched the house. The heavy velvet curtains at the window toned with the delicate green of the carpet and I could not help comparing the simple elegance with our more solid contemporary style.

The parlourmaid did not return. Instead, a young man entered the room. He was tall and slim with dark hair and friendly brown eyes.

He said: "You wanted to see my father. I'm afraid he's not here just now. He won't be in until the afternoon. I wonder if I can help?"

"I have a letter for him. Perhaps I could leave it with you?"

"But of course."

"It's from my mother. Désirée, you know."

"Désirée. Isn't that the actress?"

I thought how strange it was that Charlie, who was one of my mother's greatest friends, should not have mentioned her to his son.

"Yes," I said, and gave him the letter.

"I'll see that he gets it as soon as he comes in. Won't you sit down?"

I have always been of an enquiring nature and, because there seemed to be something mysterious in my own background, I suspected there might be in others'. I had always wanted to discover as much as I could about the people I met and I was especially interested now. So I accepted with alacrity.

I said: "I wonder we have not met before. My mother and your father are such great friends. I remember your father from the days when I was very small."

"Well, I don't come to London much, you know. I have just finished at university and now I expect I shall be a great deal in the country."

"I have heard of the country house—in Kent, isn't it?"

"Yes, that's right. Do you know Kent?"

"I just know it is down in the corner of the map . . . right on the edge."

He laughed. "That's not really knowing Kent. It's more than a brown blob on a map."

"Well then, I don't know Kent."

"You should. It's a most interesting county. But then I suppose all places are when you start investigating them."

"Like people."

He smiled at me. I could see he wanted to detain me as much as I wanted to stay, and he was trying to think of some subject which would interest me.

I said: "We're in London all the time. My mother's profession keeps her there. She's either getting ready for a play or acting in one. She has to do a lot of rehearsals and that sort of thing. And then she has those times when she's resting. That's what they call it when they are waiting for something to turn up."

"It must be very interesting."

"It's fascinating. The house is always full of people. She has so many friends."

"I suppose she would have."

"There's to be a first night soon. At the moment we are at that stage when she is getting anxious as to how it is going to turn out."

"It must be quite alarming."

"Oh, it is. She has something to do this afternoon and doesn't know when she'll be finished. That is why she has to cancel . . ."

He nodded.

"Well, I'm having the pleasure of meeting you."

"Your father must have told you a lot about her. He's always so interested in the plays. He's always at first nights."

He looked a little vague, and I went on: "So you are staying in the country when you leave here?"

"Oh yes. I shall help with the estate."

"Estate? What does that mean?"

"It's quite a lot of land . . . with farms and that sort of thing. We have to manage it. The family has been doing it for centuries. Family tradition and all that."

"Oh, I see."

"My grandfather did it . . . my father did it . . . and I shall do it."

"Have you any brothers and sisters?"

"No. I'm the only one. So, you see, it falls on me."

"I suppose it is what you want."

"Of course. I love the estate. It's my home, and now this new discovery . . . that makes it very exciting."

"New discovery?"

"Hasn't my father mentioned it?"

"I don't remember his ever mentioning anything about the estate. Perhaps he does to my mother."

"I am sure he must have told her about what has been found there."

"I haven't heard. Is it a secret? If it is, I won't ask about it."

"It's no secret. It was in the press. It's most exciting. They were ploughing up one of the fields near the river. The sea used to come right up to our land a thousand years ago. It has receded over the centuries and we're now about a mile and a half away. It happens gradually, you know. But what makes it so exciting is that the Romans used the place as a sort of port where they landed supplies, and of course all around was like a settlement. We've unearthed one of their villas. It's a fantastic discovery."

"Roman remains," I said.

"Yes, indeed. We're in Roman country. Naturally we would be. They landed first in Kent, didn't they? I know the spot in Deal . . . only a few miles from us. There's a plaque there which says: 'Julius Caesar landed here 55 B.C.' "

"How interesting!"

"You can stand there and imagine all those Romans coming ashore to the astonishment of the Ancient Britons in their woad. Poor things!

But it was good in the end. They did so much for Britain. Just imagine how excited we were to find evidence of their being on our land!"

"You *are* very excited about it, aren't you?"

"Of course. Particularly as I had studied a little archaeology. Just as a hobby, really. I did feel at one time that I should have liked to make a profession of it, but I knew what I had to do. Noblesse oblige and all that."

"But you would rather have made archaeology your career?"

"I used to think so. Then I reminded myself that it is fraught with disappointments. One dreams of making miraculous discoveries . . . but most of it is digging and hoping. For one triumph there are a thousand disappointments. I have been on digs with students. We did not find anything but a few pieces of earthenware which we hoped had come from some Roman or Saxon home of centuries ago, but they turned out to have been thrown out by some housewife a few months before!"

I laughed. "Well, that is typical of life."

"You are right. And I have been talking about myself all this time, which is an appalling lack of social grace, I believe."

"Not if the other member of the party is interested, and I have been very much so. Tell me about your own house."

"It's ancient."

"I gathered that . . . with all those centuries of Claverhams doing their duty to the estate."

"I sometimes think that houses can dominate families."

"Presenting a duty to its members who are not sure whether they wouldn't rather be digging up the past?"

"I see I shall have to be careful what I say to you. You have too good a memory."

I was rather pleased. There was a suggestion here that he believed this first meeting of ours would not be the only one.

"But it must be wonderful to trace your family back all that time," I said, remembering that I could not go back farther than my mother.

"Some of the parts of the house are really very old—Saxon in parts, but of course that has been lost in the necessary restorations which have been going on over the years."

"Is it haunted?"

"Well, there are always legends attached to houses which have been in existence for so long. So naturally we have gathered a few spectres on the way."

"I'd love to see it."

"You must. I should like to show you the Roman finds."

"We never have visited . . ." I began.

"No? How odd. We have people quite frequently. My mother likes to entertain."

I was surprised. I had not imagined there was a Mrs. Claverham.

I said: "Mrs. Claverham doesn't come to London much, I suppose?"

"Actually, she's known as Lady Constance. Her father was an earl and she keeps the title."

"Lady Constance Claverham," I murmured.

"That's right. Actually, she's not very fond of London. She might make the occasional trip . . . buying clothes and things like that."

"I don't think she has ever been to see us. I should have known if she had. I'm always there."

I could see that he thought there was something rather odd—even mysterious—about the situation.

"There are so many people coming in and out of the house," I went on. "Particularly at times like this when a new show is about to be put on."

"How exciting it must be to have a famous mother."

"Yes, it is. And she is the most wonderful person I have ever known. Everybody loves her."

I told him what it was like when a play was being put on. I told him of the sounds of singing and rehearsals, because there were always some scenes which my mother wanted to go over with certain people, and she would be inclined to summon them to the house for that.

"When she is playing a part she somehow becomes that part and we all have to get used to it. At the moment she is Countess Maud."

"And what is Countess Maud like?"

"She's a shopgirl who is really a countess and she can't make the simplest statement without bursting into song."

He laughed. "It's a musical play then?"

"That is my mother's forte. She does very little else. It's perfect for her. It is dancing and singing mostly, which she does to perfection. I shall be glad when *Maud* gets going. She's always in a state of tension beforehand, though she knows, and we all know, that she is going to be marvellous on the night. Afterwards, it settles down and in due course she will become a little bored. Then it comes off and the whole business starts again. I like the resting times. Then we are more together and have lots of fun until she gets restless and Dolly turns up with a new play."

"Dolly?"

"Donald Dollington. You must have heard of him."

"The actor?"

"Yes, actor-manager. I think he goes in for producing more than acting now."

The clock on the mantelpiece started to chime.

I said: "I have been here nearly an hour. And I only came to deliver a letter."

"It's been a most agreeable time."

"They will be wondering what has happened to me. I must go."

He took my hand and held it for a few moments.

"I have enjoyed meeting you," he said. "I'm glad you came to deliver that letter."

"I expect your father will bring you over to see us now that you are in London."

"I shall look forward to that."

"You must come to the first night of *Countess Maud.*"

"I shall."

"I'll see you later then."

"I'm going to take you home."

"Oh, it's not very far."

"I shall certainly come."

He insisted and, as I was enjoying his company, I did not protest.

When we reached the house I asked him to come in.

"I look forward to meeting your mother," he said. "She sounds delightful."

"She is," I assured him.

As we went into the hall, I heard voices coming from the drawing room.

"She's home," I said. "Someone's with her. But come up."

My mother had heard my arrival. She

called out. "Is that you, darling? Come and see who's here."

"Shall . . . ?" murmured Roderick Claverham.

"Of course. There are always people here."

I opened the door.

"Your journey wasn't really necessary," began my mother.

Charlie was sitting beside her on the sofa. He stared at my companion and I could see at once that he was deeply embarrassed.

"I was just telling Charlie that I had written him a note and you had gone to deliver it," said my mother.

She was smiling at Roderick, waiting for an introduction.

Charlie said: "Désirée, this is my son, Roderick."

She was on her feet taking his hand, smiling at him, telling him how delighted she was to meet him.

But I could see it was an awkward situation and I had made it so by bringing Charlie's son face to face with him in my mother's house.

My mother was very good at gliding over awkward situations. I felt this was like a scene in a play. Conversation seemed rather stilted and for some time Charlie himself seemed unable to speak at all.

My mother was saying, "How nice it is to meet you. Are you staying long in London?

The weather is rather lovely now. I do enjoy the spring, don't you?"

I fancied she was rather enjoying the situation, slipping with natural ease into the part she was called upon to play.

I said to Charlie: "I have been hearing about the wonderful discoveries on your land."

"Oh yes, yes," said Charlie. "Very, very interesting."

My mother had to hear about them. She said how absolutely fantastic and how proud they must be and how wonderful to think of finding something that had been there all that time.

Then she asked Roderick if he would like a glass of sherry or something. He declined and said he really had to leave and how much he had enjoyed meeting us both.

"It makes me laugh," said my mother. "There was I, sending a note to your father, when all the time he was on his way here."

Charlie left with his son soon after that.

When they had gone, my mother lay back on the sofa and grimaced at me.

"Oh dear, oh dear," she said. "What have we done?"

"What is this all about?" I asked.

"Let's pray it never comes to the ears of the formidable Lady Constance."

"I've learned this morning that that is

Charlie's wife. I never thought of Charlie's having a wife."

"Most men do have . . . tucked away somewhere."

"And Lady Constance is tucked away in this wonderful old mansion with the Roman remains."

"I should imagine she is rather like an old Roman matron herself."

"What are they like?"

"Oh—those women who know everything, can do everything, never put a foot wrong, obey all the rules and expect everyone else to do the same . . . and very likely make ordinary people's lives miserable."

"Charlie must have told you about her."

"I knew there was a Lady Constance and that's about all. The boy's nice. He takes after Charlie, I reckon."

"Charlie is one of your best friends, and he has never told you much about his wife!"

She looked at me and laughed.

"Well, it's a little awkward. Lady Constance would never allow her husband to have a friendship with a flighty actress, now would she? That's why she's never heard of me and we don't talk of her!"

"But when Charlie comes to London so often . . ."

"Business, my darling. So many men have

business which takes them from their homes. Well, I'm just a bit of Charlie's business."

"You mean she would object to his coming here if she knew?"

"You can safely bet on that."

"And now the son knows."

"I knew I shouldn't have asked you to take that letter. I realized it as soon as you'd gone. I thought you would just drop it in."

"I was going to, but the maid took me into the drawing room. I thought Charlie would be there and then Roderick came. I'm afraid it was my fault."

"Of course it wasn't. Mine if anyone's, for sending you. Come. Don't let's worry about it. Charlie's not a child. Nor is this Roderick. He'll understand."

"Understand what?"

"Oh . . . he'll be discreet, that young man. He'll sum up the situation. I liked him."

"I liked him, too," I said.

"Trust Charlie to have a nice son. Nice man, Charlie. Pity he had to get hitched up to the high-and-mighty Lady C. Well, perhaps that's why . . ."

"Why?"

"Why he comes here, love. However, it's a storm in a teacup. Don't worry. Roderick will keep his mouth shut and Charlie will get over the shock of seeing his two lives touching each other for a minute or two. And then all will be as it was before."

I was beginning to understand, and I was wondering whether it would be as it had been before.

•

Roderick Claverham's visit to the house and the effect it would have on Charlie was soon forgotten, for the first night of *Countess Maud* was almost upon us. The house was in chaos. There were feverish misgivings, momentous last decisions about changing this and that; there were fierce refusals from Désirée, impassioned appeals from Dolly and noisy reprimands from Martha. Well, we had had it all before.

And then the night itself. The day that preceded it had been one of especially high tension, when my mother had to be left alone and then suddenly demanded our presence. She was worried. Should she change the bit of business at the end of the first act? Could she try something else at that stage? It was too late, of course. Oh, what a fool she had been not to think of it before. Was the dress she was wearing in the first act too tight, too loose, too revealing or simply plain drab? This was going to be the end of her. Who would want to see her after the flop this was going to be? It was a ridiculous play. Whoever heard of a countess serving behind a counter in a linen draper's shop!

"It's because no one has that it makes a play," screamed Martha. "It's a fair play and you are going to make it a great one—that's if you can put a stop to your tantrums."

Dolly strode around striking dramatic poses, his hand to his head appealing to God to spare him from ever working with this woman again.

"Almighty God," he cried. "Why did You not let me take Lottie Langdon?"

"Yes, God, why didn't You?" said my mother. "This silly Countess Maud would just have suited her."

Then Dolly put on one of his Garrick poses and, with the resignation of a Pontius Pilate, cried out: "I wash my hands of this affair." And with an appropriate gesture he turned to the door.

He did not mean it, of course, but carried away by the drama, my mother pleaded: "Don't go. I'll do everything . . . everything you want of me . . . even Maud."

And so it went on. In earlier days I might have believed it was all coming to disaster, but now I knew they were all too professional to allow that. They did not mean what they said. They were placating Fate. Theatrical people, I had discovered, were the most superstitious on earth. They did not say beforehand: "This is going to be a great success," because if they did, Fate, being the perverse creature it was, would make sure that it wasn't. You had been arrogant to think it was your decision. So if you said it would be a failure, Fate would jeer: "Well, it won't be—it will be a success."

At last I was there in the theatre with Charlie and Robert Bouchère in a box looking down on the stage. The curtain went up on the linen draper's shop. There was singing and dancing and suddenly the line of girls parted and there was Désirée behind the counter, looking delightful in the dress, which was neither too tight, too loose, too revealing nor plain drab.

The audience burst into that loud applause which always greeted her when she appeared, and soon she was into "Can I help you, madam?" before she came out to dance round the stage in her inimitable way.

Dolly came into the box in the interval. He said the audience seemed to like it and with Désirée it could not fail. She had the audience where she wanted them from the moment she appeared.

"So you are not sorry you did not get Lottie Langdon after all," I could not help saying.

He gave me that quizzical look, as much as to say, you should know by now what that was all about.

He disappeared and we settled down to enjoy the last act.

Before the lights went down I saw that someone below in the stalls was trying to catch my attention. I felt a sudden spurt of laughter rising in me. It was Roderick Claverham. I lifted my hand and, acknowledging my recognition of him, I smiled. He returned the smile. I looked at Charlie. He was discussing the show with Robert Bouchère and had clearly not seen his son. I did not inform him that Roderick was in the theatre. I had learned a lesson. I wondered whether Roderick understood.

Then the curtain went up and we watched Désirée through the final scene with the aristocratic bridegroom declaring: "I'd love you if you were a shopgirl still," while Désirée responded with some of her most skilful top notes.

It was over. The audience was wildly enthusiastic. There was Désirée, led onto the stage by the man who would love her if she were a shopgirl still. He kissed her hand and then, to the delight of the audience, her cheek. The flowers were brought and Désirée made a curtain speech.

"Dear, *dear* people . . . you are *too* kind to me. I don't deserve it!"

"You do. You do," from the audience.

Holding up her hand in mock modesty, she told them that the greatest joy she could know was to play for them. "I knew you would love Maud. I did from the first moment I met her."

Echoes came back to me. "This stupid creature, why do I have to play such an idiot?"

It was all part of the playacting which was her life.

People were making for the exits. I caught one more glimpse of Roderick in the crowd. He turned to look at me and smiled. I looked towards Charlie. He had still not seen his son.

I went to Désirée's dressing room with Charlie and Robert after that. Martha was rapidly helping her to change. Champagne was drunk.

Désirée kissed Dolly and said: "There, I did it."

Dolly said: "You were magnificent, darling. Didn't I tell you you would be?"

"I could feel how much the audience loved it."

"It was you they loved."

"The darlings!"

"Well, you are rather wonderful, you know."

"Thanks, sweetheart. Say it again. I love to hear it. And there's my Noelle. What did you think of your mother, pet?"

"You were absolutely splendid."

"Bless you, sweet."

Robert said in his amusing French accent: "Is she . . . Noelle . . . old enough to drink the champagne, eh?"

"Tonight she is," said my mother. "Come,

darlings. Let's drink to a nice run . . . not too long. I don't think I could stand Maud for too long. But enough to make it a success and full houses to the end. And may she know when it is the right time to leave us."

We drank to Maud. It was about half an hour later when we drove back to the house. Thomas had the carriage waiting for us.

There had been a good deal of kissing and more congratulations before we parted, and in the carriage there were just Martha, my mother and myself. The streets were not very busy, for the crowds were fast dispersing.

"You must be exhausted," I said to my mother.

"Oh, my dear, I am. I shall sleep right through until tomorrow afternoon."

"Knowing that *Maud* was a great success," I said. "It was a success, wasn't it?"

"Of course. I knew it would be, darling," said my mother.

Martha looked at me and raised her eyebrows.

"Oh, one's always jittery just before," said my mother defensively. "You have to be. If you weren't, you'd go onstage flat. It's the life, darling."

As we were pulling up at the house, I noticed the girl. She was standing near a lamppost, but I could see her face. She looked rather dejected and I wondered what she was doing standing about at this time of night.

My mother was saying: "Oh, I'm so weary, and 'Can I help you, madam?' keeps going round and round in my head."

Thomas had jumped down from the driver's seat and was holding the door open. My mother alighted. I saw the girl take a step forward. Her face was still tense. Before I could alight from the carriage she was hastily walking away.

I said: "Did you see that girl?"

"Which girl?"

"The one who was standing over there. She looked as though she was watching you."

"Came to take a look at Countess Maud, I reckon," said Martha.

"Yes. But she seemed different somehow."

"Another of the stagestruck crowd," said Martha. "Thinks she's another Désirée, I don't doubt. Most of them do."

"Come in," said my mother. "I'm half asleep, if you're not."

I knew that we should all find it difficult to sleep. It was like this on first nights . . . but this night seemed different. There were two things to make it so: the presence of Roderick in the theatre, which set me wondering again about Charlie, Lady Constance and the relationship he must have with my mother; and then the girl in the street. Why had she made such an impression on me? People often stood about to get a glimpse of my mother . . . outside the theatre and occasionally outside our home, for the press had betrayed where Désirée lived. The girl must have been, as Martha had said, stagestruck: she had wanted to see Désirée at close quarters.

I should be at peace. The first night was over. Now there would be a long run and my mother and I would have more time together.

The Accident

✵

Countess Maud had settled in—another success for Désirée.

It was about three weeks after the opening night—a Thursday and a matinee. My mother had left for the theatre and I had said I wanted to do some shopping and I would come to the theatre so that I could join her after the performance and Thomas could drive us home together. He often did this. It gave us a little time together before she dashed off for the evening performance.

As I came out of the house I saw Roderick Claverham coming down the street.

"Hello," he said, and for a few seconds we stood smiling at each other.

I spoke first. "You are still in London, then?"

"I have been home and came back again."

"How are the remains?"

"No further discoveries. It would be surprising if there were. I was hoping I might see you. I've been here once or twice before with the same object in view. This time I've struck lucky."

I felt pleased because he had admitted that he was looking for me.

"Were you going to call on us?" I asked.

"I thought in the circumstances that might not be quite acceptable, would it?"

"Perhaps not."

"Whereas meeting by accident . . ."

"Would be quite another matter, of course."

"Were you going somewhere?"

"Only shopping."

"May I come?"

"You wouldn't be interested."

"I think I should."

"It is not necessary shopping. I was really going to finish up at the theatre and come home with my mother."

"Perhaps I could escort you to the theatre."

"It will be two hours before the show finishes."

"Well, we could walk round a bit. You could show me this part of London. Perhaps we could have a cup of tea somewhere? Does that seem like a bore to you?"

"Quite the contrary."

"Then shall we start?"

"Of course, you are attracted to the past," I said as we walked along. "I don't think we have anything here as ancient as your Roman remains. My governess is very interested in this area. You see, it is very much associated with the theatre and she is devoted to all that."

"Perhaps that's because she is with a theatrical family."

"There is my mother, of course, but to tell the truth Matty rather despises her achievements. People do when they find someone who has reached the top of what they consider to be a lower grade than they themselves aspire to—particularly if they haven't made even the first steps towards their goal. You see, Matty fancies herself as a great actress and thinks that she is wasting her time teaching."

"I should have thought she should have been very proud of her present pupil."

"We get along quite well. But it is acting she is really interested in. I think in her heart she knows all that is right out of reach. But don't you agree that people get pleasure out of daydreams?"

"Very likely."

"It's an easy way. Matty can live in her dreams—those moments when she is on the stage giving the finest performance of Lady Macbeth, winning the acclaim of the audience, receiving the bouquets, reading about her genius in the next morning's papers. She doesn't have to go through all the nerve-racking tensions, the hideous doubts, the nightmare of the opening performance as my mother does."

"I should have thought your mother was absolutely sure of success."

"It is because she isn't that she is successful . . . if you understand what I mean. She tells me that unless you are in a state of tension you don't give your best performance. In any case, I can tell you that being a successful actress is not easy and I am beginning to think that Matty's dreams are more enjoyable than the reality. She gets lyrical about this place and she loves being in the theatrical environment. She thoroughly enjoys our walks round here."

"As I am doing."

"We always talk a lot about the old days. It must have been exciting when the theatres were reinstated. Matty goes on at length about the Puritans under Cromwell, who closed the theatres. They thought they were sinful. Matty rails against them."

"I agree with her. I have a dislike for the sanctimonious who enjoy taking away people's pleasures with the excuse that it is good for them to be without it while all the time they are indulging their pleasure in contemplating their own virtue."

"I feel the same. But it was wonderful when the theatre came back. Almost worth having been without it! Matty is very interested in the Restoration playwrights. She has made it a subject for us to study. She says it will be good for me. I am glad she did."

"I daresay she is teaching herself as well as you."

"I am sure she is. We went to libraries and unearthed all sorts of information. *You* will understand how exciting it was. You have your Roman relics."

"I certainly do. And when you walk these streets you picture them as they were years ago."

"Yes . . . with the men in their magnificent wigs and feathered hats—and Nell Gwyn was, of course, at Drury Lane selling oranges and then becoming an actress and fascinating King Charles. It's all so romantic."

"And you do not wish to go on the stage and share in the limelight with your mother?"

"I have too much respect for her talents to imagine I share them. I can't sing and my mother has a beautiful voice. She is also a wonderful dancer."

"And, unlike Matty, she does not sigh for the classical roles."

"*Countess Maud* and suchlike are good enough for her."

"And very good she is with them."

"I saw you at the play."

"Yes, I saw you."

"You didn't stay. You must have hurried off."

"I was unsure. Better to take no action when you are wondering which is the right one."

"I suppose so. By the way, this is Vere Street. We discovered an interesting story about a theatre which was once here. It was opened by Killigrew and Davenant, who were two well-known theatrical men. They were so anxious to get the theatres started again that they opened one here only a few months after the Restoration. Matty said their enthusiasm must have been marvellous. They brought out a patent that women could play on the stage. Before that their parts were taken by boys. Can you imagine that! Women have been very badly treated through the ages. I think it is time we did something about it. Don't you agree?"

"I fear that if I don't I shall lose any regard you have for me, so I will say at once that I do."

I laughed. "I should not want you to agree with me for that reason."

"Forget that I said it. It was a foolish remark to make in a serious conversation. Yes, I do agree, but I am sure that with people like you around that situation will soon be remedied."

"The story I was going to tell you was of a wronged woman. She was one of the first women to play on the stage. She was in the theatre which was in Vere Street and she was playing Roxana in *The Siege of Rhodes.* The Earl of Oxford, Aubrey de Vere, came to see the play and conceived a passion for her. A de Vere could not marry an actress, but she would not submit without marriage. The villain then produced a bogus clergyman who arranged a sham marriage, and she did not learn how she had been tricked until it was too late."

"Not the first, I believe, to have suffered in that way."

"Matty loves to collect stories about these people. She can tell you about the arrogance of Colley Cibber and the virtue of Anne Bracegirdle."

"Tell me about the virtuous one."

"She was an actress who died in the middle of the eighteenth century, which was a time when a lot of interesting people seem to have lived. She had very high moral standards, which was rare in an actress. She used to go round helping the poor. She reminds me of my mother. She has hundreds of begging letters. People are always waiting outside the theatre with some pitiable story."

"Your mother has a lovely face. There is a softness . . . a gentleness about her. She is beautiful, of course, but she has a sort of inner beauty. I believe that when people have faces like that they are really good."

"What a nice thing to say. I want to tell her that. She will be amused. She doesn't think she's good at all. She thinks she's a sinner. But you're right. She *is* good. I often think how lucky I am to be her daughter."

He pressed my arm and we were silent for a moment, then he said: "What happened to Roxana?"

"We did discover that there was a child named Aubrey de Vere, and he called himself the Earl of Oxford. He was the son of an actress and it was said that the earl had gone through a form of mock marriage with his mother."

"That must have been the one, unless he made a habit of going through mock marriages."

"I could imagine he might. That's the maddening thing about these stories. One often doesn't know how it turned out in the end."

"One has to imagine it. I hope Roxana became a great actress and nemesis overtook the Earl of Oxford."

"Matty discovered that he was notoriously immoral, but he was witty and popular at court, so I suppose he didn't suffer for his misdeeds."

"What a shame! Look. Here is a tea shop. Would you like to sit down for a while and then we can go to the theatre in time for the end of the play?"

"I should enjoy that."

The tea shop was small and cosy; we found a place for two in a corner.

As I poured the tea, he talked about the holiday he planned in Egypt.

"An archaeologist's dream," he said. "The Valley of the Kings! The pyramids! So many relics of the ancient world. Imagine it all."

"That is just what I am doing. It must be one of the most thrilling experiences possible to get into one of those tombs of the kings . . . though frightening in a way."

"Exactly. I think the robbers of tombs had a lot of courage. When you think of all the myths and legends, you realize how amazing it is what people will do for gain."

"How exciting it will be for you!"

"You'd enjoy it, I know."

"I am sure I should."

He looked at me intently and then stirred his tea slowly, as though deep in thought.

Then he said: "My father and your mother have been really great friends for years, haven't they?"

"Oh yes. My mother has often said that she relies on him more than anyone else. Robert Bouchère is another of her friends of long standing. He is a banker in Paris and is often in London. I think your father comes first with her."

He nodded thoughtfully.

"Tell me about your home," I said.

"It's called Leverson Manor. Leverson was an ancestor but the name got lost somewhere when one of the daughters inherited and married a Claverham."

"And your mother?"

"She, of course, is a Claverham only by marriage. Her family have estates in the North. They are a very old family and trace their origins back right through the centuries. They rank themselves with the Nevilles and the Percys who guarded the North against the Scots. They have portraits of warriors who fought in the Wars of the Roses and farther back than that when they were fighting the Picts and the Scots. My father, as you know, is a gentle and kind man. He is very popular on the estate. They are all in awe of my mother and she likes to keep it that way. She gives the impression of being conscious that she married beneath her, which I suppose, strictly socially speaking, she did. Actually, she cares deeply about my father and me, her only son."

"I can picture her so well. A rather terrifying lady."

"She wants the best for us. The point is that we don't always agree as to the best and that is when the conflict begins. If only she could rid herself of the belief that her blood is slightly more blue than my father's, if only she could understand that some of us must do what we want and not what she decides is best for us . . . she would be a wonderful person."

"I can see you are fond of her and of course you would have a portion of the bluer blood to mingle with the baser sort."

"Well, I understand her. She is really a grand person and the fact is that she really is very often right."

I believed I was getting a good picture of Lady Constance and life at Leverson Manor.

How I should love to see it! Not that I ever should. Of one thing I was certain: Lady Constance would never approve of her husband's friendship with an actress, even a famous one. It was therefore wrong to expect this encounter to be other than one between casual acquaintances.

We could not linger indefinitely over the tea table, although he gave me the impression that he would have liked to.

I looked at my watch and said: "The play will be approaching the end."

We came into the street and walked the short distance to the theatre. Before we parted at the door, he took my hand and looked at me earnestly.

"We must do this again," he said. "I've enjoyed it thoroughly. I have so much to learn of the history attached to the theatrical world."

"And I should like to hear more of the Roman remains."

"We must arrange it. Shall we?"

"Yes."

"When is the next matinee?"

"On Saturday."

"Then shall it be then?"

"I should like that."

I was lighthearted as I went up to the dressing room. Martha was there.

"Not such a good house," she said. "I was never fond of matinees. They never seem the same as night. And we weren't fully booked. She won't like that. If there's anything she hates, it's playing to half-empty houses."

"Was it half empty?"

"No . . . just not full. She'll notice it. Trained eye and all that. She's more audience-conscious than most."

Contrary to Martha's expectations, my mother was in a good mood.

"Jeffry slipped when he put his arm round

me in 'I'd love you if you were a shopgirl still.' He grabbed me and pulled a button off my dress at the back, Martha."

"He's a clumsy beggar, that Jeffry," said Martha. "I reckon he looked right down silly."

"Not him. They love him . . . all that golden hair and the jaunty moustache. Half the audience are in love with him. What's a little slip? It only makes him human. They come to see him as much as me."

"Nonsense. You're the bright light of the show and don't you forget it. I haven't worked my fingers to the bone to get you taking second place to Jeffry Collins."

"Jeffry thinks he's the one who pulls them in."

"Well, let him. No one else does. Let's have a look at that button. Oh, that'll soon be put right for tonight."

"Oh, tonight . . . it starts all over again tonight. I hate matinees."

"Well, Noelle's here to go home with us."

"That's nice, darling. Had a good afternoon?"

"Oh yes . . . very good."

"Lovely to have you here."

"And," said Martha, "we'd better get a move on. Don't forget there's a show tonight."

"Don't remind me," sighed my mother.

There were one or two people at the stage door, waiting for a glimpse of Désirée. She was all smiles and exchanged a few words with her admirers.

Thomas helped her into the carriage and Martha and I climbed in beside her. She waved gaily to the little crowd and, when we had left them behind, leaned back with half-closed eyes.

"Did you buy anything nice?" she asked me.

"No . . . nothing at all."

I was about to tell her of the meeting with Roderick Claverham when I restrained myself. I was not quite sure how she had felt about my bringing him to the house. She had laughed it off, but I fancied she had found the situation embarrassing.

She had lived her life free of conventions and she had given so much to others. She had chosen to live as she pleased, and I had heard her say that if you don't hurt anyone, what harm can you do?

As long as Lady Constance did not know of the rather special friendship between her husband and the famous actress, did it matter? To moralists, yes, it did; but Désirée was never one of those. "Live and let live," she used to say. "That's my motto." But when Charlie's secret life and his conventional one touched, perhaps that was time to pause and consider.

I was unsure, so I said nothing of the meeting with Roderick.

I led her to talk of the afternoon's performance, which she was always ready to do; and finally we turned into the road and the horse pricked up his ears as, to our amusement, he always did, and would have broken into a gallop at this juncture if Thomas had not restrained him.

My mother said: "The darling knows he's home. Isn't that sweet?"

We were about to draw up when it happened. The girl must have run right in front of the horse. I wasn't sure what happened exactly. I think Thomas swerved to avoid her and then she was lying stretched out on the road.

Thomas had pulled up sharply and jumped out. With my mother and Martha, I followed.

"Good heavens," cried my mother. "She's hurt."

"She dashed right under Ranger's feet," said Thomas.

He picked her up.

"Is she very badly hurt?" asked my mother anxiously.

"Don't know, madam. But I don't think so."

"Better bring her in," said my mother. "Then we'll get the doctor."

Thomas carried the young woman into the house and laid her on the bed in one of the two spare bedrooms.

Mrs. Crimp and Carrie came running up.

"What is it?" gasped Mrs. Crimp. "An accident? My goodness, gracious me! What *is* the world coming to?"

"Mrs. Crimp, we need a doctor," said my mother. "Thomas, you'd better go. Take the carriage and you can bring Dr. Green back with you. Poor girl. She looks so pale."

"You could knock her down with a feather by the looks of her, let alone a horse and carriage," commented Mrs. Crimp.

"Poor girl," said my mother again.

She put her hand on the girl's forehead and stroked her hair back from her face.

"So young," she added.

"I think a hot drink would do her good," I suggested. "With plenty of sugar in it."

The girl opened her eyes and looked at Désirée. I saw that expression which I had seen so many times before, and I felt proud that even at such a time she could be aware of my mother.

Then I recognized her. She was the girl I had seen standing outside the house when we had come home from the theatre after the first night.

So . . . she *had* come to see Désirée. She was another of those stagestruck girls very likely—one of those who adored the famous actress and dreamed of being like her.

I said to Désirée: "I think she is one of your admirers. I've seen her before . . . outside the house . . . waiting for a glimpse of you."

Even at such a time she could be pleased at public appreciation.

The hot tea was brought and my mother held the cup while the girl drank.

"There," she said. "That's better. The doctor will soon be here. He'll see if there is any harm done."

The girl half raised herself and my mother said soothingly: "Lie down. You're going to rest here until it is all right for you to go. You'll be very shaken, you know."

"I . . . I'm all right," said the girl.

"No, you are not . . . at least not for going off. You are going to stay here until we say you may go. Is there anyone you would like a message sent to . . . someone who will be anxious about you?"

She shook her head and in a blank voice which betrayed a good deal said: "No . . . there is no one."

Her lips quivered and I saw the deep sympathy in my mother's eyes.

"What is your name?" asked my mother.

"It's Lisa Fennell."

"Well, Lisa Fennell, you are going to stay here for the night at least," replied my mother. "But first we have to wait for the doctor."

"I don't think she has been hurt much," said Martha. "It's shock. That's what it is. And you have a show tonight. You know how rushed these matinee days always are. Matinees ought to be abolished, if you ask my opinion."

"Nobody is asking your opinion, Martha, and you know how necessary it is to squeeze every penny out of the public if we are to carry on."

"I reckon we could do without matinees," persisted Martha.

"Think of all the people who can only get away one half day a week."

"I'm thinking of *us,* ducks."

"Our duty in life is to think of others . . . particularly in the theatre."

"Can't say I've noticed it."

The girl on the bed was listening avidly. I had come to the conclusion that she was not badly hurt.

When the doctor came he confirmed this.

"She only has a few bruises," he told us afterwards. "She's shocked, of course. She'll be all right in a day or so."

"I propose to keep her here for the night," said my mother.

"That's a good idea. What about her family?"

"She doesn't appear to have any."

"Well, in that case it would certainly be best for her to stay. I'll give her a mild sedative, which will ensure a good night's sleep. Give it to her when she's ready to settle down for the night. Just let her rest till then."

"And now," said Martha, "we'd better be getting ourselves ready or we'll be disappointing our audience. They've come to see Madame Désirée, not understudy Janet Dare."

"Poor Janet," said my mother. "She'd love a chance to show what she could do."

"We all know what she can do and it would not be good enough."

After my mother had left for the theatre, I went to our guest and stood by her bed.

She said: "You have been so good to me."

"It was the least we could do. How did it happen?"

"It was my fault. I was careless. I was so eager. I didn't realize the carriage was still moving. I admired Désirée so much. I've seen *Countess Maud* three times . . . up in the gallery, of course. I couldn't afford anything more. It is so maddening when someone big and broad gets in front of you. She is wonderful."

"Lots of people think so."

"I know. She is at the top, isn't she? And you are her daughter. How marvellous for you."

"Tell me about yourself. What do you do?"

"Nothing at the moment."

"You want to be an actress?" I suggested.

"You guessed."

"Well, there are so many. You know, lots of people see my mother on the stage and think it is a wonderful life. Actually it is tremendously hard work. It is not easy, you know."

"I am aware of that. I'm different from those people. I've always wanted to go on the stage."

I looked at her sadly.

"I can act, I can sing, I can dance," she said earnestly. "I tell you, I can do it."

"What have you done in that line?"

"I have been on a stage. I have sung and danced."

"Where?"

"Amateur dramatics. I was the leading actress in our company."

"It isn't the same," I said gently. "It doesn't count all that much with the professionals. How old are you? I'm sorry. I should not have asked. I am acting like an agent."

"I want you to be like an agent. I realize you know a good deal about it because of your mother. I'm just seventeen. I felt I couldn't wait any longer."

"How long have you been in London?"

"Three months."

"And what have you been doing?"

"Trying to find an agent."

"And no luck?"

"They weren't interested. It was always no experience. They wouldn't even let me show them what I could do."

"Where do you come from?"

"From a place called Waddington. It's only a little village. Nobody's ever heard of it except those who live there. It's not far from Hereford. I hadn't a chance there, of course. All I could do was sing in the church choir and at concerts I was the star turn."

"I understand."

"And when I saw your mother in *Countess Maud,* I wanted to be just like her. She's wonderful. You can feel that the audience is with her all the way."

"So you left this place near Hereford. What about your family?"

"I haven't any family now . . . nor any home. My father rented a small farm and we lived fairly comfortably until he died. My mother had died when I was five years old, so I don't remember much of her. I kept house and did a bit on the farm."

"I see, and all this time you wanted to be an actress. Did your father know?"

"Oh yes, but he thought it was just a dream. He was very proud of me when I sang in the concerts. He used to sit in the front row, his eyes on me all the time. He understood, but he was the sort of man who would say it can't be done and be resigned. I'm not like that. I have to try to make it come true."

"It's the only way of course. My mother had a hard struggle."

"I guessed she had. She would not come to

that perfection easily. When my father died I
decided I would try my luck. I would never
forgive myself if I did not. My father had a
stroke. I looked after him for six weeks before
he died. Then I sold up everything I had and
came to London."

"And you have been here for three months
and are just where you were when you arrived."

"Only much poorer."

"I'm afraid your story is not unusual. So
many people are ambitious and so few succeed."

"I know. But I am going to try. How did
your mother get on? Fighting her way. And
that is what I am going to do."

I said: "I know how you feel, but just now
you ought to be resting. I think you should take
the sedative the doctor left and sleep. But have
something to eat first. I am sure that's what
you need. Then perhaps you will feel sleepy."

"You are so kind."

I left her and went down to the kitchen.
They wanted to hear all that had happened and
listened avidly.

"Miss Daisy Ray's so kind," said Mrs.
Crimp. "She seemed to be in quite a state herself to think that her carriage had run down the
poor girl."

"You can rest assured she will do everything she can to help her," I said. "Could you send something up for her to eat?"

"A leg of chicken or something like that? Perhaps some soup?"

"That sounds just right, Mrs. Crimp."

"Leave it to me."

Jane said: "I'll take it up."

I went back to Lisa Fennell and told her that some food was coming shortly. Jane brought it. She studied Lisa Fennell with interest. She wanted to chat. They had something in common: they both aspired to attain that fame which was Désirée's.

"Everyone is so kind here," said Lisa Fennell.

"That's Miss Daisy Ray all over," said Jane. "She's always like that."

Jane went, and Lisa Fennell ate the food with relish. I wondered whether she had enough to eat. I pictured her trying to eke out her money—for I was sure there was not much. She would be wondering all the time how long it was going to last—hopeful, despairing in turn. Poor girl!

I gave her the sedative. "This will make you sleepy," I said. "It is what you need, the doctor said. You'll feel better in the morning."

I sat with her for a little while until I saw that she was becoming drowsy. It was not long before she was asleep. Then I crept out of the room.

I was waiting up for my mother when she returned from the theatre, because I knew she would want to know what had happened to Lisa Fennell.

She always went into the drawing room for about half an hour, as she said, to settle after the evening's performance. Martha often went to the kitchen to get a drink of some sort. A glass of hot milk or perhaps a glass of ale—whatever she fancied. She said it helped her to relax.

I could always tell from her mood how the performance had gone. That night I saw that it had gone well.

"What about this girl?" she asked. "What did she say her name was?"

"Lisa Fennell. She's sleeping now. She had a nice supper and then I gave her the sedative. She was soon asleep after that. I looked in at her about an hour ago. She was not aware of me. She's going to be all right."

"I do hope she's not badly hurt."

"Of course she's not," said Martha.

"You never know. These things are not always obvious at the start. They can show up later. And it was our carriage."

"She ran into it," insisted Martha.

"Thank goodness we were not going at any pace."

"I've talked to her," I said. "She wants to be an actress."

Martha clicked her tongue and raised her eyes to the ceiling.

"Poor girl," said my mother. "Has she done anything?"

"Amateur dramatics," I said.

"God preserve us!" murmured Martha. "And she thinks because of that she's another Désirée."

"Not exactly . . . she thinks Désirée is wonderful. She just wants a chance to do something like it."

I told them what she had told me.

"The best thing she can do," said Martha, "is pack her bags and go back, find some farmer to marry her and set about milking the cows."

"How do you know?" demanded my mother. "She might have talent. At least she had the determination to come to London."

"Determination is not talent, as you should know."

"It's one of the necessary ingredients to success."

"It's bread without yeast. You never get it to rise."

"Since when have you been the culinary expert?"

"I've been in the theatre long enough to know about the theatre. And for every one who gets to the top there are ten thousand trying to."

"Some of us manage it. Why not this girl? I think she ought to have a chance at least. She's done something in her village."

"Village audiences are not London audiences."

"Of course they're not. But I don't think the girl should be dismissed as no good before she's had a chance to show what she can do."

"So you are going to see if you can give her a chance, are you? Like the others you've tried to help. And what thanks did you get, eh? Some of them had the nerve to blame you because they thought you were going to hand them success on a plate, and when they didn't get it, they thought you'd stopped them. They said you were jealous. The Lord spare us from any more of that nonsense."

"I think everyone should have a chance," persisted my mother.

"She did come to London," I put in. "She's got the right spirit, and I've heard you say that that plays a big part in getting there in the end."

"We could at least see what she could do," said my mother.

"Don't forget you've got six shows a week, plus two matinees, before you start setting up the Good Samaritan act."

"I'll remember," said my mother. "But I do think everyone should have a chance." She yawned. "Good show tonight. I thought they were going to keep us there till morning with all those curtain calls. It's good when they stand up and cheer. It looks as though *Maud* is here for a very long time."

"And it looks as though it's time for your bed," said Martha tersely.

"I know," replied my mother. "I'll never get up in the morning."

I kissed her suddenly. I thought how good she was, how kind. She really cared about that girl. In the midst of all her success, her first thought had been of her, and I knew she would do everything she could to help her.

The ultimate virtue, I thought, is caring for others. On impulse I went to her and kissed her.

•

Lisa Fennell had been with us for a little more than a week. My mother had heard her sing. She thought she had quite a good voice. There was nothing that a few lessons would not put right. Her dancing was not bad either. It was arranged that she should go to a singing teacher whom Désirée knew.

Désirée could be wildly enthusiastic about a project. She was, according to Martha, a natural Samaritan and more often than not a bit of a fool over her lame ducks. It was her carriage which had been involved in the accident, she insisted, and it was only right that she should try to make up to that poor girl, who had been terribly upset. She was impecunious; she was struggling; and to my mother it seemed only natural that she should take her under her wing.

Lisa was to stay with us for the time being, until she could be satisfactorily "fixed up."

Her few possessions had been collected from her lodgings, the poverty of which had shocked both myself and my mother. I shared my mother's feelings regarding her and was as eager to help as she was. We were both tremendously sorry for Lisa.

After three lessons with the singing teacher, my mother said to Martha and me: "I can't see why Dolly couldn't give her a place in the chorus. It's rather thin, I've always thought."

"Thin!" screamed Martha. "What are you talking about?"

"The girls should be closer in that number when they put their hands on each other's shoulders and do the high kicks. Some of them have a little difficulty in reaching and it spoils the effect."

"Nonsense," said Martha. "It's one of the best of the dances."

"It could be better. Don't you think so, Noelle?"

I hadn't noticed the girls were having difficulty in stretching, but I had to agree with my mother.

"Yes," I said. "They could do with one more girl."

"I'll speak to Dolly," said my mother.

"He'll go mad," retorted Martha.

When she spoke to Dolly, I was present. She said: "I don't want Martha there. She'll side with him. But you be there, Noelle. He's got a soft spot for you and a respect for youth. He won't fly off the handle so profanely if you're there."

So I was present.

"Dolly," she said. "I think the chorus line is a little too thin."

"Thin?" cried Dolly.

"I fancy it is."

"As long as it's only one of your fancies."

"There's this girl," she went on. "She's good. It would be a wonderful start for her and it *was* my carriage. I thought, if we could squeeze her into the chorus it would be a good turn for me and just what she needs."

"I'm not in this business to squeeze people into the chorus just because they run under your horse's feet."

"This is a poor girl, Dolly. Do listen."

"Not if you're going to talk about squeezing one of your protégées into my chorus."

"*Your* chorus! Who made the show what it is? *I* did."

"With a little help from me and some others. Actors and actresses always have inflated ideas of their importance."

"Dolly, you're not such a fool as you like me to think. We could do with another girl in the chorus. You know we could."

"No," said Dolly firmly.

"Dolly, I'm asking you."

"I'm fully aware of that. You get these crackpot ideas about helping people who come along to you with a mournful tale. It's just like you. It's not the first time. Give this girl a job and you'll have thousands tracking to your door. You'll have them under your carriage wheels by the thousand. We'll have a stage full of chorus girls. There won't be any room for the principals."

"Dolly, I am only asking for one."

"Look here. I've just about had enough of your charities. Have them, if you must, but keep them out of my business."

"I hate you, Dolly, sometimes. You're so smug. Can't you see you're upsetting me? You're going to spoil my performance tonight."

Dolly struck one of his theatrical poses, pressing his hand to his forehead, his face set in lines of despair.

"What I suffer, Almighty God, who has seen fit to punish me. What have I done to suffer this woman? How can I endure this torment? She is determined to ruin me. She plans my destruction. She wants to ruin the play to which I have given all I possess. She wants to fill my stage with hundreds of simpering idiotic chorus girls."

"Shut up!" said my mother. "Who said anything about hundreds? I keep telling you, it is only one. And if you are ruined, Mr. Dollington, it will be by your own hand. Now you are making me ill . . . too ill to go on tonight. You'll have to use Janet Dare. See how the audience likes that. She won't mind playing with a chorus that's miserably thin because Mr. Dollington, who fancies himself as Garrick and Kean all rolled in one, is afraid of spending a few more pence on a show others are working themselves into the grave to keep going. Come on, Noelle, I need you to put one of those eau de cologne presses on my forehead. I can feel a splitting headache coming on."

She had taken my hand and started towards the door.

Dolly said: "All right. I don't promise anything, mind, but I'll have a look at the girl."

My mother was all smiles. The headache had evaporated.

"Dolly darling," she said. "I knew you would."

•

The result was that Lisa Fennell sang for Dolly while George Garland, my mother's pianist, accompanied her on the piano. I was there with Martha.

"It's good to have an audience," my mother had said.

Lisa sang "Can I help you, madam?" and it was a good imitation of my mother.

Dolly grunted and asked her to go through one of the dances, which she did.

Dolly grunted again, but he would not give a verdict immediately.

"Just saving face," my mother whispered to me. "Well, let him. It's going to be all right."

Later that day Dolly sent word that Lisa Fennell could start in the chorus the following Monday. He wanted her to get a little practice in dancing in the meantime.

Lisa was in a state of bliss.

"I can't believe it. I really can't," she kept saying. "To think that I am in a show with the great Désirée."

She was not more delighted than my mother, who said: "I know you are going to succeed. You've got the urge. That's what it takes."

"And to think that if I had not been run over and nearly killed . . ."

"That's life, dear," said my mother. "Something awful happens and it turns out to be good in the end."

Lisa settled into the chorus and it was clear that she adored my mother.

I said: "She imitates your voice . . . she walks as you walk, with that special swing. You're her model . . . her ideal."

"She's stagestruck, that's all. I'm there and she's making her way up."

"She's so grateful to you. You've given her her chance."

"Well, they won't be able to say she is inexperienced after this."

Lisa said to me one day: "I've been looking at lodgings. I want to get somewhere near the theatre. It's hopeless otherwise. Everything's so terribly expensive. But I suppose I can just about manage. Your mother has been wonderful. I feel I just can't encroach on her hospitality anymore."

I told my mother what she had said.

"I expect she wants her independence. People like places of their own. Dolly's a bit of an old skinflint. He says he can't pay fancy salaries to chorus girls. If they don't like what they get they can always go elsewhere."

"She did say something about lodgings being expensive."

"She's no trouble here, is she?"

"I don't think so. She's quiet and helpful and gets on well with them all."

"Well, sound her. Tell her she can stay if she likes. There's that room at the top . . . if she has any qualms. That's never used and she could be on her own up there."

When I told her, I saw the joy in her face.

"It's not only having to take something I couldn't really afford, it's being here . . . near your mother . . . right at the heart of things . . ."

"My mother said you could be on your own up there."

"I don't know what to say. No one has ever been so good to me before. Désirée is an angel."

"She's a wonderful person. I believe many people have discovered that."

When she thanked Désirée, she was told: "You'll find a way of paying me back if you want to. Not that I want paying. I tell you, dear, it's as much pleasure for me as it is to you to see you doing the work you're set on. You'll get on and I'll be the first to congratulate you."

"And to know that but for you it could never have happened."

"Oh, there are always ways, dear."

We slipped into a routine. I did not see so much of Lisa Fennell. I think she was afraid of intruding. She had the big attic room, the ceiling of which sloped on either side; and there she lived in quiet contentment. She used to sing songs from *Countess Maud* and often I thought it was my mother singing.

•

It was three months since the first night of *Countess Maud,* and the audiences were still flocking to see it. Some people came more than once. That was a sign of success.

Lisa used to come home from the theatre with my mother and Martha. I did not think Martha was very pleased with the arrangement. She was very possessive towards my mother and I was sure that she resented her interest in Lisa.

Lisa was aware of this and tried hard not to offend. In fact, it seemed to me that Lisa was aware of a good deal and was treading warily, terrified of alienating anyone.

I mentioned this to my mother and she said: "Yes, it's possible. The poor girl is very anxious to hold her job. She doesn't want to upset anyone. I know exactly how she feels. We must try to make things easy for her."

Then something happened which was significant. Janet Dare had an accident. She had gone shopping in Regent Street one afternoon, had slipped on the pavement and broken her leg in two places. It was going to be a long time before Janet was back at work.

Janet was in the chorus as well as being understudy, and the chorus line would now be as it was before Lisa came. They could get by with those, but an understudy, although fortunately rarely needed, was a necessity.

I could see the dreams in Lisa's eyes.

She approached my mother first. "I know

the songs. I know the dances . . . and I've watched every one of your performances."

"I know," said my mother. "You'd be right for the job. I can't answer for Dolly. If I suggest you, he's bound to raise objections."

"But I do know it so well. I'd practise . . . I'd rehearse . . ."

"I know, dear. You are the one for it. Leave it to me. I'll see what I can do."

Dolly was surprisingly acquiescent. I think he must have realized that Lisa Fennell was the best choice. She had modelled herself on my mother. She knew the songs.

He raised no objections and it was settled.

Lisa Fennell, in addition to her role in the chorus, was to understudy Désirée.

The Understudy

I had seen Roderick Claverham on one or two occasions. The meetings were never planned. They took place on matinee days.

I would stroll out shortly after my mother had left and he would be waiting for me in the street. There was always an element of excitement because I would be wondering whether he would be there.

I was almost sure that he would be all the same.

I think we liked it that way because both of us had a feeling that the meetings should be something of a secret, in view of the relationship between our parents.

However, I enjoyed the meetings very much. We walked a good deal: we had tea in our little tea shop, and then he took me to the theatre, where I would join my mother, and we would come home in the carriage with Martha and Lisa.

We sometimes walked down Piccadilly to Green Park. There we would sit and watch people as they strolled by, and the children feeding the ducks.

I had learned a certain amount about his home—enough to give me a fairly clear picture of it. I heard about the interesting people who had visited Leverson Manor since the discovery of the Roman remains. And, of course, I talked about myself.

I knew this was an intermediary period. We could not go on meeting like this. In a way it seemed almost furtive, for I said nothing to my mother of our acquaintance, which was extremely odd, for up to this time I had always been completely open with her. And I guessed he had said nothing to his father.

I was right when I told myself that it could not last like that. I wanted him to come and meet my mother; he wanted me to visit his home in Kent. I had a longing to do so, and a burning curiosity to see Lady Constance even more than the Roman remains.

It was Tuesday and my mother was spending the afternoon with her dressmaker. She wanted some new clothes for the show. She thought it needed brightening up a little.

I had told Roderick that I should be free on that particular day and he had immediately said we must meet.

We made our way to Green Park and as we were sitting there Roderick suddenly said: "What are we going to do, Noelle?"

"Do?"

"I mean . . . how much longer are we going on meeting like this? You haven't told your mother, have you? I haven't mentioned our meetings to my father. It seems odd. Why do we do it?"

"I think we both feel it might be a little embarrassing for them."

"Yes. I think it would be for my father."

"I suppose my mother is not so easily embarrassed. She would think it was quite normal. I really don't know what to say about it."

"Well, we have avoided mentioning it. It's absurd really. It is not our affair."

"It is just that your mother knows nothing about this . . . friendship between your father and my mother, and if she did, of course, she would not approve."

"I am sure she would not, and my father would not wish her to know."

"And because of that, you and I are caught up in this secrecy."

"I should like to call openly at your house. I want you to visit Leverson. After all, we are very good friends. At least I hope we are."

"I hope so, too."

"Well, with two of us hoping, it must be. What are we going to do about it, Noelle?"

"I really don't know."

"You see . . . you and I . . . well . . ."

"Why . . . Noelle!"

I was startled . . . Lisa Fennell was coming towards us. I felt myself flushing. Her bright curious eyes were on Roderick.

I said: "Let me introduce you. This is Mr. Roderick Claverham, Mr. Charlie Claverham's son."

"Oh! How nice to meet you."

"And this is Lisa Fennell. She is in the show . . . *Countess Maud* . . . you know."

"I was taking the air," she said. "Trying to get relaxed for the evening's show. It's a lovely day, isn't it? I love the parks in London. May I sit down with you?"

"Please do," said Roderick.

She took her place on the other side of him.

"I don't think I've seen you at the house," said Lisa.

"No," replied Roderick. "I did come once. That was a little time ago."

"I think it was before you joined us, Lisa," I said.

"Has Noelle told you how I came?"

"Yes. She did mention it."

"Wasn't it wonderful? Like a fairy story. I was almost killed, you know."

"The carriage wasn't going very fast," I said.

"And it all started from that. Désirée . . . the famous actress . . . has been so good to me." Her voice shook a little. "She is the most wonderful person in the world."

"Yes. I have heard that she is very kind."

"Do you live in London?"

"My home is in the country, but we have a small house in London. It's very useful for my father, who needs to be here quite often on business. It's very convenient."

"I'm sure it must be. I love London. So ancient . . . and modern at the same time. What a combination! Don't you think that is fascinating?"

Roderick said he did.

"Mr. Claverham has something very ancient in his own home," I told Lisa. "They have found remains of a Roman settlement on the land."

"How wonderful!" cried Lisa. She turned to Roderick. "Do tell me about it."

I listened, vaguely thinking of what Roderick was saying when she interrupted us. It had seemed important. What a pity she had had to come along at that moment.

She was listening to him, urging him to tell her more—completely unaware that her intrusion had spoilt our tête-à-tête. Roderick was too polite to show the disappointment I felt sure he shared with me.

Eventually I said: "Well, I must go back."

"And so must I," echoed Lisa. "I had no idea it was so late."

"Let's go, then," I said.

We went back to the house together. Roderick said goodbye and left us.

"What a charming young man!" said Lisa as we went in. Her eyes shone with pleasure. "Fancy Charlie's having a son like that and keeping him hidden!"

My mother returned soon afterwards. She had had a rewarding session with the dressmaker and wanted to tell me about it. She was changing the blue dress in the first act to one of deep mauve and the one in the last act was to be red.

"Those colours stand out more. Besides, it will give the show a new look. And it will be good for us all. We're getting a bit rusty. What do you think? I called on Janet Dare. Poor

dear! She's going out of her wits. She is just
longing to be back. If it has anything to do with
her, she won't be off much longer."

I thought I should tell my mother that I
had met Roderick. Lisa might mention that she
had seen him and it would appear strange that
I had not talked of it.

When we were alone I said, trying to appear
casual: "By the way, do you remember Roderick Claverham . . . Charlie's son? He came
here once."

"Oh yes, of course. What a nice young
man!"

"I've seen him . . . once or twice. I happened to run into him."

"Did you? How interesting."

"As a matter of fact, I was with him today.
Lisa was with us."

"Oh, Lisa . . . I was just thinking of her
. . . having been with Janet Dare of course.
She is so thrilled to have that job in the chorus
. . . and the understudy."

"She's eternally grateful to you. After all,
you fixed it for her, didn't you?"

"I couldn't have done anything if she
hadn't had the talent."

"She tries to be exactly like you."

"She's thinking of playing Countess Maud,
that's why. God forbid, she might have to one
day. My goodness, her nose is going to be put a

little out of joint when Janet comes back. The poor child fancies herself as understudy."

I was thinking I need not have any qualms about seeing Roderick. My mother was not greatly interested, nor was she in the least perturbed about her relationship with Charlie.

•

A few days later Jane came to my room and told me that my mother wanted to see me and would I go to her at once.

"Is anything wrong, Jane?" I asked.

"She don't look too well, Miss Noelle."

I hurried to her room, and was immediately filled with alarm. She looked most unlike her usual self.

"I've been so ill," she said. "It could have been the fish I had last night. But it was immediately after lunch that it started. I feel dizzy as well as sick."

"Why don't you lie down?"

"I've been lying down. What's so awful is that I don't think I can go on tonight."

"You certainly can't if you are like you are now. I think I ought to call Dr. Green."

"Oh no. That's not necessary. It's just something I've eaten. It will pass in time. I think you'd better get a message to Dolly, though . . . just in case it's necessary . . . which it may not be . . . but we must be prepared."

"Thomas can go right away," I said.

In half an hour Dolly was at the house in a state of great agitation.

"What's happened? Eaten something? Oh, Almighty God, what have I done to deserve this?"

"I should cut out the dramatics, Dolly. It's not the time for them. If I can't go on tonight we've got to do the obvious . . . and we ought to be busy with it right away . . . just in case it's necessary . . . which it may not be, but we have to be ready. Lisa will have to take my place."

"That amateur!"

"She's not an amateur. She's not bad, actually. You yourself have said so, though it was like getting blood out of a stone to make you admit it."

"You talk as though this is of no importance. Let me tell you, it's a disaster . . . a calamity. I've got to placate all those people who have paid to see Désirée, not some little amateur from the country."

"Anyone would think it was the first time you'd had to put in an understudy. It's nothing. Shut off the histrionics and bring out the common sense. You've got to get busy, Dolly. Of course, I might be all right. There are a few hours to go. But at the moment . . ."

"Is that girl here?" asked Dolly.

"Yes," I told him. "Shall I tell her to come down?"

"Right away."

I went to Lisa's room. She looked up expectantly.

"My mother's not well," I said. "She's been terribly sick and she's giddy. Dolly's here. She thinks she might not be able to go on tonight."

She stared at me. She was trying to hide the elation, but I could see it there. Naturally it would be. I understood.

"Is she . . . very bad?"

"No. It's only a bilious attack. She's lying down. She feels dizzy when she stands up. I can't believe she'll be fit to go on tonight. You're to come down at once. Dolly's pacing up and down like an animal in a cage, and my mother is trying to soothe him."

"He'll be furious."

"Well, you know Dolly."

"He won't trust me to do it."

"He must," I answered her. "He wouldn't have given you the job in the first place if he didn't believe you could do it in an emergency."

"And your poor mother. How awful!"

"I don't think it is anything much. She says she's probably eaten something which did not agree with her. You'd better hurry. The longer you keep Dolly waiting, the more incensed he'll be."

She hurried down and I went to my room.

This could be Lisa's chance. It was only natural that that thought should be uppermost in her mind.

•

My mother was feeling a little better but not well enough to go on that night. I wanted to stay with her but she said I ought to go to the theatre to cheer Lisa on.

"Poor girl. I know what she is going through. She's got strong nerves, though. I will say that for her. And she'll need them tonight."

"She's very earnest about it all."

"Quite right. You need earnestness, and all you've got, to succeed in this profession, I can assure you. She shouldn't be too confident, though, and I don't think she is. She's got to have that awful feeling that she's going to lose her top notes and fall flat on her face instead of into her bridegroom's arms. It's got to be a mixture of fear and confidence . . . and that's not easy to come by. Don't I know it! But this is a chance for her. If she does well, she'll be in Dolly's good books. If she fails . . . it could be the chorus for the rest of her life. Let's wish her well. She knows the songs, she knows the dances. The tricky bit is that twist at the end of the first act. Once or twice I've nearly bungled it."

So I went to the theatre and I sat, trembling for her.

The curtain was about to go up. I surveyed the audience from the box I was sharing with Robert Bouchère. Just for those few minutes we were the only ones in the audience who knew what was to come.

Dolly lifted the curtain and stood before us.

"Ladies and gentlemen, it is with great regret that I have to tell you that Désirée is indisposed and cannot be with you tonight."

There was a gasp which rippled through the stalls, to the upper circle and gallery. I looked about me apprehensively. These people had paid to see Désirée.

"I have been in Désirée's company just before coming to the theatre," went on Dolly. "She is desolate because she has to disappoint you. She begged me to ask you to forgive her and she particularly asks you, her dear public, to give Lisa Fennell a chance to show you what she can do. Désirée has absolute faith in Lisa and I am sure that, after tonight's performance, you will share that faith. I know how you all love Désirée, but you would not want her here when she should be in bed. She sends her love to you all. She is missing you as you are missing her. But she fervently knows that you will give Lisa a chance and that you will not be disappointed."

The curtain was up. The opening chorus

had begun and there was Lisa giving a fair imitation of Désirée in "Can I help you, madam?"

It was a good performance. I followed her every movement, watching for pitfalls, like the twirl at the end of the first act. The audience applauded. Some of them must have realized what an ordeal the poor girl was going through, and they had set aside their disappointment in not seeing Désirée and were giving encouragement to the beginner.

I said to Robert: "It's going to be all right, isn't it?"

"She is so like . . ." he said. "She copy, yes? It is like seeing a shadow of Désirée, you understand?"

"I see what you mean," I replied. "But I think the audience is not displeased."

"Oh no, no. But they do not forget they pay to see Désirée. It is a pity for Lisa that it is Désirée she must follow. If it were some other . . . someone not so . . . how shall we say? . . . so much herself . . . so distinguished . . . it would be better. She is good, this girl, but she is not Désirée."

I saw what he meant. She had modelled herself too closely on Désirée, submerging her own personality into achieving it. If she had tried to present herself and not a pale shadow of Désirée she would have made more impact. As it was, she was Désirée without that inimitable charm, that overpowering charisma.

I drove home in the carriage with Martha and Lisa. Lisa was exhausted yet elated.

The audience had applauded loudly at the end and someone in the stalls shouted: "Well done!"

"The press was there," said Lisa. "Oh, I wonder what they will say."

I felt protective towards her. I thought she was attaching too much importance to this. There might be a few lines in the press, but there would be more interest in Désirée's indisposition than in Lisa's interpretation of Countess Maud.

Lisa evidently believed that stepping into the breach and hearing someone in the stalls saying "Well done!" was going to shake the theatrical world.

My mother was waiting for us. She looked considerably better and wanted to hear all about it. How did the audience react? How had Lisa managed that tricky bit at the end of the first act? Had she got right to the top notes of "I'd love you if you were a shopgirl still"? And how had her steps fitted in with those of the bridegroom?

It had all gone better than she had dared hope, Lisa assured her.

"Now I shall sleep easily," replied my mother. "My dear child, I am sure you were wonderful. And Dolly . . . what did he say?"

"He grunted," said Lisa.

"What sort of grunt was it? We always know his mood by the nature of his grunts."

"Grunts of relief," I said.

"Thank goodness for that. He must have been pleased or he would have been stamping round here by now."

I said: "We must go to bed. Lisa's exhausted." I turned to my mother. "And you are an invalid. Good night, dearest mother."

"Good night, my angel."

We kissed while Lisa stood watching us; then Lisa herself went to my mother and put her arms round her.

"Thank you," she said. "Thank you. I owe everything to you."

"You owe tonight to some beastly bad fish, my dear, not to me," said my mother.

We all laughed and my mother went on: "I'm glad for you, my dear. It was a chance and you were ready to take it. That's the way to do it."

Lisa looked remorseful. "I am sorry it was because you were ill."

"Oh, come. Take your opportunities and be thankful from wherever they come."

And on that note we went to our respective rooms.

There was not a great deal in the papers next morning—just a report of Désirée's illness and that a newcomer, Lisa Fennell, had taken her place. There was no comment on how she had performed.

Dolly came round and I was eager to hear what his verdict was.

"She went through all the motions," he said. "But she's no Désirée, I can tell you that."

"The audience applauded," I said.

"They always do when it's a newcomer. Even audiences have their sentimental moments."

"So you think that's all it was."

He nodded and turned to my mother. "As for you, madam, you be careful what you eat in future. Don't let it happen again. The audience wouldn't stand for it. *Maud* would be off in a week if we had any more of that."

So, I thought, this is the end of Lisa's little triumph.

•

I was sitting in the park with Roderick. It was a week after Lisa Fennell had taken my mother's place in *Countess Maud.* I was telling Roderick about it.

He said: "I suppose that sort of thing happens often in the theatre?"

"Oh yes. It's quite a common occurrence. There is great consternation all the same when the leading player is unable to be there."

"That girl has courage to face an audience

who would obviously have preferred someone else."

"Lisa was overjoyed. She did her best to show concern about my mother—and of course she *was* concerned—but she couldn't hide her joy. After all, it was only a bilious attack . . . uncomfortable at the time, but it soon passed. As you can imagine, there was tremendous drama at the time. Dolly—that's Donald Dollington—made sure of that. I think at heart he enjoys a crisis. It gives him a chance to display his dramatic talents."

"How did the play go?"

"Quite well. I think Lisa is clever to have done it. Of course, there is something very special about my mother. It's more than being able to sing and dance. It's personality."

"The girl seems to have a pleasant personality."

"It's not the same. It was a pity Lisa had to follow someone like my mother."

"We were talking the other day . . . do you remember? . . . when she joined us."

"I remember."

"About this . . . situation. What are we going to do, Noelle?"

"You'd be very welcome at our house, you know. I mentioned to my mother that we had met and she did not seem to think there was anything extraordinary about it."

"It's a ridiculous situation. Just because

your mother and my father had a sort of romantic friendship, you and I are uneasy about meeting."

"But we do meet. Perhaps it is just our feeling and we are imagining something which isn't there."

"My father was uneasy when I appeared at your house. He has never mentioned it, actually, which is odd. I sense that he wants to keep his friendship with your mother apart from his home life."

"That implies, of course, that it was rather a special friendship."

"What of your father? He must have died a long time ago?"

"I'm not sure. My mother doesn't talk about him very much. She makes it clear that she doesn't want to. All that she will say is that he was a very fine man, someone for me to be proud of."

"She never mentions when he died, or how?"

"No. Désirée can be very firm when she wants to, although mostly she is so easygoing. She's made it clear that she doesn't want to talk about him. I sometimes wonder if they parted. You see, she had this burning ambition to succeed on the stage. It might have been something to do with that. I often wonder whether he is still alive and one day I shall see him. But she has certainly made it clear that she does not want to speak of him."

He nodded. "And then . . . of course . . . she just has friends . . . like my father."

"There's a Frenchman, too. He comes and goes just as your father does. Those two have always been coming and going, for as long as I can remember. I have always known that they were her special friends."

"Of course, she is a very attractive person and she doesn't live exactly conventionally in any way."

"Oh yes. She doesn't conform to the rules of society. I am sure she understands that your mother and Robert's wife . . . I presume he has a wife . . . most men have . . . I'm sure she understands they would not approve of her friendship with them. She would say, well, it is better they do not know. She would respect their views and wouldn't want to upset them in any way. She never makes any demands on her friends. She's fond of them . . . you see, it is her way of life."

"I do understand all that, but I am thinking of how it affects us."

"Well, no one has suggested we should not meet. We shall have to see what happens."

Roderick was not very satisfied, and I was thinking that this conversation was an indication of the way in which our friendship was progressing. We were no longer merely acquaintances.

We chatted of other things, but I knew that at the back of his mind was the thought that because of the relationship between our parents we were in a situation which he would like to change.

When I arrived home I was met by consternation.

My mother was laid low with another attack similar to that which she had had before.

Dolly was already there. He was in my mother's bedroom. She was prostrate and looked very pale.

She said: "Oh, here's Noelle. Thank God you're here, darling. I feel better when you're around. It's another of those silly attacks. Something I've eaten again."

I looked at her in dismay. It could not be. It must be something else . . . something serious. I felt a terrible anxiety creeping over me. She had always seemed so young . . . so full of vitality.

"I think we should get a doctor," said Martha.

"No, no," cried my mother. "It's my stupid digestion. I ate too much at lunch. Well, I've learned my lesson."

Lisa was there . . . anxious, on tenterhooks. She seemed as though she was trying to calm herself.

"If I'm no better tomorrow, I'll see the doctor," said my mother. "The important thing is the show tonight."

Dolly gave a repeat of his previous performance, reproaching the Almighty, demanding to know what he had done to deserve this. *Countess Maud* was set for a record run. Why should the powers that be want to ruin that? Désirée *was* Countess Maud, and here he was, in such a short time, having to use the understudy again. What was Heaven thinking of? It hadn't even been a decent interval, and here it was again.

Martha said: "Let's get down to what's what, eh? Let's see what we've got to *do.*"

It was the same as before. Lisa went on. I was not there, but I heard she had improved her performance. It was not such a blatant replica of Désirée's. But the audience was lukewarm. What could one expect? They had come to see Désirée and had been fobbed off with Lisa Fennell.

I saw her after the show. She was exhausted and less elated than on the previous occasion.

"I could do it," she said almost angrily. "But one needs practice. If I had a week's run I'd be all right."

"You're fine and you took it on at such short notice, and you haven't really had a lot of practice on the professional stage. It was really remarkable. They realize that. They don't tell you so, but they do. You know what Dolly is. He scoffs at my mother sometimes."

I was sorry for Lisa. She had tried so hard and she had done very well. It was merely that she could not compare with Désirée.

I doubted there was an actress in London who could have done that.

The next morning, in spite of my mother's protests, we called in the doctor.

Martha said it was too much of a coincidence that she should have eaten tainted food on two occasions so close together. No one else had suffered. It was better for the doctor to come.

My mother was completely restored and apologized to Dr. Green when he arrived.

"Your visit is not really necessary," she said. "It's these people who insisted on your coming. The trouble was that I had eaten something which didn't agree with me and I was a little bilious and dizzy with it, so that I could not get to the theatre last night."

"And," said Martha, "it happened just a few weeks ago."

I thought the doctor looked a little grave then. I was hustled out of the room, but Martha remained.

It was not long before the doctor came out. I heard Martha talking to him as he left.

I rushed into my mother's room. She looked at me triumphantly.

"I told you so," she said. "There's nothing wrong with me. It was something I ate."

"What . . . twice?"

"Yes, twice. It can happen, you know. It's not so difficult to understand."

"But . . . are you sure?"

"Absolutely. I am sound in every limb."

"Well, it wasn't your limbs which were in question."

"No . . . really, there's nothing. It's natural to feel a bit dizzy with a bilious attack. I think I had better have one of those food tasters . . . the sort kings and queens used to have in the old days. Don't mention it to Dolly or he'll make one of the chorus girls taster-in-chief. The fact is that there is nothing wrong with me. But I must always watch what I eat in future."

Martha came into the room. She looked immensely relieved.

"I was right," said my mother. "You wouldn't believe me, would you?"

"Well, let's thank our lucky stars that it is all right. Dolly will be here soon."

"Yes. He'll be furious with me for upsetting his show twice for nothing much."

"He'll be jolly grateful that it was nothing much. My goodness, you had me scared."

"You scare too easily, Martha."

"It did seem as though there was something to be scared about. If anything went wrong with you . . ."

"It would be the end of *Countess Maud,* it seems."

"It would be the end of more than that. I don't know where we'd be without you."

•

Lisa joined us in the park. She just happened to come across us, she said. I wondered if she had followed me. She had been very interested in Roderick.

I was sorry for Lisa. I could understand her need for company. She was hovering between euphoria and despair.

It was the day after her appearance as Maud. The papers had mentioned it. "Another disappointment for all those who had gathered together to see the incomparable Désirée to find that once again she was unable to appear. We are told it was a bilious attack which had forced Désirée to take to her bed instead of the boards. In her place was her understudy, Miss Lisa Fennell, a young dancer usually seen in the chorus. Miss Fennell tried hard. She fought her way through, faltering on some of the intricate dances, but on the whole was adequate. A talented amateur. She needs more practice in the role. Poor *Maud* can only totter along at this rate. It's a thin show and needs a personality like Désirée's to hold it up. If she is going to make a practice of taking nights off, *Countess Maud* will not last another month."

It was a wretched review, damning poor Lisa with faint praise.

Désirée said: "It's not bad, dear, not bad at all. You should see some of the stuff that came my way in the early days! You'd have thought the best thing I could have done was pack up and go home. They're like that, dear, all these critics. They couldn't do it themselves and they don't like anyone else to. You just don't take any notice of them. Most of them would give their ears to be on the stage. They can't do it, so they take it out on those who can. That's what I've always said, and if anyone ought to know, I did."

Lisa let herself be persuaded. Someone outside the stage door as she left had asked for her autograph and that had raised her spirits considerably.

As before, the press was more concerned with Désirée's absence than Lisa's presence. One bilious attack would have been passed over as something that could happen to anyone; but two aroused suspicion. There were hints. Could it be that Désirée's indisposition might be due to an inclination to take just a little too much of her favourite beverage?

This set my mother and Dolly seething with rage and resentment—even threatening to take action against the offending journalist. After a while, though, they grew calmer.

"What can you do?" said my mother.

"You've just got to take what they hand out to you."

Apart from that it seemed that the press had decided that an understudy's taking over from a well-known actress for a night—or two —was no great news.

Because it had happened so recently, on this occasion in the park, Lisa's taking over the part during my mother's enforced absence was the main topic of conversation.

Roderick listened politely as Lisa went over it all.

Poor Lisa, I thought. I supposed talking about it gave some balm to her wounded spirit. She was explaining to him the feeling of numbed terror as the curtain rose.

"I know all the numbers . . . all the steps. I've watched them from the chorus whenever I was onstage, and the chorus is used nearly all the time in *Countess Maud* . . . and yet I keep asking myself, 'Can I remember this? What's the first line after that?' Your knees knock together. You're sure the words won't come."

I put in: "My mother always says it is necessary to feel nervous if you are going to give a good performance, and you obviously did that, Lisa."

"I do hope so. But nobody noticed . . ."

"Dolly did. He was pleased with you, really. I could tell that."

"He said the show would close if Désirée had any more bilious attacks."

"Of course it wouldn't and she won't. Missing a night or two only makes the people more eager to see her."

I turned to Roderick. "Do forgive our going on about this. It was so important to Lisa."

"I can understand that," he said. He turned to her. "I wish I had been there."

"I'm glad you weren't. I'd rather you saw me when I had had a little more practice."

"I hope no more practice with *Maud,*" I said quickly. "You can only have that if my mother has more attacks and we should all be very worried if she did."

"Oh, I didn't mean that. Of course I didn't. I agree. *I* was really worried when she had that second one . . . but of course it was just a coincidence . . . as the doctor said. It can happen."

"Perhaps," suggested Roderick, "you could get the leading part in another play . . . after what you have done in this one. It must be very difficult to be called upon at a moment's notice. Everyone will know that."

"It's part of an understudy's job. I have to be grateful that I got a start at all. It is so hard to get going without friends."

"Well, you have friends now," said Roderick.

She seemed to realize that we had been talking too much about her affairs and she said quickly: "Do tell us more about those wonderful discoveries on your land. How I should love to see them!"

And so we talked, and I felt faintly resentful because once again she had interrupted my session with Roderick.

•

I went with my mother to visit Janet Dare. She lived in a small house in Islington which she shared with a friend. She was delighted to see us.

The first thing she said was: "Look! No crutches."

"Wonderful!" cried my mother. "When are you coming back?"

"I have to do some exercises first. It's the dancing, you see. That's going to take a little time. If it weren't for that, I should be back in a week or so. I hope everything's going all right and Mr. Dollington understands."

"Of course he does."

"It was wonderful of him to go on paying my salary. I don't know what I should have done otherwise."

I knew why that was. I had heard my mother arguing with him about it. Dolly had said the company could not afford to pay a girl who wasn't working, particularly in that he had

had to top up Lisa Fennell's salary on account of her taking on understudy.

"Don't be mean, Dolly," my mother had said. "What's the poor girl going to live on if you don't pay her salary?"

"What she lives on when she's out of work, I suppose," answered Dolly.

"You're a hard one, Dolly."

"Désirée, I'm in business. I've got to make the show pay or we'll all be out of work."

Finally they had come to an arrangement. The company would put Janet on half pay and my mother would make up the rest. Only Janet wasn't to know, because she'd feel awkward if she did.

I wanted to blurt this out, for I always wanted people to know how good my mother was. She, who knew me well, understood and flashed a warning glance at me.

Janet was saying: "They tell me it will be two more weeks before I should attempt to practise. I reckon it will be a month before I'm back. My legs will be stiff at first."

"You don't want to strain yourself. Lisa Fennell's quite good."

"That new girl! What a chance for her! To go on twice!"

"Due to my silly digestion."

"I read the papers. It wasn't exactly fame overnight, was it?" she added with a faint hint of satisfaction.

"That's mostly a romantic dream, you know."

"It has happened. But not to Lisa."

"She hasn't been long on the stage," I said, defending her. "She really did quite well."

"Quite well is a polite way of saying not quite well enough," said Janet. "I reckon I could have made them sit up."

"I can see that I have been a little remiss," said my mother with a laugh. "I should have had more bilious attacks."

"Oh no . . . no," cried Janet. "I didn't mean that! I was horrified when I heard."

"That's all right, dear, I understand. It's all very natural. One man's meat is another man's poison, as they say. Well, it certainly was poison in this case. However, I shall be careful in future. And don't you worry. You'll have a name one day. It's a name you want. It's funny what a name does. People have a way of thinking you're good if they've been told so. And the more they're told, the better they believe you to be. The idea is planted in their heads before they're aware of it."

When we left, my mother said: "Poor girl! It's dreadful for her. I hope she'll soon be dancing again."

•

Lisa was very interested when she heard we had been to see Janet Dare.

"It will be some time before she dances again," I told her.

"It must be awful for her. I know just how she must be feeling."

"She thinks it will be a month. My mother thinks it will be quite six weeks. If it were just singing she would be all right. It's the dancing that's difficult."

"Roderick Claverham doesn't often come to the theatre, does he?"

"No. He's in town only for spells. He's looking after the family estate."

"I suppose it is huge."

"I have never seen it, but from what he says, I gather it must be large."

"That must be wonderful. Charlie . . . his father . . . is such a nice man. What's his mother like?"

"I've never met her."

Lisa smiled secretively. "No. I suppose the families wouldn't meet. What I mean is . . . Charlie's here when he's in London . . . and he's in London quite often . . . when you consider there's this estate in the country."

Of course, Lisa Fennell was sufficiently worldly-wise to understand the situation. Charlie was so obviously devoted to my mother. They were like a married couple . . . not in the first flush of passion, but having reached that happy state of understanding and deep affection, as though they had settled down to a sober and rewarding friendship, undemanding and contented.

Lisa continued to talk of the Claverhams and I found myself telling her what I knew of the Kent mansion and Lady Constance.

She listened avidly.

"And you," she said. "You are really very friendly with Roderick Claverham."

"We've met a few times."

"Even though he doesn't come to the house."

"Well, he could. My mother would be pleased to see him."

"Yet he doesn't come. He just arranges to meet you outside."

"Oh well . . . we just meet."

"I know." She looked amused.

"He comes to London a good deal now, doesn't he?"

"People do, don't they? They like the country, but it's nice to get away from it now and then."

"He's like his father." She was smiling to herself. "How long is he staying in London?"

"I don't know."

"I thought he said something about being here till the end of the week."

"Oh yes, I remember. You are very interested in him."

"I am interested in everyone and he is very interesting. So is his father . . . and Désirée and you . . . I've always been interested in people around me, haven't you?"

"I suppose so."

But I felt she was particularly concerned with Roderick Claverham.

•

Then it happened again. It was about three o'clock in the afternoon. My mother was resting, as she often did, in readiness for the evening's performance. I went in to see her.

She was lying on her bed, and the moment I entered the room, I could see that something was wrong.

"What is it?" I asked.

"I've got that silly queasy feeling coming on."

"Oh no!" I cried, alarm creeping over me.

"It'll pass. When something like that has happened you imagine it's going to repeat itself. That's all it is. Imagination."

"Lie still, then, and perhaps it will pass."

"I hope so, darling. I think it might just be nerves. This maddening countess has been part of my life for too long."

"Oh, it hasn't been all that much of a long run yet."

"I get like this after a while . . . unsettled . . . I keep thinking of something new. I'm restless by nature. I'll be all right. Did you want something? Was that why you came in?"

"No, nothing special. I just wanted to see whether you were asleep. Do you feel any better now?"

"Not really, dear. I'm becoming afraid there's no doubt that it is that silly old thing again."

"Shall I send for the doctor?"

"No, no. He'll only say it's something I've eaten."

"What have you eaten?"

"Nothing much since the dinner last night and the milk I had after the show. I just had coffee and toast for breakfast and a little fish for lunch."

"Fish again?"

"I often have fish."

"It's very strange. I'm worried about you."

"Oh, my darling, you mustn't be. I'll be all right. Strong as a horse, that's me."

"What about those attacks? They are getting too frequent."

"Darling, I think there's no help for it. Dolly will have to be told."

I was really worried now. This was the third time over a fairly short period. Something would have to be done.

Dolly was in despair. He had got away with it twice, and now here it was again. It looked as though it were becoming a habit.

At five o'clock that afternoon my mother was certain she could not go on that night. By this time Dolly was really frantic. What was the audience going to say this time? People would think it was no use booking. You never knew what you were going to see. The press would have a field day. They were already hinting that Désirée's troubles were due to intoxication. That sort of thing did an actress no good with the public. Who was going to believe in these bilious attacks?

That was the trouble. I did not believe in them either. I was terribly afraid that there was some reason for them other than that they were due to something she had eaten.

Martha felt the same. She averted her eyes and muttered something to herself.

"Tomorrow," she said, "I'm going to get another opinion. No more of that dithering old Green."

The immediate concern was the night's show.

Lisa was in a nervous state. Like all actresses in a similar position, she had hoped for fame overnight. She had scarcely had that. I was not sure whether her performances had done her more harm than good. But she was always hopeful. This would be her third attempt and I knew she was practising the leading role all the time.

My mother said to me: "Do go tonight. I think it helps Lisa to know you're there. Robert is in town. He'll go with you."

I did not want her to know how anxious I was about her, so I agreed. The next day Martha and I would put our heads together and decide what should be done. We would call in a specialist and try to find out if there was anything seriously wrong.

Just before Lisa left for the theatre I had a word with her.

She was pale and tense.

"I've done a bold thing," she said. "I don't know what made me. I wrote a note to Roderick Claverham and asked him to come to the theatre tonight as I'm playing the lead."

I was astounded.

"What will he think?" she went on. "He probably won't come."

"Why did you?" I asked.

"I just had a feeling that I needed in the audience all the friends I could muster."

"You'll be all right," I said. "I wonder if he'll come."

"He did say he was sorry he missed my performance before."

I really could not give my attention to much except what was wrong with my mother. I wished I could talk to Martha about it. Charlie wasn't in London at the time. He would have been very understanding and would have helped us to find the right specialist. For to a specialist we were going. Martha had made up her mind about that . . . and so had I.

I was glad of Robert that night. It was his custom to take a box for as long as the play should run for all my mother's shows, so we were able to use it whenever we wanted to. It was most convenient.

Robert was very concerned about my mother, and I felt I could talk to him as openly as I could to Charlie.

He said: "This is most disturbing."

I told him that we were going to insist on her seeing a specialist tomorrow. We didn't think Dr. Green was good enough.

"You think it is something really bad?"

"Well, it has happened three times, all within a short space of time. She has to feel really ill to give up a night's performance. It can't go on. We are wondering if there is some reason for it . . . something wrong . . . internally."

"She always looks so . . . how do you say it? . . . so full of the good spirits."

"Healthy! Vital!" I supplied. "I wanted to stay with her but she wouldn't hear of it. She said Lisa would need my support."

"That is what she say to me. Dear Désirée, she think always of the others."

"Yes. And I'm terribly worried about her."

He took my hand and pressed it.

"We will do something," he promised.

I looked down below. In the tenth row of

the stalls I saw Roderick. He looked up at the box and waved. So he had come to see Lisa.

I was wondering what would happen when Dolly came out onto the stage and said his piece. The audience listened aghast, then the murmuring started.

Dolly looked distraught, his hand to his brow, his pose one of acute melancholy. He faced them bravely.

"Désirée is desolate. She hopes you will forgive her. Believe me, if she were fit to stagger onto this stage, she would have done so."

One or two people walked out. We waited in trepidation for more to follow. There were some anxious moments, and then they settled down.

They had come to see a show. It was an evening's outing, and although it might not be what they had expected, they would stay.

The curtain went up; the chorus was singing; it parted and there was Lisa. "Can I help you, madam?" She was giving it everything she had. I thought she was good.

Let them like her, I prayed.

Dolly came silently into the box and sat down, watching the audience rather than the stage.

After a while the tension eased. It was not going too badly. I felt even Dolly relax a little, but he was still watchful, still alert.

In the interval he left us.

Robert said: "It goes well, eh? Not bad? The young girl . . . she is no Désirée . . . but she is good, eh?"

I said: "Yes. It's the third time she's done it and she improves every time."

"It is a trial for her."

The door opened and Roderick looked in.

"Hello," I cried. "I saw you below. Robert, this is Roderick Claverham, Charlie's son. Roderick, Monsieur Robert Bouchère."

They exchanged courtesies.

"It was good of you to come," I said. "Lisa will be pleased."

"How is your mother?"

"It's another of those horrible attacks. We're going to make her see a specialist. Martha is going to insist, and I agree with her. She can't go on like this. How are you enjoying the show?"

"Very much. I am somewhat far from the stage, but it was the best seat I could get at such short notice."

I looked at Robert. I said: "This is Monsieur Bouchère's box. He kindly allows us to use it."

Robert said quickly: "You must join us. Here you get a good view of the stage, except for the one corner. It is the right one. But that is rarely of importance."

"How kind of you. I shall be delighted."

"You are staying in London long?" I asked Roderick.

"No. My visits are brief. There is a good deal to do at home."

"And your father?"

"He is at home now. I expect he will be coming to London soon."

The bell was ringing and the curtain was about to rise.

I noticed with interest how Roderick watched Lisa.

"She's doing well," I said. "I'm glad."

He nodded.

The final curtain had fallen. Lisa took the applause with obvious gratitude. It did not last very long. If my mother had been there, they would have called her back and back again.

We went into Lisa's dressing room to congratulate her. She was half elated, half apprehensive and looked frail and vulnerable. I felt sorry for her and I sensed that Roderick was, too. Her great chance had not really brought her what she had hoped for.

Roderick said: "I wonder if I could take you out to a little supper . . . you and Noelle and perhaps Monsieur Bouchère?"

"What a lovely idea!" cried Lisa.

Robert said: "You must excuse me," and I added that I wanted to get back at once to see how my mother was.

Lisa's face fell and Roderick looked disappointed, too.

Robert said: "Why should you two not go, yes? It is good for you, Mademoiselle Fennell . . . to sit over supper . . . and what is it you say? . . . relax . . . release the tension. What you have done tonight is a stress . . . is it not? Yes . . . it will be good for you to sit . . . and talk . . . to laugh . . . to forget. I will take Noelle home."

"Thomas will be there with the carriage for Martha and me," I said.

"Then we shall all go in the carriage . . . the three of us . . . leaving these two to their supper."

Roderick was looking expectantly at Lisa. I told myself he was implying that he would like to go back to the house to discover how my mother was, but Lisa was looking so dejected, and Robert was right when he said she needed to relax. As for Roderick, having made the invitation, he could scarcely take it back. So it was decided that Roderick and Lisa should have supper while the rest of us went back to the house.

When we arrived Robert said he would wait to hear the news of my mother, and as soon as we were in the house Martha and I went immediately to her room.

Martha knocked at the door. There was no answer.

"Asleep," she whispered to me. "A good sign."

She opened the door and looked in. Moonlight showed me that my mother was not in her bed.

Hastily we went into the room. And then we saw her. She was lying on the floor and it struck me that her head was in a very unnatural position. Then I saw that there was blood on her face.

I ran to her and knelt beside her. She looked strange . . . unlike herself.

I called to her in anguish. She did not move; she did not answer; and some terrible instinct told me that she would never speak to me again.

•

When I look back over the night that followed, it is just a jumble of impressions. There is the memory of all the household crowding into that room. Robert was amongst them. They were all shocked, unable to accept this terrible thing that had happened.

Dr. Green arrived.

He said: "She must have fallen and cut her forehead on the edge of that dressing table as she fell . . . and she has suffered further injuries."

She was taken to the hospital, but by that time we all guessed that nothing could be done.

We had lost her. I was trying to think what it would be like without her, never to hear her voice again . . . her laughter, her gaiety, her easygoing acceptance of life. All that was gone . . . taken from us in the space of a few hours.

It was not possible to accept it at first. I wondered whether I should ever be able to. Life would never be the same again. I just could not imagine it without her. I could not bear to. She had been right at the heart of my life, and now she was gone, in one night.

Why had I not been there? I could have caught her before she fell. I could have saved her. While I was at the theatre, completely unaware, talking to Roderick, Lisa and Robert . . . this had been happening . . . and she was gone . . . forever.

It was past midnight when Lisa came in. She was flushed and elated. She had clearly enjoyed the evening with Roderick.

She took one look at me and said: "What's happened? What's wrong?"

I said: "My mother is dead."

She went pale and stared at me.

I said: "She got out of bed. She must have had a dizzy spell. She fell. She injured herself . . . and . . . it's killed her."

"No," said Lisa. "Oh *no* . . ."

Then she fainted.

When she recovered, she kept saying: "No,

no, it can't be. She'll get better, won't she? She couldn't die . . . just because she fell."

I did not answer. I just turned away. She caught my arm. There was anguish in her face. She had really cared for my mother. But of course she had. Everyone had cared for my mother. I had thought in my heart that Lisa was too preoccupied with her own success, her own chance to show the world what she could do. It was natural. But she had really cared for my mother. She looked stunned. Yes, she had really cared deeply.

I got her to her room and asked Mrs. Crimp to bring her a hot drink. Mrs. Crimp was only too glad to have something to do.

"I can't believe it," she kept saying. "What shall we do without her?"

I could not answer that question.

The household was numbed by the shock. It was no longer the home we had known.

The papers were full of the news about Désirée.

"One of our greatest musical comedy artistes, Désirée had revolutionized the genre; she had brought it into favour. She was too young to die." She had been cut off in her prime. She would be sadly missed. There were lists of all the shows in which she had appeared. Cuttings from the papers were reproduced.

There were reporters lying in wait for us.

Jane's opinion was asked. "She was a lovely lady," said Jane.

Mrs. Crimp said: "Her sort are rare. There'll never be another like her."

Lisa was interviewed more than any. Lisa was the understudy. "I owe everything to her. She was wonderful to me. She gave me my first chance."

I read the reports again and again. The newspapers were soaked with my tears. I wanted to read the laudatory notices . . . sometimes I would smile, remembering what she had said of some of those roles. Then my misery would descend on me. I could not rid myself of memories. They came flooding back. Going into a room when I was very young. "Is this a party?" and people laughing, frightening me a little until I was caught up in her loving arms.

People had loved her, but none more than I. I was the one closest to her; for me was the greatest loss.

Charlie was heartbroken: Robert was deeply unhappy: Dolly was despondent. The theatre was closed for a week out of respect for Désirée. And then what? demanded Dolly. It was doubtful that *Countess Maud* would continue. Dolly was deeply grieved, but, like the rest of us, what he was really mourning was the loss of Désirée. Like us all, he had loved her.

Then we heard that, in view of the suddenness of her death, there would have to be an inquest.

•

What an ordeal that was!

We were all there—the servants, Martha, Lisa, Charlie, Robert and Dolly. Lisa sat beside me, tense and nervous.

There was no question as to my mother's death: it was due to a fall during which she had broken her neck, and there were multiple injuries which had resulted in instant death. But because Dr. Green had reported that she had been subject to bilious attacks which had come in rather rapid succession and for which the only explanation was that these were due to food she had eaten, a coroner's inquest had seemed desirable.

Two doctors gave evidence. Traces of poison had been discovered in the stomach, although the poison was not the cause of death . . . only indirectly. The sickness and dizziness which had made her fall had, however, been due to the fact that she was suffering from the effects of this poison.

They talked of *Euphorbia lathyrus,* and I began to understand why men had been sent to examine the garden. The doctors explained that they were referring to the plant commonly known as spurge . . . caper spurge in this case. It would have been in bloom at the time of the death and could have contributed to it. In this plant was a milky substance which was a drastic purge and irritant. The results of taking it could be sickness and diarrhoea—and in some instances this could result in dizziness.

It was clear that the deceased had been a victim of such poison, and as there was a bush of caper spurge in the garden, it seemed likely that it came from this.

Perhaps she had been unaware of the unpleasant quality of this plant and had touched it on those various occasions after which she had been taken ill.

We were astounded. My mother had never expressed any interest in the garden, such as it was—a small square behind the kitchen with a few shrubs growing round it, one of which was evidently this caper spurge.

I could not imagine her going down to the garden or, if she did, noticing the plants, but the assumption was that on those occasions when she had suffered the attacks she had been in contact with this plant.

There was a seat in the garden. Yes, she had been seen by Mrs. Crimp on one or two occasions, though not recently, sitting on it. The caper spurge was near the seat. The conclusion was that by some means she had managed to get the poisonous juice on her hands and it had touched the food she ate soon afterwards.

To some it might seem a possible explana-

tion. Not so to me, who knew her so well. It did
transpire that some people were more suscepti-
ble to the poison than others. It was assumed
that the deceased may have been one of these.
But death was not due to the poison. It was the
fall which had caused that.

The verdict was Accidental Death.

It was over. She had gone forever. A blank
and empty future lay before me.

What now? I asked myself. What shall I do?
I did not know and I did not greatly care. All I
could think of was: she has gone forever.

•

A few days passed. They were bleak, meaning-
less. I was too numbed still to take in the situation and to realize fully the drastic change in
my life.

Charlie and Robert were a wonderful help.
I saw them every day. I felt they were both
trying to impress on me that they were my
friends and were going to look after me.

Dolly was quite desolate, and it was not
only because *Countess Maud* would have to
come off, since it was no good without Désirée.
Lisa was quite ill. She stayed in her room and
seemed to want to be alone.

I learned of my financial position. My
mother had earned a considerable amount of
money when she was working, but she had
spent lavishly and the life of even a successful

actress had its unproductive periods. She had lived up to her income and, when debts were paid, there would be just a little for me. Invested wisely, it would bring in a small income, enough perhaps for me to live modestly. The house was mine, but I should not be able to keep a houseful of servants.

My first thoughts were for the Crimps. They, with Jane and Carrie, had been part of my life. Matty had been making plans to leave, because, as she had said, I should not much longer be needing a governess.

Then Robert said he would buy the house from me. He needed a place in London. He had for some time been tired of staying in hotels. He would keep the servants and, of course, I must consider it my home for as long as I wanted to.

I said: "You do not really want the house, Robert. You're just buying it because you know how worried we all are here."

"No, no," he insisted. "I do need a place. Why should I seek . . . when it is here? It is . . . her house. I feel it is what she would want. She talked much of you. She asked me to look after you . . . if ever there was a need. You understand?"

I did. He had loved her. He was doing this for her.

There was the question of Lisa.

"She should not be disturbed," he said.

"She is much upset. She was very grateful to Désirée. She grieves much. No, she must stay . . . if that is her wish. We will not disturb her."

Mrs. Crimp said she had always known that Monsewer Robber was all right and, even though he was a foreigner, he was quite the gentleman. She and Mr. Crimp would look after him. They could not hide their relief that their future was safe.

Then there was Martha. She had already spoken to Lottie Langdon, who had always wanted her and had even on one or two occasions tried to lure her away from Désirée.

"I couldn't stay here," she said. "Too many memories. We'd been together too long. But now she's gone and it's no good wanting her back because she's not coming. I have to keep reminding myself of that. I know what she'd say if she were here, God bless her. 'Be sensible, Martha. I've gone and you're still here. You've got to go on. It was good while it lasted, but it's over now. You're valued in the profession and you know Lottie Langdon always wanted you. She always said you were the best.' That's what she would have said. Charlie will look after you. She always said Charlie came first. He was the most reliable, in spite of that old dragon he married. Robert will keep this place going . . . for her sake . . . and it will always be a home for you. I don't know anyone who was loved as she was. And she deserved it, that she did. I can't stay here. It's best for me to get away . . . and be quick about it. As for you, Noelle, you ought to do the same . . . even if it's only for a little while. If there's anything I can do . . . But I think Charlie wants to talk to you."

She was right. Later that day, Charlie came to me and said: "I want to talk to you seriously, Noelle."

When we were in the drawing room, he said: "Your mother and I were, as you know, very great friends."

"I know that."

"For many years the friendship persisted. I knew her as well as anyone. I loved her deeply, Noelle."

I nodded.

"My dear, dear child, you were always first with her. She was a wonderful woman . . . unorthodox, yes . . . not always acting in a manner acceptable to society . . . but what is that beside a warm and loving, caring heart?" He paused, too filled with emotion to go on.

I waited, sharing his feelings.

"She asked me to look after you," he continued. "She said: 'If I were to go and Noelle needed someone, I'd like it to be you, Charlie.' That is what she said. And it is not only because of that. I'm very fond of you, Noelle."

"You have been wonderful to me, Charlie, always . . . you and Robert."

"There are too many memories here, Noelle. I've been talking to Martha. We agree, you ought to get away. It's very necessary. It's all too close here. I know you will never forget her, but you have to try."

"It wouldn't be any good. I shall never forget her."

"All grief, however deep, is softened by time. I want you to come to Leverson Manor. I want to have you there . . . under my care."

I stared at him in amazement.

"But . . . I have never been there . . . neither I . . . nor my mother. It was . . . apart. We always knew that. Your wife would not want me there."

"*I* want you and it is my home. I promised Désirée that I would look after you. More than anything, I am determined to keep my promise to her."

"You can't do this, Charlie. Our two families have always been kept apart."

"It's different now. I am going to take you to Leverson. You must come. Think about it."

I did think about it. It seemed incredible. To go there . . . after all these years. It was impossible. But Charlie was determined.

For a short period I was thinking of something other than the loss of my mother. To leave this house of memories . . . I thought with sudden pleasure, I shall see Roderick. See him often . . . learn about the estate and some of those exciting remains which had been found on it. For the first time since I had seen my mother lying dead on the floor of her room, I had thought of something else, and the curtain of gloom and melancholy had lifted a little.

•

Charlie went home that day—I supposed to prepare his family for my possible arrival. I could not believe that the formidable Lady Constance would ever allow me to enter her home. But it was Charlie's home, too, and I had seen how determined he could be. He had been devoted to my mother, and that devotion was now directed towards me. I considered the prospect of seeing more of Roderick, and I felt that I was being propelled into agreeing to accept what might be an extremely embarrassing situation. I had to think of my future. I must take Martha's example. She was unsentimental, full of common sense, and she had said, rightly, that when a situation became unbearable, the sooner one moved away from it, the better.

I should have a small income. Thanks to Robert's bounty, I should have a roof over my head. What did women in my position do? Of slender means, fairly well educated: well, there were only two paths open to them. They became governesses or ladies' companions. I could not see myself as either. Governesses usually came from highly respectable backgrounds

—very often from vicarages; ladies who found themselves faced with the necessity to earn a living. The daughter of a famous musical comedy actress would scarcely fit in.

So . . . I needed to think of Charlie's proposition.

It was, after all, what my mother had wanted, and she had sought the best for me. I needed time to think. On the other hand, it was desperately important that I draw myself out of this maze of misery in which I was caught.

Charlie settled the question temporarily.

After a few days he returned.

"Could you be ready to leave by the weekend?" he asked.

"But . . ."

"Let us have no buts," he said firmly. "You are coming."

"Your family . . ."

"My family will be ready to welcome you," he replied with an air of finality.

And that was how I went to Leverson Manor.

KENT

Leverson Manor

I had been expecting a pleasant manor house, but when I saw Leverson Manor I was completely overwhelmed. As the carriage which had been sent to meet us at the station approached the house, I saw that, with its machicolated tower and embattled gatehouse, it dominated the landscape.

I was too bewildered then to notice details, but later, when I began to learn a little about its architecture, I was able to appreciate the intricate cornices, the finials, and the traces of the changing modes of the centuries which intermittent restoration had imposed upon it.

At this time it seemed to have an air of cold defiance—a fortress, ready to defend itself against all comers. It was not merely a stone edifice but a living thing. Through four centuries it would have seen much coming and going —births, deaths, comedies and tragedies. I wondered what it was about to see now. I should be part of this house—for a time at least. I was asking myself what it would hold for me.

Apprehension descended on me as we drove under the gatehouse into a cobbled courtyard. I had a feeling that the house itself was watching me, assessing me, despising me as a being from an alien world, who did not belong here, who knew nothing of life except what had been gathered from the noisy streets of London and the somewhat artificial world of theatrical circles. I was not an ordinary visitor. I was becoming more and more uncertain of the wisdom of coming to this place.

As we alighted from the carriage, Charlie laid a reassuring hand on my arm, and then I knew that he was acutely aware of my apprehension.

"Come along," he said in a voice which was

meant to be cheerful. He swung open the heavy iron-studded door and we went into a hall.

Now I felt I had really stepped into the Middle Ages. I glanced up at the hammer-beam roof, the whitewashed walls hung with swords, pistols, shields and blunderbusses. Two flags were crossed at one end of the hall—one displaying what I presumed to be the family's emblem and the other the Union Jack. Near a staircase, like a sentinel, was a suit of armour. The floor was tiled and our footsteps echoed through the hall as we walked. There was a dais at one end, on which was a large open fireplace, round which I imagined the family gathered after eating at the large refectory table in the centre of the hall.

The windows, two of which were of stained glass, were emblazoned with the family arms and denoted its participation in famous battles. The light from these windows, faintly tinted as it was, gave an uncanny ambience to the place.

Again I told myself I should not have come. I had a ridiculous but certain feeling that the house was telling me that. I did not belong here in this place with all its traditions. I wanted to run out, go straight to the station and back to London as fast as I could.

Then a door opened at the top of a short staircase, which led up from the right side of the dais.

"Noelle. It *is* good to see you." And there was Roderick hurrying towards me.

He took my hands. "I was so delighted when I heard you were here."

Charlie looked on benignly and I felt some of my fears slipping away.

"You two seem to know each other," he said.

"We met once or twice in the street," I told him.

"I was desperately sorry to hear about your mother," said Roderick.

"It was necessary for Noelle to get away," said Charlie.

"You're going to find some interesting things here," said Roderick.

"I think the house is most . . . unusual. I have never seen a house like it before."

"Oh, there isn't one, is there?" replied Roderick with a laugh, looking at his father. "At least, that is what we like to think."

"We're proud of it," said Charlie. "Though I'm afraid we take it for granted, having spent all our lives here. We like to see how it affects people. We have never really lost that, have we, Roderick?"

"Certainly not. The house is a bit of a hybrid, really. That's what happens to these old places. They need bolstering up over the years and you see the ideas in vogue during one century intruding on another."

"Surely that makes it all the more interesting?"

The gloom was dispelling and I felt a great lifting of my spirits. I had been right to come, after all. Roderick was here . . . and Charlie. They would help me . . . protect me if need be.

Then Charlie said to Roderick: "Where is your mother?"

"She is in the drawing room."

My sudden burst of relief evaporated. I guessed that Lady Constance had only accepted my coming here because she had been obliged to.

"We'd better go up, then," said Charlie; and we mounted the short staircase to the door through which Roderick had come into the hall.

We passed through several rooms, under arches and up and down little staircases, past walls hung with magnificent tapestries and portraits. I scarcely noticed them. And after a long time, it seemed, we came to the drawing room.

Charlie opened the door and we went in. Vaguely I was aware of a room with heavy drapes at the windows, a highly polished wooden floor covered in rugs, tapestries and linenfold panelling. And there, seated on a thronelike chair, was the woman I had often visualized and never thought to meet: Lady Constance.

We advanced towards her, and Charlie said: "Constance, this is Miss Noelle Tremaston. Noelle, my wife."

She did not rise. She lifted a lorgnette and surveyed me, which I felt was a gesture meant to remind me of my insignificance. Although I resented this, I stood there quite meekly. There was something about her which demanded homage.

"Good day, Miss Tremaston," she said. "Your room has been made ready for you, and one of the maids can take you to it. You will need to recover from your journey, I am sure."

"Good day, Lady Constance," I replied. "Thank you. It was not really a very long journey."

She waved her lorgnette and pointed in the direction of a chair, indicating that I might sit.

"I gather you have come from London," she said.

"Yes, that is so."

"I don't care for the place. Too much noise . . . too many people, and some of them can be most unpleasant."

Roderick said: "A good many people find London fascinating, Mother, and there are unpleasant people everywhere."

"That may be so," she retorted, "but everything in London is on a bigger scale, and that means there are more of them." She turned to me. "I gather your mother was involved with the theatre." There was a certain distaste in her voice. "You will find it very different here. We live quietly in the country."

"I find the house very interesting," I said.

"That is good of you, Miss . . . er . . ."

"She is Noelle to us," said Charlie with a hint of firmness in his voice.

"And there have been some wonderful discoveries on your land," I said.

"Noelle wants to see the Roman remains," added Roderick.

"H'm," murmured Lady Constance. "But now she will want to see her room. Ring the bell, Roderick, please."

Roderick obeyed and very soon a maid appeared.

"Take Miss . . . er . . . Tremaston to her room, Gertie," said Lady Constance. "And make sure that she has everything."

"Yes, your ladyship," said Gertie.

Roderick was smiling at me reassuringly, Charlie a little apprehensively, as I followed Gertie out of the room.

We went up and down more stairs and through more rooms.

"This is the Red Room, miss," said Gertie when we reached our destination. "It's to be yours. See, it's all in red. Red curtains, red carpets and red on the bed." She giggled at the rhyme, which I imagined had been said many times to the occupants of the room.

"There's the Blue Room, the White Room . . . but they're not used very much. You'll get lost in this house at first. Rambling old place, it is. But you get used to it. They've brought your bags up so you can unpack. Want any help? . . . No? Well, all you have to do is ring if you do. There's hot water and towels here and in about half an hour I'll come and take you down. Her ladyship don't like anyone being late."

When she had gone I sat down on the bed. It was a four-poster, probably at least a hundred years old. I touched the red curtains and felt my uneasiness growing.

Lady Constance was hostile. Naturally she would be, so that should not surprise me. I thought of the streets of London; the carriages taking people to and from the theatre; of my mother, laughing, carefree, full of gaiety. No wonder Charlie had turned to her. She was everything that Lady Constance was not. I longed for her more than ever. I felt lost in an alien world. Such a short time ago everything had been happily predictable—and now there was complete change.

I wanted to weep helplessly. I wanted to go back to Désirée's comforting security; and instead of Désirée's warm loving-kindness, I was confronted by the frigid dislike of Lady Constance.

But Roderick was here, I reminded myself.

He and Charlie wanted me to be happy. I was not alone.

I washed and changed. I was ready to face Lady Constance.

•

During the first days at Leverson Manor, there were occasions when I told myself I should have to get away. It was only the insistence of Charlie and Roderick that I should stay which made me feel that I could not leave at once.

It had soon become clear to me that Lady Constance tolerated my presence only because it was impossible for her to do otherwise.

I saw here a new man in Charlie. I had thought him mild and easygoing, but at Leverson Manor he was master of the household and somehow, formidable as Lady Constance was, he had made her understand this. I also realized more fully how deeply he had loved my mother. I knew that he was lost and lonely without her—a feeling so intense, which we both shared. Silently, he was begging me not to go. It had been *her* wish that we should be together if an occasion like this arose. It had, and he was going to look after me, and it gave him a modicum of comfort that he could do this.

Then there was Roderick. I cannot deny that I drew comfort from him. Like his father, he was determined that I should stay and, bruised and lonely as I was, I was in a measure grateful. I was living in a strange, unreal world between those happy carefree days which I had believed would go on forever and the dreary wilderness of life without Désirée which I must face sooner or later.

In time, I reminded myself, I should consider my situation. Perhaps it would be good for me to do some work. It might indeed be necessary that I did. In the meantime I had to get through the days: I had to learn to suppress my sorrow: and Charlie and Roderick were helping me to do that.

Sometimes I felt that she was watching over me tenderly, urging me to stay with Charlie. She trusted him. Her greatest concern had always been for me. To be without her was utter desolation.

"Try to take an interest, love," I could almost hear her saying. "Perhaps we'll be together someday. I never thought much about these things, but there are times when you have to face them, and if you can get a bit of comfort from believing it, that's not a bad way. Be patient. You've got to go on living. I trust Charlie. He's the one I want to look after you."

Roderick suggested that I should learn to ride.

"It's necessary here in the country," he said.

The riding lessons were a success. Roderick was a good and patient teacher and I began to find the exercise exhilarating. I improved so rapidly that for several hours at a stretch I could forget my mother.

"In a week or so you'll be a good horse-woman, Noelle," Roderick told me. "Then we can go farther afield. There is a good deal for you to see."

He was so delighted that I had to show my pleasure for his sake; but I must say that I did feel uplifted by my aptitude on a horse, and it was certainly good to be able to put aside the black desolation, if only for a few hours.

One of the first things Roderick wanted to do was show me the Roman ruins.

The countryside was very flat around Leverson. From my bedroom window I could see the land stretching out almost to the sea. Roderick had explained to me that at the time of the Roman invasion the sea must have come within a quarter of a mile of the house. Now there was a mile and a half between it and the sea.

When he took me to inspect the finds, he glowed with enthusiasm.

"I always wanted to show you this," he said. "Remember?"

I did remember, and the memory saddened me. We had mentioned the secrecy of our meetings, and we had wished that this need not be. Our wish had been granted, but at what a cost!

Roderick saw at once that he had saddened me and was immediately remorseful.

I said: "It's all right. Yes, I did want to see them. You made them sound so interesting."

"It is one of the most exciting discoveries in the country. It was a sort of fuelling station, but a very important person must have been in charge of operations, and had to have his villa nearby. You see the mosaic pavings . . . lovely reds and whites . . . chalk for the white, sandstone for the red. It's all so ingenious . . . and modern in a way. It was a tragedy the Roman Empire disintegrated. If it had not, we might not have slipped into the Dark Ages." He laughed. "Oh, forgive me. I go on and on about all this. It grips you, you know."

"I am sure it does . . . and I like to hear it. Is that a cottage over there?"

"Not exactly. It's Fiona's domain . . . her workshop."

"Fiona?"

"Fiona Vance. You'll meet her. She's probably there now . . . working away. I'll explain. You asked if it was a cottage. In a way it is. It certainly was once. Then it was derelict, and no one thought much about it. It was isolated . . . falling apart. We did consider clearing it away altogether . . . and then there was this discovery and the cottage was right in the centre of it. When excavations started, and they were finding all sorts of pottery . . . weapons

. . . and things like that, work had to be done on them. That is when Fiona came."

"What does she do exactly?"

"Work continuously. She's dedicated. You see, most of the artifacts are found in fragments. They have to be fitted together . . . like a jigsaw puzzle. Only experts can do it. Pieces of wood . . . metal . . . pottery . . . they all have to be treated in different ways. Without expert knowledge much could be lost."

"And Fiona has this special knowledge?"

"Yes. It's interesting how it came about. She lives with Mrs. Carling, her grandmother . . . a peculiar old lady. She's really rather odd . . . some superstitious people would say she is a witch. They don't like to offend her . . . afraid she'll fix the Evil Eye on them. You know the sort of thing. She's devoted to Fiona. She's looked after her since she was a baby . . . that was when Fiona's parents died. Their carriage overturned and they were killed together when Fiona was about a year old. She's quite different from the old lady. However, you'll see for yourself."

"She sounds very interesting . . . so does the grandmother."

"You'll find lots to interest you here, Noelle."

"You and your father are so good to me."

I heard my voice tremble and he said

quickly: "We're going to show you all this place has to offer. We want you to be happy here. I know how difficult it is just now, but it will get better."

"Tell me more about Fiona."

"Well, it all started when she found some coins in her garden. There was quite a fuss about it. It was an indication of what might be here . . . right on our doorstep. Sir Harry Harcourt . . . have you heard of him? He's one of our leading archaeologists . . . he's been out to Egypt recently and made the most fantastic discoveries. You must have heard of him."

"Yes. I know his name."

"Well, he made a personal visit to Mrs. Carling's garden, and I fancy was rather impressed with Fiona. She was about sixteen at the time, and he offered her a job in one of his concerns. Old Mrs. Carling didn't want her to go, but Fiona's heart was set on it. And of course, it was a wonderful opportunity. Fiona was hooked . . . and she was a good worker. So when all this happened, she was sent here to look after the bits and pieces which were coming to light in fairly large quantities once they started digging around. Old Mrs. Carling was pleased because it brought her granddaughter back, and Fiona was content. She's a kind girl and hated to disappoint her grandmother. So . . . Fiona could do the work she wanted to and at the same time feel no remorse. And the workshop is only a stone's throw from Mrs. Carling's house."

"I look forward to meeting her."

"I am just going to show you our greatest find, and then we'll look in on Fiona. There, look. This is the remains of the villa. Mind how you go. The ground is uneven. You'd better take my arm."

I did so and he pressed my hand against him.

"You need to watch your step. This is part of the villa. This mosaic paving is some of the best-preserved in Roman Britain. Now I must show you what I consider the most important of all. It reveals how civilized the Romans were. Be careful here. Fiona was wondering if we should fence some of this off."

"Do many people come here to look at it?"

"Now and then. Particularly when there is some new discovery and it's mentioned in the press. What I want to show you is the bath. At a time when cleanliness was not the major pre-occupation of most of the world's population, the Romans were very particular about it. This bath has been revealed in almost perfect condition. There are three pools. The tepidarium, the warm, the calidarium, the hot, and the frigidarium, the cold, which I believe they plunged into at the end. A very spartan people these. Look, you can see how deep they were. Don't go too close. It would not be very pleasant to fall in. Sir Harry was very excited about it. Every now and then some party comes down, intent on further exploration. I can tell you, it has altered things at Leverson. It has given us some notoriety in the archaeological world. So excuse me if my enthusiasm runs away with me."

"It's quite fascinating and I love to hear about it."

"You will hear lots about it, I can assure you. Oh, look! There is Fiona. She's heard our approach, I think."

A girl had emerged from the cottage. She was wearing a green smock which was very becoming to her flaxen hair. I noticed that her eyes were green, accentuated by the colour of the smock. Her face creased up with pleasure at the sight of Roderick. Then she was looking at me with a curiosity which she tried in vain to suppress.

"Oh, Fiona," said Roderick. "I was just talking about you."

"Oh, dear," she said, in mock dismay.

"Extolling your virtues, of course. This is Miss Noelle Tremaston, who is staying with us."

"Good afternoon," she said. "I heard you were here. News travels fast in this place."

Roderick laughed. "Miss Tremaston . . . Noelle . . . already knows who you are: Miss Fiona Vance, our archaeological expert."

"He flatters me," said Fiona. "I'm an amateur."

"Oh, come. That's overmodest. You should see the work she has done on some of our finds. We're getting a good idea of the kind of ornaments and pots which were used on this site . . . all thanks to Fiona's careful work. Are you going to ask us in, Fiona?"

"I was hoping you would suggest it."

"Let's go, then," said Roderick. "Miss Tremaston wants to see some of the marvels you've produced."

She smiled at me. "I've only fitted together what was already there," she said. "I was just going to make a cup of coffee. Would you care for some?"

"We'd enjoy that," Roderick answered for us, and I immediately agreed.

It was indeed a cottage which had clearly been converted into a workshop. There were two rooms made into one. Benches had been set up and these were crowded with oddments and various tools, some of which I did not at that moment recognize as such but which afterwards Fiona explained to me were bellows to blow away loose earth, coarse metal sieves, ladles, steel rods for inserting into the ground which were called probes, as well as brushes of different sizes. There were containers of all sorts, glues and bottles of several kinds of solution; and in the centre of the room was a stove on which stood a pan of hot water.

Leading from this room was a small alcove, part of a kitchen. In this was a deep sink and a tap. There was an old stove there and a cupboard, from which Fiona took cups and a coffeepot.

There were four small chairs with wicker backs and on these she asked us to be seated while she went into the alcove and made the coffee.

Roderick told me that the cottage had not had to be changed very much. The stairs near the old kitchen led to two rooms upstairs, the bedrooms, and they were left just as they had been.

"That is where Fiona has a rest when she is tired."

"That is not true!" retaliated Fiona from the alcove. "I'm never tired during the day. I bring a sandwich with me most days and make coffee. Sometimes I take them upstairs just to get away from all the muddle and the smell of some of the products I have to use."

She brought in the coffee in cups on a tray.

"Are you staying long at Leverson?" she asked me.

I hesitated and Roderick said: "We are trying to persuade her to."

"And you come from London, I believe?"

"I do."

"I daresay you'll find it a little dull here."

"Shame on you, Fiona!" cried Roderick. "With all this on your doorstep! I've just been showing her the baths."

Her eyes shone. "Aren't they wonderful?"

"I have never seen anything like them before," I told her.

"Few people have . . . in such condition. Isn't that so, Roderick?"

"See how proud we are. Fiona, you are worse than I am."

They exchanged glances, and I wondered about the relationship between them. He was obviously fond of her and she . . . well, perhaps it was too soon to say, but I fancied she was of him.

She went on to talk about the vase she was piecing together.

"It's an unusual one," she was saying. "There is too much missing as yet. It's disappointing."

"There is quite a unique pattern on it."

"Yes. That's what is so maddening." She shrugged her shoulders and smiled at me. "Well, that's all part of the job," she went on. "There is often something which could be made perfect . . . but the essential parts are missing."

"The coffee is delicious," I said.

"Thank you. I hope you will look in whenever you are this way."

"Shouldn't I be disturbing your work?"

"No, not at all."

"Fiona loves to talk about it, don't you, Fiona?"

"I suppose so. By the way, I've made a sketch of that drinking vessel . . . how I think it should look if completed. Of course, we've only a fragment so far. It's at home. Come and have a look at it when you're passing."

"I will," said Roderick.

It struck me that, as I wondered about her, she might have similar thoughts about me. She might be asking herself how friendly *I* was with Roderick. She was watching me intently. I could not say in a hostile manner. She had been charmingly welcoming and friendly towards me.

It occurred to me that she must be in love with him.

As we walked back to the manor, talking about what we had seen that morning, I was preoccupied, thinking about my own feelings for Roderick.

•

Unsettled as my position was, I was being drawn more and more into life at Leverson Manor. My feelings were not only mixed; they went from one extreme to another. I was becoming more and more interested in the house.

Sometimes it seemed to welcome me, at others to reject me.

On one occasion I was lost. In those first days it was easy to lose one's way. There were so many doors: one could easily miss the one for which one looked and find oneself in a hitherto unexplored part of the house.

It was during my first week that this happened to me. I had come from my room and turned into a corridor which I had thought would take me to the staircase. When I realized my mistake, I tried to retrace my steps. I felt sure I was going in the right direction and would in due course come to the hall.

However, I found myself in a part of the house which I had never seen before. I came into a room with several windows and portraits along the wall facing them. The light was strong, for it was early morning and I had been on my way down to breakfast. The room faced east. There was a deep silence. I often felt this in the house when I found myself alone. It was rather disconcerting. There was a table in a corner and beside it a piece of unfinished tapestry on a frame; in another corner of the room was a spinning wheel.

I looked about me. I guessed this was one of the older parts of the house. I tried to fight off that familiar feeling which came to me now and then that I was being watched. It was most uncanny.

I should have tried to retrace my steps immediately, but there was something about the place which made me pause.

I glanced at the pictures on the wall. There were about six of them in ornate frames, and the subjects wore clothes of several early periods. I studied them—Leversons and Claverhams, I guessed. The eyes of some seemed to look straight at me and they made me feel uneasy. As I stared, their expressions seemed to change and to regard me with derision, distrust and dislike.

I was growing very fanciful since I had come here. It was because, in spite of the welcome I had had from Charlie and Roderick, in my heart I knew I should not be here. I wondered what my mother would have been like if she had married Charlie and come to live here. The house would have been different then. She would have dispersed that aura of formality. She would have snapped her fingers at the past.

I moved towards the unfinished tapestry in the frame. I recognized it at once. It was the house itself, in all its splendour. I recognized the coat of arms worked in blues, reds and gold.

There was a rustle behind me. I started guiltily. Lady Constance had come silently into the room and was watching me.

"You are interested in my work, Miss Tremaston?"

"Oh yes . . . it is quite splendid."

"You know something of tapestry work?"

"I have never done any."

"This is the house, you see. The house is very important to me."

"I know. It is such a magnificent place."

She had approached me and was standing close to me, watching me intently.

"Ever since I came here I have done my best to maintain the standards laid down by our ancestors."

"I am sure you have."

"I am determined that nothing shall disturb that."

"Yes," I said. "It would be a pity if anything were to."

"Were you . . . er . . . looking for something?"

"Oh no . . . no. I lost my way."

"It is so easy to lose one's way when one is not accustomed . . ." Her voice trailed off.

I felt myself shiver slightly. I had a great urge to turn and run away . . . right out of this house.

I said feebly: "I was going down to breakfast."

"Oh yes. You go back the way you came. At the end of the corridor you will find the staircase. It leads down to the hall. The breakfast room is on the right."

"I realize now the way I should have gone. Thank you."

I was relieved to escape. She was telling me to go, that I did not belong here. It was in every gesture, every inflection of her voice. I must go . . . soon.

But later that day, when I was having my riding lesson in the paddock, Roderick made me feel how glad he was that I was here, and I wanted to stay.

•

The uncertainty was soon back with me. I could go to London. Robert had impressed on me that I must use the house whenever I wanted to. He was particularly anxious that I should regard it as my home. It was what my mother would have wanted; and, as with Charlie, now that she was gone, he could only be comforted when he was doing what she would have wanted.

This must necessarily be a waiting period. In the meantime I must try to resign myself with serenity for whatever fate was in store for me. I was less unhappy than I had thought possible during the riding lessons with Roderick and sharing with him the enthusiasm for the Roman remains, in which my interest was growing apace. I was becoming friendly with Fiona and sometimes, when Roderick was busy, I went alone to the cottage. Fiona showed me how to clean pottery with a soft brush in order to loosen the dirt. I would picture as I did so the people who had used such utensils in their ordinary daily lives. I discovered the fascination of delving into and seeking to re-create the past. It was a wonderful way in which to escape from the present.

I tried to forget Lady Constance, and indeed did not see a great deal of her. She would appear at dinner, but other meals she often took in her room. I always sat next to Charlie on those occasions and he would talk to me, protecting me, as it were, against the faintly disguised shafts which came from Lady Constance. Not that she took a great deal of notice of me. Her strategy was to treat me coolly, as a guest whom she hoped would not stay long. No one else seemed to be aware of that, but for me the implication was there.

I had struck up a friendship with Gertie, the maid, who had been given the task of looking after me. She brought my hot water night and morning and cleaned my room.

She was a girl of about seventeen who had come to the family at the age of twelve. She had taken a liking to me, perhaps because I was less formal than most of the guests who came to Leverson Manor. I enjoyed chatting to her.

She knew that I was the daughter of Désirée and was overawed by the fact.

"I saw Désirée once," she told me. "It was

a few years back . . . when my sister got married. He was comfortably off, her young man . . . had two stalls in Paddington, in the market there . . . cockles and mussels. He did a thriving trade. When they were engaged, he took me and my sister to the theatre. It was lovely. He said, 'I'll take you to see the great Désirée. That's what all London's doing.' We went to see her in *Gypsy Girl.*"

I closed my eyes. I remembered it well. There had been the usual quarrels, my mother refusing to wear some of the costumes, Dolly stamping out and being allowed to go . . . and then coming back and making some compromise over the costumes. And the longing for the old days was almost unbearable.

Gertie did not know that. "She was lovely," she went on. "She had big gold rings in her ears . . . and the way she danced with Lord James . . . all round the stage she went . . . it was lovely."

"I remember it well," I said.

"And now you're here, miss. That's ever so exciting."

I could see my connection with Désirée played a big part in my attraction for her, and in due course I think it made her more frank with me than she would have been with anyone else.

She told me that Lady Constance was "a bit of a tartar."

"Everything's got to be just as she wants it. Otherwise you're called to her. There's a warning once, but next time you could be out. She's always talking about trad-something."

"Tradition," I suggested.

"Yes, miss, that's it. Everything in the house has got to be just right . . . and just like it was in bygone days."

"I can imagine that."

"She can be hard on people. There was Emmy Gentle."

"One of the maids?" I asked.

Gertie nodded. "She was a wild one. More fond of the men than housework. She'd be larking about with anything in trousers that came her way. And she was always breaking things. Sometimes you could cover up for her . . . but there was this precious china. She was warned once . . . twice. Then there was a third time. That was it. It wasn't easy to get another place . . . not without a reference. Emmy couldn't find anything. Then she went to the bad."

"To the bad?"

"Well, yes. That's what they call it. You should have seen her. All decked out, she was. She had a dress of real silk. She said it was better than being Lady Constance's slave. But it just shows you . . . you've got to be careful with her ladyship."

Gertie told me about her home. "There was

eight of us . . . only two old enough to go out
to work. I send home a little bit. Not much, but
it's a help."

She had made me see that, like most members of the household, she went in fear of Lady
Constance. The case of Emmy Gentle had been
a lesson to them all.

Gertie went on: "Her ladyship don't like
that Miss Vance seeing so much of Mr. Roderick."

"Doesn't she?" I asked. "Why?"

"Well, she'd be afraid, wouldn't she? After
all, who is she? That old grandmother of hers is
a witch, some say. Emmy Gentle went to her
once when she was in a bit of trouble. Emmy
always said she did her a power of good. Oh,
Miss Fiona's the young lady all right. Had a
good education, they say. Old Mrs. Carling saw
to that. She'd want the best for her. Then there
was that Sir Harry Something. He taught her a
lot about those old Roman things and he gave
her a job. She went away and came back. Oh,
she's quite the lady, but she's not the sort Lady
Constance would want for Mr. Roderick."

"And . . . er . . . Mr. Roderick?"

"I reckon he'll go his own way. Him and
the master are ones for having their own way
. . . for the things that matter to them . . .
though they're soft enough in some things.
Alike they are. But I reckon when the time
comes Mr. Roderick will choose without his

mother's help. All the same, there's sure to be fireworks if he did. But we'll see. She wants a real lady for him . . . someone with a grand title. Well, she is *Lady* Constance herself . . . and she don't like you to forget that."

"Yes, as you say, it will be for Mr. Roderick to decide."

"Yes . . . but there is that old Mrs. Carling . . . she's one to get what she wants, and they say she's got powers . . ."

I was silent, wondering about the wisdom of carrying on such a conversation with a servant in a house where I was a guest. I said how interesting it was that the Roman remains had been discovered on Leverson land. But to Gertie the past was not of the same interest as the immediate present, and the conversation came to an end. I left her then to get on with her work.

•

One day I called at the cottage and instead of Fiona I found a strange woman there. I guessed at once that it was Mrs. Carling, of whom I had heard so much.

She was certainly unusual—tall and straight with dark abundant hair, which she wore in plaits round her head; large Creole earrings dangled from her ears. But what struck one immediately were her bright, penetrating eyes. They were luminous and gave the impression that they were seeing something invisible to others. The manner in which they were fixed on me made me feel faintly uneasy, for she gave me the impression that she was probing into my mind, trying to discover things which I did not wish to be revealed.

I said: "You're Mrs. Carling, I'm sure. I've heard so much about you. I'm Noelle Tremaston."

"Of course. And I have heard much about you. I am so pleased to meet you at last. And how are you liking this part of the country?"

"It's very interesting . . . and particularly the discoveries."

She nodded. "Fiona's gone off. Someone found something in a garden. She has gone to see if it's ancient or modern. You'd be surprised how many people think they've found something of value since all this started!"

"I suppose that is inevitable, and you never know whether it is going to be something of real importance."

"Do sit down. Would you like some coffee?"

"No, thanks. I've just had lunch."

"Fiona may not be long. She went out an hour or more ago."

I sat down.

"She's completely caught up in all this," she said.

"I can understand how absorbing it is."

"H'm," she said. "She and Roderick Claverham . . . they are a pair of enthusiasts."

"I know."

She was looking at me anxiously. "And you, my dear. I know you have suffered a terrible loss."

I was silent, and she went on: "Forgive me. I shouldn't have mentioned it. But I am . . . aware. Perhaps you have heard something of me."

I nodded.

"Fiona is fond of you already. I should like to help."

"Thank you . . . but there is nothing anyone can do. It has just . . . happened."

"I know, my dear, but you are young. If at any time I could help . . . I don't know whether you've heard, but I have been blessed with a certain gift."

She was making me feel rather uncomfortable, for as she spoke she was watching me so intently.

I said: "Yes, I have heard."

"I've had my sorrows, so I understand full well," she went on. "I lost my daughter when she was twenty-two years old. She was my life. I took Fiona and she became my consolation. There are always consolations in life, my dear. We do well to remember that."

"I try to remember it."

"I knew of your mother, of course. I know

she was a wonderful person as well as a famous one. I know what it feels like to be suddenly bereft. There is some good to come, even out of such suffering. It helps us to understand the suffering of others. I just wanted you to know that."

"Thank you. You are very kind."

"One of these days you must come to see me. I could perhaps help in some way."

"It is good of you."

"Promise me you will come."

"Thank you. I will."

She went on: "I have said what had to be said and that is enough. Tell me about yourself. Tell me what you think of the excitement over all these relics. The Claverhams are delightful people, are they not? Senior and Junior, I mean. We couldn't have better squires of the neighbourhood. Such a wonderful family . . . going right back through the centuries. Roderick is going to be just like his father. It is what the neighbourhood needs. I am sure they are very kind to you."

"Yes, they are."

She looked at me somewhat roguishly. "And her ladyship?"

I was taken aback and she laughed. "She has grand ideas about certain things, that one. But Mr. Claverham is a good and kindly man and his son Roderick takes after him."

Suddenly she seemed to change her mind.

Perhaps it occurred to her that she was being a little too frank on such a short acquaintance and she began to talk of the village and what a difference the discoveries had made, how glad she was that Fiona had found the work she loved so close to home—such absorbing work which she was able to share with Roderick. She talked of some of the people in the village and how she had managed to cure them of certain ailments because she had a herb garden where she grew all sorts of medicinal plants which her special knowledge helped her to use to advantage.

"Some of them call me a witch," she told me. "Years ago I might have been burned as one. Think of all the good women who met that fate. There are white witches as well as the other sort, you know. White witches bring nothing but good. I am one of that kind . . . if you can call me one. I want to help people. I want to help you."

I was relieved to hear the sound of horse's hoofs. Mrs. Carling rose and went to the window.

"It's Fiona," she said, and in a few moments Fiona came into the cottage.

"Oh, Noelle," she said. "How nice to see you. You've met my grandmother."

"We have been getting along very well," said Mrs. Carling.

"I had to go to Jasmine Cottage," said Fiona to me. "They found some fragments of china in the garden. Someone must have thrown an old milk jug out a few years ago." She smiled ruefully. "We get that now and then. But of course we have to look at everything. We can't afford to let anything pass."

"Of course not," I said.

"Well, I'm glad my grandmother entertained you. Thanks, Granny."

She looked a little uneasy and, having met the grandmother, I could understand that.

"I daresay you'd like some refreshment, Fiona," said Mrs. Carling.

"Oh, I would," said Fiona.

When Mrs. Carling left us to make the coffee, Fiona looked at me almost questioningly. I knew she was wondering what her grandmother had said to me.

I told her that we had had a very interesting chat and she seemed relieved.

We were drinking the coffee which had been prepared when Roderick arrived.

He told us that he had been to see one of the tenants and, as he was passing, he couldn't resist calling. He looked pleased to see me there. I knew he was delighted that Fiona and I got along so well.

Fiona explained about her visit to the cottage to inspect the broken milk jug.

Roderick laughed. "Another?" he said. "Well, no doubt there will be lots more."

"The trouble is, one can never be sure."

"No stone must be left unturned," quoted Roderick. "Who knows? You might find the discovery of the century. How is the vase coming along?"

"Slowly. I'm getting so many pieces of various things that I don't know how I get them all in this place."

"You'll have to have a room at the Manor."

"I might even want that."

"Why not? There's plenty of room. All you have to do is ask."

"I'll remember that," said Fiona.

"Well, she is certainly overcrowded here," said Mrs. Carling, smiling benignly on her granddaughter.

When Roderick and I were leaving together to return to the Manor, Mrs. Carling took my hand and looked at me earnestly.

"I do want you to come and see me," she said.

"Thank you. I should like that."

"Please promise me."

"I will come."

"I think you will find it . . . useful."

We said goodbye, and when we had left the cottage, Roderick said: "What did you think of the old lady?"

"She's very unusual."

"Unusual! Some people think she is slightly mad."

"She did say that she could have been burned as a witch two hundred years ago."

"Lucky for her, then, that she was not born earlier."

"I think she is devoted to Fiona."

"There is no doubt about that. Fiona is a very admirable young lady. She certainly does not take after her grandmother. No flights of fancy there. Fiona has her feet firmly planted on the ground. She is wonderful to her grandmother, who, at times, must be something of a trial to her."

We reached the house. I went in while Roderick took our horses to the stables.

•

I heard from Lisa Fennell. She wrote:

Dear Noelle,

I have not written before, as I have been ill. I am still at the house. Monsieur Bouchère has said I may stay until I find something suitable. Mrs. Crimp has been an angel. I don't know what I should have done without her—and of course Monsieur Bouchère's kind hospitality.

I was so terribly shocked by your mother's death. I was very fond of her. Her wonderful understanding and help meant so much to me. I shall never forget how she helped me. She was the most wonderful person I ever met.

That she should die like that . . . at the height of her powers . . . and so suddenly

. . . really shattered me. I had a slight cold at the time. It developed and with the shock I became really ill.

I can't stop thinking of her and what we have all lost . . . including the theatre, which will never be the same without her. I was so depressed . . . so wretched. She had come into my life like an angel of mercy . . . and then to be taken away. I felt guilty because I was taking her place when it happened.

I've recovered now. I am going to throw myself into my work. I have been very lucky. Mr. Dollington has given me a part in his new show, Rags and Tatters. *It will be opening in a few weeks. At which theatre, I am as yet uncertain. We are into rehearsals madly, as you can guess. Lottie Langdon is taking the lead. Mr. Dollington is very sad. Something seems to have gone out of him.*

But we all have to go on, don't we?

I do hope you will come and see the show. Perhaps you could persuade Mr. Claverham to come with you. I should so enjoy seeing you again.

With my best regards,

Lisa Fennell

Here it was back . . . the heartbreaking memories . . . Lisa under the horse's hoofs . . . bringing her into the house. Désirée's concern . . . bullying Dolly into giving Lisa a place in the chorus.

It would always be like that.

• • •

A few days passed and I was no nearer to making a decision about my future. One moment I wanted to stay at Leverson Manor, the next I felt an urgent desire to get away. The main reason for this was, of course, Lady Constance. At dinner I would often find her eyes on me. It was an uncanny feeling. Once, when I was talking to Roderick in the garden, I glanced up at the house and saw a shadow at a window. I knew it was Lady Constance, and I had the feeling that she was willing me to go. But whenever I suggested that I should, there were loud protests from Roderick and Charlie.

I should soon be having a meeting with the solicitor who had looked after my mother's affairs; and when he told me exactly what the position was, I must make plans.

The estate kept Charlie and Roderick busy. It was very large and they were often out all day.

Roderick said: "When you are a little more practised, you will be able to ride out with me and see something of the estate . . . meet some of the tenants. I think you will enjoy that."

He spoke as though I should be at Leverson Manor indefinitely, and I reminded myself— though not him at that time—that as soon as I had seen the solicitor, I must bestir myself and decide on my future.

My friendship with Fiona grew quickly. She was very interested in the theatrical world and over cups of coffee we talked a great deal. I found it comforting to talk of Désirée to someone who had not known her. I explained about the shows and the way she had worked. I could smile, remembering the first nights, the tension before them and the relief when they were over, the people who had come to the house, the dramas, the triumphs.

In her turn, she talked to me about her life, how good her grandmother had been to her.

"Sometimes," she said, "I fear I shall never be able to repay her. She spent more than she could afford on my education. Sometimes I fear she has made me too much the centre of her life and I shall disappoint her. She has never said so, but I believe she would rather I was not interested in all this. I remember one day she said to me, 'You are growing up, Fiona. I want the best for you. My daughter, your mother, meant everything to me and when she died there would have been nothing at all if she had not left you.' Soon after that, I found the coins in the garden and everything changed. She hints that she led me to the coins. She had a premonition that they were in the garden and I should find them and they would change my life . . . lead me on to my destiny. Well, the

coins aroused Sir Harry Harcourt's interest,
and he gave me a chance. You see, my grandmother believes she has special gifts and naturally she wants to use them for getting the best
for me."

"What is that?"

"I suppose most people . . . parents . . .
grandparents . . . think it is a good marriage
for their charges. They want security through
what they call a good marriage. I think I could
have a very happy life . . . working like this.
But my grandmother probably wouldn't agree
on that. And your mother . . . I expect she
planned something like that for you."

"I suppose she would have wanted me to
marry in time. But what I wanted was to be
with her and for things to go on as they always
had done. I rather think she wanted the same.
And then . . . suddenly . . . it was all over."

"Let me show you how the vase is coming
on. I wonder if I shall ever be able to complete
it."

I looked at the pieces she was working on
and she showed me some sketches of what she
thought it might have looked like when it was
complete.

I told her then that her grandmother had
invited me to call on her.

"Yes, I heard her asking you. She's very interested in people who come here, and she is
particularly interested in you."

"Because of my mother," I said.

Everything seemed to lead back to her, and at any moment my grief could overwhelm me.

Fiona understood and we talked of other things.

•

The following afternoon I found myself making my way to Mrs. Carling's house. I found the place easily. It was a large cottage, surrounded by shrubs, and there was a gate with a short path to the door. It was very quiet. I paused for a moment, wondering whether I wanted to go on. There was something very strange about the woman and I was a little disturbed by the probing nature of her interest and the manner in which she would suddenly lean forward and peer into my face.

I noticed some unfamiliar plants in the garden at the side of the house. Herbs, I supposed. Did she make them into concoctions which she supplied to people like Emmy Gentle in their troubles?

The door was overhung by creeper, which also grew round the windows. I thought of Hansel and Gretel in the witch's house.

Did Roderick ever come here? I wondered. I sensed that he was fond of Fiona. But then he made me feel that he was tender towards me. There was something very kind in Roderick's nature. He was considerate to everyone. It came naturally to him. I felt that it would be unwise to imagine that there was something special for me simply because of his kindness.

I lifted the brown knocker and I could hear the sound of it echoing through the house. I stood waiting. It would be pleasant if Fiona was there, and perhaps Roderick would call and join us.

The door opened. Mrs. Carling was smiling delightedly at me. She was wearing a long flowing gown with a tiger-skin pattern; the Creole earrings swung as she held out her hand to me.

"Come in. Come in," she cried. "I am so glad you decided to come. I had a feeling you were hesitating."

"Oh no. I wanted to come."

"Then let us go in. I know we are going to have an enjoyable afternoon. I have been looking forward to this ever since we met. It's more cosy than in that room of Fiona's . . . all those bits and pieces and brushes and things . . . playing about with things people used long ago. It's like disturbing the dead, as I say to Fiona."

"Perhaps they would be rather pleased that we are so interested in them . . . if they could know it," I said.

"Maybe. Maybe. You'd like a cup of tea, I am sure. I have the kettle on the boil."

"Thank you."

"I'll get Kitty to bring it in. She's my little maid."

We were in a room with two small windows, each fitted with leaded panes. The heavy curtains made the room dark. The furniture was heavy, too, and there were several pictures on the walls. One was of a saint being stoned to death and another was of a woman, her body strapped to a stake of wood, her hands folded in prayer; she was standing in water and it was clearly meant to imply that when the tide rose she would be submerged. I read the title. "The Christian Martyr." There was another picture of a big black cat with green eyes. The paint was luminous and it was most effective and inclined to be eerie. The creature seemed alive.

I felt oppressed and wished Fiona would appear, but I supposed at this time she would be working.

Mrs. Carling sat opposite me.

"I must explain about Kitty," she said. "She's a little backward. She came here one day, wanting me to do something for her. She had heard I cured people of some ailments. I took an interest in her. She had not had much of a chance, really. I thought a little care might help her. She could only stutter when she came to me . . . but she is improving. She is one of a large family. The father worked in the mines. Kitty's brothers joined him and her sisters went into service. No one wanted to employ Kitty.

They didn't want her at home. Well, she came here and I took her in. I've trained her as well as I can. She's a good child. She's very grateful to me."

"How kind of you."

She smiled at me benignly. "I like to help people. Some of us are given special powers and we are meant to use them. If you don't they can be taken from you."

It was not long before Kitty brought in the tea. She was young, about sixteen, I imagined. She had a gentle self-deprecating manner and was clearly very eager to please.

Mrs. Carling indicated where she wanted the tray. Kitty set it down and gave a shy glance in my direction. I smiled at her; she returned the smile, which illuminated her face. I warmed to Mrs. Carling, who had clearly helped the poor girl considerably.

Mrs. Carling patted Kitty's shoulder. "Good girl," she said, and when she had gone, Mrs. Carling said: "Poor child. She is so anxious to do well. Now tell me, how do you like your tea?"

As we partook of the tea and little cakes, we talked. I asked how long she had been here.

"I came here with Fiona," she told me. "It was when her parents had died and I had her to myself. So this has been our home all these years. The only time I was here alone was when she went away to school and then, of course, to

Sir Harry Harcourt's place. It was a blessing that she came back to me because of the work here."

"You must have been rather sad when she went away."

"Oh yes. But it was best for her and I knew she would come back. So I was able to endure the separation."

"It must be very interesting to know such things."

"Nothing is entirely fixed in life, you know. Disaster can threaten, but there are ways of avoiding it."

"You mean it is up to a person whether he or she is involved in tragedy."

"I just mean that there are times when it can be avoided."

"So these things are not destined to happen."

"Not exactly. They can be in our paths . . . but if we are aware of them, we can stop them happening."

"How interesting!"

"It is just one of those gifts one is born with. You, my dear Miss Tremaston, are at this stage at a turning point in your life. That much I can sense immediately."

I thought: She knows my mother has died and she will have heard how devoted we were. She probably guesses there will not be a great deal of money. It is a natural assumption.

She went on: "It may possibly be that I can help you."

"I think it is a matter which will evolve naturally."

"Maybe. But I want to help you."

"It is very kind of you."

"We are meant to help each other. We have been divinely endowed for that purpose and must not forget it. My dear Miss Tremaston, I know you need help. That is why I was so anxious that you should come to see me. You need help . . . urgently. When we have finished tea, I shall take you to my private sanctum. I have seen so many people there . . . and I believe have benefitted them. I am convinced that now I can be of help to you."

I was both repelled and fascinated. There seemed to be something false about her and yet I could almost believe in her powers.

We left the tea tray and she led me up a short staircase to a room which had similar leaded windows and the same kind of heavy drapes, but being slightly higher, it was a little lighter. The first thing I noticed was the table covered with a green baize cloth and on a wooden stand was a large glass ball.

Mrs. Carling was standing close to me.

"It helps," she murmured, "if you will take a seat here. I shall sit opposite."

I sat down.

"Give me your hand." She held mine across the table.

"Ah, I feel the waves coming over to me. We are in tune. My dear, I am going to be able to help you."

Her heavy breathing was disrupting. I kept my eyes on the glass ball.

"Oh . . . I am aware of it now. My dear child, it is very close. You are threatened. Oh yes, it is there. I cannot but see it . . . I feel it . . . it is very close . . . oh, very close. How glad I am that I decided to speak to you. Oh yes . . . yes. It was time."

I watched her while she laid her hand on the ball. She was staring into it.

"Danger," she whispered. "Danger."

"Where?" I asked. "From what?"

"I cannot quite see. It's there . . . vague . . . menacing. No . . . I cannot quite see. But I know it is there."

"You mean at Leverson Manor?"

She was nodding. "Enemies," she said. "They are lying in wait . . . watching . . . waiting. Oh yes, this is a warning. No time to lose. You must go. Soon . . . it will be too late."

"But what is this danger?"

"It is there . . . hovering over you. I see this black cloud. It is evil. I can tell you nothing more . . . only that it is there . . . near. It comes nearer . . . nearer. It is almost upon

you. It is here . . . in this place. This is where
danger awaits you. You must get away from
here. You must not delay. There is still time."

She fell back in her seat, breathing heavily.
"No more," she murmured. "No more . . .
but it is enough."

She leaned forward once more and looked
into the ball.

"It is gone," she said. "There is nothing
more. You have had your warning. That is
enough."

Her breath was now coming in short gasps.
"It is always so," she muttered. "It is exhaust-
ing."

I said: "Do you mean that you see me
threatened . . . in that piece of glass? Then
you must have seen who . . ."

She shook her head. "It is beyond our understanding. I see symbols. I sense that you are
in danger. You have just suffered a great loss.
You are alone . . . bewildered. This I knew
when I first met you. And I knew, too, that
there was some menace. You are in dangerous
waters. That is all I can tell you, and you can
avoid this danger by leaving this place. It could
only happen here."

I said: "Should I go back to the Manor and
tell them that you have advised me to leave?"

She smiled slowly. "They would laugh.
Lady Constance thinks that it is Lady Constance who rules the universe, not Almighty

God. His ways are mysterious and a closed book to such as she is. Do not tell them you have seen me. Pack your bags. Make excuses if you must, but do not tell them what you have learned from me. You will not be understood."

I rose unsteadily to my feet. I was considerably shaken by the experience even though I was inclined to be sceptical. This dark room seemed sinister and my strange companion was almost convincing me that I was in the presence of the supernatural.

I even felt then that my decision was being made for me. The thought occurred to me that I might be receiving guidance from my mother. If it were possible for her to come back to help me, I knew she would do so.

Then my thoughts had turned to Lady Constance. I knew that she hated me and wanted me gone.

"I can see you are distressed," said Mrs. Carling. "Don't be, my dear. You have had your warning. You and I clearly have been brought together for a purpose. Go back to London without delay and in a short time you will know what you have to do. This is not the place for you. That much is clear. The danger is here."

"I am so uncertain. If only my mother were here . . . but then, if she were, none of this would have arisen."

"It is no use saying if, my dear. Life moves on. What is to be will be."

"Then perhaps I cannot avoid this . . . calamity which is waiting for me."

"You can. You can. That is at the root of it. That is why I knew I had to see you. I had to look into the future for you. It was meant. I sensed it the moment I saw you . . . no . . . before—when I heard you were here. Go back, pack your bags . . . leave while there is time."

I murmured: "I have to think about it."

She smiled at me resignedly. "Your fate is in your hands. It is so with us all."

I felt I had to get away.

I said: "Thank you, Mrs. Carling, for all you have done to help me."

"I had to do it. It was my duty. The best repayment you can make is to get yourself out of danger."

As I walked away from the cottage, the feeling that I had had a glimpse of the future began to recede. In the open air normality returned.

How had I allowed myself to be duped— even momentarily—by such a theatrical performance? Surely I, of all people, should know when people were playing a part. Of course, there was a certain atmosphere in the house. There was hostility towards me in the Manor. Perhaps I should go. My presence was obviously offensive to Lady Constance.

Mrs. Carling was right in one thing: I should leave Leverson Manor, but not because of any imminent danger. Mrs. Carling had been playing a part as surely as I had seen my mother do many times. There was a certain power in having knowledge which others did not possess. Mrs. Carling certainly had convinced herself that she had.

I went straight up to my room.

My problem was beginning to solve itself. I faced the facts. I was unwanted in some quarters of Leverson Manor and welcome in others.

But Mrs. Carling was right. I should get away. Yet when I encountered Charlie and Roderick that evening, I realized that I could not announce my impending departure without some reasonable excuse other than that an old woman who was possibly a little unbalanced had read my fate in a crystal ball.

•

I spent a sleepless night and awoke with the conviction that I must find a suitable excuse, and Charlie should be the one to receive it. He must understand Lady Constance's aversion to me and surely he must have some guilty feelings about bringing me into the household. If I told Roderick that I intended to go, he would find all sorts of reasons why I should not. Charlie must realize the position and perhaps agree that, much as he wished to carry out my mother's instructions to look after me, bringing me into his household was not the best way of doing it.

I awoke in the morning and went, as I usually did, to the window to look out on the splendour of the gardens, which were at their best at this time of day. It was fortuitous, for the first person I saw was Charlie, sitting on the wicker seat on the lawn, and he was alone.

Now was the time. I hastily washed and dressed, hoping that he would still be there when I was ready to go down. By good fortune he was. He called a cheery "Good morning" as I came out of the house and I went over to him.

"It's a glorious morning," he said.

"Charlie," I told him. "I have to talk to you."

"Sit down," he said, looking at me anxiously. "Is anything wrong?"

"Yes, it is. I have to go, Charlie. I can't stay here."

He was silent for a few moments. Then he asked: "Is it . . . my wife?"

"Well, yes. She doesn't want me here."

"She will change."

"I don't think she will. After all, it is asking a lot of her."

He brooded for a moment. "She will grow accustomed to having you around," he said, with more hope than conviction.

"No, Charlie, she will not. And I have decided that I must go."

"Where to? And what will you do?"

"I have to make up my mind. The blow came too suddenly. It was the last thing I expected. She was so well . . . and she had such vitality . . . and then, to go like that."

He held my hand and pressed it. He understood; he felt the same.

"What can I do, Charlie?" I asked.

"There is always a home for you here. I promised her . . ."

"I know. But she would be the first to understand that I have to go, and the sooner, the better."

"To London?"

"Just at first. I thought I might get some post."

"Post? What sort of post?"

"Governess. Companion. That is what most people do when they are in my position."

"It would not do for you, Noelle. You have your mother's independent spirit."

"An independent spirit is all very well if you have the means to support it. I know roughly what my position is. I shall have to consider."

"My dear Noelle, there is no need to think about that. I am going to give you an allowance."

"Thank you, Charlie, but I could not accept

it. I want to stand on my own feet. When the
solicitors have worked things out in detail, I
shall know exactly where I stand and what I
can do. Very shortly I am going to Mason, Mason & Crevitt and everything will be clear. In
the meantime I shall go back to London. Robert will let me stay in the house for a while."

"Robert bought the house so that it would
always be a home for you . . . in the way it
always had been."

"I cannot take that from him, any more
than I can take an allowance from you. I shall
not be entirely penniless. Compared with some
people, I shall be affluent. Charlie, I have to get
away."

"I have sworn to look after you, Noelle. I
promised your mother. She made me swear."

"Yes, I know you promised her, but she did
not foresee difficulties. And . . . I have made
up my mind."

He sighed. Then he said: "Very soon I shall
be going abroad on business. Probably the day
after tomorrow. I shall be away for several
weeks. Promise me this. You will not go until I
come back."

I could almost hear the voice of Mrs. Carling: "You must get away at once."

She seemed a long way from reality. Out
here in the fresh morning air, I could tell myself that it was ridiculous to be influenced by an
old woman with a crystal ball. It smacked of

theatrical melodrama. I was sure Charlie would have laughed it to scorn if I had told him.

"That's a promise, then," he said. "I tell you what we'll do, Noelle. Why not go and see your solicitor now? You could travel up to London with me and stay at our place, or your old home. It need only be for a night or two. You could hear what the solicitor has to say and then we could discuss it when I get back. How's that?"

"Yes. It sounds sensible."

"You don't want to rush into anything. You're shocked, Noelle, still. We all are. It was so sudden and she meant so much to us. We can't think clearly. I want to know you are under my roof. That is what she wanted. I don't want you to be in London . . . alone. So let's fix it, shall we? You and I will go to London. I shall be going off to the Continent at once. You'll stay there for a day or so and then come back here. I promise you that when I return to Leverson, we'll go into all this thoroughly."

"Yes," I said. "That seems a good idea."

I was relieved. In spite of the hostility of Lady Constance, the warning from Mrs. Carling and the feeling that I should not be here, I did not want to leave Leverson.

The Fire and the Rain

Charlie and I arrived in London in the late afternoon. I was deeply moved to be back, and the familiar sights gave me mingling feelings of pleasure and pain. Everywhere there was so much to remind me of her. Charlie and I said little, but we understood each other's mood because we shared it.

I was staying at his London house. I could have gone to my old home, but I thought that would have been too painful just yet, and there was a certain anonymity about Charlie's pied-à-terre, something impersonal which suited me at the moment.

The following day Charlie left for the Continent and I went to Mason, Mason & Crevitt. The result of that interview was the assurance that the capital left by my mother would bring me in a small income—enough to live on frugally—so there was no immediate need to think of augmenting it. The position was much as I had thought it to be. If there had been an urgent need, I should have had to take some action. I almost wished there had been something more positive.

I decided that I would not return to Leverson yet.

It was inevitable that I should call at my old home. I had walked past it and resisted the impulse to knock at the door. I kept remembering too much, even in the street. There was the spot where Lisa Fennell had fallen in front of the carriage and so come into our lives. There was the window where I used to watch for my mother's return from the theatre.

I had felt then that it would be unbearable to go inside.

But the next day the urge to go in was too strong to resist.

When I knocked at the door, it was opened

by Jane. She stared at me for a second and then her face broke into a wide smile.

"Miss Noelle!"

"Yes, Jane," I said. "It is."

"Oh, come in. I'll tell Mrs. Crimp."

"I was passing," I began, "and I . . ."

But she was not listening. She ran through the hall and I followed. "Mrs. Crimp! Mrs. Crimp! Look who's here!"

And there was Mrs. Crimp, her face creased with emotion. She rushed towards me and enfolded me in her arms.

"Oh, Mrs. Crimp," I said, my voice trembling.

"There!" said Mrs. Crimp. "Oh, Miss Noelle, it is good to see you."

"I passed yesterday, but I couldn't . . ."

"I know. I know. Come along in. Oh, Miss Noelle, it brings it all back, it does." She took a handkerchief and wiped her eyes. Then she straightened herself and said briskly: "You'd better come to my room. I want to hear how you're getting on."

"And how are you getting on, Mrs. Crimp?"

"Oh . . . it's not the same. 'Caretakers,' I said to Mr. Crimp. 'That's what we are!' When I think of the old days . . . I tell you, I could sit down and have a good cry."

I felt my face twist in misery, and she went on: "We've all taken it bad. Well, there was no one like her. Never was and never will be. She was one on her own. But it's gone and we've got to try to forget. But . . . what wouldn't I give to have her back. Come to my room and we'll have a little chat. Jane, tell Carrie to bring up some of that special wine and the biscuits to go with it. I baked a fresh batch of them only this morning."

I felt I should not have come. It was too painful. Every part of the house reminded me.

We sat in her room and she said: "How are you getting on with Mr. Charlie?"

"Oh, there's a beautiful house, but I am not sure whether I shall be staying there. I have to make plans, you see."

"We were hoping you'd be coming back."

"It isn't my house now, Mrs. Crimp."

"Well, Monsewer Robber wouldn't mind. He's an easygoing gentleman. Not here much. It's a funny sort of arrangement. Here we are, qualified butler and housekeeper, and no one to buttle and housekeep for. Different from the old days. My goodness, the comings and goings then. Now Monsewer Robber looks in for a while and that's all. Gives us a free hand to keep the place going. I reckon he'd be glad if you came back to us, Miss Noelle. He was here two weeks ago. Wanted to know if you'd been back. I think he'd like you to make use of the place. That Miss Fennell seems to have made it her home."

"Is she getting on all right?"

"She's in that *Rags and Tatters.* It's not doing bad, they say . . . and it's not doing so well. How could it without . . . ? Miss Fennell's pleased with herself. We hear her often practising the songs. She's always saying she's going to get a place of her own . . . but I suppose this is convenient and free . . . so you can't blame her. We like to have someone about the place. It makes it a bit more lively. Monsewer Robber doesn't mind. I think he'd rather there was someone here from the old days."

"Is Miss Fennell here now?"

"No. She's popped out for a bit. She'll be pleased to hear you called. I'd have thought you might have stayed here. I'd have your room ready in a jiff. The place is all the same. Her rooms are not touched. Monsewer Robber didn't want them to be. When he comes here he goes to her room and stays there quite a bit. I really get worried about him. He was so fond of her."

"I know."

"You're not thinking of coming back?"

"My plans are rather uncertain at the moment."

"We'd like to have you here," she said wistfully. "I was saying to Mr. Crimp only the other day, I said, 'If Miss Noelle came back, it would be a little like the old days.' "

"People can't go back, Mrs. Crimp."

"That's a fact, if ever there was one. Mr. Crimp and me . . . we get really down sometimes thinking of the old days. There was always something going on . . . that Mr. Charlie and that Mr. Robber and them all popping in, and as for that Dolly . . . he was a regular caution. Then there was that Martha Gee. She was a real old battle-axe, she was."

I drank a glass of wine and complimented her on her biscuits, remembering how she had always loved receiving compliments.

"It's like the old days, sitting here talking to you, Miss Noelle," she told me. "You'll have to have a word with Jane and Carrie. We don't have a carriage now. No use for it. We're a small household. Monsewer Robber would be so pleased if you was to come back. We understood he took the house so that you could use it. Now it seems he's done it all for that Miss Fennell. That's all very well, but she's not the family, is she? Mr. Crimp and me . . . we're always hoping you'll come back."

There was a pleading note in her voice, and I said: "I can't say anything at the moment, Mrs. Crimp. I have to see how things go."

"You like it in the country with that Mr. Charlie's family, do you?"

"Well . . . it's not my home, you see . . ."

"You'd be better with us. Oh, I know there's all this to remind you. Every day something comes to me and I say, this is where she did this . . . or that. There's no getting away from it. But I wouldn't want to go away. I like to be in the old place, even though it's so different without her."

"I understand what you mean. I like to be here . . . and on the other hand there are all the memories to remind me."

We sat in silence for a few moments thinking of her, then I said I would go.

"Just have a word with Jane and Carrie . . . and would you like to look at her rooms? Maybe not. Perhaps later. As I said, they're all kept as they were. Monsewer Robber's orders. When he comes here he goes up there. He even sleeps in her bedroom sometimes. He's a funny man, that Monsewer Robber. Well, he's a foreigner. He's not like Mr. Charlie. You know where you stand with him."

I had a talk with Jane and Carrie and I was gratified, for they showed as clearly as Mrs. Crimp had that they were delighted to see me.

How different from Lady Constance!

Perhaps I should come back . . . for a short while at least. Would it help me to sort out my life back in that house where her presence permeated the household so strongly?

I steeled myself to go to her rooms. They were just as she had left them. Her clothes were hanging in the wardrobe: I could smell her perfume still. It was almost as though she lingered on . . . reluctant to go.

In those rooms I could feel that she was somewhere close, looking down on me, caring for me, trying to guide me in the way I should go.

•

It was late afternoon when I returned to Charlie's house. I felt emotionally drained and a little comforted.

I had not been in the house half an hour when I was told that there was a visitor for me in the drawing room.

I went downstairs. There was Lisa Fennell. She looked well and prosperous.

She took both my hands and kissed them.

"They told me you had been," she said.

"It was so good to see them."

"I wished I had been at home. As soon as I heard you had called, I came right over. I can't stay. I have to get to the theatre, but I had to see you first. How long will you be in London?"

"I only came for a day or so but I may stay longer."

"Oh, you must. Noelle, how are you . . . really?"

"I'm all right, thanks. And you?"

"All right. It has been awful . . . I can't forget. You're better with Charlie."

"He is going to be away for a few weeks."

"And what about . . . ?"

"Roderick? Oh, he's at Leverson Manor, of course. It's a vast estate. Roderick and Charlie have to spend a lot of time on it."

"I daresay they do. I suppose you and Roderick see a lot of each other?"

"Yes. He's been teaching me to ride. I shall soon be proficient, he tells me."

"That must be interesting. And Charlie, of course, is a dear man. And his wife . . . ?"

"Oh yes, Lady Constance."

"I expect you get along well with her."

"She is rather formal."

She nodded, sensing the meaning in my words.

I said quickly: "But tell me, Lisa, how are you getting on?"

"I can't grumble. It's good to be working."

"I heard. In *Rags and Tatters*. What sort of a show is it?"

"The usual song-and-dance affair."

"And all is going well?"

"Not badly. Front row of the chorus, and what do you think? Dolly has made me understudy to Lottie Langdon."

"That's good, is it not?"

"I think so. I shall never cease to be grateful. I owe everything to your mother."

"Well, she made Dolly take you in in the first place."

"She was wonderful."

Neither of us spoke for a moment. Then I said: "We've got to try to forget the past."

"It's not easy."

She smiled in an attempt at brightness. "You must come and see *Rags and Tatters* while you're here."

"I'd like to."

"It's playing to full houses at the moment. But Lottie is not . . ."

"No. No one could be."

"I could get a good seat for you the night after tomorrow. Dolly would see to that."

I hesitated. It would be an excuse to stay on and there was only one reason why I wanted to return to Leverson, and that was to see Roderick, whom I realized I was missing more than I had thought I would.

I said quickly: "That would be very nice, Lisa. I'll look forward to seeing you."

"That's fixed, then. The night after tomorrow."

•

Roderick arrived in London. I was preparing to go out, in a somewhat listless fashion, when there was a tap on my door.

I called: "Come in." And there was Roderick.

My pleasure must have been obvious. He seized my hands, laughing.

"I thought I'd look you up," he said. "It's a long time since I saw you."

"Three days," I said.

"It seemed longer. When are you coming back?"

"I . . . I'm not sure."

"I thought you had just come up for a meeting with the solicitor. Surely you have had that by now? I thought I would come and see what was delaying you."

"Oh, Roderick, how nice you are!"

"I'm only being truthful. We missed you."

We? I thought. Lady Constance?

"Roderick," I said. "You must see that I can't go on encroaching on your family's hospitality."

"What nonsense! My father would be most put out if he heard you say that."

"And your mother?"

"Oh, she'll come round in time."

I sighed. I could not believe that. At the same time, I was pleased that he wanted my return so much that he brushed it aside. I should have liked to talk to him seriously about my position, but that was too delicate a matter to be lightly discussed.

"How did the meeting go? Fruitfully, I hope."

"As expected. I have enough to live . . . quite humbly . . . so that gives me time to de-

cide what I shall do without making rash decisions."

He looked pensive, and I thought he was
going to say something, but he seemed to
change his mind. After a pause, he said: "What
else have you done?"

"Do you remember Lisa Fennell?"

"Of course. She was the understudy."

"That's right. I've seen her. She is still at
the house. Robert said she could stay until she
found somewhere to live. She is in something
called *Rags and Tatters.* I am going to see it
tonight."

"By yourself?"

"That won't matter. I shall know people in
the company. Dolly will be there, of course.
He'll bring me home."

"I think you should have an escort. I shall
come with you."

"Oh? Would you like that?"

"Nothing better. I shall go right away to see
about the seats."

I was feeling happier.

"That won't be necessary. Lisa's in the
chorus. She said something about seats. I must
let her know there will be two of us."

"It is going to be a very interesting evening," he said.

●　●　●

It was wonderful to be with him. We lunched near Hyde Park and afterwards went for a walk there and sat by the Serpentine. During that time he persuaded me to go back with him the next day. I have to admit I needed little persuasion. My visit to London had shown me that there was nothing there for me but poignant memories from which I could not escape.

Moreover, I was facing my true feelings for Roderick. In his company I was happier than I thought it possible to be after losing my mother, and I was beginning to think that he was the only one who could give me compensation for what I had lost.

During that day in Hyde Park, I was almost happy.

Lisa had told Dolly that I proposed to come to see the show with a friend, and he had arranged seats in the stalls. I knew it would be an emotional experience, going to the theatre where my mother had last performed, and I steeled myself for it.

When the curtain rose, I quickly identified Lisa. I watched her closely. She was outstanding. She sang the songs with special verve and danced abandonedly. I was not surprised that Dolly had chosen her to understudy Lottie Langdon. Lottie herself was a very professional performer, but she lacked the charisma which had been so much a part of my mother's personality.

The play was a trivial piece, but no more so than *Countess Maud,* yet it lacked flair, which meant that it lacked Désirée.

Dolly came to us in the interval. He wanted to know how I was getting on, and looked at me with such tenderness that I felt a rush of emotion.

"If there is anything you want, you know . . ."

"Oh, Dolly," I said. "I know."

"That's the spirit. What do you think of the show?"

Roderick joined me in saying that it was most enjoyable.

"Not bad," said Dolly. "If only . . ." He sighed sadly.

"How's Lisa Fennell getting on?" I asked him.

"Not bad," he said again. "Not bad at all. She's enthusiastic, I'll say that for her . . . and that's half the battle. She's no Désirée, of course, but then, who ever would be?"

We were silent for a moment, thinking of her.

"I'd like to see Lisa after the show," I said.

"Go along to her dressing room. You'll see her there. It's the second of the chorus rooms. You know the way."

"I know it well."

"Are you going to be long in London?"

"No," answered Roderick. "We are going back tomorrow."

"Charlie well?"

"Yes. He's on the Continent at the moment. He'll probably be away for some weeks."

"Well, I must leave you. Bound to be some drama backstage. Never knew a show without them. I'll be seeing you again soon, Noelle. You know there'll be a seat for you at any of my shows."

"Thank you, Dolly."

He kissed me and left us; and after the show was over we went to the chorus dressing room and found Lisa.

She was delighted to see us.

"You must come out and have supper with us," said Roderick.

Her face lit up with pleasure. "That would be wonderful! Can you give me a few minutes to change?"

While we waited for her, we talked to the doorman, who was overjoyed to see me.

"It seems a long time since you used to come here," he said to me. "Things don't seem the same. Désirée was wonderful. Always a cheery word and a smile. It's not the same without her."

I thought: There is everything and everyone here to remind me.

Lisa was animated at supper that night. She

was so excited about her career, which was progressing well.

"Of course, I am only in the chorus," she explained. "But that's going to change. The fact that Dolly has made me understudy to Lottie shows it. What I'm waiting for is the chance to show them what I can do."

I could not help thinking of her chance which had come through my mother's illness . . . that slight indisposition which had resulted in her death.

"The opportunity will come one day," said Roderick. "The great thing in life is to be ready for it when it does."

"I know that's true. I shall be ready. I'd love to be in something better than *Rags and Tatters.*"

"You will," prophesied Roderick.

She was smiling at him. "Now tell me about yourself and that wonderful place where the Romans were."

"Noelle is very interested in it."

"Yes," I agreed. "It is quite fascinating. I have been allowed to help clean some of the fragments of pottery and things which have been found."

"How wonderful! I should love to see it."

"You must come down one day," said Roderick.

I could not help wondering what Lady Constance's reaction would be if she were confronted by a dancer from the chorus of *Rags and Tatters*. It was a thought which depressed me, reminding me as it did of my own reception.

I was rather silent, and Roderick, with his quick understanding of other people's feelings, realized that the theatre had brought back memories. It was too soon to have come back.

I should have more chance of putting the past behind me away from London. I was right to have decided to go back with Roderick . . . for a time at least.

•

I was greeted coolly by Lady Constance, who managed to convey that she was disappointed and had hoped that I might stay in London. Gertie was delighted to see me. It was from her that I learned the news.

"The weather's been something shocking. It started to rain the day you left and has hardly stopped since. The river overflowed and there was a bit of trouble near all that Roman stuff. Stands to reason . . . all that digging. Then Grace tripped down the stairs and hurt her ankle."

Grace was one of the maids who looked after Lady Constance's rooms. She was more mature than most of them and had been with the household since she was thirteen.

"I hope she wasn't badly hurt," I said.

"Well, she's had to lay up. Mustn't put her foot to the ground, so the doctor says. Lady Constance sent for the doctor. So it's me that has to do her ladyship's rooms now." She grimaced.

"And that does not please you, Gertie?"

"You know what her ladyship is like. She's that particular. I'd rather look after you, miss."

"Thank you, Gertie, but I expect Grace will be better soon."

"Can't be too soon for me."

I went to see Fiona. She welcomed me warmly and told me about the flooding and the land falling in. "It's not far from the mosaic paving," she said. "I was very excited when it happened. I thought it might reveal something. I daresay there will be some investigation soon, but the land is too soggy at the moment. As soon as it's a little drier, they'll probably get to work on it."

"I wonder if they will discover something else."

"It's a possibility. We'll have to wait and see. In the meantime, have a look at this drinking vessel. Look at the intricate engraving on it. I'm having a lovely time piecing it together."

While she was showing me, Mrs. Carling arrived. There was a certain reproach in the look she gave me which I knew meant that she was disappointed in me for not taking her advice to stay away.

"Miss Tremaston has been to London," said Fiona. "She and Roderick came back yesterday."

"Travelled together, did you?"

"Yes," I answered. "He came to London while I was there. So . . . we came back together."

"London must seem exciting . . . after this," said Mrs. Carling.

"Oh, it is very pleasant here. And all this . . ." I waved my hand towards the site. "I find it most exciting."

She gave me a penetrating look, and Fiona said: "I'll make some coffee."

"I'll do that," put in Mrs. Carling. "You get on showing Miss Tremaston those things."

As we sat drinking the coffee, I was aware of Mrs. Carling's attention, which seemed to be fixed on me.

I guessed she was really hurt, and a little angry, because I had not taken her advice.

•

It was midmorning. Roderick had gone off early with the agent on estate business, and I was wondering what I should do. I should have liked to ride out somewhere . . . perhaps down to the sea or through some of the little villages in the neighbourhood, but I was not really proficient enough to go out alone. Very soon I hoped to be.

I decided I would stroll down to see Fiona, which was becoming quite a habit. She seemed to like my company and clearly enjoyed talking about the artifacts and how she was treating them.

I was descending the stairs past those rooms which were occupied by Lady Constance when I noticed the door of one of them was open.

Gertie must have heard my footsteps, for she came out.

"Miss," she whispered. "I have to show you this . . . it's what I've found." She put her fingers to her lips, and added: "Come in."

I hesitated. This was Lady Constance's bedroom, where Gertie had been working since Grace was unable to.

"You must see," went on Gertie. "You'll be ever so interested."

Still I held back.

"Look . . . I'll show you . . ."

She retreated into the room. I still stood at the door. I watched her go to the dressing table; she opened a drawer and took out a book. It was fairly large . . . a kind of scrapbook. She spread it out on the dressing-table top and looked over her shoulder at me conspiratorily, jerking her head in a beckoning manner.

I should have refused, I knew, but I acted on impulse and tiptoed into the room.

Gertie pointed to the open book.

I approached and gasped, for I could see a picture of my mother there. I remembered that picture well. It was taken while she was playing in *Sweet Lavender*. I knew the dress . . . a lavender-coloured crinoline. There was a mauve velvet band about her neck with some brilliants in the front.

I could not stop myself then. I went closer.

"Désirée, Miss Lavender, dominates the stage," I read. "Her scintillating presence can even light up this dull piece."

I felt the tears in my eyes, and for a few seconds I forgot to wonder why a picture of my mother should be in a scrapbook which must belong to Lady Constance.

"It's all about her, miss," Gertie was saying. "Look." She turned a page. There were pictures of my mother . . . sometimes with other actors and actresses. "Désirée in *Passion Flower*"; "Désirée in *Red Roses for May.*" The cuttings were all about her. "Désirée, looking exquisite, brought something to the tired old songs." *"The Girl from the Country:* a poor thing but Désirée's own."

The scrapbook was full of these pieces. Someone had taken the trouble to cut them out and paste them in this book.

I was completely absorbed. Once again my memory was betraying me.

Then suddenly I was struck with horror. A

shiver ran through me. I knew instinctively, before I turned, that we were being watched.

Lady Constance was standing in the doorway.

She advanced towards us. Her eyes went to the scrapbook. She said in icy tones: "I was wondering to what I owed your presence in my room."

"Oh . . ." I stammered. "I was passing . . . and I just stopped to speak to Gertie."

Gertie was trembling. With a nervous gesture she closed the book and put it into the open drawer from which she had taken it.

"I thought you would have finished at least ten minutes ago," said Lady Constance to Gertie. "Grace never took so long."

I muttered something about just going out. She nodded at me and, overcome by embarrassment and guilt, I escaped.

My thoughts were in a turmoil as I went out of the house. I felt the cool breeze on my heated face. What a terrible situation! How could I have been so foolish? I had allowed myself to pry into her secrets.

There was no doubt in my mind that she was the one who had cut out those pictures, who had pasted the notices into the book, who had read them and suffered over them and been tortured by them.

I had known the depth of Charlie's feelings for my mother, and so had Lady Constance.

• • •

Gertie was frightened. She told me that she had
indeed "cooked her goose." Now she was waiting for the blow to fall.

"She didn't say much," she went on. "But if
looks could have killed, I would have dropped
down stone dead. It's just that I know she'll be
watching me all the time . . . looking for
trouble. I know she is just waiting to pounce
. . . and I don't know what I'll do, miss, I really don't. You see, how will I get another
place? Stands to reason, she wouldn't give me a
reference, would she? And there's all them at
home . . . too young to go out and earn. You
see, miss?"

I did see and I was desperately sorry for
her.

I also had some pity for Lady Constance,
for I felt I knew what had helped to make her
what she was. I could not stop thinking of how
she must have felt for all those years. She must
have loved Charlie. I had sensed that. Charlie
and Roderick were everything to her. And
through the years she had known of her husband's devotion to Désirée. Naturally she had
wanted to know as much as possible about her
rival. She had made a scrapbook about her career. It was pitiable. Poor Lady Constance!
And poor Gertie!

The accident to the bust on the stairs happened three days later.

The bust was of one of the members of the family in the uniform of a general. It was placed on a carved mahogany pedestal and stood on a landing in between the second flight of stairs and the third.

It was one of Gertie's duties to clean the stairs. I had heard her refer to the bust as "the old un with the cap and the whiskers." The whiskers had been sculpted with skill and the peaked cap and uniform suggested a somewhat formidable general of great dignity.

"He gives me the creeps," Gertie said of him. "I always think he's watching if I do the corners right and that he's just about to give me a telling-off. Yesterday he wobbled. That thing's not strong enough for him. He's too grand for it."

As I came onto the stairs, Gertie was beside the bust with a feather duster in her hand.

"Hello, miss," she said. "Off out?"

I said I was.

"Going to that Miss Vance, I reckon. You like those old bits and pieces they've found, don't you?"

"Yes, I do."

She was smiling at me rather indulgently. She moved a little closer to the bust and, as she did so, she swayed slightly and clutched at the pedestal for support. The figure swayed for a fraction of a second, then it clattered to the floor. I jumped back, for it was very heavy. I stared at it in horror while Gertie looked on in utter dismay.

"Gawd help me! This is the end," she murmured.

We both must have noticed at the same time that the tip of the general's nose was lying on the carpet beside a piece of his ear. I thought flippantly: The general will never look the same again.

My flippancy was short-lived when I looked at poor Gertie's face, which was woebegone with hopeless fear. I was ashamed that I could have been amused even for an instant.

I made a sudden decision.

"I'll say I did it," I told Gertie. "I'll say I was passing the plinth. It was insecure, I brushed against it accidentally and immediately it toppled off."

Hope shone in Gertie's face. "Oh, miss, you couldn't do that!" she said.

"I could."

"Her ladyship will be very angry."

"I shall have to accept that."

"She don't like you very much already, miss . . . not any more than she likes me."

"But you would lose your job. As for me . . . well, she can't dislike me more than she does already, and if she asks me to go, I can do so. It's different with me."

"The master wouldn't let you go. Nor would Mr. Roderick. They like you too much. And she does take notice of them."

"Leave it to me, Gertie."

"Oh, miss, you're just wonderful!"

"I'd better see her right away."

Resolutely I went up the stairs. Gertie was looking at me with something like adoration in her eyes.

I knocked at the door of Lady Constance's sitting room and she called: "Come in."

"Good afternoon," she said coldly.

"Good afternoon," I replied. "I am afraid there has been an accident."

She raised her eyebrows.

"I am very sorry," I went on. "As I was passing the bust on the stairs, I must have touched it and it fell off the pedestal. I am very much afraid that it has been damaged."

"The bust? You mean the general?"

"Yes," I said. "The bust on the landing."

"I'd better see what harm has been done."

I followed her down the stairs and, as I did so, saw Gertie making a hasty exit.

Lady Constance stared at the statue in dismay.

"Dear me," she said. "It has been in the family ever since it was made."

"I can't tell you how sorry I am."

She was staring at the tip of the general's nose.

"It is most unfortunate."

I felt deflated, but all the time I was thinking of Gertie, who was saved—at least for a time.

•

After that, I was very much aware of Lady Constance's eyes upon me. She seemed to be watching me at every moment. Although nothing more was said about the broken bust, it was constantly on our minds. I thought she was gloating over my discomfiture, hoping I would commit some other offence, something which would make it impossible for me to stay on.

I promised myself that, as soon as Charlie returned, I would tell him I must get away. I had, however, promised to stay until his return, so I must do so. On the other hand, I could go to London for a short visit again. The truth was that I did not want to. I did not know which was worse: to stay here, under the resentful eyes of Lady Constance, or to return to the perpetual memories of London.

I was living in a world of despair in which there was a faint glimmer of hope that, through Roderick, I might escape to a brighter future.

I confessed to myself that I stayed because of him.

All the same, I began to get an obsession about Lady Constance. I had nightmares and in my dreams I was afraid of her. In one, she came to my bedside and offered me a glass of wine, which I knew was poisoned. I awoke screaming: "No . . . no!"

In daylight I could laugh at myself. I reasoned: You have suffered a great shock . . . far greater than you realize. You are not your normal self. Lady Constance naturally does not want you here. It was a mistake on Charlie's part to bring you here and when you realized the position you should have retired gracefully, even though it did mean hurting Charlie. And let's admit it, it was not really what you wanted to do. It was all because you needed affection, reassurance, and Charlie, who had been your mother's friend of long standing, was the best able to give it—so she had thought. Moreover, there was Roderick. But, for all that, you had to accept the animosity—even malevolence—of Lady Constance.

But the situation was decidedly uncomfortable and, in addition, I had allowed the vague warnings of Mrs. Carling to unnerve me a little. When I was out in the fresh air, I thought of her as a harmless old lady who liked to imagine herself a seer. There was no harm in listening to her, humouring her, when I was in her company; but in the middle of the night, after a frightening dream, she seemed a significant figure, and I told myself I should listen to her prophecies of the evil which was overhanging my life, and I could not stop thinking of the hatred which I was sure Lady Constance felt towards me.

When I looked at the matter calmly, I could tell myself that I was in a vulnerable state, and just because one terrible tragedy had overtaken me, that did not mean that others were waiting to beset me. I must wait patiently for Charlie's return and then make plans. Meanwhile, I must forget the dislike Lady Constance felt for me and the mystic warnings of a fanciful old woman.

At the back of my mind was the problem of my feelings for Roderick. I was falling in love with him, and I felt sure he had some special feeling for me.

One morning Gertie came to my room full of excitement. She set down the hot water and turned to me.

"Oh, miss," she said. "There's been a fire in the night. What do you think? It was at the cottage . . . you know . . . the one where Miss Vance does her work."

I sat up in bed. "How terrible! Is there much damage?"

"No . . . hardly any. Thanks to the rain, they say. It's been pouring cats and dogs all through the night. It must have started just after the fire. Farmer Merritt was driving his dog-cart home late at night and saw smoke coming from it. He gave the alarm. Then, of course, there was the rain . . . heavy stuff, so there wasn't the damage there might have been."

"Oh, dear. I wonder what Miss Vance will do."

"It's not all that bad, they say. Makes you wonder, though. Good job nobody was there."

Everyone was talking about the fire.

I saw Roderick at breakfast. He said he had already been over to take a look at it.

"It's the upper rooms," he said. "It's a good thing we had that torrential rain . . . and of course Tom Merritt's just happening to be out that way. He'd been coming home late with his wife. They'd been visiting a friend, and they took the shortcut past the remains. He was able to give the alarm and it was soon under control."

"Poor Fiona."

"She'll be there this morning. Why don't you come along with me? I shall be going over there shortly."

I said I should like to.

As we walked over, he said: "One wonders how a fire could start in such a place."

"You don't think . . . ?"

"It was deliberate? Good heavens, no. Why should anyone want to?"

"There are people who have odd ideas . . . disturbing the dead and that sort of thing."

He laughed. "I don't know of anyone who

would feel all that consideration for the Romans."

"Well, there must have been a reason."

"Was there lightning last night? The place might have been struck perhaps."

"That's a possibility."

We found Fiona already there. She was most distressed.

"How could it have happened?" she cried. "I really cannot understand."

"Never mind," said Roderick. "What harm's done?"

"The rooms upstairs are in a mess. Something will have to be done about the roof. Fortunately everything is all right down here."

"All the artifacts in perfect order?"

"It seems so . . . just as they were."

"That's something to be thankful for."

"Let's have a look at the damage upstairs," said Roderick.

We mounted the stairs. There was a bed in each room and these were decidedly damp. There was one part of the ceiling through which one could glimpse the sky.

Roderick said: "That can be put right today . . . preferably before there is more rain."

"We have to be grateful to the rain."

"And to Tom Merritt," added Roderick.

"It would have been such a blow if the whole place had been damaged."

There were footsteps on the stairs and we

all looked towards the door, which opened to disclose Mrs. Carling.

"I've come over to see the damage," she said. "Oh, my goodness! You won't be able to work here, Fiona."

"Downstairs is all right. You wouldn't know there had been a fire."

Mrs. Carling pursed her lips. "This will need a good deal of repairing," she said.

"There is not a great deal of damage, when you come to assess it," said Roderick.

"All the same . . ."

"Let's go down and have a look," went on Roderick.

He led the way downstairs, and we stood in the room where Fiona worked.

"You see," said Fiona to her grandmother, "there is nothing much changed down here. Fortunately farmer Merritt saw it in time . . . and then there was the rain."

"I haven't seen rain like it for years," said Mrs. Carling.

"Providence looking after us," commented Fiona lightly. "It would have been a tragedy to have lost anything down here."

"Oh, sometimes good comes out of evil," said Mrs. Carling, staring ahead, as though into the future.

Fiona looked at her quickly.

"Well," went on Mrs. Carling. "You might have had a better place to work."

"But this is ideal," cried Fiona. "It's right on the spot. I have everything at my fingertips. It couldn't be better."

"You know I could always find a room for you at the Manor," said Roderick.

"There, Fiona!" cried Mrs. Carling. "That would be very nice."

"It *is* nice of you," said Fiona, "and thanks for suggesting it. But it is best here. You see, there is nothing like being on the site, as it were."

"I have offered it before," said Roderick. "After all, it's all on Leverson land."

"I'm perfectly all right here," insisted Fiona. "And it won't take long to put the roof right."

"It will be repaired today," Roderick assured her. "It must be. Then, of course, the stuff up there will have to be taken out. What do you want in its place?"

"Just a few bits and pieces. A chair or two . . . a table. Some of what's up there may still be all right."

"Well, that will be sorted out. You're sure I can't tempt you to come up to the Manor?"

Mrs. Carling was watching her granddaughter intently. "It would be very nice," she said, almost coaxingly.

"I'm sure it would," said Fiona firmly. "But I'm perfectly all right here."

Mrs. Carling pursed her lips. For a moment

she looked almost venomous. I could see she was very displeased with Fiona.

She said she had to leave us, and rather abruptly did so.

"Poor Granny," said Fiona. "She has always thought I shouldn't be working here in this place. She says it is like a shack."

"Well, the offer is open," said Roderick. "I'd find a comfortable room for you."

"I know. But you do understand, don't you? It wouldn't be the same. I want to be here . . . close to everything."

"Of course," said Roderick.

"When it's all patched up, it will be as good as ever."

"I'm going off now to arrange that patching-up. We must get the roof done. It looks as though we might be getting some more rain soon. So . . . it's imperative."

When he left us and we were alone together, Fiona said: "The idea of having a room at the Manor doesn't appeal to me at all."

"No? Wouldn't you be more comfortable?"

"Decidedly not. Her ladyship would not like it. As a matter of fact, she is not very fond of me."

"She does not like me either."

"Of course not. She does not like any young woman not of her choosing to be friendly with her son."

"I see."

"You and I both come into that category. She thinks we have designs on Roderick, and she is preserving him for higher things. It's rather amusing. She would do anything to keep me from seeing more of Roderick. Just imagine what it would be like if I were on the premises! It's bad enough having me here. I am sure she wishes that the site had never been discovered."

My spirits rose a little. It was comforting to find someone in the same position as I was— although I suppose her resentment for me had sprung from Charlie's relationship with my mother, although she would have noticed my growing friendship with Roderick.

"So that is why you don't want to have a room in the house?"

"Well, if I thought it would be better for the work, I would put up with Lady Constance's disapproval. But I don't think it would be, and it's true that I think this is better for work."

Her work, I thought, seems more important to her than Roderick's presence, and that thought gave me a certain pleasure and relief.

•

The mystery as to how the fire in the cottage had started was the main topic of conversation in the neighbourhood for several days. Theories were put forward, and the favourite one was that a tramp had got in and set it alight. Some asked why should he want to destroy a place which was his shelter. The answer was that he lighted a pipe and started it that way; then it got out of control, so he ran off and left.

Gertie told me what was being said. She had thought—and this was the general view—that Miss Vance would have had a room at the Manor. Mr. Roderick had been heard to say that this was what she should do—at least while the place was being repaired.

"Poor Miss Fiona," said Gertie. "Such a nice lady . . . a real lady. Never gave herself airs. A regular life they say she has with that old grandmother."

"She never says . . ."

"Oh no. She wouldn't . . . not about her own grandmother. But she's a strange one, that Mrs. Carling."

"I believe she has something of a reputation."

"Oh yes. Well, she's good with girls in trouble. Those things she grows in her garden work wonders, and she tells the future, some say. They can go to her and she can see what's going to happen. She tells you what you should do and what will happen to you if you don't."

"And you believe this? Have you any proof?"

"Well, there's some as say they have. But she's an odd one. She does queer things. She walks about the place at night."

"How do you know?"

Gertie was silent for a few seconds, and then said: "Well, I'll tell you, miss. It's that little Kitty."

"The maid of hers?"

"Yes, miss. I'm sorry for her. Half scared out of her wits, she is. I've made a sort of friendship with her. She was carrying a load from the shops some little time back, and the handle of the bag broke and there was everything, all over the place. She just stood there, looking as if she was going to cry. I said to her, 'Look here. That's not the end of the world, you know.' I picked up the things for her and put them into the bag. Then I tied up the handle somehow, so she could carry it. You wouldn't believe it, miss. You'd have thought I'd saved her life. She looked on me as though I was some sort of god. You can't help liking that sort of thing. As for her . . . she's like a little waif . . . never had a chance. That family of hers didn't want her. Treated her shocking . . . and all because she was tuppence short. Then she went to old Mrs. Carling, and she's like a slave to her. I took quite a fancy to poor little Kitty. I suppose it was because she thought I was so wonderful."

I laughed. "I think you're wise in a lot of ways, Gertie."

"Well, thank you, miss. I had a word with Kitty. I told her she could always come to me and I'd give her a hand if there was any trouble. You should have seen her. Her face . . . it made me feel I was something."

"Oh, Gertie, you are. You are indeed."

"Oh, I've got my head screwed on all right, miss. I see her now and then. She always runs up to me. She tells me things. You know, they sort of come out. She thinks Miss Fiona is a saint with what she has to put up with. As for the old lady, she can act very strange sometimes, and Miss Fiona tries to keep it all looking as normal. It seems to me that Mrs. Carling does certain things to make her prophecies come true."

"What do you mean?"

"I think it seems as though she gives things a little push, to make them go the way she wants."

"I suppose, when you make prophecies, you should see that there is a good chance of their coming true."

"Well, you might say that. It's a pity Miss Fiona don't come here to do her work. It would be better than that old cottage. Mrs. Carling was really put out about Miss Fiona not taking a room at the Manor when it was offered. She goes on and on about it till Miss Fiona nearly loses her patience. Still she goes on. 'After all I've done for you,' and that sort of thing. It really upsets Miss Fiona. Mrs. Carling says it's asking for trouble when you don't take the chance when it's given you. No good will come of it. Of course, you can't get much out of Kitty. I just piece it all together. Anyway, I don't reckon Miss Fiona has much of a life with all that going on."

Descent into Danger

❧❧

There was a great deal of heavy rain during the next few days, and Roderick told us that the water was having an effect on some parts of the land. The fact that over the centuries it had been gradually reclaimed from the sea meant that it was soft and in places inclined to be soggy; and there were one or two places where there was a danger of subsidence.

"We've had this trouble before," he said. "It

follows this sort of weather. We have to keep a watchful eye on things."

"What can you do?" I asked.

"The most important part is to keep people off it until we can bank it up or do something about it. All the digging which has been going on since the discoveries hasn't helped, of course. When my father comes home we'll have to talk about it. In the meantime we are putting up a few warning notices in what we feel may be vulnerable spots."

We discussed it over dinner that evening.

"It can't be long before your father is home," said Lady Constance.

"No. He'll soon be back now. There's more damage been done to the cottage than we thought at first. I do think Miss Vance ought to come here for a while anyway. She would be so much more comfortable than with the workmen there."

"It's her choice," said Lady Constance sharply. "You offered her a room, didn't you?"

"Yes, I did."

"And she wouldn't take it. I should have thought that was an end to the matter."

Roderick looked at his mother steadily. "I believe she won't come because of you."

"I? What have I to do with it?"

"You are the mistress of the house. If you show clearly that you don't want her here, she can't very well come, can she?"

Lady Constance caught my eye guiltily, and I felt sorry for her.

I said: "I understand Miss Vance prefers to work near the site."

Roderick replied: "That is what she says, but I am sure, Mother, that if *you* invited her, she would come . . . if only temporarily— while the work is done."

"Is that what you expect me to do?"

"I don't expect it, but I should be pleased if you did."

"I can't see why. *My* wishes don't enter into the matter."

"But they do. Look. It is going to be very uncomfortable for Miss Vance while they are cleaning things up at the cottage. If you invited her to come here temporarily, I am sure she would agree to come."

"But she has already refused."

"Because she thought you did not want her. Moreover, she didn't realize what an upheaval it was going to be. It will certainly disrupt her work."

"Very well. I'll have a word with her."

"You will?" cried Roderick with obvious pleasure.

"As you feel I should and are blaming me for the woman's being in such dire straits, I'll have a word with her. I'll go over to see her this afternoon."

I was amazed, and so was Roderick. In fact,

he was delighted. I was interested to see how Lady Constance basked in his approval. There was no doubt of her affection for her son. He and her husband were the two she cared about. I thought of the scrapbook and how she had kept cuttings about my mother, knowing of Charlie's love for her, and I could guess how deeply she had suffered. Her resentment of me was completely understandable, and it was insensitive of Charlie to have brought me here. That was another reason why I should go as soon as possible. I understood Lady Constance's coolness to Fiona. In fact, there was a good deal I was beginning to understand about Lady Constance. I was changing my attitude towards her. I could pity her: I could excuse her resentments because I knew the reason for them. She who had been so proud had been bitterly humbled: she who had determined to be strong, to rule her household and plan the best for her husband and son, was vulnerable.

The next day Roderick went off early. It continued to rain during the morning and cleared up after luncheon, which we took in our rooms. I was glad of that. I did not want to have to face Lady Constance alone.

I was wondering what she would say to Fiona and what Fiona's response would be. Fiona could be forthright. The outcome would be interesting to me, because in a way Fiona's case was not unlike my own.

It was my custom to call on Fiona in the afternoon. I very much wanted to hear the result of the interview and I must delay my visit until it was over.

I had seen Lady Constance set out after luncheon. She was walking the short distance from the house to the site. She looked brisk as she set out, as though she were going into battle. She carried a black umbrella. It was not raining at the time, but there could well be another shower or two.

I guessed the meeting would be brief.

I should hear all about it from Fiona. An hour passed while I sat at my window, waiting for the return of Lady Constance. I was surprised that she was so long. The walk would be about fifteen minutes there and fifteen back. An hour had passed. What could they be talking about for the rest of the time?

Could I have missed her return? That was hardly likely. It might be that she had gone on somewhere else. That was not likely, but I supposed just possible.

It was half an hour later when I decided I would call on Fiona. Lady Constance must have left by now and if by some chance she had not done so, I should have to make some excuse and come away.

I put on my outdoor clothes with stout walking shoes and took an umbrella with me.

It was a somewhat bleak day and the countryside looked a little desolate. Everything was damp and there was rain in the air, although it was not actually falling. There was scarcely any wind and dark clouds loured low in the sky.

When I came near the site, it started to rain. I put up my umbrella and took the path which led up to the cottage.

It looked different. There were pieces of loose earth spattered about. They must have been disturbed by the heavy rains, I thought.

I glanced over at the baths and the mosaic floor. They looked just as usual. Then . . . too late . . . I saw the yawning gap before me. I tried to stop sharply, but as I did so, the ground beneath me gave way. I tripped forward, my umbrella flew away and I was falling . . . down into darkness.

•

I was stunned and bewildered for a few seconds before I realized what was happening. This was one of the spots Roderick had talked about. The soil was giving way beneath my feet. It was in my eyes. I shut them tightly for a few seconds. I tried to clutch at something, but the damp earth came away in my hands.

My fall was not rapid. It was impeded by the obstructing soil which gave way under my weight. And then . . . suddenly I was falling no longer. I opened my eyes. I could not see much, but the hole through which I had fallen was still there and it let in a little light.

I was standing on something hard. I felt a mild relief because I was no longer falling.

I was able to put my hand down and touch what I was standing on. It was smooth and felt like stone. Fragments of soil were still falling round me and onto the shelf on which I was standing. I listened to the sound of their fall. It was now intermittent and I saw that the hole through which I had fallen remained, so there was still a little light from above coming in.

I felt a great relief. At least I was not entirely buried. Someone must come. But who? They would discover that the land had subsided. But how long could I stay here?

I perceived that it would be impossible to try to climb up. There was nothing but damp loose earth to cling to. Then I began to feel very frightened.

I heard something. A cry. "Help . . . help me . . ."

"Hello," I said. "Hello."

"Here . . . here . . ."

I recognized Lady Constance's voice.

A thought flashed into my mind. It had happened to her. She had been going to call on Fiona, just as I had been. She would have taken the same path.

"Lady Constance," I gasped.

"Noelle. Where . . . are you here?"

"I fell . . ."

"As I did. Can you move?"

"I . . . I'm afraid to. It might . . ."

I had no need to explain. She was in the same position as I was. At the moment we were safe . . . but how did we know whether the slightest movement might set the earth falling down on us, burying us alive?

My eyes had grown accustomed to the darkness. I appeared to be on some sort of stone floor. There was earth scattered all over it. I could see something dark . . . a shape moving slightly. It was Lady Constance.

"Can you move very slowly . . . this way?" I said. "We seem to be in some sort of cave. It's lighter where I am. The hole is still above. I'm afraid to move because the earth round me is very loose. But there seems to be a sort of ceiling."

She started to crawl slowly towards me. There was a sound of falling earth. I held my breath. I was desperately afraid that the soil would fall in and bury us.

I said: "Wait . . . wait."

She obeyed and all was quiet. I said: "Try again."

She was close now. I could see her vaguely.

She put out a hand and touched my arm. I grasped her hand.

I could sense that her relief matched mine.

"What . . . what can we do?" she whispered.

"Perhaps they'll come and rescue us," I said.

She did not speak. "Are you all right?" I asked.

"My foot hurts. I'm glad you're here. I shouldn't be. But . . . it makes two of us."

"I understand," I said. "I'm glad you're here."

We were silent for a while, then she said: "This is the end of us perhaps."

"I don't know."

"What can happen, then?"

"We'll be missed. When Roderick comes back. Someone will come to look for us. We must keep very still. We must not disturb anything. When they miss us they'll come to rescue us."

"You're trying to comfort me."

"And myself."

She laughed, and I laughed with her. It was quite mirthless laughter, a defence, perhaps, against fate.

"Strange," she said, "that you and I should be here."

"Very strange."

"It's good to talk, isn't it? I feel so much better now. I thought I was going to die alone. I was very frightened."

"It's always good to share something, I suppose . . . even this."

"It's a help. Do you really think we shall get out of this?"

"I don't know. I think we may have a chance. Someone might come along."

"They might fall down with us."

"They might see what has happened in time. They'd get help."

"Should we call out?"

"Would they hear us?"

"If we heard them, they might hear us. There's a gap there. You can see the daylight."

"While that's there, there is hope."

"You're a sensible girl," she said. "I'm afraid I haven't been very good to you."

"Oh . . . that's all right. I understand."

"You mean about Charlie and your mother?"

"Yes."

We were silent for a few moments. She was still holding my hand. I think she was afraid something would happen to separate us. I, too, felt comforted by her closeness.

She said: "Let's talk. I feel better talking. I know what happened about the bust."

"The bust?"

"On the stairs. I know Gertie broke it and you took the blame."

"How?"

"I was watching from the top landing. I saw the whole thing. Why did you do it?"

"Gertie was terrified of being sent away. She sends money home to her family. She was afraid you would dismiss her and wouldn't give her a reference. It seemed the simplest thing to do."

"I see. That was good of you."

"It was nothing much. I was going away soon. It seemed better to let you think it was my fault."

"How did you know all this about Gertie?"

"We talk. She tells me about her family."

"You talk thus . . . to the servants?"

"I suppose that shocks you. I was brought up in a different way . . . where differences in class were not nearly so important as human relationships. People were people in our household, not servants and employers."

"That was Désirée, was it?"

"Yes. She was like that. She was friendly with everyone."

"And you take after her."

"No. I'm afraid there was only one Désirée."

Silence again. I thought it was a pity the subject of my mother should be brought up at a time like this.

But she was still holding my hand.

It was not good to be silent. It made us frighteningly conscious of our desperate plight.

"I had no idea that you knew about the bust," I said.

"I was watchful."

"Of me?"

"Yes, of you."

"I was aware of it."

"Were you? You gave no sign. I can't tell you how glad I am that you fell down where I did. I'm a very selfish woman."

"No . . . no. I understand. I am glad you are here."

She laughed and moved closer to me.

"Strange, is it not? We must keep talking, mustn't we? When we talk, fear seems to recede . . . but it's there. I think we may be going to die."

"I think there is a good possibility of rescue."

"You say that to comfort me."

"As I told you, I also say it to comfort myself."

"Are you afraid of dying?"

"I had never thought of it till now. One seems to be born with the idea that one will go on forever. One can't imagine a world without oneself."

"That's called egoism, isn't it?"

"Yes, I suppose so."

"So you have never had to be afraid until this happened?"

"That is so. I'm afraid now. I know that at any moment the earth can fall in and bury us."

"We shall be buried together. Does that comfort you?"

"Yes, it does."

"It comforts me, too. It is strange that I should draw comfort from you when I think how I resented your coming to Leverson."

"I am sorry. I should never have come."

"I'm glad you did now."

I laughed. "Because if I had not, I could not have joined you here."

"Yes . . . just that." She laughed with me. Then she said: "Well, there is something more. We are in this strange position and down here we are getting to know each other more than we ever would in an atmosphere of security."

"It is because we are facing possible death. That must draw people close."

"Let's go on talking," she said.

"I am listening, too," I said. "If we hear anything from above, we must be ready to call . . . to let them know we are here."

"Yes. Could we hear them?"

"I don't know. I think we might."

"But let's go on talking . . . softly. I can't bear the silence."

"Are you comfortable?"

"My foot hurts."

"I expect you have strained something."

"Yes. It's a small thing when one may be facing death."

"Don't think of that."

"I'll try not to. You found my book of cuttings. You looked at them with Gertie."

"I'm sorry. She called me in and when I saw . . . it was irresistible."

"What did you think of it?"

"I thought it was very sad."

"Why?"

"Because it told me how you must have felt through all those years."

"I knew everything she was playing in . . . what they said about her. I understood it all. He was besotted about her."

"Other people were, too."

"She must have been a wonderful person."

"To me she was the most wonderful person in the world."

"A good mother, was she?"

"The best."

"That seems unlikely. A woman like that! What would she know about bringing up children?"

"She knew about love."

Silence again. I realized she was weeping quietly.

"Tell me more about her."

So I told her. I told her how Dolly came with his plans and how they quarrelled and abused each other. I told her about all the dramas, the last-minute changes, the first-night nerves.

It was like a dream . . . sitting in a dark hole with Lady Constance, talking of my mother. But it helped me as it did her, and at that time we were overwhelmed with gratitude for the other simply for being there.

I thought: If we ever get out of here, we shall be friends. We can't go back to our old relationship after this. Each of us has shown the other too much of our inner selves.

How strange it was that, in that nightmare situation from which we both feared we might never emerge alive, Lady Constance and I had become good friends.

I could just see from my watch that two hours had passed. We listened for some sound from above and heard nothing. I feared the coming of the night, for that would mean there was no hope of rescue till morning.

Roderick would return to the house. He would quickly learn that we were missing . . . both his mother and I. Where would he go to look for us? Could he possibly be led to this spot?

"How long have we been here?" asked Lady Constance.

"It is more than two hours since we found each other."

"I was here before that. It seemed very long. That was the worst part."

"It must have been more than an hour. I saw you leave the house. I knew where you were going, as you had said. It must have been shortly after you left when you fell."

"To be down here . . . alone. That was terrible."

"How lucky we were to land on this stone. I don't know what it is. It seems like a sort of ledge. It's very solid . . . and there's the gap above it. That has saved us, I think. I wonder what it can be."

"I should not like to have sat on soft earth. One would not feel safe."

"That's what I mean. We have been very lucky to strike this."

"Let us hope our luck continues."

She had to talk. She could not bear the silence. She told me about her early days in the grandeur of her ancestral home, where there was always a shortage of money. Charlie, of course, was very rich. Not quite on their level socially, but the family accepted that. He was so very helpful, and therefore a marriage was agreed on.

"But, you see, I loved Charlie," she went on. "He was the kindest man I had ever known. He was so different from the others. I married Charlie because my family wished it, but I fell in love with him. More than anything, I wanted him to love me. He did . . . to a certain extent . . . but then, of course, there was Désirée."

"I am sure she would have been upset if she had known she caused you suffering. She never wanted to hurt anybody. Life was a light-hearted affair to her. She had her men friends. It was very jolly. Do you understand?"

"It is not easy to. Charlie was my husband . . . and she had no husband."

"My father died a long time ago. I never knew him."

"I see. And after that she thought other people's husbands were hers for the taking."

"She never thought of it that way. She did not exactly *take* anyone. They came to her. They were all friends together. Life was to be enjoyed. That was her philosophy. She wanted to enjoy it, and everyone around her to do the same."

"Never mind the heartbreak she caused."

"She did not know of it. She would have sent Charlie back to you and told him to be a good husband if she had known."

"But life is not like that. She must have been very beautiful."

"She was, but she had more than beauty. Does it hurt you . . . to talk about all this?"

"I want to know. I can see her now more clearly than I ever did. I used to think of her as a wicked siren."

"A siren . . . but never wicked. She would never have willingly hurt you. Sometimes I think that she let herself believe that everyone looked on life as she did. Listen . . ."

We were silent, straining our ears.

There was nothing.

"I thought I heard a voice," I said, and we fell silent, still listening.

"Ah . . . there it is again."

"Hello . . . hello!"

"Let's shout," I cried. "Hello! Hello! Down here."

Lady Constance shouted with me. There was silence while we waited breathlessly.

"Someone's there," I whispered. "They must be looking for us."

We turned and embraced each other in our relief. I think we were both near tears.

We sat holding each other . . . tense . . . listening. There was no sound. The disappointment was intense.

"Let's call again," I said, and shouted: "We're here. We're down here."

Then I heard a voice. It was Roderick's.

"Can you hear me? Can you hear me?"

"Yes, yes."

"Don't move. Wait. We're coming."

There was a dark shadow above.

Someone was up there.

"Noelle . . . Mother . . ."

"We're here," I cried. "We're here . . . together."

"Thank God. Don't move, whatever you do. This can be dangerous."

There was a pause which seemed to go on for a long time but could not have been more than five minutes. Then Roderick was there again. There must have been others with him, for I heard several voices.

He shouted down: "We're lowering ropes. Attach yourselves to them. Tie them round your waists. We're going to pull you up."

We kept our eyes on the opening and we saw the ropes descending. I seized them. First I helped Lady Constance to tie one round her waist. Then I did the same for myself.

"Are you ready?" called Roderick.

"You must go first," I said to Lady Constance.

"Suppose more earth falls down."

"I'm tied to the rope. I'll be all right."

"Noelle, Noelle." It was Roderick.

"I'm here," I answered.

"We are going to start now. We are going to bring you up together. Hold on to each other and make sure the ropes are securely tied. Ready? Now . . ."

Arms about each other, Lady Constance and I were lifted. We moved upwards, dislodging earth as we went. I heard stones rattling on the shelf which we had just vacated. Nearer and nearer to the top . . . and then the fresh air was enveloping us, and we were standing on terra firma. The air seemed intoxicating. And most wonderful of all, there was Roderick. He had his arms round both of us.

"You've given us a fright," he said, his voice strained with emotion.

Then they were untying the ropes. Lady Constance could not stand up and she was taken to the carriage which was waiting for us. Earth fell from my clothes and I staggered and would have fallen if Roderick had not caught me. He was holding me tightly.

"It is wonderful . . . wonderful . . . to have you safe," he said. "Oh, Noelle . . . when you weren't there . . ."

I said: "I felt you would come. All the time, I felt it. It just kept me from despair."

He held me firmly for some seconds and I was happier in that moment than I had been since my mother died.

"I love you, Noelle," he said. "You're never going away from me again."

"I never want to."

We stood close for a few seconds.

He said: "We'll talk. First we've got to get you both back . . . make sure you've suffered no harm. Dearest Noelle, I thank God I found you."

I was in the carriage. Lady Constance was lying back, her eyes closed. She was almost unrecognizable; her face and clothes were streaked with dirt and her hair was straying from its usual austere order. I suddenly realized how I must have looked when Roderick was saying he loved me.

Lady Constance opened her eyes and smiled at me. All the warmth and friendship I had felt when we were in danger was still there.

This was the most bewildering experience. I had been plunged into disaster, to find that there could be a happy life for me.

I felt I was living in a dream from which I should awake at any moment.

•

The rest of that night seems rather hazy. I was more shocked than I had first realized. I was taken to my room, where the first thing I wanted to do was throw off all my clothes and get into a bath. This I was allowed to do before the doctor arrived.

I was amazed at the quantities of soil which fell from me. It was in the pockets of my coat, in my shoes . . . everywhere.

I soaked myself in the hip bath, and my soiled clothes were taken away.

I was in bed when the doctor visited me and proclaimed that no bones were broken, though I had plenty of bruises, and, as I had had a terrible shock, I must have hot food and then take a sedative he would leave for me. Then I must see whether I was well enough to get up next morning.

I was content to do this. I did not want to
think of that experience, because I could not do
so without recalling those terrifying moments
when I had fallen and thought the earth was
going to bury me alive. I wanted to be alone to
think of Roderick with his arms about me,
showing me so clearly how happy he was because I was safe. I wanted to think of his saying
he loved me. I also wanted to remember what
Lady Constance and I had said together in
those moments of revelation. That was enough
for this night.

As for Lady Constance, she was suffering
from a sprained ankle and acute shock, and
would stay in bed until the doctor saw her
again.

•

I slept deeply and awoke the next morning feeling refreshed. I was longing to see both Roderick and Lady Constance.

I stretched out in my bed, savouring the
comforts of sheets and soft pillows.

I looked round the room and out of the
window. Everything seemed so beautiful and
precious as I remembered how I had thought I
might never see any of it again.

How lucky we had been to be discovered so
soon . . . for it was comparatively soon. We
might still be there. I shuddered at the thought.

I wondered whether I should get up, what it

would be like to see Roderick again. It would be different between us after his declaration. I had thought he might have been on the point of telling me he loved me on one or two occasions, but he had not done so, and that had set doubts in my mind. Yesterday it was such an emotional moment that the words had slipped out.

I was glad. I felt joyous, full of hope for a future which had previously been filled with misgivings. It had been worthwhile to have been nearly buried alive to hear those words.

The door of my room was slowly opening. Gertie came in. She was looking excited and expectant.

"I just looked in to see whether you was awake, miss," she said. "And if you'd like something. I thought I wouldn't knock, which might wake you if you wasn't already awake like."

"Thank you, Gertie. I am awake."

She came towards the bed, her eyes wide, looking at me as though I were a different person from the one I had been before.

"I'm ever so thankful you're safe, miss."

"Thank you, Gertie."

"And it was because of me, in a way. It was an awful thing, and to think, if I hadn't been able to . . . well, miss . . . I can't tell you how pleased I was to be the one . . . after all you did for me. I was able to do something for you."

"What do you mean, Gertie?"

"Well, it was her, wasn't it? . . . Kitty. Her coming here like that . . . to me. All upset she was. She knew, you see. She's here now . . . won't go back. Mr. Roderick said she was to be given a room. Reckon there might be a job for her here. And her ladyship wouldn't say no to that, seeing it was her who saved her, too."

"I don't understand what all this is about, Gertie."

"Well, it was her that come here. She was in a terrible state. She didn't know what to do, so she came to me. I told you how we got on, after I'd helped her with the bag and she looked on me like I was something special. So when she was frightened she came to me. She told me old Mrs. Carling had taken away the notice."

"What notice?"

"Warning people not to use the path."

"There was a notice?"

"Not when you was there, because she'd taken it away, hadn't she? Real mischief. Kitty reckons it was so's you'd fall in. Mrs. Carling knew you went almost every afternoon to see Miss Vance, and she guessed you'd be along. And there you was . . . just as she'd planned it."

"Gertie. I can't believe this. Mrs. Carling took the notice away in the hope that I would be trapped!"

Gertie nodded and looked wise. "She's been off her head these last weeks. They've had a terrible time with her. She set fire to the cottage because she wanted Miss Vance to come up and work at the Manor."

"Set fire to the cottage!"

Gertie looked knowledgeable. "She wanted Mr. Roderick for Fiona. She goes about muttering to herself. Kitty heard. So she wanted her up at the house, and you out of the way. I reckon that's the long and the short of it."

"It cannot be true."

"Well, why did she take the notice away? Kitty saw her go out on the night of the fire and she knows she took paraffin with her. Then she actually saw her take the notice away. She went out and waited there. She saw you go down. She didn't see Lady Constance, but she saw you. She didn't know what she ought to do. After a time she came to me. You could have knocked me down with a feather. I soon spread the news. They got Mr. Roderick right away, and he called the men all together with ropes and things. So they got you out. But Kitty was afraid to go back after what she'd done. That's why she's here. I've got her in my room. I have to keep telling her it's all right and she's done a good thing in telling on her old mistress. I tell her she's not got to worry about going back to Mrs. Carling anymore. I'm going to look after her."

"Oh, Gertie . . ."

She rushed to me and flung her arms round my neck. We hugged each other for a few moments.

"I'm that glad you're safe, miss, I'm forgetting my place. You're safe and sound and I had a part in bringing you back. Now, can I get you something to eat? Some coffee . . . some toast?"

"Just that, Gertie, and some hot water. I'm longing to get up."

"I'll see to it," she said.

I lay back in bed, marvelling at what I had heard and wondering if it could possibly be true.

•

I hastily washed and dressed and ate a little breakfast. I must admit I felt light-headed, but that was due to everything which had happened in such a short time rather than any physical disability.

My mind was a jumble of memories: those horrifying moments when I had fallen, my conversation with Lady Constance, the rescue, all that Gertie had told me—and all dominated by Roderick's telling me he loved me.

More than anything I wanted to see Roderick.

When I was ready to go down, I went to the window, and there he was, seated on the wicker seat, looking up at my window. He saw me immediately.

"I'm coming down now," I called.

I ran out of the room and down the stairs. He was striding towards me, taking my hands in his.

"Noelle . . . how are you this morning? It's wonderful to see you! I have been sitting here . . . waiting . . . since Gertie told me you were going to get up."

"I wanted so much to talk to you."

"And I to you. Did you sleep well?"

"I knew nothing since I took the doctor's sedative and woke to find the sun streaming into my room."

"I've had nightmares . . . dreaming that we couldn't get you out."

"Well, forget them, because here I am."

"And you are always going to be here, Noelle. Let's sit down and talk. I love you, Noelle . . . so much. I've been wanting to tell you for a long time. I was afraid it was too soon . . . your mother was so recently dead, and I knew you were still living with your grief. I was afraid you could not think of anything else. I told myself I must wait until you had recovered a little. But yesterday it came out. I couldn't stop it."

"I'm glad."

"Does that mean you love me, too?"

I nodded and he put his arm round and tightened his hold on me.

"We shan't want a long engagement," he said. "My father will be pleased. He'll see it as a way of keeping you here."

"I'm so suddenly happy," I said. "I never thought to feel like this again. It all looked so grim. I hated being in London. There were so many memories of her . . . and I was away from you. Then you came and it was bearable. I was wondering what I should do . . . and now there is a chance to be happy again."

"We certainly shall be."

"What of your mother? Have you heard how she is this morning?"

"Still sleeping. She is very shocked. She will need a long rest."

"She has other plans for you."

He laughed. "Oh," he said. "Marriage. She will come round when she sees it's inevitable. Don't think of obstacles. There are not going to be any . . . and if there are, we shall quickly overcome them."

"I'm thinking about it all the time."

He kissed my hair gently. I thought: How can I be so suddenly happy? Yesterday was so different. Today I am in another world . . . and all because yesterday I nearly lost my life. The birds were singing more gaily; the grass glistened with tiny globules of morning dew; the flowers were more colourful and fragrant because of the recent heavy rain: the whole world had become more beautiful because I was happy.

For a few moments we were silent. I believe he, as I, was savouring the beauties of nature around us while we thought of the future which would be ours.

I said at length: "Gertie told me a strange story this morning."

"Yes," he said. "About Kitty the maid and Mrs. Carling."

"Is it true, then?"

"That she took the sign away? It seems so. Tom Merritt had put it up during the morning with four or five others in those places he considered to be dangerous. It was warning people not to use those parts until someone could get to work to test their safety."

"Gertie said that Kitty saw her take it away and didn't know what she ought to do about it."

"Yes, that's so. It had certainly been removed. Kitty saw her do it. These people watch what goes on and Mrs. Carling knew . . . and so did Kitty . . . that you often went to the cottage in the afternoons. So Kitty waited and saw you fall. She didn't know what she ought to do, but she eventually told Gertie. Thank God she did. We should have found you eventually, but she helped us get there more quickly."

"Do you think Mrs. Carling really did take the sign away?"

"She is mad, you know. We have suspected that for some time. Fiona was very worried about her strange behaviour . . . which was getting worse. She has always been fanciful . . . eccentric . . . but this was different. Fiona has had a terrible time looking after her. Mrs. Carling has been taken to a hospital for the mentally unstable. She was caught trying to set fire to the cottage again. Thank God that maid of hers finally had the good sense to come to Gertie. That helped us get you out without the delay there might have been. I can't stop thinking of what might have happened. You could so easily . . ."

I said: "We were fortunate to have landed on a kind of ledge."

"A ledge?"

"It seemed like stone of some sort. Otherwise we could have gone right down. The earth was so damp and soggy. I am glad I was near your mother. I want to see her as soon as I'm allowed to. Do you think I shall be able to?"

"But of course. We'll go together and tell her . . ."

"Oh . . . no. She shouldn't have another shock so soon. Roderick, will you leave it to me . . . just for a while? I think it may be possible that I could explain it to her."

"Don't you think it would be better to come from me?"

"I should have thought so . . . but after yesterday . . . well, we were together down there all that time . . . not knowing whether we should ever come up. That sort of thing does something to you. I think it may have done to your mother . . ."

"If you think it is best."

"Perhaps I'm wrong. It is different here in the house from what it is in a damp dark hole which can collapse on you at any moment."

"It will be all right. When she sees how pleased my father will be . . ."

I was unsure, but I could not let anything cloud my happiness at that moment. I wanted to savour every minute. Nothing must stand in the way of my happiness.

•

The doctor called later that morning. He saw me in my room and told me that he thought I had recovered from my shock. The bruises would in time disappear and I had clearly not broken any bones, which was a mercy. We had been lucky to have been rescued comparatively quickly. He thought I should not allow myself to become exhausted and that I should remember I had been through a very trying experience. Apart from that, I might carry on as normal.

He was a little longer with Lady Constance. She, too, had emerged from the accident with a good deal of luck. She must undoubtedly rest on account of her ankle alone, and she must keep to her room for a while. He hoped that shortly she would be none the worse for what she had endured.

When I asked if I might be allowed to see her, he said: "Certainly. A little chat will do her good. She doesn't want to be made to feel she's an invalid. Just remember that a shock like that can have an effect which may not be immediately apparent."

So I went to see Lady Constance.

She was sitting up in bed, looking very different from when I had last seen her. Her hair was neatly drawn away from her face to make a coil on the top of her head, and she was dressed in a negligee of pale blue. As I entered the room, I had the feeling that she had left my companion of misfortune far behind and had reverted to the familiar and formidable mistress of the household who had intimidated Gertie and—I had to admit—myself.

I approached the bed. I knew she was trying to make a barrier between us, struggling to return to that haughty arrogance which had been her shield.

"How are you, Noelle?" she said coolly.

"I am well enough, thank you. And you, Lady Constance?"

"Rather shaken still, and my ankle is painful. Otherwise, apart from feeling tired, I am all right."

Her eyes held mine for a moment. I guessed she was remembering and regretting those confidences. Was she debating whether they could be set aside, forgotten? No. That could hardly be. Could they be put down to the somewhat hysterical ramblings of someone who was face to face with possible death? She was a proud woman and, now that she had returned to the safety of everyday life, she would be remembering, and resenting afresh, the indignities and humiliation she had suffered through her husband's infatuation for another woman.

"It was a terrible ordeal we suffered," she began, paused, and then added: "Together."

"It was a comfort to have someone to share it with," I said.

"A comfort indeed."

I saw the tears on her cheeks then, and I knew that the battle with herself was nearly over. Boldly I went closer to the bed and I took both her hands.

"It was indeed a terrible ordeal," I repeated, "and yet I cannot be entirely sorry that it happened."

She was silent.

I went on: "To talk together . . . to understand . . ."

"I know," she said with emotion. "I know . . ."

I realized then that it was for me to take the initiative. Her pride was holding her back.

"I hope," I said, "that, now we have found friendship, we are not going to lose it."

She gripped my hand and replied quietly: "I hope that, too."

The barriers were down. It was as though we were back together in that dark and dismal hole.

She took a handkerchief from under her pillow and wiped her eyes. "I am being foolish," she said.

"Oh no . . . no."

"Yes, my dear Noelle. We shall always remember what we went through together, but, as you say, there is some good in everything. And it has made us friends."

"I was afraid it was just for then. I was afraid it would not last."

"It became too firm for that . . . even in that short time. But it was not exactly so sudden. I have always admired you . . . just as I did . . . her."

"We shall start from now," I said. "The rest is in the past. It is the present which is important. I feel happier and hopeful now."

She did not ask for explanations, and I think because she was afraid of showing more emotion, she said: "You have heard that that madwoman removed the warning sign."

"Yes."

"They have put her away. It was she who set fire to the cottage. What a danger she was!"

"Yes," I replied. "It was fortunate that Kitty, the maid, saw what she had done."

"The poor child is a little retarded."

"But sufficiently aware to tell Gertie what she had seen."

"She can't go back, of course. We shall keep her here. I wonder what Fiona Vance will do now."

"It will be a relief to her, I expect, to know that her grandmother is being cared for. I fancy she was something of a trial to her and must have been for some time. She never mentioned it or complained."

"I daresay something will be arranged."

We were silent for a few seconds, then Lady Constance said: "My husband will be home soon, I daresay."

I made a hasty decision.

"Lady Constance," I said, "there is something I want to say to you. I don't know how you will take this. If I don't tell you now, Roderick will soon. But if it is going to upset you . . ."

"I think I know what it is," she said. "Roderick wants to marry you. That is it, is it not?"

I nodded.

"And," she went on, "you want to marry him. I have seen it coming."

"And you, Lady Constance?"

She lifted her shoulders, and I went on: "I know you expected your son to marry someone very different from me. I know you wanted the highest in the land for him . . ."

She did not reply for some moments. When she spoke, it was almost as though she were talking to herself.

"I am not a very happy woman. For years I have brooded. All those years my husband was with her. She was everything that I was not, the sort of person a man can be at peace with . . . happy with . . . the sort who doesn't make demands. I realize now that was something I was doing constantly . . . trying to make people what they were not . . . to fit in with what I wanted them to be. I sought the wrong things in life. When we were in that dark hole, I saw things which I had never seen before. It was as though a light had been thrown on the past, and I began to ask myself how much of what had happened had been due to myself. If I had been different . . . loving . . . lighthearted . . . not setting such store by material things . . . perhaps it would have been different. I saw clearly your care for Gertie . . . your love for your mother. I began to see that I had made misjudgements, set too much store on the less important aspects of life. I saw how foolish I had been to dislike you because you were your mother's daughter . . . because you had not such a grand pedigree as I have. Noelle, I shall be grateful to you always. I shall be happy to continue our friendship through our lives, and I hope you will never go away from this house."

I could not stop myself. I put my arms round her and, for a few moments, we clung together.

I said: "I am so happy. I have never felt such happiness since I lost my mother."

Shock

Roderick and I were in a state of bliss. It was so wonderful to bask in the approval of Lady Constance. In spite of her exhaustion—which was great—she looked younger and took a great interest in our plans. I had never seen her so animated before. The change had been so sudden and there were times when I expected her to revert to the old Lady Constance, when I would see a trace of that icy aloof manner towards the servants, but even with them her manner had softened.

I was sure they were aware of it.

She was always warm and friendly towards me. Sometimes it was hard to believe that the change would last, but I was beginning to accept it and I was sure she herself only had to look back to that time we had spent together, so highly charged with emotion . . . to realize how happy she could be in her newfound understanding of others . . . and herself.

I went over to see Fiona, taking a different route because the path was now fenced off and men were working on it.

Fiona greeted me warmly.

"My dear Noelle, what a dreadful thing! I am so relieved and delighted that you are all right. I blame myself in a way. I knew she was getting more and more strange. I didn't want people to know. I thought I could manage her."

"You must not talk like that. Of course you did your best. I had no idea that she was so ill."

"She was the victim of obsessions. I should have been more alert. It did not occur to me that it was she who had set fire to the cottage, though I had had hints . . ."

"Whatever made her do it?"

"Let's have a cup of coffee. Then we can talk."

"I'd enjoy that."

She went into the little kitchen.

"How are you getting on with the repairs upstairs?" I called.

"It's coming back to normal. It *is* good to see you here. Thank goodness Kitty saw what she did."

"Gertie's a kind girl. It was so good of her to befriend Kitty in the first place."

"I am glad Kitty is up at Leverson. It's better for her there. You see, she had some notion that my grandmother had saved her. After all, she did take her in when the poor girl must have been rather desperate. Kitty felt she had to serve her without question. It will be healthier for her up at the Manor."

"And Gertie will keep an eye on her."

She came in with the coffee.

"Now," she said, "we can talk. Yes, my grandmother wanted me to marry Roderick. That was at the root of the trouble."

"Oh," I said.

She smiled. "I heard," she went on, "about you two. Congratulations! I saw it coming, of course, but the marvellous thing is that Lady Constance is pleased about it."

"How news travels!"

"I was saying my grandmother had obsessions and this was one of them. She thought if she made the cottage uninhabitable, I should have to go to work in a room in the Manor, which would bring me into closer contact with

Roderick. Hence the fire. Then she saw an obstacle in you. She quite rightly saw how things were between you and Roderick."

"How did she know that?"

Fiona looked at me with an indulgent smile. "It was rather obvious, you know."

"She saw us so rarely together."

"Once was enough. And she wanted to remove you from the scene."

"She did warn me that danger was threatening me here."

"Yes, she wanted you to go away."

"I see now."

"And then, when you wouldn't, she looked for opportunities."

"She was taking a chance. Someone else could have fallen into the trap . . . and Lady Constance did before me."

"She was not really thinking as normal people think. She was ready to take the chance to remove you . . . and, you see . . . from her point of view . . . it worked."

"Her mind must be very distorted."

"Poor Granny. She became very strange once before. That was after the death of my mother. She had a stay in hospital then . . . but she recovered and I went to her, and caring for me seemed to help her. Of course, she always believed in her special powers and such things, but that did not intrude too much on normal life at that time. She gave me the utmost care. It was when I was growing up and became interested in archaeology that it started up again. She was obsessed by my future. She wanted a grand marriage for me and Roderick was the one she chose. She had discovered that I was corresponding with a student whom I met when I was with Sir Harry Harcourt. He's studying archaeology. We got to know each other and have kept in touch. It's a . . . very firm friendship."

"I'm glad."

She flushed slightly. "So you see, my grandmother's dreams are all her own."

"Poor lady. Does she know what has happened?"

"I don't think so. When I last saw her, she was talking about my mother as though she had recently died. So I could see she was back all those years."

"I hope she will be all right."

"I think she will be in that hospital for some time."

"And you are managing all right without Kitty?"

"Oh yes. Mrs. Heather comes in and cleans up the house. She cooks me a meal every evening, as she says so that I can have something good inside me at least once a day. So, you see, I am managing very well. In fact, it is a relief to know my grandmother is having the best possible care."

"It was a terrible experience," I said, "both for me and for Lady Constance. But in some ways it seems to have straightened out a lot of difficulties."

There was a knock on the door. Fiona opened it and one of the workmen stood there.

"There's something down there, miss," he said. "You know . . . where the path gave in. It's stone or something."

I said excitedly: "It must be the ledge on which we landed."

"We dug down a bit, miss," went on the man. "Looks like some sort of Roman stuff."

•

That was the beginning. Excavations had been going on for some days and there was great jubilation when it was discovered that the stone ledge onto which Lady Constance and I had fallen was part of the floor of what could be a temple.

The existence of this could possibly have been the reason why our fall had not been deep and had made our rescue easier than it might have been. In fact, it may well have saved our lives.

Fiona and Roderick were in a state of great excitement. I shared this to some extent. It added a new zest to the days, and I would go down to the site with Roderick to watch. Several people from the archaeological world had come down to inspect the find and now some work was being done on it. The assumption was that the temple was an extension of the villa, and this might give rise to further interesting revelations. Each day something new came to light. Part of a statue had been found before what was an altar. And there were traces of a trident, and part of what could be a dolphin. The new discovery was known as the temple of Neptune.

In the midst of all this excitement, Charlie returned.

He was delighted to hear about the discovery, and I was looking forward to telling him the news about Roderick and myself.

That night remains clear in my memory.

We were at dinner, and the main topic of conversation was the temple of Neptune.

"Which," said Roderick, "means that our site here could prove to be one of the most interesting in the country."

"That might well be," said Charlie. "How did they come to find out what was down there?"

"Of course, you haven't heard," said Lady Constance. "There was an accident."

Charlie looked from one to the other of us in concern.

"An accident," he repeated.

"It's all over now," said Lady Constance. "And all this has come out of it. If we hadn't fallen, Neptune and his temple might never have seen the light of modern day."

We gave Charlie a brief account of what had happened. He was dismayed.

"What a lot has happened since I have been away," he said. "Thank God you are all right."

"The temple was helpful," I explained. "You see, we fell into it, which probably saved us from being buried in all that loose earth."

"There is something else," said Roderick. He was looking at me and smiling.

"Well?" said Charlie.

"Noelle and I have decided . . . well, we are going to be married."

I was watching Charlie closely. I saw his face frozen for a moment, and then it seemed as though an expression of dismay crossed his face. I was amazed. I had expected him to be delighted.

I immediately thought: He is worried about Lady Constance. I wanted to tell him that he had no need to be.

He smiled, but I fancied it was a forced smile.

"Oh," he said. "I see."

Lady Constance put in: "We don't want there to be any delay."

"You . . . seem pleased," said Charlie.

"I am," replied Lady Constance firmly. "Very."

"I . . . I see," said Charlie.

He was smiling. Of course he was pleased. After all, why should he not be?

•

It was about ten o'clock next morning. I was preparing to go out with Roderick, and we were to make our first call at the temple.

Gertie came to me. She said: "Mr. Claverham wants you to go to his study, miss."

"Now?"

"Yes, miss. He said now."

I went down immediately. I was surprised to see that Roderick was there.

Charlie said: "Come in, Noelle. Shut the door. I have something to say to you both. I am afraid this will come as a terrible shock to the two of you. I blame myself. I should have seen the possibility. I have been pondering all night as to what is the best thing to do, and I have come to the conclusion that the only thing is to tell you the truth. You have to know. There can be no marriage between you two. You, Noelle, are my daughter. Roderick is your brother."

PARIS

At La Maison Grise

I was sitting in the train which was taking me to London. I was still reeling from the blow. When Charlie had told us, we had been too stunned to take in what it meant at first. With a few words he had shattered our dreams; the whole world was falling about us. We could only see our lives in ruins.

I do not know how I lived through the next few days. We talked. Was Charlie sure? All the time, he had known, he said. There had been no secrets between him and my mother.

"You should never have met," he said. "I should have known better than to bring you down here. I am to blame. I thought Roderick would marry Fiona Vance. They seemed to have such interests in common. Your mother would have been so distressed if she knew what had happened. The last thing she wanted was to harm anyone . . . least of all you, Noelle. She loved you more than anyone. She always wanted what was best for you."

There was no way out of the situation. Whichever way we looked, we came face to face with the impossibility. Then I saw that there was only one thing for me to do, and that was to go away.

Where could I go? What could I do?

There was my old home . . . Robert Bouchère's now. I could go there for a while. He had told me I must always regard it as my home. I could stay there while I tried to make some sense of my life, to start again, to try to build something out of the ruins.

Charlie said: "You must let me look after you, Noelle. In view of our relationship, it is only right that I should do so. I shall make you an allowance."

I was not listening. I could only think: I always wanted to know my father. Oh, Charlie, why did it have to be you!

Poor Charlie was deeply distressed. His infidelity towards his wife had lain heavily on his conscience, and now this. The sins of the fathers visited on the children. Both his children . . . Roderick and myself . . . must pay the cost of his sin.

He was a most unhappy man—as unhappy as we were.

I wrote to Mrs. Crimp and told her that I should be coming to stay until I made plans. What plans? I wondered.

I cannot bear to dwell on that time. Even now, I want to put it out of my mind. The death of my beloved mother, to be followed so soon by this dark tragedy, overwhelmed me.

I just wanted to go to my old room, to shut myself in, to pray for strength and the will and the power to pick up the shattered fragments of my life and try to rebuild something from it.

Through the familiar streets where I had ridden with her on our way back from the theatre . . . back to the house . . . the house of memories. Briefly, I had believed I had escaped from the clinging past . . . only to find that I had stumbled into a second tragedy as great as the first.

I knew I had to stop brooding on my misfortunes. Self-pity never helped anyone. I had to force myself to look around me, find an interest in something . . . anything to take me out of this melancholy into which I had fallen.

Mrs. Crimp welcomed me warmly.

"I'm right glad to see you, Miss Noelle, and so will Mr. Crimp be. Your room is ready . . . and you can have your dinner when you want it."

"I don't feel much like eating, Mrs. Crimp, thank you."

"Something on a tray perhaps? Something you could have in your room?"

"That sounds nice."

Lisa Fennell was coming down the stairs. She ran to me and embraced me.

"I was so thrilled when Mrs. Crimp told me you were coming," she said. "How are you?" She was looking at me anxiously.

"Oh . . . all right," I answered. "And you?"

"Fine! Let's go to your room. Mrs. Crimp says it is ready."

She was watching me intently, and when we reached my room, she said: "My poor Noelle. Something terrible has happened, hasn't it? Is it . . . Charlie?"

I shook my head.

"Lady Constance has been difficult?"

"No . . . no." I hesitated. Then I thought: She will have to know. It is better to tell her now.

I said: "Roderick and I were to be married."

She opened her eyes wide, and I felt my lips

tremble. "But," I went on, "he is my brother, Lisa. My half brother. Charlie is my father."

Her jaw dropped. "Oh, my poor, poor Noelle. So that is why you have come back."

I nodded.

"I see . . . what a dreadful thing! I suppose one might have guessed."

"Yes . . . I suppose so. I just thought of them as very good friends. Rather naïve of me, I suppose."

"What are you going to do?"

"I don't know. I haven't thought beyond getting away. I'll have to think where I'm going from here."

"And . . . Roderick?" asked Lisa.

"We were both bewildered. Everything was going well. Lady Constance was reconciled . . . and then Charlie came back and told us . . . and everything was shattered. Oh, Lisa, I don't know how I can bear it. My mother . . . and now this . . ."

Lisa nodded and the tears came into her eyes.

"That was terrible," she said.

"And now, when I thought I was going to be happy again, this happened."

"You must stop brooding on it, Noelle. You have to find an interest . . ."

"I know. Tell me, Lisa, how are things with you?"

"I've got a job, and I believe Dolly looks on

me as one of his regulars now. Lottie Langdon was off one night and I had a chance to take the lead. The audience gave me quite a good reception. Lottie's not as hard to follow as your mother was. I think I did rather well, actually. It all helps. I am sure Dolly will give me a place in his next. *Rags and Tatters* can't last much longer, and he is already considering something. Well, Dolly always is considering something."

"I'm glad things are going well with you."

"You must come and see the show again. It's improved since you saw it. But I reckon it's on the way out."

I knew that I had been right to come to London. I felt the influence of my mother here and the first tragedy superimposed itself on the most recent one; but I had learned to live without her; I had even been contemplating a happy life. Now I must learn to live without either of the two people whom I had loved best in the world.

Everyone helped a great deal. Dolly arrived. He had heard, through Lisa, what had happened, and was all sympathy. He was amazingly gentle. I was to let him know if I felt like a visit to the theatre. Even if it wasn't his show I wanted to see, he'd make sure I had a good seat and was well looked after. There was a camaraderie among theatrical folk and the daughter of Désirée would be welcome any-where.

The days flowed on. It was existing. That was all I could call it. I awoke each morning with a cloud of depression settling over me, and I went through the days in a blank despair.

Lisa thought I should do some sort of work.

"Work is the best thing at such times," she said.

I wondered if I should go to a hospital. There would be some voluntary work I could do, I supposed.

Lisa thought that might be a little depressing, which was the last thing I needed. Perhaps Dolly could help?

"What good should I be in the theatre?" I asked.

Martha came to see me. She had heard from Lisa the reason for my return.

Martha was deeply shocked. "It would have broken her heart if she'd known what trouble she'd caused you. I always thought there was something special between her and Charlie. And he was so fond of you, too. And you, of course, were the apple of her eye. She'd have done anything for you. What a turnabout, eh? And it was you she was thinking about all the time. It was always 'What's best for Noelle?' I used to say to her: 'You make a god of that child. You want to think of yourself.' And now, because of all this . . . well, I reckon she's crying her eyes out in heaven, if she's looking down and seeing what's happened. What are you going to do about it, love? I reckon you ought to do something."

"I could go right away from here. I *have* to do something, Martha. What do people like me do when they are left as I am? There are only two courses open to them, as I've said so often. Governess to some peevish child, or companion to a demanding old woman."

"Can't see you doing either of them, I'm sure."

"I don't know. It would be different. I could be a little dignified, too, because I would not depend entirely on my salary, as most of those poor people have to. I'd have a certain independence."

"You're not seriously thinking of that, are you?"

"The trouble is, I am not seriously thinking of anything. I am just drifting along."

That was exactly what I was doing; and I should have gone on doing so but for the arrival of Robert Bouchère.

•

Robert was surprised and pleased to find me at the house, but when he realized how unhappy I was, he was overcome with sorrow and sympathy.

"You must tell me all about it," he said. "Tell me exactly what happened."

So I told him. He was deeply shocked.

"You had no idea?" he said.

"No. It did not occur to me."

"Have you ever wondered about your father?"

"Yes."

"And asked your mother?"

"She was always evasive. She only told me that he was a good man. Well . . . Charlie is a good man."

"His friendship with her went back a long way."

"Yes, I know. I should have guessed perhaps."

"He was insistent on taking you to his home."

"I realize why now. I'm afraid I have been innocent . . . and very naïve. I just thought they were great friends. I should have thought that, as I knew him so well and was fond of him . . . she would have told me."

"My dear Noelle, you have suffered two great shocks. You are bewildered, and the best thing for you to do is to make plans. You must take some action. I think it would be good for you to go right away from here."

"Where should I go?"

"As Charlie did, I promised your mother that, if the need arose, I would look after you.

It would seem that the need is now here. Why should you not come to France with me . . . to my home . . . if only while you have time to make some decision about your future? You would be in a new place. It would all be so different. You could start again . . . make a new life. I could believe that here you will not find that easy. Here you remember too much. She is still here . . . in this house. Do you feel her presence?"

"You have left her rooms exactly as they were," I said. "How could they change? Everything here reminds me of her . . . you, too."

"That is why you should get away. You nurse your grief, *chère* Noelle. That is not good. You must get away . . . leave it behind you."

"Go away . . ." I said bluntly. "Go right away. You have never told me much about your home, Robert."

"It would perhaps be interesting for you to discover?"

"Would they . . . want me there?"

"Who? There is my sister, my great-niece . . . and there are occasional visits from my nephew . . . my sister's son."

"I thought you had a wife."

"She has been dead eight years. What do you say to this plan?"

"I had not thought to leave the country."

"It is best to leave the country. Thus you

get right away. Everything will be different in France. You will start a life that is new entirely. Who knows? Perhaps this will be best for you."

"Robert, you are good to me."

"But of course. I have promised her that, if Charlie is not there, I shall stand . . . what is it you say? . . . in his shoes?"

"Yes, Robert. That's right. It is so kind of you to care as you do."

"My dear, I am fond of you. Your mother was very dear to me. I know that her great concern was for you. She made me promise . . . and if she had not done so . . . it would have been my duty . . . even if it did not give me great pleasure . . . which it does, as you know well. What do you say?"

"I must think about it. I had wondered whether to try to get some post . . . perhaps in a hospital . . . where I could do something for sick people."

He shook his head. "It is you who need to be looked after. You just come with me."

"Shall you think me ungrateful if I say I should like to consider it?"

He waved a hand. "I give you one day . . . two days . . . but you must come. It is right for you. I promise you, there will be a new life . . . new people . . . new country. This will fade."

"Robert, thank you, thank you. I will think of it very seriously. I think you may be right.

But I do need to collect my thoughts. Please give me time."

"I give," he said, with a little smile.

•

I was wavering. Since Robert had made his suggestion, my interest was stirring and my melancholy had lifted a little. I knew I was wrong to steep myself in sorrow as I was doing here. I had to move on. I must stop thinking of what might have been and accept the fact that there was never going to be a life with Roderick. I had to move on: and here was Robert, throwing me a lifeline.

He was good to me during those days. I knew that he was very anxious that I should go with him. He wanted to do his duty towards my mother's daughter, because he had cared so deeply for her. His desire to look after me was as earnest as Charlie's had been.

This time I must be more careful. I must know what I was going to do. At least Robert did not have a wife who would have resented his friendship with my mother. I would sway in my intentions. I would ask myself whether it would not, after all, be better to stay here. To look for some work to do.

"Robert," I said. "Tell me about your home."

"I do have a place in Paris," he said. "But

my home is about five or six miles outside the city."

"In the country?"

He nodded. "It is a pleasant old place. It survived the Revolution . . . miraculously . . . and the family have been there for centuries."

"A stately home, I suppose?"

"Well, La Maison Grise might just qualify for that description."

"La Maison Grise? The Grey House."

"It is so. Built of that grey stone which stays where it was put . . . no matter wind or weather."

"And your family?"

"There are not so many of us now. There is my sister, Angèle. She has always lived there. Daughters often stay on, even after they are married. When Angèle married her husband, Henri du Carron, he helped with the estate. It worked out well. I had business in Paris and he was there to look after things."

"And he died?"

"Yes. Quite young. He had a heart attack. It was sad. Gérard was only seventeen when it happened."

"Gérard?"

"He is my sister's son . . . my nephew. He will inherit La Maison Grise when I die."

"You have no children?"

"No, alas."

"You have not mentioned your wife."

"It is eight years since I lost her. She had been an invalid for some years."

"So at La Maison Grise there is just your sister and her son."

"Gérard is there rarely. He has a studio in Paris. He is an artist. Angèle runs the house, and there is Marie-Christine."

"You have mentioned a . . . great-niece, is it?"

"Yes. She is my great-niece and Gérard's daughter."

"So Gérard is married."

"He is widowed. It was a tragedy. It is three years since she died. Marie-Christine is now . . . well, twelve, I suppose."

"So your household consists of your sister, Angèle, who is Madame du Carron, and her granddaughter, Marie-Christine? Is she there all the time, or does she live with her father?"

"She visits him now and then, but La Maison Grise is really her home. My sister naturally looks after her."

"So it is a small household. Do you think they would mind my visiting you?"

"I am sure they would be delighted."

I was thinking seriously about going. There did not seem to be any complications.

So I made up my mind to visit La Maison Grise; and it was comforting to discover that the decision lifted my spirits considerably.

• • •

Robert and I had had a smooth sea crossing and on landing had taken the train to Paris, where the family coach had been waiting for us. It was a somewhat cumbersome vehicle with the Bouchère arms emblazoned on its side. I was introduced to Jacques, the coachman, and after our luggage had been put into the carriage we set out.

Robert made light conversation and, as we drove through Paris, he pointed out certain landmarks. I was bewildered by my first glimpse of that city of which I had heard so much. I caught glimpses of wide boulevards, bridges and gardens. I listened to Robert's explanations, but I think I was too concerned with what I should find at La Maison Grise to be greatly influenced by the city just then. That was something I could discover later.

"Prepare for a longish drive," said Robert as we left the city behind us. "We are going south. This is the road to Nice and Cannes, but they are a long way off. France is a big country."

I sat back, listening to the clop-clop of the horses' hoofs.

"It seems almost as though they know the way," I commented.

"Oh, they do. They have done it so many times, and it is usually these two who make the journey. Castor and Pollux—the Heavenly Twins. They are, I regret to tell you, not really apt names. They are far from heavenly, those two! But they can always be trusted to get us home. You will see how they prick up their ears and make an extra spurt when we are within a mile of home."

I wondered whether Robert was a little nervous. He seemed to be trying hard to make cosy conversation.

It was late afternoon when we reached the house. We had come through an avenue of trees and had gone about half a mile before it came into view. It was appropriately named, for it was indeed grey, but the green foliage around it robbed it of the sombre aspect it might otherwise have had. At either end were the cylindrical towers, aptly named "pepper pot," which are characteristic of French architecture. In front of the house were several stone steps leading to a terrace, and this gave a delightful touch of homeliness and softened the effect of the harsh grey stone.

We had pulled up, and two grooms appeared. Robert alighted and helped me down.

One of the grooms asked if we had had a good journey.

"Yes, thank you," said Robert. "This is Mademoiselle Tremaston. We shall have to find a horse for her to ride while she is here."

The groom spoke in rapid French.

"He says he will be there to help you choose. I'll take you to the stables tomorrow and we shall fit you up."

A terrible sense of loss crept over me, as I remembered my lessons with Roderick. I was longing with great intensity to be back at Leverson. I knew I should never forget. Why had I thought I might, merely by coming away?

Robert was saying: "I want to show you some of our villages. You'll find them interesting. They are different from those in England."

"I shall look forward to that," I said.

He took my arm and we mounted the terrace steps. I noticed that the shrubs in the white tubs were very well cared for.

I commented on them and Robert said: "That is Angèle's doing. She said the house had an unwelcoming look, and they help to dispel that. Perhaps she is right."

"I can imagine that would be so."

We were facing an iron-studded door. It opened suddenly and a manservant stood there.

"Ah, good day, Georges," said Robert. "We're here. This is Mademoiselle Tremaston."

Georges was a small man with dark hair and bright, alert eyes. He studied me and bowed. I sensed this was a somewhat formal household.

I stepped into a hall, at the end of which was a staircase, and at the foot of this was a woman. She came forward to greet me and I knew at once that she was Madame du Carron, Angèle, for she was sufficiently like Robert for me to guess that she was his sister.

"Welcome, Mademoiselle Tremaston." She spoke English with a pronounced French accent. "I am happy that you have come."

She took my hands and I immediately thought: How different from Lady Constance. I reprimanded myself. I must stop continually harking back.

"I am happy to be here," I said.

"And you have had a good journey?" She looked from me to Robert. "Welcome to La Maison Grise. It is good to see you, Robert. It is trying, is it not . . . that journey? La Manche . . . what you call the Channel . . . it can be a monster."

"It was quite a benevolent monster this time," I replied lightly, "which was fortunate for us."

"But it is a long journey. What would you wish? To your room . . . or perhaps some refreshment . . . some coffee . . . a glass of wine?"

I said I should like to go to my room first and wash.

"That will be best. Berthe!" she called.

Berthe must have been hovering near, for she came at once.

"This is Berthe. She will look after you. Berthe . . . hot water for Mademoiselle."

"Certainement, madame." Berthe gave a quick smile in my direction, accompanied by a brief curtsy.

"Come this way," said Angèle. "When you are ready, we can have a long talk. We can get to know each other, is that not so? That is . . . if my English will let us. Perhaps you have some French?"

"A little. I think perhaps your English might be more reliable."

She laughed, and I felt we had made a good start.

I was taken to my room. It seemed dark until Angèle opened the shutters: then the light flooded in and showed me how pleasant it was. The carpet and curtains were in a shade of pale pink; the furniture was delicate, and I felt I had stepped back a hundred years, for there was an elegant eighteenth-century atmosphere about the place. On one of the walls was a delicate tapestry—a charming reproduction of Fragonard's "Girl on a Swing."

I gave an exclamation of pleasure.

"You like it?" asked Angèle.

"I think it is enchanting."

"Then I am content. Robert says it is very important that you feel . . . how is it? . . . *comme chez vous.*"

"At home! You are so kind," I said.

"Robert tells me of your great sorrow. We wish to help."

"I am grateful to you."

"Let me show you this." She crossed to one corner of the room and drew back a curtain, disclosing an alcove in which was a large cupboard and a table on which stood a ewer and washbasin. On the floor was a hip bath.

"We call it the *ruelle*."

"How very convenient," I said. "Thank you so much."

She took my hand and pressed it. Then she withdrew hers and seemed a little ashamed to have shown such emotion.

She said briskly: "Berthe will bring along the hot water. Your bags are here. Perhaps you would like to come down in an hour, say? I will come for you then. Is that too long?"

"I think it will be just right, thank you."

At that moment, Berthe came in with the hot water.

"Do you need help to unpack?"

"Thank you, no. I can manage."

"In an hour, then?"

"Yes, please."

I was alone.

How different from the welcome I had received at Leverson Manor! I must stop thinking of Leverson. It was far away . . . out of my life. It must be. It would have been better if I had never seen it . . . never known Roderick.

I tried to concentrate on my new surroundings. They were extremely interesting. I wanted to know more about Robert's life here, his widowed sister, and, of course, there was the great-niece and her father.

I was beginning to think I was right to have come.

I unpacked, and by the time I had had a bath and changed into a blue silk dress, the hour was nearly up. I sat by the window looking out over the lawn to what seemed like a small copse. I could see that the grounds were extensive.

There was a knock on the door. It was Angèle.

"Am I too soon?"

"No, no. I am ready."

"Then, please come."

Robert was waiting for us and with him was a young girl who I guessed was Marie-Christine.

Robert said: "I hope you liked your room."

"It is charming," I told him, and turned towards the girl.

"This is Marie-Christine," said Robert.

"How do you do?" she said in English, while making a little curtsy, which I thought charming.

"I am so pleased to meet you," I said.

She regarded me steadily.

"I believe," said Robert, "that Marie-Christine has been practising her English so that she could greet you in your own language."

"How very nice of you," I said.

She continued to watch me, and I could not help feeling vaguely uncomfortable under such scrutiny.

"Dinner is served," said Robert. "I am sure you are hungry. I am."

I was not really so, being completely absorbed in my surroundings.

"We are eating in the small dining room today," said Angèle. "As there are only four of us, that is more suitable."

It was not really small, and was furnished in the same elegant manner as what I had seen of the rest of the house. Robert sat at one end of the table, Angèle at the other. I was on Robert's right, Marie-Christine on his left. There were two servants to attend to us—a kind of butler supervising and a parlourmaid to hand round the dishes. Robert had said it was a small household, but there seemed to be numerous servants.

As we ate, Angèle asked about my home in London. I told her that I had no home in London now and Robert looked at me a little reproachfully.

"You know the house is for your use," he said.

"That is kind of you, Robert," I said. I turned to Angèle. "In fact, I have been staying with friends in the country. I am really not sure what I am going to do."

"Your bereavement, of course," said Angèle. "I am sorry."

There was a brief silence. I broke it by saying to Marie-Christine: "Do you have a governess?"

"Oh yes, Mademoiselle Dupont." She grimaced slightly, to indicate that Mademoiselle Dupont was a little severe.

I smiled. "Does she teach you English?"

"Oh yes. But she does not speak it as well as you do."

Everybody laughed.

"Well, perhaps you will learn a little from me while I am here."

"Oh yes, please. I want to."

"Marie-Christine cannot bear not to know everything," said Angèle indulgently. "She does not like to be . . ." She paused. "Outside any matter. Is that not so, Marie-Christine?"

"Certainly."

"Well, it is the right idea, if one wants to learn," I said.

"Do you like riding?" she asked me.

"Yes, I do. I learned to ride not long ago. When I lived in London, there was little opportunity."

"I'll take you with me," she promised. "I am a very experienced rider."

"My dear child," protested Angèle.

"Well, I am good. Jacques said so. And we have to tell the truth, don't we? You will be safe with me, Mademoiselle Tremaston."

"I am sure I shall, and I shall look forward to riding with you."

"Tomorrow, then," she said. "It has to be afternoon. Mademoiselle Dupont will not release me in the morning."

"I shall look forward to it."

Robert was looking on benignly. He was obviously delighted that I was getting on well with his family. And I felt comforted because they all seemed determined to make me happy here; and that night, when I retired to the elegance of my eighteenth-century bedroom, my feeling was that I had been wise to come.

•

The next morning, Berthe brought my hot water at seven-thirty and told me she would be back with my *petit déjeuner*.

I guessed that everyone took their breakfast in their bedrooms. Breakfasts here were not the meal they were at home, with a sideboard full of delicacies like devilled kidneys, eggs, bacon and kedgeree.

My French was adequate enough to enable me to deal with Berthe, and I told myself it would improve during my stay in France.

In due course, Berthe arrived with a tray,

on which was hot crusty bread, a pot of coffee and a jug of hot milk.

I was surprised not only that was I able to consume it with relish but that I was also looking forward to the day's experiences.

I found my way down to the hall and to the garden. The air was fresh and the scent of flowers was everywhere. I made my way to the pond in the centre of the lawn, in which two nymphs stood, their arms entwined. I could look back at the house now. I studied the towers, the grey walls and the shuttered windows. The sun glinting on the stones picked out little brilliants here and there. Grey, menacing in a way . . . but there was the terrace with the white tubs of flowering shrubs, and the green climbing plant, the tentacles of which clung in places to the grey stone as though determined to soften it.

"Good morning." Robert was coming towards me.

How kind he was! How eager to make me happy. Charlie had been the same, and his kindness had led me to that acute unhappiness. How I yearned to be back in the old days, which I had believed would never end.

"I trust you slept well," said Robert.

"Very well indeed. My room is lovely. I feel like Madame de Pompadour."

"Oh . . . nothing so grand as that! But we do want you to be comfortable here."

"I can see that. If I am not, it will be no fault of yours or your sister's."

He put his hand over mine. "Dear Noelle," he said. "I understand how it is. We are going to try to make you put all that behind you. It is the only way."

"I know. If only it were as easy as it sounds."

"It will come in time. Angèle was saying she was going to show you the house this morning."

"That will be interesting."

"And this afternoon, you have promised to go riding with Marie-Christine."

"She seems to be a nice girl."

"She's a little difficult at times, I understand. Angèle makes excuses for her. She lost her mother . . . and being brought up with older people . . . Mademoiselle is something of a dragon, I believe. However, come to the stables. I want to choose a suitable mount for you."

"Now?" I asked.

"Why not?"

We walked across the garden to the stables. Jacques was there.

He said: *"Bonjour,"* and Robert spoke to him about the horse. Jacques was ready. He produced a small chestnut mare. Her name was appropriately Marron. She was docile and not one for tricks, said Jacques. She liked a nice steady rider, and she could be trusted.

"It seems we have the right horse for you, Noelle," said Robert. "For a beginning, at least."

He explained to Jacques that I should be riding with Mademoiselle Marie-Christine that afternoon and Marron should be prepared. Jacques asked at what time. Well, *déjeuner* was at one o'clock. What about two-thirty? He was sure that would be all right.

When we left the stables we met Angèle, who was looking for me.

"I wish to show Noelle the house," she said. "These old houses can be a little . . . unexpected . . . you lose your way . . . but you quickly learn. It is only at first that it is a little . . . baffling."

Robert passed me over to Angèle and we began our tour of the house. She explained that, like many old houses, it had been repaired over the years. There had been additions and embellishments which make a house change its character. It must be different now from when it was first built.

"That is what makes it so interesting," I said.

"Well . . . perhaps, in a way. In this hall, you see . . . there used to be a fireplace in the centre of the room . . . a sensible place to have a fireplace, for people could sit round it."

"But dangerous," I said.

"As all fires are, I suppose. You see, the smoke used to go up through a hole in the ceiling. Well, the roof has been repaired so many times that you can't see it now. But you can see the outline on the floor."

"Yes, I see."

"Then there are the weapons that were used in battles. These are relics of the Hundred Years' War, when your country was fighting mine. And here are the weapons from the Napoleonic Wars, when we were enemies once more."

"I hope we never are again."

"Let us hope. Our Emperor is eager for friendly relations with England. We have commercial treaties and that sort of thing. Then there are our interests in the Suez Canal. So let us hope that we never go to war with each other again."

"The Emperor, I believe, is very popular here in France."

"Oh yes . . . but he has his enemies. What ruler has not? The Empress Eugénie is beautiful and charming. There is a son and heir. So . . . all seems well. They are gracious and handsome, and wherever they go the people cheer them. Robert and I are sometimes invited to certain functions and we have been received with the utmost graciousness."

"It seems that all is well, then."

"Who can say when all is well? We remember that it is not so very long ago that we were in revolution. That is something a country does not very easily forget."

"There would be no reason now."

"People find reasons," she said soberly. "But what a dismal conversation! It is all those weapons. I shall suggest to Robert that they be removed and we put up tapestries in their place. They are far more attractive. Well, this is the great hall and, apart from the removal of the central fireplace, it is almost the same as it has been through the ages."

"It is very impressive."

"Now, through there are the kitchens. We'll leave those. The servants will be there."

We went up a staircase and she took me through several rooms. They were all furnished in a style similar to that of the room I was occupying. Most of them were shuttered.

We mounted more steps and I was taken through a gallery in which several portraits hung. We paused to look at them and she pointed out members of the family, among them Robert and herself.

"This is my husband," she said. "And here is Gérard."

I paused before Gérard. He was more interesting to me because he was living and I should probably meet him.

He wore a dark coat with a white cravat;

his hair looked almost black against his white skin. He had dark blue eyes and he reminded me of Marie-Christine. It was natural that there should be a likeness. Was she not his daughter? There was the same restlessness in his eyes which I had detected in hers; it was as though they were burdened by something . . . one might say haunted.

Angèle said: "You find my son, Gérard, interesting?"

"Yes. He looks unhappy."

"It was a mistake to have it painted at that time. But it was all arranged, you see. It was painted by Aristide Longère. Do you know his name?"

"No."

"He is one of our fashionable painters. Oh yes, it was a mistake to have it painted so soon after . . ."

"After . . . ?"

"He had just lost his young wife. It was a terrible time."

"I see."

We moved away. "This is our father . . . mine and Robert's."

I could not stop wondering about Gérard as we went on through the gallery.

"This leads to the north tower," she said when we were confronted by a spiral staircase. "Gérard's quarters are here when he comes to

La Maison. It is the north light you get here. He likes that. It's ideal for his work."

"May we go in?"

"But certainly."

We came to a door at the top of the staircase. She opened it and we were in a large room with several windows. There was an easel at one end and canvasses stacked against the wall.

"Gérard works mostly in Paris," said Angèle. "So he is not here for much of the time. Then he has this tower. He has his bedroom and other rooms up here, so we call the north tower his studio."

"You must miss him when he is so often in Paris."

She shrugged her shoulders. "It is best for him. There he has his artistic friends. Here . . . he remembers . . ."

"His wife must have been very young when she died."

She nodded. "They were young when they married. Gérard is now thirty-two. It was three years ago when she died. Marie-Christine was nine then, so Gérard must have been twenty when she was born. It was far too young. Neither Henri, my husband, nor I wanted it, but . . ."

She lifted her shoulders in a familiar gesture. "Now he has his work. He has his life in Paris. It is better so. Down here . . . oh . . . no . . . it all happened here."

I nodded. I knew all about memories.

I saw the portrait then. I guessed who it was before I asked. She was very beautiful in a wild, gypsy kind of way. Her hair was reddish brown and she had light tawny eyes. There was a wilful, wayward look about her mouth, and her eyes were mischievous. She was very attractive.

"That is Marianne," said Angèle.

"Marianne . . . ?"

"Gérard's wife. Marie-Christine's mother."

"She's very beautiful."

"Yes," said Angèle quietly.

I wondered how she had died. I felt there might be some mystery and therefore it was something I could not ask just yet. I sensed that Angèle was wishing she had not brought me up to the north tower.

The tour of the house continued. In the west tower was the schoolroom.

"We had better not interrupt Marie-Christine at her lessons," said Angèle, though doubtless Marie-Christine would not mind that.

She did mention Gérard again during the tour. She said: "I suppose one day he might come and live here. He'll inherit it in due course. Perhaps he'll marry again. I always hope he will."

I told her how interesting I had found the

house. "Although," I added, "I don't yet feel capable of finding my way about."

"That will come," she said, smiling.

•

That afternoon's ride with Marie-Christine marked the beginning of our friendship. I think her interest in me was as great as mine in her. We were both frustrated by the language difficulties, and her determination to overcome this was as strong as mine.

I did manage to gather a little information. She told me that she had been riding since she was two and had her first pony.

I replied that I had lived in London and did not start until I went to stay in the country, and that was not very long ago.

"Did someone teach you?"

There was that terrible desolation sweeping over me again. I could see Roderick so clearly, holding the leading rein, urging me on.

Marie-Christine was quick to observe my change of mood.

"Who taught you?" she asked.

"A friend at the house where I was staying."

"Was it fun?"

"Oh yes . . . yes."

"Do you ride with your friend when you are at home?"

"No . . . not now."

She was thoughtful, looking for words.
"What's London like?"
"It's a very big city."
"Like Paris?"
"There is a similarity about all big cities."
"Little ones are nice. Villemère is not far from here. Only a mile or so. There is a café where they sell the most wonderful *gâteaux*. You sit under the trees and drink coffee and eat it. You can watch the people if you like."
"I should like that."
"I wish we could talk more easily. When you have to hunt for words all the time, you can't say all the things that matter. I know, I'll teach you French and you can teach me English. This is too slow."
"That seems a good idea."
"All right. Let's begin."
"We can do that by talking. We could read together, too. That would be a help."
Her eyes shone. "Let's do it. Let's start today."
"As soon as we can."
"I hate waiting. Start now."
So we spent the afternoon giving each other little tests, correcting where necessary. It was amusing and stimulating.
It was one of the most pleasant hours I had spent since Charlie had said those words which had shattered my happiness.

• • •

I was with Marie-Christine every day. She was amazingly quick to learn when she wanted to, and even in a week she was grasping a fair command of the English language. I think my French progressed at a slightly lower rate; but communication between us was growing.

I had made the acquaintance of Mademoiselle Dupont. She was middle-aged, completely absorbed in her profession, respectful to me and pleased that I was helping to improve Marie-Christine's English. So there was no trouble from that quarter. Moreover, both Robert and Angèle were delighted by the friendship between us and I think Robert was congratulating himself that he had done the right thing by bringing me to France.

It was true my sadness had lifted a little. I still thought of Roderick every day and knew in my heart that I would never forget him, never cease to hanker for what I had lost; but at least I was finding some small consolation and I was grateful to Robert for bringing me here, to Angèle for being so understanding and perhaps most of all to Marie-Christine, who had provided me with an interest.

I was amazed at how quickly time was passing. Marie-Christine had decided to become, as she said, my *patronne*. She showed me the little town of Villemère; we sat outside the café and sampled the excellent *gâteaux* and coffee. She introduced me to Madame Lebrun, who owned the café—a large, rather formidable lady who sat in the cash desk and counted the francs with an avid interest—to her small, mild husband, who did the baking, and to Lillie, the waitress, whose lover was at sea. I found I could laugh again when we wandered round the stalls on market day, which was every Thursday in Villemère. I was hunting for bargains and feeling triumphant when I secured one. Marie-Christine knew a great many people. *"Bonjour, mademoiselle,"* they would call as we passed. Marie-Christine told me they were all very interested in *la mademoiselle anglaise.*

I was surprised that I could take the interest I did in the life around me, but when I saw wives and husbands laughing together my deep melancholy would return. That close companionship was something I should never know; but at least there were times when I could feel pleasure . . . however fleeting.

I owed that mostly to Marie-Christine. Reading together, talking, our outings, her obvious interest in me, were the greatest help I could have.

She talked continuously. She was constantly asking questions. She wanted to know about my life and was very interested in theatrical circles.

"Mademoiselle Dupont says it is good for me to learn about the English theatre. She says your Shakespeare is the greatest poet that ever lived. He must be very good, for Dupont usually thinks the French must be better than anyone else. I wonder it wasn't Racine or Molière or someone like that."

"The theatrical world in which I moved is not quite the sort to win Mademoiselle Dupont's approval."

"Tell me about it."

So I told her about *Countess Maud* and *Lavender Lady,* the songs, the dances, the clothes, the first nights, the tussles with Dolly; and she was entranced.

"I love your mother!" she cried. "And she died!"

"Yes."

"She was young to die, wasn't she?"

"Oh yes."

"Why do beautiful people have to die young?" She was thoughtful for a moment. "Well, I suppose if they were old, they wouldn't be beautiful anymore. So that's why beautiful people die young."

I had a picture of my mother which I carried with me. I showed it to her.

"She's lovely," she said. "You're not like her."

I laughed. "Thank you," I said. "As a matter of fact there couldn't be anyone like her."

"We both had beautiful mothers . . . you and I . . . not just ordinary beautiful but beautifully beautiful."

I was silent, thinking about Désirée, radiant after a first night, talking all the time . . . the mishaps which had nearly resulted in disaster . . . the man in the front stalls who had been waiting at the stage door while she slipped out at the back. Memories . . . memories . . . I could never escape.

"It makes you sad, thinking of your mother, doesn't it?" said Marie-Christine.

"Yes . . . but she is gone."

"I know. So has mine. Tell me, how did your mother die? She was young, wasn't she? Well . . . not old. My mother wasn't old either."

"She had been ill. It was nothing much . . . just something she had eaten. The doctors thought it was a plant which grew in our garden."

"A poison plant!"

"Yes. It was called caper spurge. It grows wild. If you get the juice on your hands and taste it . . . it can make you ill."

"How terrible!"

"It's nothing much. It just upsets you. It makes you sick and giddy. Well, she was feeling sick and giddy. She got out of bed and fell over. She struck her head against a piece of furniture and that killed her."

"How strange . . . because my mother died . . . not by falling against a table but by falling off a horse. It is a bit like your mother, is it not? They both fell. They were both young. They were both beautiful. Perhaps that is why we are friends."

"I think it is more than that, Marie-Christine."

"You still think a lot about your mother, do you not?"

"Yes."

"I do of mine. I think about her a lot and the way she died."

"Marie-Christine, we have to try to forget."

"How can you make yourself forget?"

"I suppose by looking ahead and trying to put what is past behind you. Stop thinking about it."

"Yes. But how?"

It was a reasonable question. How did one forget?

•

I had been at La Maison Grise for four weeks and I had no desire to leave it. I had come no nearer to making a decision as to what I should do with my life; and I was now beginning to remind myself that I could not be a permanent guest, however hospitable my hosts.

Robert went to Paris fairly frequently on banking business. He had a small house there and would stay for several days at a time. Both he and Angèle said I must certainly pay a visit to the capital. I could shop and see some of the sights.

I asked Robert if he would see much of his nephew while he was there.

"I doubt it," he said. "He seems to be working all the time and I imagine does not want interruptions. I don't think he's aware of anything else at such times, so I shall wait for him to invite me to the studio. Then he may come and stay here for a week or two. He does that now and then. It gets him away from Paris for a while."

"Then he works in the north tower?"

"Yes, that's right."

"Robert, do you realize I have been here for a month?"

"Well?"

"I can't go on taking your hospitality."

"That sort of talk makes me angry. You are taking nothing that we do not want to give you. You are very welcome. Angèle says Marie-Christine is so fond of you. She has been far less difficult since you have been here. Mademoiselle Dupont says you have done excellent work on her English . . . something she never could have done. So please, don't talk like that anymore. You are feeling better, are you not?"

"Yes, I am. I forget . . . for periods . . .

then it all comes rushing back. But there are moments when I am happy."

"That's good. I knew it was right for you to come here. You should have come in the first place."

"You are good to me, Robert. I know how you felt about my mother, but that does not mean you have to extend that devotion to me."

"I beg of you to stop talking nonsense, Noelle, or I shall be really angry, and I do not like to be angry. Tell me about Marie-Christine. How have you managed to change her?"

"I think we got off to a good start with the language."

"And now you are together riding or something every day?"

"She takes pleasure in introducing me to the life here . . . and I tell her about my childhood." I paused and he nodded, realizing there must be omissions. "It makes an interest for her."

"Then please do not talk of leaving."

"I don't want to go, Robert."

"That is the best news I could hear."

So I was lulled into a sense of security. There need be no decisions yet.

•

I was beginning to realize that it was not easy to know Marie-Christine. She had her moods and could be full of high spirits one moment and fall into near melancholy the next. It was this trait in her character which intrigued me. From the beginning of our acquaintance I sensed there was some secret matter which troubled her—but only at times.

Once I said to her: "Marie-Christine, is there something on your mind?"

She pretended not to understand, as she did now and then when I asked a question which she was not eager to answer.

Now she said: "On the mind? What is that?"

"I mean, is something troubling you?"

"Troubling me? Oh yes, Mademoiselle Dupont says my mathematics are terrible." She pronounced the word in the French manner, drawing it out to make it sound horrific.

I laughed at her. "I think it is something more important than mathematics."

"Mathematics are of the utmost importance, Mademoiselle Dupont says."

"What I mean is, Marie-Christine, is something worrying you . . . something that you might like to talk about?"

"Nothing is worrying me," she said firmly. "As for those silly old mathematics, who cares?"

But still I wondered. But I understood. Had I not secret sorrows of my own which I could not bring myself to discuss with anyone?

One day she said: "I am going to take you to see my Aunt Candice."

I was surprised, because I had never heard Robert or Angèle mention such a person.

"She's my mother's sister," Marie-Christine told me as we walked our horses out of the drive.

"She lives near here?"

"Not far. It takes about half an hour. She and my mother were twins."

"She doesn't visit La Maison very often, does she?"

"No, she doesn't. Grand-mère Angéle has asked her. So has Grand-oncle Robert. At least they used to. They don't anymore. She doesn't really want to come. I suppose it brings it all back . . . and she wants to forget. In any case, she does not come."

"But you see her often?"

"Not often. I go there, though . . . sometimes. I think I remind Tante Candice of my mother too much and she doesn't like to be reminded."

"You've never told me about your aunt before."

"Well, I can't tell you everything . . . yet. There has to be time."

We rode on and very soon were taking a direction which was new to me.

We came to a stream.

"The mill is not far from here," said Marie-Christine.

"The mill?"

"Moulin Carrefour. That's the name of the house. It's on the crossroads, really. That's where it gets its name. It's not a mill anymore. It was my great-grandfather who was the miller."

"I'm finding all this a little hard to follow. It might be helpful if you explained a little to me about the place and the people you are taking me to."

"I told you, I was taking you to see my Aunt Candice, and she lives at Moulin Carrefour, which was once a mill on the crossroads."

"I have already gathered that, but . . ."

"Well, my great-grandfather was the miller, but my grandfather made a lot of money gambling or something, and he said he wasn't going to be a miller all his life. So he closed the mill down and became one of the nobility. But he disgraced himself by marrying a gypsy girl from nowhere. She had two daughters, Candice and Marianne. Marianne was the most beautiful woman who ever lived. She went to Paris and became an artist's model. She married my father and I was born . . . and when I was nine years old she died. Tante Candice lived on at Carrefour with Nounou."

"With whom?"

"Their old nurse, of course. Nounou would never leave Candice. She will be there, too."

"And Candice . . . she did not marry?"

"No. She and old Nounou just live together. I don't think they will ever forget Marianne."

"It is strange that they don't visit the house."

"It's not strange at all . . . really. Not when you know them. Candice hasn't been for three years."

"Not since her sister died."

"Yes, that's right. Come on. I'll show you the place where my mother fell. It's an unlucky place. Someone's horse threw him there at exactly the same spot where my mother died. It's called the *coin du diable*. You know what that means?"

"Devil's Corner. There must be a reason for these accidents."

"They say it is because people come galloping across the field and forget they come out suddenly at the crossroads and have to pull up sharply. Look. It's just here."

She had drawn up suddenly. I did the same. We were looking across a stretch of grass. There were the crossroads by a stream which could have been the tributary of a river flowing nearby. And there was the mill house. The windmill dominated it, and behind the house were what I presumed to be barns.

Victoria Holt

On the gate opening onto a path which led to the house were the words "Moulin Carrefour."

"Is your aunt expecting us?" I asked.

"Oh no. We are just paying a call."

"She might not wish to see me."

"Oh, she will. And she likes to see me. So does Nounou."

She dismounted and I did the same. We tied our horses to the gatepost and went up the overgrown path.

Marie-Christine took the knocker and let it fall with a resounding bang. There was silence. I felt a little uneasy. We were unexpected. What had suddenly put the idea of visiting her aunt into Marie-Christine's head?

I was thinking with relief that no one could be at home when the door opened and a face was peering round the edge of it. It belonged to a grey-haired woman who must have been in her late sixties.

"Oh, Nounou," said Marie-Christine. "I've come to see you. And this is Mademoiselle Tremaston, who has come from England."

"England?" The old woman was peering at me suspiciously, and Marie-Christine went on: "Grand-oncle Robert was a friend of her mother and she was a very famous actress."

The door was opened wide and Marie-Christine and I stepped into a darkish hall.

"Is Tante Candice home?" asked Marie-Christine.

"No, she is out."

"When will she be back?"

"I'm sure I don't know."

"Then we'll talk to you, Nounou. How are you?"

"My rheumatism is troubling me. I think you'd better come up to my room."

"Yes, let's do that. Perhaps Tante Candice will not be long."

We went up some stairs and along a corridor until we came to a door which Nounou opened. We entered the room and Nounou signed to us to sit down.

"Well, Marie-Christine," she said. "It is a long time since you have come to see us. You should come more often. You know Mademoiselle Candice does not care to go up to La Maison Grise."

"She would come if she wanted to see me."

"She knows you'll come here if you want to see her. Are you comfortable, Mademoiselle . . . ?"

"Tremaston," said Marie-Christine.

I said I was very comfortable, thanks.

"I am showing Mademoiselle Tremaston our countryside . . . interesting places and people and all that. And you and Tante Candice are part of that."

"How do you like it here, mademoiselle?"

"I am finding it all very interesting."

"It's a long way to come . . . from England. I haven't been away from this place since before Marianne and Candice were born. That's going back a bit."

"Nounou came here when they were born, didn't you, Nounou?"

"Their mother died having them, you see, and someone had to look after them."

"They were like your own, weren't they, Nounou?"

"Yes, like my own." She was sitting there, staring into space, seeing herself, I imagined, arriving at this house all those years ago, come to look after the motherless twins.

She saw my eyes on her and said almost apologetically: "You get caught up with the children you care for. I was nurse to their father. He was a bright one, he was. I looked on him as mine. His mother didn't care all that much for him. He was a good lad. He had a magic way of making money. It wasn't going to be the mill for him. He always looked after me. 'You'll never want while I live,' he used to say. Then he got married to that gypsy girl. Him, who'd been such a clever boy all his life . . . to go and do that! Then he was left with two baby girls. She wasn't meant to bear children. Some are, some are not. He said to me, 'Nounou, you've got to come back.' So there I was."

I said: "I expect that was where you wanted to be."

Marie-Christine was smiling blandly. I could see she was rather pleased by the turn the conversation was taking. She was looking at me with pride because, I imagine, Nounou was finding me a sympathetic listener.

"Everything was left to me," she was saying. "They were my girls. Marianne . . . she was a beauty right from the start. Born that way, she was. I said to myself, 'We've got a handful here.' Everyone was after her when she grew up a bit. If you'd seen her, you would have understood why. Mademoiselle Candice . . . she had looks, too, but there was no way she could hold a candle to Marianne. And then . . . she died like that."

She was silent for a few moments and I saw the tears on her cheeks.

"How did you get me talking like this?" she asked. "Would you like a glass of wine? Marie-Christine, you know where I keep it. Pour out a glass for Mademoiselle. I'm not sure about you. Perhaps watered down."

"I don't want it watered down, Nounou. I will take it as it is," said Marie-Christine with dignity.

She poured the wine into glasses and handed it round, taking one herself.

Nounou lifted her glass to me. "Welcome to France, mademoiselle," she said.

"Thank you."

"I hope you will come again to see us." She wiped her eyes, in which there were still tears. "You must forgive me," she went on. "Sometimes I get carried away. It is sad to lose those who have meant so much to us."

"I know," I told her.

"One forgets it is only important to oneself. That girl was my life. She was so beautiful . . . and to think of her carried off. Sometimes it is more than I can bear."

"I do understand," I said.

"Now tell me about yourself."

"I am staying here for a while."

"Monsieur Bouchère was a great friend of your mother, Marie-Christine tells me."

"Yes," put in Marie-Christine. "When her mother died, Mademoiselle Tremaston came to us . . . to get away from the place where it happened. She is planning what she will do."

"I hope all will go well with you, my dear. Do you like this wine? I make it myself. France is the country of the best wines."

Nounou was clearly regretting her outburst and, having betrayed her emotions over the death of Marianne, was now trying to lead the conversation along more conventional lines. We chatted for a while about the neighbourhood and the difference between the French and English way of life—and in the midst of this, Candice arrived.

We heard her coming and Marie-Christine leaped to her feet.

"Tante Candice, Tante Candice . . . I am here with Nounou! I've brought Mademoiselle Tremaston to see you."

Candice came into the room. She was tall, slim and good-looking, and she reminded me faintly of the picture I had seen of her twin sister, Marianne. Her colouring was similar to that of the girl in the picture, but more subdued; her eyes were more solemn and she completely lacked the expression of mischief which had made the other so arresting. She was a pale shadow of her sister.

She seemed very self-contained and quickly recovered from the surprise of seeing Marie-Christine with a visitor.

I was introduced to her.

"I heard you were at La Maison Grise," she said. "It's hard to keep secrets in a village. Marie-Christine is looking after you, I see."

"We are great friends," announced Marie-Christine. "I am teaching Mademoiselle Tremaston French and she is teaching me English."

"That seems a very good arrangement. You knew Monsieur Bouchère in London, I believe."

"Yes, he was a friend of my mother."

"Her mother was a famous actress," said Marie-Christine.

"I have heard that," said Candice. "Tell me, how are you liking France? It is different, I suppose."

"Yes, it is, and I am enjoying it."

"And La Maison Grise is an interesting house, is it not?"

"Very."

"Have you been to Paris yet?"

"No . . . not yet."

"You will go, of course."

"I hope to . . . soon. We have talked of it. We shall shop . . . and I hope to see Marie-Christine's father's studio."

Her face hardened perceptibly. I thought immediately: She has strong feelings about him, and she cannot hide them at the mention of his name.

She said: "Paris is a very interesting city."

"I very much look forward to a visit."

"Do you intend to stay long in France?"

"She is going to stay for a long time," said Marie-Christine. "Great-uncle Robert says she must regard La Maison as her home."

I said: "My plans are undecided."

"Because her mother . . . the famous actress . . . is dead," put in Marie-Christine.

"I am sorry," said Candice. "Death can be . . . devastating."

I thought: The memory of Marianne haunts this place. Candice feels it no less than Nounou.

Candice said lightly: "This house was an old mill. I must show you round while you are here. It has just been an ordinary residence since my grandfather's day, but it still retains some of the old characteristics."

"I should love to see it," I said.

"Then let us go now. We'll come back to you later, Nounou."

Nounou nodded and we left her.

"It has been my home always," said Candice. "One gets attached to such places. Of course, I never knew it when the mill was working."

She showed me the house. It seemed small after La Maison Grise, but then most houses would be. It was comfortable and cosy.

"The Grillons live on the top floor," she told me. "They look after everything. Jean does the garden and looks after the horse and carriage. He is a very useful man to have about the house. Louise cooks and does the housework. There are just the two of us, and they are adequate. Nounou used to do quite a bit, but she is getting past it now. I'm afraid she meanders on about the past. I hope she wasn't boring you."

"She was telling Mademoiselle Tremaston about my mother," said Marie-Christine.

I noticed an expression of faint annoyance cross Candice's face.

"Oh yes," she said. "It's an obsession with her. She never got over my sister's death. She brings up the subject continually . . . even with people who can't possibly be interested. Sudden death is such a shock."

"I know that well," I told her. "My mother died unexpectedly when she was young."

"Then you will understand and forgive poor Nounou. This was our room . . . the nursery. Nounou cleans and polishes here herself. It's her domain, really. I think she sits here and remembers little incidents from the past. I don't know whether it is good for her or not."

"I expect she gets some satisfaction from it. People do from memories."

I saw the two little beds . . . the dressing table . . . the window that looked out on the stream and the windmill.

"It's very picturesque," I said.

She took me out of doors and we walked through the garden to the stream.

"We used to play in the mill when we were children," said Candice. "Nounou was terrified. She was always afraid there would be some accident."

We walked back across the garden to the house. Nounou was waiting for us in the salon. I thanked them both for their hospitality and told them how much I had enjoyed the visit.

"You must come again," said Candice.

Marie-Christine was smiling with satisfaction as we mounted our horses and rode away.

"There!" she said. "You've met Tante Candice and Nounou."

"It was very interesting, and they were very kind."

"Why shouldn't they be?"

"Sometimes unexpected callers are not welcome."

"Tante Candice is my mother's sister and I am her niece. Nounou was their nurse. That means they should always be glad to see me."

"She does not seem very anxious to see the family into which her sister married, and you are part of that."

"That's because she blames my father for my mother's death."

"Blames your father! I thought it was a riding accident."

"All the same, she blames him. I know she does. That's why she doesn't come to La Maison."

"Who told you this?"

"No one. I just know."

"You have a vivid imagination, Marie-Christine."

"You disappoint me. You sound just like old Dupont."

"Tell me . . ." I began. But Marie-Christine had set her face in stubborn lines and rode on ahead of me, and in due course we reached La Maison Grise.

It had been an interesting and unusual afternoon.

•

I mentioned the visit to Angèle. She was somewhat taken aback.

"Marie-Christine took you there! Really, she can be quite mischievous at times. We don't have very much contact with Candice. It's due to her. She never seems to want to see us. It may be that memories are too painful. We were never on very friendly terms . . . although Marianne was constantly at the mill with her sister and the old nurse."

"It must have been a terrible blow to them both."

"You met the nurse, did you? She doted on the two girls. I think the shock was rather much for her. One of the servants here is friendly with Louise Grillon, and occasionally a little gossip seeps through. The old nurse was particularly devoted to Marianne, and she hasn't been the same since she died. That's according to Louise Grillon. Gérard was a fool to marry the girl. It was not exactly a *mariage de convenance.* We were all disappointed, but he was quite besotted about her. An artist's model! Well, she was supposed to be very attractive."

"She seems to be, from her picture."

"She was painted by several artists. They saw her and wanted to paint her. She is in several galleries. The most famous one of them all was done by a Norwegian . . . or he might be Swedish . . . Scandinavian anyway. Lars Petersen. Poor Gérard. I think he was a bit put out. Naturally he thought he was more qualified to do *the* picture."

"She must have been outstanding to arouse such attention."

"She was reckoned to be exceptionally beautiful."

"You must have known her well."

"I can't say that. She and Gérard were in Paris most of the time."

"And Marie-Christine was here?"

"Yes. That seemed the best place for a child to be. I've looked after her all her life. Marianne was not much of a mother. Overaffectionate at times and then forgetting all about the child."

"I see."

"It was really quite unsatisfactory from the start. Even when Marianne was here, she was at the mill more often than in this house. She was very close to her sister and, of course, the nurse encouraged her to go there." Angèle shrugged her shoulders. "Well, it is all over now."

"And your son was in Paris most of the time."

"He always was. His art is his life. I've always known that. We wish he had been more

conventional. He could have gone into banking
with Robert, or law with his father . . . and
then of course, there is the estate . . . not
large, but it demands a certain amount of time.
But he knew what he wanted to do even when
he was a child . . . and that was paint. Marie-
Christine should not have taken you to visit
them like that."

"I think the idea came to her on the spur of
the moment."

"So many of Marie-Christine's ideas come
like that."

"Well, they were very affable and have invited us to go again."

Angèle lifted her shoulders in that familiar
gesture of resignation, and I think she must
have been only mildly displeased that I had met
them.

A few days later she suggested that we
should at last make the visit to Paris.

"Robert has a small house there in the Rue
des Merles," she told me. "There is a *concierge*
and his wife who live in the basement. They
guard the place during his long absences and
look after him when he is there."

I was excited and immediately made prepa-
rations for the visit.

The Portrait

❧

I was enchanted by Paris—that city of gardens and bridges, dark alleyways and wide boulevards, whose turbulent history seemed to be encapsulated in its ancient buildings and monuments.

I wanted to see everything, and both Robert and Angèle were delighted and proud to show me.

I was overwhelmed by the majesty of Notre

Dame. It exuded the past. Robert said what a tragedy it had been that during the Revolution the mob had sought to destroy it.

"Fortunately Napoleon came to power just in time to prevent its being broken up and sold," he added with satisfaction. "And then Louis Philippe, before his abdication twenty years or so ago, he did much to restore the old magnificence and necessary work has been done."

I could have spent hours there, absorbing the ancient ambience, dreaming of the past, of St. Denis, its first bishop, who had become the patron saint of France, or Peter Abelard and his love for Héloïse.

We walked a great deal. One must walk to see Paris. We visited the Louvre; we sat in the Tuileries; we spent hours in Les Halles; we crossed the Pont Neuf, the oldest of all the bridges, and I was both fascinated and repelled by the decorations on the parapets. Those grotesque masks would remain in my memory forever.

Robert was very interested in the work of Haussmann, which he said had changed the face of Paris in the last few years; the work had been necessary after the vandalism of the people during the Revolution. Robert was quite clearly proud of his city, and he enjoyed showing it to me. I noticed how he delighted in my admiration, which I did not have to assume. I had always been intrigued by big cities. I suppose it was because I had been born and bred in one of the largest. I had loved London, but my desire to be back there was smothered by persistent memories. Paris I could enjoy without reservation, from Montmartre to the Rue de Rivoli, from Montparnasse to the Latin Quarter. I could revel in it all.

I would return to the house exhilarated.

"You are incapable of fatigue," said Robert.

"It is because everything I see stimulates me."

"I knew you should come to Paris," commented Angèle. "We waited too long."

Marie-Christine was at my side most of the time. She was developing a new interest in the city.

She said: "I've already seen most of this before, but with you it's like seeing it afresh."

There came the day when we called on Gérard.

As I expected, he lived in the Latin Quarter. I was in a state of high expectation when we set out. I had been hoping for some time to pay this visit, and wondered why it had already been postponed on two occasions.

We were to arrive at three o'clock.

I noticed a certain tension in both Robert and Angèle. Marie-Christine had changed, too. She seemed a little remote. I wondered why the prospect of a visit to Gérard should have this effect on them all.

We made our way along the Boulevard St. Germain, past the church of that name. I knew it had been built here on the site of a Benedictine abbey as long ago as the eighth century, but the present church, which now replaced it, dated back only to the thirteenth.

The studio was at the top of a tall building. We had to climb a great many stairs to reach it. The last flight brought us up to a door on which was a card bearing the name "Gérard du Carron."

Robert knocked and the door was opened by a man—Gérard himself. I recognized him at once from the picture I had seen in the gallery.

He cried: *"Ma mère, mon oncle et ma fille!"* He turned to me, smiling, and went on in English: "And you must be Mademoiselle Tremaston. Welcome to my studio."

We were ushered into a big room. There were several large windows and a fanlight in the sloping roof. The room contained a couch, which was probably a bed by night, some chairs, a table on which stood an array of tubes and brushes, and there were two easels, and canvasses stacked against the wall. It was the room of an artist. Glass doors opened onto the roof, which was flat, and the view across Paris was spectacular.

"How good of you to call on me," said Gérard.

"We wanted to come before," Angèle told
him. "We thought you might be busy. How are
you, Gérard?"

"I am well, and there is no need to ask you.
You look radiant. How is my daughter?"

"Learning English," Marie-Christine told
him. "And I can speak it very well."

"That's excellent."

"Noelle . . . Mademoiselle Tremaston, is
teaching me. I'm teaching her French. We're
both a lot better than we were."

"That is indeed good news," he said.
"Thank you, Mademoiselle Tremaston, for being so instructive to my daughter."

I smiled. "The benefits are mutual."

"I can hear you have succeeded very well
already. Your French is charming."

"Unmistakably English," I said.

"Well, therein lies its charm. Now, my dear
family, refreshments, I think. I shall give you
coffee."

"And I shall make it," said Angèle.

"*Chère Maman,* I am not really so helpless
as you imagine me to be, but perhaps I should
not leave my guests. So if you would be so
good."

Angèle went through a door to what I presumed to be a kitchen. Robert and I were given
chairs, while Marie-Christine sat on the couch.

"This is a real artist's studio," said Marie-Christine to me. "There are lots like it in Paris."

"Not lots, *chère enfant,*" said Gérard. "Some, it is true. I like to think I was lucky in acquiring this." He had turned to me. "It's ideal, really. The light is magnificent, and don't you think the view is inspiring, Mademoiselle Tremaston?"

"I certainly do," I assured him.

"You look over Paris without effort. I can tell you, there are numerous artists in this city who would give a great deal to have such quarters."

"There are other artists here in this place," Marie-Christine told me.

"Artists abound," said Gérard. "This is the Latin Quarter and Paris is the centre of the arts, you know. And it is here where artists forgather. Day and night they congregate in the cafés, talking of the great things they are going to do . . . always, alas, *going* to do."

"One day they will talk about the great things they have done," I said.

"Then they will be too grand to live here, or to frequent such cafés. They will do that elsewhere. So you see, there will always be talk of what they are going to do."

Angèle called: "Gerard, I can't find enough cups."

He smiled in my direction. "You will excuse

me." He went into the kitchen. I heard their voices.

"*Chère Maman,* you always think I am starving."

"This chicken will last you a little while. It's all ready to be eaten; and I have brought a *gâteau* to go with the coffee."

"*Maman,* you spoil me."

"You know it worries me to think of you . . . living like this. I wish you would come home. You could paint in the north tower."

"Oh . . . it is not the same. Here I am with my own kind. There is only one place for a struggling painter to be, and that is Paris. Are we ready? I will carry the tray. You bring that magnificent *gâteau.*"

He set the tray on the table, pushing aside the tubes and brushes. Angèle cut the cake and handed it round.

Gérard said to me: "My mother thinks I am on the verge of starvation. In fact, I live very well."

"You can't live on art," said Angèle.

"That, alas, appears to be true, and I can't think of anyone here who would not agree with you. Tell me, what have you been doing in Paris?"

We talked about our sightseeing.

"It is all so fresh to Noelle," said Robert. "It has been a delight to show her round."

"It has been wonderful," I said.

Marie-Christine put in: "This *gâteau* is delicious."

"And your home was in London?" asked Gérard of me. "We have an Englishman in our community here. You see, we live a sort of communal life. We all get to know each other. We meet in cafés and in each other's apartments. Almost every night we are fraternizing somewhere."

"Talking about the wonderful pictures you are going to paint," said Marie-Christine.

"How did you guess?"

"Because you just told us. All you are *going* to do. That is what you talk about in cafés."

"It stimulates us. Yes . . . they all must come to Paris."

"I hope you will show Noelle some of your work," said Robert. "I am sure she would like to see it."

"Really?" he asked, looking at me.

"But of course I should like to."

"Don't expect anything wonderful, something like Leonardo, Rembrandt, Reynolds, Fragonard or Boucher."

"I should imagine you have a style of your own."

"Thank you. But is it your natural politeness which makes you show such eagerness to see my work? I would not wish to take advantage of your gracious manners and bore you . . . which might well be the case."

"How can I know how I shall feel until I
see it?"

"I tell you what I will do. I will show you a
few, and if I detect signs of boredom, I will
desist. How is that?"

"It sounds a good idea."

"First tell me how long you intend to stay
in France."

"I am not sure."

"We hope for a long time," said Angèle.

"I am going to insist that she stay," said
Marie-Christine.

"It would be a tragedy to miss your English
lessons."

"Is that Madame Garnier still looking after
you?" asked Angèle.

"Oh yes, she is."

"The kitchen floor needs cleaning. What
does she do here?"

"Dear old Garnier. She has a wonderful
face."

"Have you been painting her?"

"Of course."

"I think she is quite repulsive."

"You do not see the inner woman."

"So, instead of cleaning . . . she has been
sitting for you?"

He turned to me. "You were saying that
you wished to see some of my pictures. I will
begin with Madame Garnier."

He took one of the canvasses and set it on

an easel. It was the portrait of a woman—plump, merry, with a certain shrewdness about her mouth and more than a touch of cupidity in her eyes.

"It's certainly like her," said Angèle.

"It's very interesting," I said. Gérard was watching me intently. "One feels one knows something about her."

"Tell me what," said Gérard.

"She likes a joke. She laughs a great deal. She knows what she wants and she is going to get it. She is somewhat cunning and is going to make sure she gets more than she gives."

He was smiling at me, nodding his head.

"Thank you," he said. "You have paid me a very nice compliment."

"Well," said Angèle, "I have no doubt it suits Madame Garnier very well to sit in a chair smirking instead of getting on with her work."

"And it suits me very well, *Maman.*"

I said: "You promised to show us more of your pictures."

"I feel less reluctant after your verdict on this one."

"Surely you have no doubts of your work," I said. "I should have thought an artist must have complete belief in himself. If *he* does not, will anyone else?"

"What words of wisdom!" he said with a touch of mockery. "Well, here we are. This is the *concierge.* And here is a model whom we use sometimes. A little conventional, eh? Here is *Madame la concierge.* Too accustomed to sitting . . . not quite natural."

I thought his work very interesting. He showed us some scenes of Paris. There was one of the Louvre and another of the Tuileries, a street scene and one of La Maison Grise, including the lawn and the nymphs in the pond. I was slightly startled when, turning over the canvasses, he revealed a picture of Moulin Carrefour.

"That's the mill," I said.

"It's an old one . . . painted some years ago. You recognized it."

"Marie-Christine took me there."

He turned it against the wall and showed me another picture, of a woman at a stall in the market. She was selling cheese.

"Do you sit in the street and paint?" I asked.

"No. I make sketches and come back and work on them. It is not really satisfactory, but necessary of course."

"You specialize in portraits?"

"Yes. The human face interests me. There is so much there . . . if one can find it. So many people try to conceal that which would be most interesting."

"So when you paint a portrait, you are trying to discover what is hidden?"

"One should know something about the subject if one is going to do a really good portrait."

"And all the people you have painted are subjected to this . . . scrutiny."

"It makes you sound like a detective," said Robert. "You must have lots of information about people you paint."

"Not really," said Gérard, laughing. "What I discover is for me alone . . . and it is only with me when I am working on the picture. I want to do something which is true."

"Don't you find that people don't really want to look so much what they are but what they would like to be?" I asked.

"The fashionable painter is usually the one who does just that. I am not a fashionable painter."

"But if a flattering picture gives pleasure, what harm is there?"

"No harm at all. It is just not what I want to do."

"I should like to be flattered," said Marie-Christine.

"I daresay most people would," added Angèle.

"Do you think you really discover what secrets people are trying to hide?" I asked.

"Perhaps now and then. But the portrait painter often has a vivid imagination, and what he does not discover, he will imagine."

"And does not always come up with the right answer."

"What he likes to do is come up with some answer."

"If it is the wrong one, his endeavours might seem to have been wasted."

"Oh, but he has greatly enjoyed the experience."

"It seems to me," said Robert, "that one should be wary of having one's portrait painted, if in the process one must submit to an analysis of one's character."

"I can see I have given a false impression," said Gérard lightly. "I am really talking of an exercise practised for the artist's pleasure. It is completely harmless."

A shadow fell across the glass door which opened onto a roof, and I saw a figure there. A very tall man was looking into the room.

"Hello," he said, in deeply accented French.

"Come in," said Gérard unnecessarily, for the visitor was already stepping into the room.

"Oh . . . I'm intruding," he said, surveying us. He smiled on us all. He was very blond, and in his late twenties, I imagined. His eyes were startlingly blue, and there was something overpowering about him—not only because of his size. His forceful personality was immediately apparent.

"This is Lars Petersen, my neighbour," said Gérard.

I had heard the name before. He was the man who had painted Marianne.

Gérard introduced me. The newcomer obviously knew the others.

"It is delightful to see you all," said Lars Petersen. "You must forgive my calling in such a manner. I came to borrow some milk. Have you any, Gérard? If I had known you were entertaining, I would have drunk my coffee without milk."

"We have some coffee here," said Angèle. "It might be a little cold . . ."

"I'd like it however it comes."

"We have milk here, too."

"How kind you are to me."

"Do sit down," said Angèle, and he took his place on the couch beside Marie-Christine.

"You're a painter, too, are you not?" she said.

"I try to be."

"And you live in the next studio . . . and you have come across the roof."

"Well, it is not so hazardous as you might think. We can walk about on that roof, and there is actually a path from studio to studio. My studio is exactly like this one. They are a pair."

Angèle gave him the coffee, for which he thanked her profusely.

I thought Gérard looked mildly annoyed and was wishing his neighbour had not joined the party. The big man certainly had an effect. He was soon dominating the conversation . . . talking a great deal about himself: how he had been a student in Oslo and had suddenly had the idea that he must be a painter.

"It was like St. Paul on the road to Damascus," he told us. He had suddenly seen the light. So he packed his bags and came to Paris . . . the Mecca of artists. Such friendly people. So like himself. "There we are, in our garrets . . . poor but happy. All artists should be happy." He was looking rather mischievously at Gérard, who would, of course, not be exactly poor, coming from such a family. And was he happy? I did not think he was, which might have something to do with the death of his young wife.

"To starve in a garret is an essential part of the flowering of great art, so they say," went on Lars Petersen. "So we are all living from day to day, knowing that we are on the road to fame and fortune, and the hardships of the present are the price to pay for the glories of the future. One day the name of Lars Petersen . . . and Gérard du Carron . . . will stand with that of Leonardo da Vinci. Never doubt it. That's what we believe, anyway. And it is a nice comfortable belief."

He told us how he had come to Paris. He had struggled for a few years . . . going from lodging to lodging. And then he had sold a few pictures. One of those pictures was a success. People talked of it.

I was perceptive on that day. I was immediately aware of the expression on Gérard's face. It was fleeting, but it was there. He was thinking of Lars Petersen's portrait of Marianne which had attracted so much attention.

"If you have one success, people get interested," went on Lars Petersen. "I began to sell pictures. It was a step up. That's what everyone needs. Now I have a fine apartment . . . just like this one. It's an exact replica. And where could you find anything more suitable to our needs?"

He talked on, and I had to admit he was amusing. Though his French was fluent, he would often search for a word, throwing up his head and clicking his fingers, as though summoning someone to supply it. Someone—Marie-Christine, for instance—usually did. She was greatly amused by him, and I could see that she was enjoying the visit more since Lars Petersen had appeared.

He described his own country, the magnificence of the fjords. "Fine scenery. Paintable, but"—he lifted his shoulders and shook his head—"people would rather have the Louvre or Notre Dame . . . than all the wild scenery of Norway. Yes, yes, if you want to succeed, you must serve your apprenticeship in Paris.

Paris is the magic word. You cannot be great without Paris."

"So Gérard assures us," said Robert. He glanced at Angèle. "I think, my dear, that it is time we left."

"It has been such fun," cried Marie-Christine.

"You are not far away in the country," said Lars Petersen. "Just a few miles from Paris, is it not?"

"Yes," replied Gérard, "you should come to Paris more often."

"We will," cried Marie-Christine.

"It has been good to see you, Gérard," said Angèle. "Do come home soon."

"I will."

Gérard had taken my hand.

"I have so much enjoyed meeting you. I am glad you are in France. I should like to do a portrait of you."

I laughed. "After all your warnings?"

"There are some people one sees and wants to paint. I feel that about you."

"Well, I'm flattered, but I should be a little wary, shouldn't I?"

"I promise you, the process would be painless."

"We are going back the day after tomorrow."

"As we were saying, you are not far away.

Would you agree? It would give me great pleasure."

"May I think about it?"

"Please do."

"Would you come to La Maison Grise?"

"I would rather do it here. The light is so
good. And I have everything I need here."

"It would mean my staying in Paris."

"For a week or so. Why not? You are here
now. You could stay at the house. It is only a
short way from there to the studio."

I felt quite excited. It had certainly been a
stimulating afternoon.

•

Later that day Angèle came to my room.

She said: "I wanted to hear what you
thought about the visit to Gérard."

"I enjoyed it. It was very interesting."

"He worries me, really. I wish he would
come home."

"But you know how he feels about his
painting."

"He could do it at home."

"It wouldn't be the same. Here he is with
those people. Imagine the café society . . . the
talks . . . the aspirations and the rivalries
. . . all his friends who understand what he is
talking about. Naturally he is happier here."

"It was different when his wife was alive.
She could look after him."

"He seems to manage very well with Madame Garnier."

Angèle made a contemptuous gesture.

"And there is that man living close."

"He is certainly a character."

"I suppose you know him quite well."

"He has been a neighbour of Gérard's for some time. He's always been very garrulous when I have seen him . . . talking about himself most of the time."

"Gérard has asked to paint me."

"I know. I heard him. That would be nice."

"Do you think so?"

"I am sure it would."

"I said that, after all these revelations, I was put on my guard."

"Oh, that was just idle talk. Besides, you have no dark secrets."

"Still . . ."

"I think he could do a good portrait of you. Some of his are really quite beautiful."

"He did a great many of his wife, I suppose."

"Oh yes. She was his chief model. There are some lovely ones. It was a pity there was all that fuss about the one Lars Petersen did. I think some of Gérard's were as good. It's just a matter of what takes the critic's fancy."

"He did not show us any that he had painted of her."

"No . . . I think he doesn't want to look

back on all that. It seems to be too recent . . . even now. But you must let him paint you."

"I think it would be rather amusing."

"We'll arrange it. We have to come to Paris again. I can't really leave the household much longer now, so we must get back. But we can come again . . . in a few weeks' time. I'd come with you and you could go off to the studio every day. I expect he'd want to work in the mornings. The light is best then. Oh yes, certainly, we'll arrange it. Say in about three weeks' time."

I began to feel quite excited by the prospect. I was really rather intrigued by the bohemian life. I found Gérard's conversation interesting; and I was sure he had many friends as amusing as Lars Petersen.

•

When we arrived back at La Maison Grise, there was a letter waiting for me. It was from Lisa Fennell.

I felt uneasy when I saw her handwriting. I realized that the visit to Paris had helped me take a few steps away from the past. I had certainly been stimulated—especially by my meeting with Gérard and the glimpse I had had into his way of life.

I felt a sympathy for him. He had lost his young wife as I had lost the husband I had never had, so I felt there was a bond of a kind between us.

And now I was brought back with a jolt to that other world from which, such a short time before, I had escaped.

I took the letter to my room so that I might read it without interruptions.

My dear Noelle,

I have been wondering a great deal about you. In fact, I have never ceased to think of you since you left. How are you? I am sure you are feeling better. Robert is the kindest man I know, and you did right to go with him.

The show finished and it will be some weeks before we open with the new one. There is a place for me in it, Dolly has promised. Only in the chorus, though. I think Lottie Langdon is going to take the lead. I'm hoping to get the understudy. But at the moment I am resting.

What do you think? I went down to Leverson. I wanted you to know that I had been.

You see, there was a good deal in the papers about that discovery of the Neptune temple. Apparently it's a great find and all that about how the landslide had revealed it made good news. I was quite fascinated, and I wrote to Roderick, saying how I should like to see it.

He came up to London. I was still working then and he came to the show. We had dinner afterwards. He seemed very sad. He wouldn't talk about you, so we discussed this temple and he asked me down for a weekend, so that I could see it. I went. It was fascinating. I loved it all. I met that nice Fiona Vance, and she showed me some of the work she was doing. I had a most interesting weekend. Lady Constance was very cool towards me. Clearly she didn't approve. I understand how you must have felt.

Apart from that, I enjoyed it very much. I became so interested in what Fiona was doing. She showed me how to brush off the earth and stuff from some of the drinking vessels, and I was ever so sorry when I had to go.

Fiona said it was a pity I didn't live nearer. Charlie was there. He is very unhappy, too. I am sure you are never far from their thoughts.

Both Charlie and Roderick said I must come again. Lady Constance did not add her invitation to theirs!

Well, perhaps I shall go again. I do find all those Roman relics quite fascinating.

I am still at the house. Please tell Robert I feel ashamed about keeping on there, but I am so comfortable and the Crimps don't really want me to go. They don't like caretaking, as they say. They've been used to a household where things are going on. I know I don't make much difference, but I'm there, and they are always interested in what's happening at the theatre. So I just linger on.

Try to find out from Robert whether he really thinks I ought to go. But really, it does seem rather unnecessary and it means a lot to me to be able to stay here.

I expect I shall soon be working again. I

hope so. I shan't see any more weekends at Leverson in that case.

Well, I thought I ought to let you know that I had been there and seen them. Perhaps I'll see you *sometime. Are you making plans?*

Oh, dear Noelle, I do hope that things will go right for you . . .

The letter fell from my hands.

So, she had been there. She had seen Roderick and Charlie and Lady Constance. They had been sad, she said.

Dear Roderick. What was he thinking of now? Would he forget me in time? I knew I should never forget him.

·

I found peace and a certain amount of contentment sitting in that studio, gazing across the city while Gérard du Carron worked on my portrait.

I seemed farther away from the past than I had been since tragedy had first struck me. It seemed as though once again a way of escape was opening out before me.

I was seated on a chair with the light falling full on my face while Gérard stood at his easel. Sometimes he talked while he worked; at others he lapsed into silence.

He told me about his childhood at La Maison Grise, how he had always loved to be in the

north tower. He had sketched from an early
age; he had been deeply interested in pictures.

"I used to study those in the picture gallery.
I would be up there for hours at a time. They
always knew where to find me. They thought I
was a strange child. And then suddenly I knew
I wanted to paint.

"Life was smooth and comfortable. My father was a quiet man . . . a fine man. I wonder what would have happened if he had lived.
If . . . one is always saying if. Do you say it,
Noelle?"

"Constantly."

"Why are you so sad?"

"How do you know I am sad?"

"You try to hide it, but it is there."

"You know about my mother?"

"Yes. I know of her sudden death. Robert
was very fond of her, and that is why you are
here. He promised her he would look after you.
It is for that . . . and of course because he is
very fond of you. Does it hurt to speak of her?"

"I am not sure."

"Try it, then."

So I talked of her. I told him about our life,
of the productions, the dramas and Dolly. I
kept recalling incidents and found that I could
laugh at some, as I had at the time.

He laughed with me.

He said: "It was a tragedy . . . a great
tragedy."

Madame Garnier would come, and the kitchen was full of noise. I fancied she thought the noise was necessary to show how hard she was working. She was a little resentful of me at first, but after a few days she was more amicable. We had both had our pictures painted, and that made a bond between us.

She told me that hers was going into some exhibition. People would come and look at it and perhaps buy it.

"Who would want me hanging in their salons, mademoiselle?"

"Who would want me?"

She had a habit of nudging me and bursting into laughter. She brought in bread, milk and such things, for which I discovered she overcharged outrageously. I had suspected this because of the cupidity I had seen in her eyes in the portrait. I had put it to the test and found it to be true. I was impressed by Gérard's perspicacity.

I said to him one day: "Do you know Madame Garnier cheats you over the food?"

"But of course," he said.

"And you don't tell her so?"

"No, it's a small matter. I need her to bring the food. So let her have her little triumphs. It brings her satisfaction. She thinks how clever she is. If she thought I knew, she would lose that satisfaction. Is there not a saying in English, 'Let sleeping dogs lie'?"

I laughed at him.

I used to go into the kitchen when the morning sitting was over and prepare a meal, which we would share. Angèle sometimes called and we would go back together. She was staying in Paris with me. Robert had had to go back to La Maison Grise to deal with some business on the estate. I knew Marie-Christine was put out because we had gone away without her. She would have liked to accompany us, but Mademoiselle Dupont had said lessons must not be further interrupted.

I sometimes stayed at the studio for the afternoons. Often when we were lunching together, people would call. I was beginning to know some of Gérard's friends. There was Gaston du Pré, a young man from the Dordogne country. He was very poor and was fed mainly by the others. He often appeared at mealtimes and shared what was being eaten. Then there was Richard Hart, son of a country squire from Staffordshire, whose lifelong ambition had been to paint. There were several others, chief among them Lars Petersen, the most successful of them all, since he had achieved some fame through his portrait of Marianne.

He dominated the company on all occasions, partly because he was more successful than the others and partly because of his ebullient personality.

It was a lighthearted life and, after a few

days, I felt myself caught up in it. I awoke every morning with a feeling of pleasure. I was enjoying the experience as I had not expected to enjoy anything again.

I looked forward to my little skirmishes with Madame Garnier. I had refused to allow her to continue to overcharge on her purchases, and pointed out the discrepancies to her. She would look at me, her little eyes screwed up to make them even smaller. But she respected me. I imagined her theory was that if people were stupid enough to allow themselves to be cheated, they deserved what they got. So there were no real hard feelings.

I liked to make the meal and often brought in the food. She did not object to this, for there was no profit to be made now, and it enabled her to do less work and to leave earlier. So even though I had spoilt her profitable enterprise, I had made life easier for her in other ways.

Gérard was very amused when I told him of this, and I found I was laughing a good deal.

Most of all, I enjoyed the sitting periods when we talked.

Our friendship grew fast, as it does in such circumstances, and I began to think that life would be dull when the portrait was finished.

One day, when he was working, he said: "There is something else which makes you unhappy."

I was silent for a few moments, and he

stood watching me, his brush poised in his hand. "Is it . . . a lover?" he asked.

Still I hesitated. I could not bear to talk of Roderick. He was quick to interpret my feelings.

"Forgive me," he said. "I am inquisitive. Forget I asked."

He returned to the canvas, but after a short while, he said: "It is not good today. I can work no more. Let us go out and I will show you more of the Latin Quarter. I am sure there is still much you do not know."

I understood. My mood had changed. It seemed that Roderick was close to me. I had lost my serenity.

As we came out into the street, the atmosphere enveloped me and raised my spirits a little. There was a smell of hot baking bread in the air, and from one of the houses came the sound of a concertina.

We went into the Church of St. Sulpice, and walked through the little streets with their shops containing rosaries and images of the saints.

"We call it St. Sulpicerie," he told me.

He showed me the house in which Racine had died. Then he took me to the Place Furstenberg, where Delacroix had had his studio.

"He's only recently died," he said, "but his studio has become a shrine. Do you think one day people will come along to my studio and say: 'Gérard du Carron lived and worked here'?"

"I am sure it will be, if you are determined to make it so."

"You believe, then, that we have the power to do what we want with our lives?"

"We have circumstances to contend with. Who of us knows what tomorrow will bring? But I do believe we have the power in us to overcome adversity."

"I am glad you feel like that. It is a wonderful creed . . . but not always easy to follow."

We came to a café with gaily coloured awnings, under which tables were set.

"Do you need refreshment?" he asked. "Perhaps not. But it would be pleasant to sit here. I find it soothing to the spirit to watch the world pass by."

So we sat and drank coffee and watched the people while Gérard amused himself—and me —by speculating about their lives.

There was an old man walking painfully with the help of a stick. "He has led a merry life," said Gérard. "And, now he is coming to the end of it, is wondering what it was all about. Ah! The matron with the shopping bag full of goods; she is congratulating herself that she has beaten down the prices of the butcher, the baker and the candlestick maker, little knowing that, being aware of her methods, they have put the prices up before she arrived."

Two young girls came along, arm in arm, giggling. "Dreaming of the lovers they will have," said Gérard. "And there are the lovers. No Paris street can be complete without them. They are unaware of anything but each other. And there is the young girl with her governess, dreaming of freedom when she will no longer need a governess. The governess knows that time is not far off and her heart is heavy with apprehension. Where will she find her next post?"

"I can see what you mean about knowing your subjects. Would you like to paint some of these people?"

"Most of them. Though some show too obviously what they are. I look for those with a touch of mystery."

We bought some pâté and took it back to the studio. Gérard produced a bottle of white wine and we sat on the couch and drank it with the pâté.

"I believe," said Gérard, "that you are getting a taste for *la vie bohème.*"

"Perhaps I was born into it."

"I think that may be so. That is why you have taken to it. My mother is a little shocked by the way I live. She cannot understand why I do not return to La Maison and live what she calls the life of a country gentleman."

"That would not suit you in the least," I said.

After a short pause, he said: "You are less sad now."

"You have cheered me up."

"So our little jaunt was just what you needed?"

"Yes. And I can't think why I should want to hide the truth from you."

"I should like to know, of course."

"It was like this: Your Uncle Robert and a man called Charlie were two of my mother's greatest friends. She was always surrounded by people. They came and went. But there were three of them who were always around: Robert, Charlie and the producer Dolly. When my mother died, Charlie insisted on taking me to his home. He had a son, Roderick. I had met Roderick and knew him quite well before my mother's death. She did not know of our meetings. They were not exactly secret, but I had not mentioned them. Charlie had promised my mother that he would always look after me if need be, and he took me to his home. Roderick and I fell in love. We were going to be married. Then Charlie told me that I was his daughter and so Roderick and I were brother and sister."

He was looking at me in amazed horror.

"And so," he said, "that was the end . . ."

I nodded. "That is why I am sad. After the shock of my mother's death, I wanted to start again. I know I could have done so . . . with Roderick. You see, my mother and I were so close. We had always been together. I could not imagine a life without her . . . and then . . . with Roderick, it seemed there was a chance."

He moved closer to me and put an arm round me.

"My poor, poor Noelle, how you have suffered!" he said.

"We were saying we have to accept the blows life gives us . . . but we do have the power to rise above them . . . if only we can find it."

"You are right. We have to do this. And we can . . . I am sure we can."

"I did not want to talk of this to anyone."

"But you were right to talk to me. I understand. You see, I have lost my wife."

He stood up suddenly and went to the window.

Then he turned and said: "The light is still good. I could work for a while. It will make up for playing truant this morning."

•

Then came the day when the portrait was finished. I was sad to think that period was over. There would be no more sittings, no more intimate conversation, no longer an excuse for me to go to the studio every day. There was no doubt that it had been a stimulating experience.

I studied the portrait while Gérard watched me with a certain apprehension.

I knew it was good. I was not the beauty Marianne had been, but there was a haunting quality about it. The likeness was there—and something else. It was the face of a young woman, innocent to a certain extent, and in a way unmarked by life, but there was in the eyes an expression of something which told of a secret sorrow.

I said: "It is very clever."

"But do you like it?"

"I think it betrays something."

"Something you would rather was not there?"

"Perhaps."

"It is you," he said. "Whenever I see it, I shall feel that you are here."

"Well, I suppose that is what a portrait should be."

Lars Petersen came in.

"I am all agog," he said. "Where is the masterpiece?"

He came and stood before the easel, legs apart. He always seemed to fill a room when he was in it.

"It's good," he announced. "You've done it this time, Gérard."

"You think so?"

"We'll see. It's got depth. It's the picture of a beautiful girl, too. There is nothing that pleases like a beautiful girl."

"It's not really beautiful," I said. "But it *is* interesting."

"My dear Mademoiselle Tremaston, I venture to say an artist knows best. It is the picture of a beautiful girl. Come on. Where is the champagne? We must drink to the success of our genius. Excuse me one moment."

He disappeared through the door and across the roof.

"He likes it," said Gérard. "I could see he liked it. He really thinks it is good."

Lars Petersen came back with a bottle of champagne.

"Glasses!" he demanded imperiously.

I brought them out and he opened the bottle and poured out the wine.

"It's good . . . good," he cried. "It's almost as good as my creation. Gérard . . . success! Noelle is going to launch you as Marianne did me. Not quite so well . . . but almost."

He was laughing. I wondered how the reference to Marianne would affect Gérard; but he just drank the wine and his eyes were shining.

Lars had convinced him that the portrait was good.

•

Angèle and Robert agreed with the verdict and there was talk of an exhibition. Gérard had now gathered together enough pictures which he considered to be worthy and there was a great deal of discussion about the arrangements.

We stayed on in Paris, and I was frequently at the studio. I helped Gérard to decide which pictures he would exhibit. Lars Petersen was often present to give his judgement. Others came, too, but as Lars was such a near neighbour, he was constantly in and out.

Madame Garnier grew in importance because her portrait was to be one of the exhibits. We chose some scenes of the country, but mainly of Paris; portraits, however, were really Gérard's forte, and they predominated.

Angèle and Robert shared in the excitement of preparation for the exhibition. Angèle did say that Marie-Christine was continually asking when I was coming back.

"We shall all be up for the exhibition, of course," said Angèle, and I knew that soon we should have to leave Paris. But there would be other visits. I should look forward to them.

The exhibition was fixed for September and I realized it was nearly six months since I had come to France.

I returned with Angèle to La Maison Grise, where I was met by a reproachful Marie-Christine.

"What a long time you've been away!" she said. "Does it take so long to paint a portrait? My English is getting awful. One needs constant practice. I bet your French is pretty awful, too."

"I have been getting a lot of practice."

"Which I don't with my English. It was mean of you to stay so long. Did you like sitting?"

"It was interesting."

"I expect I'll have my portrait painted someday. That's what happens if you have an artist in the family. You get painted. Are you going to the exhibition?"

"Yes."

"You'll be famous."

"I? What have I done?"

"When my mother's portrait was painted, everyone was talking about her. Everyone knows who Marianne was."

"They won't be wondering about me."

"Why not?"

"Your mother was very beautiful."

She looked at me critically. "Yes," she said slowly, "she was. So it must have been because of that."

She seemed mollified. *I* was not going to be famous, so perhaps I would settle down, return to La Maison Grise and continue teaching her English.

I received another letter from Lisa.

I had written in answer to hers and told her that I was feeling better. Robert and his family were so kind to me, and he was the sort of man from whom it was easy to accept hospitality, as she had found. I was feeling cut off from the old life. Here everything seemed so different. I had done the right thing in coming, of course, but I could not stay here indefinitely, though everyone seemed not to want me to go . . . so here I was.

Dear Noelle [she had written],

Dolly's *Cherry Ripe* got off to a wonderful start. Everyone said Lottie was splendid. It was just her piece . . . less song and dance than usual, and you know she was always shaky on her top notes.

There's a trapdoor in some of the scenes. The hero comes climbing through it in the first act. He's pretending to be a workman, but of course he is a millionaire in disguise.

Dolly had made me understudy, which I thought was good for me. I was longing for a chance to show them what I can do. I was really every bit as good as Lottie.

Well, my chance came. My chance! There was an accident! The trapdoor gave way and I fell. It was quite a long way down and I've done something to my back. Dancing is out of the question for the time being. I've got to rest. I have been to two doctors, and they can't make up their minds what I've done. Dolly is furious. It's such a bore. I know I could have had a real chance with Cherry.

I expect I shall be resting for a few weeks. Well, it has given me a chance to catch up with my correspondence.

*I think of you so much, and wonder how you
are getting on. It is quite a long time since you
went away.*

*I saw Robert when he came to London.
What a dear he is! He insists on my staying in
the house, and the Crimps would hate me to go.
He said he thought France was doing you a lot
of good, and he was going to do his utmost to
keep you there. He said his great-niece had
taken a fancy to you! It sounds cosy.*

*By the way, I went to Leverson again. There
is such a lot of activity about that Neptune temple.*

Do write and tell me your news.

My love,

Lisa

•

Time was speeding by. There was all the activity concerning the exhibition. I went to Paris
again with Angèle and was at the studio frequently. I enjoyed preparing a meal and then
we would eat together, very often joined by one
of Gérard's friends, when conversation would
be mainly about art.

Lars Petersen was at that time using a
model called Clothilde. It occurred to me that
they might be lovers. When I asked Gérard, he
laughed and said that Lars often indulged in
romantic adventures. It was a way of life with
him.

I was becoming more and more drawn into

the circle, and I very much missed these occasions when we went back to the country. All the same, I could never escape from my longing for Roderick. I even toyed with the idea of writing to him. But I knew that would be folly. There was nothing either of us could do to alter the situation. It was safer for us to be separated. To see him again would only intensify the pain. I had to cut him right out of my life. There could never be a brother-and-sister relationship between us. If we could not be together as lovers, we must remain apart.

I was glad to find that, in spite of everything, I could still be interested in other people. I was always telling myself that perhaps in time I should feel differently.

It was strange to see my face encased in a rather magnificent brass frame looking down on me from a wall. It certainly was an arresting picture. It was because of the subtle hint of tragedy which Gérard had brought into an otherwise young and innocent face. He had done it with remarkable skill. Had I really looked like that? I wondered.

I walked along the line. Some of the views of Paris were enchanting, but it was the portraits which would attract attention. Madame Garnier looked down at me. I could see her calculating how much she was going to make on her purchases, and I was reminded of her sly smile when I confronted her with her misdeeds and her calmness in brushing them aside. There she was, with all her failings and her virtues. I was beginning to think that Gérard was a very clever artist.

They were exciting days. I was often at the exhibition. I found it difficult to keep away. Gérard was delighted by my enthusiasm.

My picture was talked of, and in the notices which were given of the exhibition, I was mentioned at length.

"Noelle is the pick of the bunch." "Noelle takes the palm." "Study of a young girl who has a secret to hide. Deserted by her lover?" "What is Noelle trying to tell us? It is an arresting portrait."

Madame Garnier was commented on, too. "A fine study." "Full of character." "Gérard du Carron has come far in the last years and should go farther."

I was pleased when someone wanted to buy my portrait and Gérard refused to sell it.

"It's mine," he said. "I shall always keep it."

•

After the exhibition, we went back to La Maison Grise. I had written to Lisa telling her about my stay in Paris. I did not hear from her for some time, so I presumed she was back at work and busy.

When I first returned, Marie-Christine was

inclined to be aloof, but I soon realized that was because she had been hurt by my long absence.

One day, when we were riding together and walking our horses side by side through a narrow lane, she said: "I believe you liked being in Paris better than you do here."

"I did enjoy being in Paris," I said, "but I enjoy it here, too."

"You won't stay here always, though, will you? You'll go away."

"I know you have all made me very welcome, but I am really only a guest. This isn't my home."

"It feels like it to me."

"What do you mean?"

"It feels as though you are part of my home . . . more than anyone else."

"Oh . . . Marie-Christine!"

"I've never had anyone like you before. You're like my sister. I always wanted a sister."

I was deeply touched. "That's a lovely thing you have said."

"It's true. *Grand-mère* is kind, but she is old, and she never really liked my mother, and when she looks at me, she thinks of her. My mother noticed me sometimes, and then she seemed to forget. My father didn't notice me much either. My mother always wanted to be in Paris. My father was always there as well. Uncle Robert is kind . . . but he's old, too.

I'm just 'the child' to him. They've got to look after me. It's not really that they want to. It's a duty. What I want is a family . . . people to laugh with and quarrel with. People you can say anything to . . . and you feel they're there, however horrid you are to them . . . they can't get away because they are family."

"I did not realize you felt like that, Marie-Christine."

"You, too. You'll go away, I know you will. Look how you went to Paris. We used to have fun doing English and French. Your French was very funny."

"So was your English."

"Your French was a lot funnier than my English."

"Impossible!"

She was laughing. "You see? That's what I mean. We can be rude to each other and we still like each other. That's what I want, and then you go off to Paris. I reckon you'll be going there again soon."

"Well, if I do, I don't see why you shouldn't come, too. There's room in the house there."

"And what about Mademoiselle Dupont?"

"She could come, too. You could do your lessons there and learn something about the history of the city . . . right on the spot."

"My father wouldn't want to see me, though."

"Of course he would."

She shook her head. "I remind him of my mother, and he doesn't want to be reminded."

For a few seconds we rode in silence. We came to the end of the lane and she broke into a canter. I followed her. I was a little shaken by our conversation, during which she had revealed the intensity of her feelings for me.

She called over her shoulder: "I want to show you something."

She pulled up sharply. We had come to a lych-gate. She leaped from her saddle and tethered her horse to a post at the side of the gate. I dismounted. There was a similar post on the other side of the gate, so I tied my horse to this.

She opened the gate and we went through.

We were in a graveyard, and she led the way along a path. All around us were the graves with their elaborate statues and an abundance of flowers.

She paused before one which was presided over by an elaborate carving of the Virgin and Child.

I read the inscription on the stone: "Marianne du Carron. Aged 27 years. Departed this life, January 3, 1866."

"That," said Marie-Christine, "is where my mother is buried."

"It's beautifully tended."

"We never come here."

"Who looks after it?"

"Nounou mostly. Tante Candice perhaps.

But Nounou is here every week. She comes on Sundays. I've seen her often. She kneels down and prays to God to care for her child. She calls my mother her child. I've been close to her and heard. I never let her see me, though."

I felt a great tenderness towards her. I wanted to protect her, to help to make her happy.

I took her hand and pressed it, and we stood in silence for a few seconds.

Then she said: "Come on, let's go. I just wanted to show you, that's all."

•

Not long after my return, Gérard came to La Maison Grise. He had been very busy, he told us. Following the exhibition, he had several commissions.

"It was due to your portrait," he said. "It attracted so much attention, so I have you to thank."

"It was you who did the work. I only sat there."

"I could not have done it without the sitter." He went on: "I shall be busy here. I've brought some work with me. I can do it just as well here as in Paris, and it will be a change to be in a different environment."

He spent a lot of time in the north tower. Angèle was delighted to have him home. I knew that she worried about him. She confided to me that she thought his rather disorganized way of living had many disadvantages. She was sure he did not have regular meals, nor did he get enough to eat.

"And," she added, "he has never got over the shock of Marianne's death. I am sure that is one of the reasons why he likes to be in Paris. It brings it back too vividly here."

"Yes, Marie-Christine has shown me where it happened."

"So close to her old home. It was terrible. The old nurse came out of the house and found her lying there. It was a terrible shock for her. She was devoted to Marianne."

"It must have been terrible for her."

"Well, he is home for a while, and I am glad of that."

So was I.

I could talk to him about his work and his friends, of whom by now I had met so many. Sometimes he would ride with Marie-Christine and me in the afternoons. I noticed he always avoided the road that led to Carrefour.

Robert was pleased that he was there. He would become quite animated over the dinner table. They discussed politics, and I acquired a certain insight into affairs of which I had known nothing before.

I discovered that Robert admired their Emperor Napoleon III, nephew of the notorious Napoleon, who had married the glamorous

Empress Eugénie. Gérard was slightly less enthusiastic.

"He understands what the people need," insisted Robert.

"He is obsessed by making France great," retaliated Gérard. "He wants power. He is his uncle all over again."

"His uncle made France a great power," Robert insisted.

"And finally ended up in Elba and St. Helena."

"That was ill luck."

"It's always ill luck," said Gérard.

"You must admit the Emperor has promoted public works. He has brought in good things. For another thing, he has lowered the price of bread."

"Oh yes, he cares for France. I don't dispute that." He turned to me. "Are we boring you with our politics?"

"Far from it," I assured him. "I am discovering my ignorance and am delighted to learn something."

"It is just that some of us are a little uneasy. I don't like what is happening with Prussia. I think the Emperor is inclined to underestimate their strength."

"Nonsense," said Robert. "A petty German state! To think it can stand up to France!"

"The Emperor is well aware of the humiliations heaped on us by the Congress of Vienna."

Gérard turned to me. "That was just after the defeat of Napoleon I. We were at our lowest ebb at that time."

"That is so," added Robert. "And the Emperor wants to make France great again. He wants to change the European balance of power."

"He was pleased to have an alliance with your country after the Crimean War," said Gérard to me. "And after that, there followed war with Austria, in an attempt to expel that country from Italy."

"He proved himself a great military commander at Solferino," Robert reminded Gérard.

"I am afraid he will go too far."

"He has brought prestige to our country," insisted Robert. "Don't forget, Louis Philippe fell because he let France slip into becoming a minor power in Europe."

"The present Napoleon is determined not to do that, but I am afraid his attitude with Prussia may get us involved in trouble."

"Prussia!" said Robert contemptuously.

"To be reckoned with. Aren't they trying to put a Hohenzollern on the throne of Spain?"

"This is something the Emperor will certainly not allow."

"If he can stop it," said Gérard. "Well, let us hope it will all blow over. We don't want

388· Victoria Holt

trouble with Prussia. This wine is good, Uncle
Robert."

"I am glad you appreciate it. How is the
work going?"

"Not too badly. I shall have to go back to
Paris soon. By the way, Noelle, Petersen is really serious about doing your portrait."

"Why don't you agree?" said Angèle. "You
enjoyed sitting for Gérard. It would be interesting to see what he did."

"He can't bear that my portrait of you has
brought me some credit," said Gérard. "He
wants to show that he can do better."

"Give him a chance to prove that he is
wrong," said Angèle.

I said I should like to. "I wonder whether
Marie-Christine could come to Paris with me.
Mademoiselle Dupont could come, too, so that
Marie-Christine could have her lessons. She
was very put out about being left behind."

"She has taken a great fancy to you," said
Angèle. "I am glad of that. I can't see why she
shouldn't go."

"I shall look forward to it very much," I
said.

"Then," said Angèle, "that's settled. When
do you want to leave, Gérard?"

"At the beginning of next week, I think.
Does that suit you?"

I said that it did.

When I saw Marie-Christine and told her

that I was going to Paris the following week, her face fell. I quickly added: "Would you care to come? Mademoiselle would of course accompany us, and I am sure you would find it very educational."

She threw her arms round me and hugged me.

"I suggested it," I said, "and they all agreed that it would be a good idea."

•

Lars Petersen was delighted that I had agreed to sit for him.

"From the moment I saw you, I wanted to paint you," he said. "That is how it happens. I knew at once."

"Well, I suppose I should be flattered."

"You know you have an interesting face."

"I didn't, but it occurs to me that you noticed it after Gérard's success."

He looked at me roguishly. "I cannot allow him to steal a march on me, now can I? He painted a good picture. I must paint a better one."

"I see there is a great deal of rivalry."

"But of course. There is more rivalry in art than in anything else. We are watching those around us. Each of us wants to be the great artist who will live forever, whose name is known to millions. That is the great achievement. So naturally we are watchful of our rivals."

His conversation was racy and amusing. I learned a good deal about Lars Petersen. He was without doubt extremely attractive and lived a merry life. He was not serious about anything but his art; he was immensely ambitious, determined to make a name for himself and to enjoy himself on the way to success. It was impossible not to like him.

I watched the progress of the portrait. It was good but it lacked that subtle quality which Gérard had brought to his. Perhaps that was because I had not opened my heart to him as I had to Gérard. There was not the same rapport between us.

Gérard used to come in at the end of the morning sittings, and the three of us would eat together. After that, I would go back to the house and spend the rest of the day with Marie-Christine. We went sightseeing with Mademoiselle Dupont. I learned a great deal of French history, for Mademoiselle Dupont had a habit of turning every jaunt into a history lesson. Marie-Christine and I exchanged secret glances, and sometimes we found it hard to restrain our laughter.

We frequently visited Gérard's studio, and on these occasions usually managed to elude Mademoiselle Dupont. Gérard came to the house, too, so we saw a good deal of him during the visit.

There was one disconcerting incident which baffled me.

I was in Lars Petersen's studio when he needed some special paint of which he had not sufficient. He knew Gérard had some and said he would go and get it from him. So I was left alone in his studio.

As I sat idly there, waiting for his return, I noticed that a piece of cloth had been caught in the door of a cupboard and was partially protruding. It was probably a duster, I thought. I had made a habit in Lars's studio, as in Gérard's, of putting things in their place, for they were both inclined to be untidy. So I rose, went to the cupboard, and opened the door with the intention of putting the duster right inside; but as I did so, a stack of canvasses fell out. I was putting them back when I saw a sketchbook among them. Picking up the canvasses, to my amazement I saw that one of them was a picture of a nude woman in a pose which could only be called provocative. It was, without doubt, Marianne.

I felt myself flushing. I was obviously not meant to see what was in this cupboard. I hastily put the canvas back and stacked in the others. The sketchbook was lying on the floor. I picked it up and glanced through it. It was full of pictures—all of Marianne in various stages of nudity.

I threw the sketchbook into the cupboard, shut the door, and went back to my seat.

The painting and the sketches were the work of Lars Petersen. She must have posed for him thus.

I felt deeply shocked, for I felt there was something behind this.

Lars had come back into the room.

"All is well. This is just what I needed."

He went on working, but I could not stop thinking of those pictures. Marianne *must* have posed for him in such a way.

She was an artist's model. Was this the manner in which she posed? I could not help thinking that there must have been some special relationship between Marianne and Lars Petersen.

Marianne

✿

It was a week after I had returned from Paris when I received the letter from Lisa. When I read it, I was so profoundly shocked that I had to read it several times before I could believe it was true.

She wrote from Leverson Manor.

My dear Noelle,
There is so much to tell you, and I want you to hear it from me. I could not bear that you should hear it from any other source.

I wrote to you about my accident. I thought it was nothing much at first, but how wrong I was! After three weeks resting, the doctor gave me a terrible shock. He said I had injured my back permanently and, far from getting better, it was getting worse. Imagine my feeling! I had gone on that night, ready to show everyone that I was every bit as good as Lottie Langdon . . . and I would have done it, too. It was really my great chance . . . and then . . . this happened.

Dolly was kind in his way, but all he really thinks about is the production. I knew there was no hope of getting a place in anything else. I was finished.

I was so wretched. I just wanted to die. My life . . . all my ambitions . . . had come to nothing.

Then Roderick came to town and saw me. He was horrified by the change in me. Oh, he was so good to me, Noelle. You know he would be. He has always been good and kind to people in trouble. He understood as nobody else did what I felt like. I was frantic, really. I could not think what I should do now I could no longer work.

He took me down to Leverson Manor. Lady Constance was none too pleased, but Fiona was very good to me. She made me interested in helping her, which I was able to do. She was getting married to a young man she had met some time before through her work. He had come down to Leverson because there was a lot of work over this Neptune temple. He was now helping her and they will live in Fiona's house, now that her grandmother is away in the hospital.

I don't know why I'm going on like this. I suppose it is because I am trying to bring myself to tell you.

I am not at all sure how you'll take it, after what happened between you two. I was so desperate. I was in despair. I even thought of killing myself. I might have done so if it had not been for Roderick. He knew what was in my mind. Nobody understood as he did. I had not only lost the work which meant so much to me . . . but a means of livelihood. You can imagine how I felt.

Well, we both had to make something of our lives, and then suddenly he said he would look after me. He would marry me.

And that is what has happened, Noelle.

I feel so different now. Charlie is very good to me. He is such a kind, good man, and so is Roderick.

Lady Constance is very angry, but you know how calm and cool she can be . . . at the same time letting you know how much she resents you.

I didn't care. I had a reason to go on living.

Noelle, forgive me. I know just how you must be feeling. But it wasn't to be, was it?

Roderick says we have to make something of our lives, and that is what we are doing.

I do hope something very good will turn up for you . . . as it has for me. Sometimes we can't have what we want in life, can we? We just have to take what is there.

My loving thoughts are with you.

God bless you and bring you some hope of happiness . . . as Roderick and I have found.

Lisa

I was stunned. Roderick and Lisa . . . married! I kept remembering scenes from the past. That first meeting in the park; that night she had taken my mother's place; Roderick had been there; she had asked him to come and see her performance. Of course, right from the beginning, she had been in love with him.

Somewhere at the back of my mind, I had hoped that a miracle might happen, that everything would come right. How foolish I had been! How could it ever come right? And now . . . this was the end. He was married to Lisa.

I had to forget. I had to stop thinking of him.

I put the letter into a drawer, but I could not forget it. Again and again, I took it out and read it.

•

I had told Robert. He was deeply touched.

"Robert," I said. "I feel adrift . . . floating aimlessly with no destination in sight. I am just being carried where the tide takes me. I can see it all clearly. Lisa . . . her career in ruins

. . . lost as I am now. I know that he loved me, but he would understand Lisa's plight so absolutely. He was always understanding and thoughtful of other people. She was helpless, I believe on the verge of suicide, and he saw one way of helping her . . . giving her a home . . . security . . . helping her to fight back."

"It is a terrible tragedy, Noelle. I wish I could help more. I think you are happier here than you can be anywhere else."

"I can't stay here indefinitely, Robert."

"Why not? Regard it as your home."

"But it is not my home. I am doing nothing with my life."

"You do a great deal. Marie-Christine is a different girl since you came. We have always been worried about her. Poor child, she has not had much of a life. And we are so fond of you . . . Angèle as well as myself. So is Gérard. Don't think of leaving us, please."

"I don't want to go," I said. "I can't think what I should do."

"Then stay. You should go more to Paris."

So I stayed.

The weeks were slipping away. It was nearly two months since I had received Lisa's letter. I had replied briefly, thanking her for letting me know, and wished her and Roderick a happy future. I had heard nothing since. And it was better so.

Lars Petersen had an exhibition, and I was

caught up in that. He showed my portrait, which was bought for some national collection. He was delighted. Gérard had the painting of me hanging in his studio.

"I like to see it," he said. "It inspires me every day."

Marie-Christine and I, with the ubiquitous Mademoiselle Dupont, were more frequently in Paris than in the country.

While they were at their lessons, I would go to the studio. I had taken to shopping in the markets, which was always an exhilarating experience, and I would take in something tasty for *déjeuner*. It was becoming a habit. Gérard and I would sit together, often joined by Lars Petersen or some impecunious artist looking for a free meal.

Robert was right when he said that the bohemian life was good for me.

Gérard had noticed the change in me, and one day, when we were alone, he asked me what had happened.

I could not resist telling him. I said: "Roderick is married. I shouldn't mind, but I do. It is the best thing for him. He has married Lisa Fennell, who was understudy to my mother. She had an accident and that was the end of her theatrical career as a dancer, which was what she did best. I think he was sorry for her. He liked her, too. He was always interested in her career. On occasions I had a twinge of jealousy.

And now . . . she is married to him. She will spend her life with him as I had intended to spend mine."

"My poor Noelle. Life is cruel. Troubles do not come like single spies but in battalions. Does not your Shakespeare say that?"

"I believe he did, and it is true in my case."

"But there must be a turnabout. Things will change and then everything will go right. It is a law of nature."

"I shall never forget Roderick."

"I know."

"He will always be there, and always there will be the knowledge of what I have lost."

"I understand."

"Because of Marianne . . ."

"I shall never be able to forget Marianne," he said.

A shadow fell across the door. Lars Petersen looked in.

"Something smells good," he said. "Is there a little to spare for a poor hungry man?"

•

I seemed to have become haunted by Marianne. I knew exactly what she had looked like. I could not get out of my mind those sketches I had come across in Lars Petersen's cupboard.

I asked questions about her. I talked to Marie-Christine. I tried to talk to Angèle. All they would say was: "She was very beautiful."

"The most beautiful woman in the world," said Marie-Christine. "She had the sort of looks people could not help noticing," said Angèle. "She found the country life dull. She could not have been much more than fifteen when one of the artists who had come down to see Gérard caught a glimpse of her. He wanted to paint her, and that was the beginning of her modelling career. She went to Paris. But she came back fairly frequently to see her sister and the nurse."

There was very little I could discover which I did not already know. Yet I continued to think of her, because she had bewitched Gérard as well as others.

I suggested to Marie-Christine that we visit her aunt again.

"I think they were rather pleased to see you when you called last time," I said.

"All right," said Marie-Christine, "although *I* don't think they care much whether I go or not."

"Well, you are Marianne's daughter, so let us go."

We went and were received warmly enough. Polite questions were asked about my impressions.

"You are almost one of us now," said Candice.

"I have certainly been here quite a long time."

"And you have no desire to leave us?"

"It is very pleasant here, and I have not made any plans to do so."

"We won't let her go," said Marie-Christine. "Every time she mentions going, we tell her she is not to."

"I can understand that," said Candice, smiling.

She wanted to show us the garden, and while we were all walking round together, I had an opportunity of being a little apart with Nounou.

I said: "I wanted to talk to you about . . . Marianne."

Her face lit up.

"I'd like to hear more about her," I went on. "She sounds so interesting, and you know more of her than anyone, I imagine."

"Interesting! We were never dull with that one around! Candice doesn't talk of her much . . . especially before Marie-Christine."

"You must have lots of pictures of her."

"I look at them all the time. It brings her back. I'd like to show you, but . . ."

"It's a pity. I should love to see them."

"Why don't you come one day . . . alone? In the morning, say. Candice would be out. She goes out in the morning . . . shopping in Villemère. She takes the trap. She visits friends there, too. In the morning . . . come alone."

"That would be very interesting."

"I'll show you my pictures of her. Then we can talk in comfort."

Candice was saying: "I was showing Marie-Christine this holly bush. There are lots of berries forming on it. They say that means a hard winter."

•

That was the beginning of my visits to Nounou.

It was easy to call during the mornings when Marie-Christine was at her lessons and Candice was out. There was a conspiratorial air about the visits which suited our moods—mine as well as Nounou's. They took my mind off my obsessive wondering about what was happening at Leverson Manor. I imagined their riding over to the site, marvelling at the discoveries, drinking coffee with Fiona . . . and perhaps her new husband . . . a cosy little quartet. I would torture myself with these imaginings, and it was a mild relief to ride over to Carrefour and chat with Nounou. I asked myself what I should say if Candice returned unexpectedly, or even happened to be there when I called. "Oh, I was passing and I just looked in." I supposed perhaps she would accept that, but I doubted it.

Nounou revelled in our meetings. There was nothing she liked so much as to talk about her adored Marianne.

She showed me pictures of her. There was

Marianne as a child, showing signs of that great beauty, and as a young woman, proving how that early promise was justified.

"She was a sorceress," said Nounou. "All the men wanted her. She was restless here in this place. It was too quiet for her. Candice was the serious one. She tried to hold her back. She wanted her to marry well and settle down."

"Candice didn't marry."

"Well . . . she lived under the shadow of her twin sister. It was always Marianne whom people noticed. Without her sister, she would have seemed a very nice-looking girl. She ought to have married some nice young man. But there was always Marianne. And then this artist came down to see Monsieur Gérard, and he took one look at her and wanted to paint her. That was the start for her, and when Marianne wanted something, there was no stopping her. So she went to Paris. First one wanted to paint her and then another. She was famous. They were all talking about Marianne. Then she married Monsieur Gérard."

"You were pleased about that?"

"It was a good match, of course. The Bouchères were always the big people round here. Well, there it was . . . what you'd expect of our beauty. He was always painting her."

"So it was a happy marriage?"

"Monsieur Gérard . . . well, he was as

proud as proud could be. He'd got the prize, hadn't he?"

"And they lived mainly in Paris?"

"Oh, they were here now and then. She was always coming over here. Couldn't desert her old Nounou. She was always my girl. She'd tell me things."

"So you knew a great deal about what was happening?"

Nounou nodded sagely. "I could see there were things going on, and she was only going to tell me half of them. Oh, she was a wild one. Then, for that to happen to her . . . to see her there, dead at my feet! I felt I would die . . . I wished I had before I'd seen that. I just can't bear to think of it . . . even now."

We were silent for a while. I could hear the clock on the mantelpiece ticking away the seconds . . . reminding me that time was passing. I must leave before Candice returned and Marie-Christine finished her lessons.

"Come again whenever you feel like it, my dear," said Nounou. "It's good to talk to you . . . though it brings it all back. Still, it makes me feel she is close to me . . . like she used to be."

I said I would come again to see her soon.

•

We were in Paris again. Marie-Christine was always excited by these visits, and Robert and

Angèle thought it was good for us to make them; and as the house was there, they said why not use it.

I always felt an upsurge of my spirits when I came into the city. When I was away from it, I missed the free and easy way of life lived by Gérard and his friends. The studio had become part of my life, and I believed that there I was more able to put thoughts of Roderick out of my mind.

I looked forward to our lunches, particularly when they were uninterrupted. Gérard was becoming one of my best friends. There was a bond between us: I had lost Roderick; he had lost Marianne. That made for a deep understanding which no one else could quite give.

I talked to him about Roderick. I told him about the Roman remains and the fearful adventure when Lady Constance and I had come near to being buried alive, and how Mrs. Carling had removed the warning notice.

He listened with the utmost interest.

"You have been through a great deal," he said. "It seems that it all began with the death of your mother. My poor Noelle, how you have suffered!"

"You, too," I said.

"Differently. Do you think you could ever forget Roderick?"

"I think I shall always remember."

"Always with regret? Even if . . . there were someone else?"

"I think Roderick would always be there."

He was silent for a moment, and I said: "And you . . . and your marriage?"

"I shall never forget Marianne," he answered.

"I understand. She was so beautiful. She was unique. No one else could take her place. You loved her . . . absolutely. I understand, Gérard."

"Noelle," he said slowly, "I have been on the point of telling you several times. I have to talk to someone. It is like a great burden on my mind. I hated Marianne. I killed her."

I gasped. I could not believe I had heard him correctly.

"You . . . killed her?"

"Yes."

"But she was thrown from her horse!"

"Indirectly . . . I killed her. It will haunt me all my life. In my heart, I know I was responsible for her death. I killed her."

"How? Her nurse told me she found her in the field near Carrefour. She had been thrown from her horse. Her neck was broken."

"That's true. Let me explain. I quickly learned how foolish I'd been. She never cared for me. I came from a rich family. All she wanted was flattery, admiration and money. There was plenty of the first two."

"How can you say you killed her?"

"We were at La Maison. We quarrelled. There was nothing strange about that. She taunted me. She repeated that she had never cared for me. She had married me because I was a good match for an artist's model. She hated me, she said. She was mocking . . . taunting me in every way. I said to her: 'Get out of this house! Get out of my life! I never want to see you again!' She was taken aback. She thought she was so desirable that she could act as she pleased and still be irresistible. She changed immediately. She said she had not meant what she said. She did not want to leave me. We were married and we must be together. We must make the best of things. I said to her: 'Go! Go! Get out of my life! I never want to see you again.' She started to cry. 'You don't mean that,' she said. Then she went on: 'Forgive me. I'll be different.' She knelt and clutched at me. I did not believe in her tears. She wanted to stay with me because life was easy and comfortable . . . but at the same time she wanted to go her own way. I had had enough. I could endure no more. I saw her beauty as evil. I knew my only chance of a peaceful life was to be rid of her. I wanted to forget I had married her."

His face was distorted with grief and pain.

He went on: "I said: 'Get out of here. Go . . . go anywhere . . . but keep away from me.' She said: 'Where could I go?' 'I don't care,' I told her. 'Only get out before I do you some harm.' She was crying, begging me to forgive her. Then suddenly she ran out. She ran down to the stables. She took her horse and was gone. The next thing I heard was that she was dead."

"She had had an accident."

"She had an accident because she was in such a state of despair. She was galloping madly and she came suddenly to the crossroads. She was not caring where she went because she was so upset . . . *I* had upset her . . . turned her out . . . and she was thrown. You see, I killed her. It haunts me and I know it will throughout my life."

"So . . . you did not love Marianne."

"I hated her. And I am responsible for her death."

"That's not true, Gérard. You did not plan to kill her."

"I told her to get out . . . out of my life, and she was so distraught that she lost hers in doing it."

"You are wrong to blame yourself."

"I do blame myself, Noelle. I should not have been so harsh with her. I should have said we would try again. I had married her . . . made my vows. I drove her away because I was tired of her . . . and because of her state of mind, she died. Nothing will convince me that I am not responsible for her death."

"Gérard," I said, "you have to forget this. You must stop blaming yourself."

"Perhaps I shouldn't have told you."

"I'm glad you did. I understand more now. It was not your fault. You must see that. Lots of people quarrel. You have explained it to me, and I must tell you that, as a looker-on, I think it is ridiculous to blame yourself."

"No, Noelle, I was there. I saw her stricken face. I know she was superficial, heartless . . . but her position meant everything to her. She liked being secure. And when she was in danger of losing that, she went off . . . riding recklessly. She could have wild moods, she could be fiercely unreasoning and angry. She was killed because of what I had done to her. That is murder, as surely as taking a gun and shooting someone."

"It is not the same. It's not deliberate, for one thing."

"You will never make me see that, Noelle."

"Gérard," I said. "I have made up my mind, and that is exactly what I am going to do."

He smiled at me, and I said: "I am glad you told me."

•

Gérard's revelation had amazed me. It astounded me that the melancholy brooding I had seen at times was not a longing for Marianne but due to a sense of guilt.

It was two days after his confession that he said to me: "I have felt different since I told you. I feel as though I have shed the burden to some extent. You are the only one I have told. I could not bring myself to talk of it to anyone else. With you, it seemed natural to do so."

"You did right to tell me, Gérard. I think I can make you see that you must not blame yourself."

"I cannot stop doing it. I never shall. She was so distraught when she left. Not that she cared for me. She saw the comfortable life disappearing. Of course, she could have gone back to Carrefour, but that was what she had escaped from, and was the last thing she wanted. She could have gone back to Paris and become a full-time model. But she was at times lazy and extravagant. It was rather an unexpected trait in her character that she wanted the security of marriage."

"Gérard," I said, "it is over. She is gone. You must forget her, stop blaming yourself. Put her out of your mind."

"As you should Roderick."

I was silent, and he said: "You see, it is easy to tell others what they should do."

"I know. Other people's troubles always seem to have a solution. It is only one's own that do not."

"I must forget Marianne. You must forget Roderick. Noelle, could we perhaps do that together?"

I looked at him in surprise. "Together . . . ?" I murmured.

"Yes. I have grown very fond of you. These days when we have been together have been wonderful for me. Why shouldn't we stay together?"

"You mean . . . ?"

"I mean, why don't you marry me? I have felt different since you came . . . different about everything. I know you will go on thinking about Roderick. But he has gone out of your life. He can never come back. You can't go on grieving for him forever. You have to start afresh. There is a chance for us both together."

He was looking at me appealingly. It was true that our friendship had grown; we understood each other. I could find a certain relief from my memories when I was with him.

But there had only been one man whom I had wanted to marry, and though I could not marry him, that did not mean that I could easily turn to someone else.

And yet I was fond of Gérard. The most enjoyable times since I had lost Roderick had been spent with him.

I was bewildered, and he knew it.

He took my hand and kissed it. "You are

uncertain," he said. "But at least you do not give a definite no. So the idea is not entirely repulsive to you."

"No. Of course not. I am fond of you, Gérard. I look forward to being in the studio more than anything else, but I am so unsure. I think it would not be fair to you. You see, I loved Roderick. I still love him."

"Yet he has realized he has a life to lead. He is now married."

"I think he did it because he was sorry for Lisa. It was pity."

"No matter what, he has married. Think about what I have said. You might come to realize that it is best . . . for both of us. Think about it, will you?"

"Yes, Gérard," I said. "I will."

•

I did think about it. It was never out of my mind. I was very fond of Gérard. I was drawn to the life of the studio. It had given me great pleasure to prepare meals for him; and now I was overwhelmed by a desire to comfort and care for him. I wanted to banish from his mind forever that notion that he had been responsible for Marianne's death.

In a way I loved him. Perhaps if I had never known Roderick, that would have been enough. But Roderick was there. The memory of him would never go away. I knew that for the rest of my life I would dream of him.

And yet I was fond of Gérard.

And so my thoughts went on.

I would go to the studio as usual. There was always a great deal of coming and going, with the usual talk; but something else was cropping up. It had gradually seeped into the atmosphere for some time now. I sensed a general uneasiness; there were differences in opinions, and the young men were fierce in their arguments.

"Where is the Emperor leading us?" demanded Roger Lamont one day. "He thinks he is his uncle. He will end up at St. Helena if he is not careful."

Roger Lamont was an ardent anti-royalist. He was young, dogmatic and fiery in his views.

"You'd have another revolution on our hands if you had your way," said Gérard.

"I'd rid France of this Bonaparte," retorted Roger.

"And set up another Danton . . . another Robespierre?"

"I'd have the people in command."

"We did once before, remember? And look how that turned out."

"The Emperor is a sick man with grandiose ideas."

"Oh, it will work out all right," said Lars Petersen. "You French get too excited. Let them get on with their business and we'll get on with ours."

"Alas," Gérard reminded him. "We are involved, and their business is ours. We live in this country and its fortunes are ours. We're in trouble financially. The press is not free. And I think the Emperor should restrain himself in his quarrels with the Prussians."

They would go on arguing for hours. Lars Petersen was clearly not particularly interested. He interrupted them to talk about a certain Madame de Vermont, who had given him a commission to paint her portrait.

"She is in court circles. I'll wager that before long I'll have the Empress sitting for me."

Roger Lamont jeered, and Lars turned to me. "Madame de Vermont saw your portrait and asked the name of the artist. She immediately engaged me to paint her. So you see, my dear Noelle, that it is to you I owe my success."

I said how delighted I was to have been some use to him. And I was thinking how pleasant it was, sitting here and listening to their talk. I felt I was one of them.

It was a pleasant way of life. Was it possible that I could truly be part of it for the rest of mine? At times I believed I could, and then the memories would come back. I would dream of Roderick, and in those dreams he was urging me not to marry anyone else: and when I awoke the dreams seemed so real.

But *he* had married Lisa Fennell. That was the final gesture. He had accepted our fate as irrevocable. Surely I must do the same?

It was impossible. I could not do it, I told myself. Then I would shop in the markets, buy some delicacy, take it to the studio and cook it. And I would say to myself: This might be the way for me. But later . . . there would come the doubts.

Dear Gérard! I wanted so much to make him happy. I thought a great deal about Marianne. I could not believe that she was the kind of girl who would ride recklessly because she was so upset. I thought she was too superficial to have cared very deeply.

I wished that I could put an end to his terrible feelings of guilt. Perhaps I could discover something from Nounou.

I was obsessed by Marianne, and when our stay in Paris came to an end, I was almost eager to return to La Maison Grise, because I had a belief that from Nounou I might glean some useful information.

When Gérard said goodbye, he asked me to come back soon, and I promised I would.

"I know it is not what you hoped for," he said. "But sometimes in life one has to compromise . . . and the result can be good. Noelle, I shall understand. I shall not reproach you for remembering him. I am prepared to take what you can give. The past hangs over me as it does

over you. We can neither of us expect to escape
entirely. But we should be good for each other.
Let us take what life has to offer."

"I think you may be right, Gérard, but as
yet I am not sure."

"When you are, come to me . . . come at
once. Do not delay."

I promised I would.

•

When I returned to La Maison Grise, I lost no
time in calling on Nounou.

She was very pleased to see me.

"I've missed your visits," she said. "I can
see that Paris fascinated you as it did Marianne. It is that sort of city, is it not?"

I agreed that it was.

I was not sure how I could get round to
asking her what I wanted to know. When I was
in Paris, I had felt it would not be difficult.

We talked about Marianne, as we always
did. She found more pictures. She talked of her
hosts of admirers. "She could have married the
highest in the land."

"Perhaps she realized that after she had
married Monsieur Gérard, and regretted the
marriage."

"Oh, that family has always been highly
thought of. She did very well for herself.
There's none that could deny that."

"Apart from the prestige the marriage brought, was she happy in it?"

"She was happy enough. She was greedy, my girl. As a child she would stretch out her little hands and say 'Want it' whenever she saw something that took her fancy. I used to laugh at her. 'Mademoiselle Want It,' that's what I called her. I'm just going to put some flowers on her grave. Would you like to walk over to the cemetery with me?"

I was wondering what I could say to Nounou. I kept forming phrases in my mind. "If she had quarrelled with her husband, and he had told her to go, how would she have felt about that?" She would ask me how I could possibly have got such an idea into my head. I must not betray what Gérard had told me.

I watched her tend the grave. She knelt and prayed for a few moments. And as I stared at the gravestone, with her name and the date of her death, I could picture her beautiful face mocking me.

I am dead. I am buried. I shall haunt him for the rest of his life.

No, I thought, you shall not. I will find some way of freeing him from you.

Which sounded as though I had made up my mind to marry him. But later on I felt I could never marry anyone now. Roderick had gone out of my life, taking all my hopes of a happy marriage with him.

• • •

Robert had gone to Paris. He said, before he left, that the situation was getting somewhat grim. The Emperor was losing patience with Bismarck. He saw in him the enemy of all his plans for the greatness of France.

"It is a good thing," Robert had said, "that Prussia is only a small state. Bismarck won't want trouble with France, though he is as arrogant and ambitious for Prussia as the Emperor is for France."

He thought he would be in Paris for some little time.

"When you feel like coming to the house, you'll be welcome. Gérard will be delighted, too."

I would go, I promised myself. But first I wanted more talks with Nounou.

Before I could do so, there was devastating news. It was a hot July day. Marie-Christine and I were in the garden when Robert unexpectedly returned from Paris. He was very excited.

We saw him go into the house and hurried after him. Angèle was in the hall.

Robert announced: "France has declared war on Prussia!"

We were all astounded. I had heard the discussions in the studio, but had not taken them very seriously. This, of course, was what they had feared.

"What will it mean?" asked Angèle.

"One good thing is that it can't last long," said Robert. "A little state like Prussia against the might of France. The Emperor would never have gone into this if he had not been certain of a quick victory."

Over dinner, Robert said he would have to go back to Paris almost immediately. There would be precautions he would have to take, just in case the war was not over in a few weeks. He supposed he would be kept in Paris for a while.

"You should stay here in the country until we see what is going to happen," he went on. "Paris is in a turmoil. The Emperor, as you know, has for some time been losing the sympathy of the people."

The next day Robert went back to Paris. Angèle accompanied him. She wanted to make sure that Gérard was looking after himself.

I was wondering what was happening at the studio. We were avid for news.

Several weeks passed. It was early August when we heard that the Prussians had been driven out of Saarbrücken, and there was great rejoicing. Everyone was saying that this would be a lesson to the Germans. However, within a few days the news was less good. It was only a small detachment which had been driven out of

Saarbrücken, and the French had failed to take advantage of their small success. They were, therefore, routed and had retreated in confusion into the Vosges Mountains.

There were grim faces everywhere; there was murmuring against the Emperor. He had plunged France into war on the flimsiest pretext, because he wanted to show the world that he was another such as his uncle. But the French people did not want conquest and vainglorious military success. They wanted peace. And this was certainly not success. It was humiliating failure.

Through those hot August days we waited for news of the war. Not much seeped through to us, and I guessed that was a bad sign.

Robert came back for a brief visit. He advised us to stay in the country, though he must go back. Things were getting very difficult in Paris. The people were very restive. Students were gathering in the streets. The cafés and restaurants were crowded with people who wanted to arouse others to action.

The days of revolution were not far enough in the past to be readily forgotten.

I was seeing Nounou now and then. She had little interest in the progress of the war. I had not up to that time found an opportunity to bring up the matter which was very much in my mind. I wondered a great deal about Gérard. He was serious-minded and would, I knew, be deeply perturbed by the war.

Opportunity came suddenly. I was with Nounou one day and she was talking about Marianne. She had found a picture of her which she had forgotten existed. She had not seen it for years.

"It was at the back of one of the albums, tucked away under another picture. She must have hidden it. She never liked that one."

"May I see it?" I asked.

"Come up," said Nounou.

She took me to that room which I thought of as Marianne's room. There were pictures of her on the wall, and on the table were those albums which were for Nounou a record of her darling's life.

She showed me the picture.

"She looks a little bit saucy here, does she not? Up to tricks. Well, that was like her—but it shows more on that one."

"And she wanted it to be hidden?"

"She said it was too revealing. It would put people on their guard."

I studied it. Yes, I thought, there was something about it . . . something almost evil.

"I'm glad I've got her pictures," said Nounou. "In my young days, there wouldn't have been all these pictures. That Monsieur Daguerre brought them in. I don't know what I'd do without my pictures."

"If she didn't like the picture, I wonder she did not destroy it."

"Oh no . . . she'd never destroy any of her pictures. She'd look at them as often as I did."

"It sounds as though she was in love with herself."

"Well, why shouldn't she be? Everyone else was in love with her."

"She was happily married, wasn't she?"

There was a slight pause. "Well, he was madly in love with her."

"Was he?"

"Oh yes. Everybody was. He was jealous." She laughed. "Well, you could understand that. Every man was after her."

"Did she quarrel with her husband?"

Nounou was thoughtful and a smile curved her lips.

"She was a clever girl. She liked things to go the way she wanted them to."

"Most people do, don't they?"

"They want them, but with her—she thought they ought to, because she was so beautiful. If they didn't go the way she wanted, she'd make them."

"That must have been trying for him."

"Well, she was a handful. Didn't I know it? There were times when she drove me to distraction. But it didn't change my feelings for her . . . one little jot. She was mine . . . and there was no one like her. She told me everything . . . or most things. I was always there —old Nounou—to help sort out her troubles."

"Did she tell you about her quarrels with her husband?"

"There was very little she held back from me."

I took a chance and said: "I am not sure that he was as besotted about her as you think."

"Why do you say that?"

I decided that I could be on the verge of discovery, and for Gérard's sake I was going to do everything I could to find out what I wanted to know, even if it meant distorting the truth a little.

I began: "The day she died . . ."

"Yes?" said Nounou eagerly.

"One of the servants heard them. There was a quarrel. He told her to go. He had had enough of her. It doesn't sound as though he were so desperately in love with her."

She was silent for a second, and a slow smile crossed her face.

"It's true," she said. "But that was what she wanted. Here." She rose and went to a cupboard. "Look at this."

She opened a door and disclosed a travelling bag.

"That's her bag," she said. "Can you guess what's in it? Her jewellery . . . some special clothes. I tell you, she was clever. He did tell her to go. But that was what she meant him to. She led him to it."

"Then why was she so upset?"

"Upset? She wasn't upset. She had it all worked out. I knew. I was in on the secret. She played on him. He was meant to say what he did. She provoked him into it. It was all working out as she'd planned. Don't you think I knew? She told me everything. I knew what was in her mind."

"Why did she want him to tell her to go?"

"Because *she* was the one who wanted to go. She wanted to be free . . . but she wanted it to come from him. She'd been bringing things over to me and I was keeping them for her. She wanted him to turn her out. She didn't want it to be said that she'd left him for another man. But that was what she was going to do. I can see her now, her eyes alight with mischief. She said, 'Nounou, I'm going to make him turn me out. I can do it. Then I shall go to Lars. Lars wants it that way. He doesn't want it to seem as though he'd come between us. He wants it to be that I go to him after Gérard has turned me out. Lars doesn't want trouble. And this is the way.' I've seen this Lars. A fine, upstanding young man. More her sort than Monsieur Gérard. Of course, Monsieur Gérard had the family . . . the standing . . . but he was too serious for a girl like her. She'd have been better off with Lars. But let me tell you, it was her arranging. She wanted Monsieur Gérard to turn her out, and she got her way, I reckon. She and Lars worked it out between them. Lars could say, 'Well, you let her go . . . and so no hard feelings.' You see, they were friends . . . living close to each other. Oh, it would have been a good way . . . and then that to happen."

"So the quarrel was arranged by her," I mused.

"I'm sure of that. She told me, didn't she? I reckon he cursed himself for saying it after. But she was a siren. She could get anyone to say anything she wanted them to."

"And she was going off to her lover?"

"All the things she wanted to make sure of keeping were here, waiting for her. In a day or so, he was coming down to fetch her."

"But . . . she died. It wasn't because she was so worried about being turned out that she was reckless."

"Not her. She wasn't worried. She was full of joy. I could picture her, laughing and singing to herself . . . galloping along. At least she died in triumph."

"So it was excitement at the thought of the future that made her careless. She was thinking of being with her lover . . . of her lucky escape from her husband . . ."

"There's not a doubt of it! I knew her. She'd do reckless things. She'd have been so pleased by the turn things were taking. She could be reckless at times. I know. Who knows better? She thought she had a charmed life. Everything had gone her way . . . and there she was, on the threshold, you might say, of the life she wanted. She'd always had a fancy for that Lars. And then . . . right when she was ready to start the life she'd been wanting for a long time . . . death came." The tears were on her cheeks. "I'll never forget her . . . my bright and beautiful girl."

I was elated. I thought: I will go to Gérard tomorrow. I will tell him that he was mistaken. She had been planning to go to Lars Petersen. They had been lovers for some time. I would tell him about the sketches and the picture I had seen in Lars's studio.

Surely now I could wipe out his guilt.

I did not go to Paris, for the next day the news came to us.

The Emperor with his army had surrendered to the enemy at Sedan, and he was a prisoner of the Prussians.

•

The days now seemed like a hazy dream, for we had only vague ideas of what was happening. Fragments of news did reach us now and then, but we were very much in the dark.

Before the end of the month, Strasbourg, one of the last hopes of the French, had surrendered, and we knew that sooner or later there would be an onslaught on Paris. We were very worried about Gérard and Robert and Angèle.

The Germans were advancing across France, fighting pockets of resistance as they went. They were all over the North of France, and Paris was under siege. Each day we expected the invading forces to come our way.

Mademoiselle Dupont feared for her mother in Champigny and went to join her; we waited in trepidation for what each day would bring.

Marie-Christine and I had grown even closer during that period. She was now fourteen years old and mature for her age. I tried to make life as normal as I could and gave her a few lessons every day. It kept our minds from wondering what was happening in Paris and when we would be drawn more closely into the war. Sometimes we heard gunfire in the distance, and we were rarely apart.

During those months, I began to realize how much my life here had meant to me.

A hundred times a day I assured myself that I would marry Gérard if we came out of this alive. I would make him see that he was in no way responsible for Marianne's death. Nounou had made that clear enough. I would try to forget Roderick. I would make a new life for myself. Marie-Christine would be very pleased if I married her father, and she had become very dear to me.

At least the terrible catastrophe which had
struck France had made me see which way I
must go.

Each day I wondered how long this situation could continue. We heard that Paris had
been bombarded, and I could not stop thinking
of the studio and wondering what would happen there. Would the friends congregate there
now? They would not be talking of art now
. . . but of war. They would be thinking of
food, for we heard that hunger was stalking the
streets of the capital.

We were lucky to escape the army. We were
surrounded by Prussian units, though we did
not see them, but we knew they were there. We
could not stray far from the house and we lived
in expectation of death every hour of the day;
but we survived.

Then we heard that the Prussians were in
Versailles. It was January when Paris, threatened by famine, surrendered.

•

It was a bitterly cold day when Marie-Christine
and I drove into Paris.

One of the coachmen took us. He had a
daughter living there and was eager to find her.

That was a day of bitter sadness.

We went to the house first. It was no longer
there. There was just a gap and a pile of broken
bricks and rubble where the house had been.

There were a few people in the street. No one could tell us what had become of those living in the house. It seemed there was nothing very unusual about such a house. There were many in a similar condition.

"Let us go to the studio," I said.

To my relief, I saw that the building was still standing. I had been terrified that that, too, might have been destroyed.

I mounted the stairs. I knocked at the door. There was no answer. I went across to that other door. To my immense relief Lars Petersen answered my knock.

"Noelle!" he cried. "Marie-Christine!"

"We came as soon as we could," I said. "What has happened? The house is gone. Where is Gérard?"

I had never seen him solemn before. He seemed like a different person.

"Come in," he said.

He took us into the familiar studio, with its easels, the tubes of paint, the cupboard in which were the portrait and sketches of Marianne.

"Is Gérard not here?" I asked.

He did not speak.

"Lars," I said. "Tell me, please."

"He would have been all right if he had stayed here."

I stared at him blankly.

"But . . . nowhere in Paris was safe. It was just bad luck."

"What?" I stammered. "Where?"

"He was at his uncle's house. He was worried about his mother and his uncle. He wanted them to get back to the country somehow. But it wasn't possible. Not that there was any safety anywhere in France. War is terrible. It destroys everything. Life was good . . . and then the Emperor quarrels with Bismarck. What is that to do with people like us?" he finished angrily.

"Tell me about Gérard."

"He was there. He never came back. The house was destroyed with everyone in it."

"Dead . . . ?" I whispered.

Lars looked away. "When he did not come back for two days, I went there. I found out. Everyone in it was killed. There were nine people, they said."

"Gérard, Robert, Angèle . . . all the servants. It can't be."

"It was happening all round us. Whole families . . . that is war."

I turned to Marie-Christine. She was looking at me blankly. I thought: This child has lost her family.

I took her into my arms and we clung together.

"You should go back," said Lars. "Don't stay here. It's quiet now, but Paris is not a good place to be."

• • •

I can't remember much of the drive back to La Maison Grise. The driver had been jubilant when he arrived to take us back. He had found his daughter and her family. They had all survived the bombardment of Paris; but when he heard what had happened, horror took the place of his delighted relief.

As for myself, I could only think that I should never see Gérard again; I could not stop thinking of my good friends Robert and Angèle . . . gone forever.

I felt an extreme bitterness towards fate, which had dealt me one blow after another. My childhood had been made up of fun and laughter and so soon I had been brought face to face with tragedy . . . not once, but three times. Those whom I had loved had been taken from me.

I felt desperately lonely, and then I reproached myself when I considered Marie-Christine. She was robbed of her family; she was alone in a world of which, because of her tender years, she could know very little.

She became in a way my salvation—as I think I did hers. We needed each other.

She said to me: "You will never go away from me, will you? We'll always be together."

I replied: "We shall be together as long as you want it."

"I want it," she said. "I shall always want it."

And the weeks began to pass.

•

It was March when peace was ratified at Bordeaux. The terms were harsh. France had been utterly humiliated, and there was a great deal of uneasiness and resentment. Alsace and part of Lorraine were to be ceded to the German Empire, and France was to pay an indemnity of five billion francs, and there would be a German occupation until the money was paid. The Emperor had been released and, as there was no longer a welcome for him in France, he had gone to join the Empress in exile in England.

France was in turmoil. In April there was a communist uprising in Paris and a great deal of damage was done to the city before the rising was suppressed in May.

Things were beginning to settle.

We heard that a cousin of Robert's had inherited the house and estate. It did not pass to Marie-Christine, as the old Salic law, which ordained that female members of the family could not inherit, seemed to apply to the families of the nobility.

However, Marie-Christine would be comfortably off financially. Robert had left me some money and the house in London, which he had always intended should be reverted to me.

Lars Petersen came to see me.

He had changed a good deal; he had lost some of that old exuberance and was more serious.

He was going home, he told us. Paris had lost its charm for him. It was no longer the lighthearted city, refuge of artists. He had had enough of Paris, and there were too many memories for him to be contented there.

I told him that Marie-Christine and I would be leaving. La Maison Grise was passing into the hands of Robert's cousin and Robert had left my old home in London to me.

"Who would have thought things would have turned out like this?" said Lars. "Gérard . . . dear old Gérard . . . I was fond of him, you know."

He shook his head sadly. I fancied he might be feeling a little guilt and remorse, remembering perhaps that once he had intended to take Gérard's wife to live with him.

Marie-Christine and I sadly watched him drive away.

It was a few days later when the cousin came to La Maison Grise. He was very pleasant and delighted with the house, which he had never thought would come to him.

I explained that we were preparing to leave for London, which we should do very soon, to which he replied graciously that we must not feel we had to hurry.

He stayed a night, and when he had gone, I said to Marie-Christine: "It has been decided for us. I wonder what you will think of London."

"I shall like it if we are together," said Marie-Christine. "And it will be different, won't it?"

"Different, yes."

I was thinking of the people at home . . . the house of memories. My mother's room . . . I could see her clearly . . . reclining in her bed, her beautiful hair spread out on her pillow; ranting against Dolly . . . and most of all, I could not forget the nightmare of seeing her lying dead on the floor.

The French episode was over. I could ask myself: If Gérard had lived, should I have married him? Should I have been able to build a new life . . . a life when memories might have ceased to fill me with regrets?

I should never know.

CORNWALL

The Dancing Maidens

We settled into the house. The Crimps had welcomed us warmly. They were obviously delighted, not only that we were there but because the house was now mine.

Mrs. Crimp did say to me some days after our return that this was how it should be. That Monsewer Robber had been a nice enough gentleman, but it was a funny sort of setup, if you asked her. And now it was all back where it

belonged. "With you, Miss Noelle," she added
with satisfaction.

Mrs. Crimp was eager to explain everything. There were only two maids, Jane and
Carrie. That was all they'd needed, with them
being sort of caretakers, and the house not used
as a residence.

"You might want to change, Miss Noelle."
I said I would see.

"And that Miss du Carron. I suppose she's
a mademoiselle. Will she be staying here?"

"Yes. It will be her home as well as mine.
She lost all her family. She is Monsieur Robert's great-niece. He, her father and her
grandmother were all blown up when the Germans shelled Paris. They were in a house there
when the Germans were trying to take the city.
A shell demolished the house and everyone in
it."

"Wicked beggars . . . and that poor
mite."

"We have to help her, Mrs. Crimp. She's
suffered a terrible loss."

Mrs. Crimp nodded, and I knew she would
be especially kind to Marie-Christine.

Marie-Christine herself seemed to be recovering from the shock of her loss. It had been
good to come to an entirely new environment.
She was interested in London. I took her
round. We walked in the parks; we visited the
Tower of London; we looked at historic build-

ings and the theatres where my mother had worked. She was enchanted by it all.

We had not been there long when Dolly called.

"I heard you were back in London," he said. "It's good to see you." He looked at me searchingly. "How are you, my dear?"

"I'm all right, Dolly, thanks."

"I heard about Robert. Tragedy, that stupid war. And you've brought his niece back with you."

"His great-niece. She has lost her family . . . her father, grandmother and Robert. It is dreadful, Dolly."

"I see that. And she likes to be with you. It is good for her that you are here."

"And for me, too, Dolly."

"Yes."

"Do you hear anything of Lisa Fennell?" I asked.

"Oh, that girl. She had an accident. Turned out worse than we thought. She married . . . married Charlie's son, as a matter of fact."

"Yes. She wrote and told me."

"Charlie hardly ever comes to London now. I haven't seen him for ages."

Marie-Christine came in and I introduced her.

"I knew your uncle well," Dolly said. "You'll have to come and see one of my shows."

Marie-Christine looked pleased at the prospect.

"Lucky Lucy," he went on. "It's playing to packed houses . . . so far. Lottie Langdon's good."

"She's Lucky Lucy, of course?" I said.

"Of course. You must come. I'll see you get the best seats. I am glad you are back in London, Noelle."

It was right to have come. Marie-Christine was recovering from the shock, and I think she was able to do that better here away from the scene of disaster. She was young and resilient, and had never been especially close to her family. I think I had begun to mean more to her than any of them, even before the tragedy.

She was maturing quickly. I supposed it was inevitable that such dramatic events would have that effect.

I was delighted to see how much she enjoyed *Lucky Lucy.* Dolly came round to see us in the interval, and afterwards took us backstage. Marie-Christine was introduced to Lottie Langdon in all her finery. Flushed and triumphant from the acclaim of a delighted audience, Lottie was very gracious to Marie-Christine, and affectionate towards me.

Marie-Christine was in good spirits, but for me the evening had been too reminiscent of the past. I could not sleep that night. On a sudden impulse, I had a desire to be in my mother's room. I wanted to be there, as I had on those mornings when she had slept late and I had crept into her bed to talk.

I went down to her room. I lay on the bed and I thought of her.

There was a full moon that night, and it set a silvery glow over everything. I felt that she was near me.

I don't know how long I lay there, lost in memory.

Then suddenly I was startled, for the door was slowly opening.

Marie-Christine had come into the room.

"Noelle," she said. "What are you doing here?"

"I couldn't sleep."

"It was going to the theatre," she said. "It reminded you."

"Yes, I suppose so."

"It must have been a wonderful life."

"It was."

"And she was as beautiful as Lottie?"

"Much more beautiful."

"We both had beautiful mothers."

I said: "Marie-Christine, what are you doing out of bed at this time?"

"I heard you leave your room. I peeped out and watched you. I wasn't going to do anything about it, but you stayed so long, and I thought I had better go and see."

"You *are* looking after me, Marie-Christine."

"We are going to look after each other, aren't we?"

"Yes. For as long as is necessary."

She came to the bed and lay there beside me.

"I thought you were going to marry my father," she said. "I should have liked that. It would have made you my stepmother."

"I couldn't feel closer to you if you *were* my stepdaughter."

"I think it would have been very good for you. You liked him very much, didn't you?"

"Yes."

"So if he hadn't died . . ."

"I am not sure."

"But if he asked you . . ."

"He did. I told him I couldn't just then. I wanted time to think."

"Why?"

"It's a long story."

"Was there someone else you loved?"

"Yes, there was."

"And he didn't love you?"

"Yes, he did. But we found we were brother and sister."

"How?"

"It's too complicated to tell quickly. We met and fell in love, and then we learned of our relationship."

"I can't see how . . . and why you didn't know."

"I'd known his father for a long time. I thought he was one of my mother's friends. She had a lot of friends. They had been lovers and I was born. He lived in the country with his wife and son. These things happen."

"With people like your mother, I suppose."

"She didn't live according to the laws laid down by society."

"How dreadful for you!"

"If my mother hadn't died, it would have been different. She would have seen what might happen and stopped it in time. But she died . . . and this happened."

"No wonder you look sad sometimes."

"I have been very unhappy. It is hard to forget, Marie-Christine."

"If you had married my father, that would have been good for us all."

"Perhaps. But we shall never know."

"And now you have come back to the house where you lived with your mother. What happened to . . . your brother?"

"He is married now."

"So he found consolation."

"I hope so."

"Noelle, *you* should find consolation. You could have done with my father. He was miserable about my mother. He was happier when you came. You could have helped each other."

"It was not to be, Marie-Christine."

"Well, we have to start from . . . now. We have come back to this house. It is our house . . . and it is the place where *she* lived. Everywhere you remember her. This room is just as it was when she was here. That should not be so, Noelle. It's our house now . . . yours and mine. We're going to live here. It's going to be different from what it was before. There must be no going back to all these memories. We're going to start on this room. I know this is what your mother would want."

"What do you mean . . . you are going to change it?"

"I'm going to get rid of all the clothes in that wardrobe. We're going to have new curtains . . . new carpet. We're going to have white walls instead of pale green. We are going to take the furniture out . . . perhaps put it in the attic, or even sell some. Everything is going to be new, and when it is finished it shall be *my* room . . . not hers. Then you will stop remembering and being sad. She will have gone. There won't be all those things to remind you. What do you think of my idea?"

"I . . . I'll consider it."

"Don't do that. Say yes, I think it's a good idea. Because it is. Here in this room . . . I have a feeling she is telling me what to do. She's saying: Look after Noelle. Stop her thinking of the past. Tell her I'd rather she forgot me if thinking of me makes her sad. That is what she is saying to me."

"Oh, Marie-Christine!" I said, and we clung together for a few moments.

She said: "It's going to be exciting. I think we'll have yellow curtains, because yellow is the colour of sunlight, and we're going to send out all the shadows and bring in the sun. We shall have a blue carpet. Blue and yellow. Blue skies and yellow sunshine. Oh, do let's do it, Noelle!"

"Perhaps you are right . . ." I began.

"I *know* I'm right. We are going to start tomorrow."

•

It was Marie-Christine who found the letters.

She had thrown herself wholeheartedly into the refurbishing of my mother's room. She had chosen curtain materials and they were being made. She had decided on the carpet, and at this time she was preoccupied with the furniture.

She was obviously enjoying the task, and I was touched by her desire to do what was best for me.

She was happier than she had been since she lost her family. She was right, too. One should not make perpetual shrines to the dead. It was a way of nursing one's grief.

She came bursting into my room, her eyes

shining. She was brandishing some papers in her hand.

"You know the bureau?" she said. "I was going through it. I thought it was one of the pieces that could go into the attic. Behind one of the drawers there was another little drawer. If you didn't know it was there, you could have missed it. I just put my hand at the back to see if there was anything stuck there . . . and found it. There were letters in it. I think they could mean something."

"What letters?" I said. "My mother's . . . ?"

"They're written to her, I think. She must have kept them. She was Daisy, wasn't she? They're all addressed to 'My dearest Daisy.' "

"You've read them?"

"Of course I've read them. I think it's an important discovery."

"Her private letters . . ."

Marie-Christine looked exasperated. "I tell you, they could mean something. Here. Read them. They were in order. There is no date on them . . . but I found them like that."

She handed them to me.

I read the first one.

> Meningarth,
> near Bodmin
>
> My dearest Daisy,
>   I was astounded to hear the news. I feel

very proud, too. I don't suppose it's possible, but would you feel like coming back, now this has happened? I understand, of course, how you feel, my darling. I know you hate the place and what you went through here. I know you said you never wanted to see it again. But I have a faint hope that this might possibly make a difference. Won't it be difficult up there?

You know I want to do everything to make you happy. And there would be the child.

My love to you forever,

Ennis

Marie-Christine was watching me closely. "Read the others," she said.

Meningarth
near Bodmin

My dearest Daisy,

I knew what your answer would be. I know about your dreams of fame and fortune. You can't give up, particularly now there is a chance of its coming true. If you came back here, it would be the end of that.

So you have good friends up there. They will do everything for you . . . far more than I can. They are rich and the sort of people who like to have you around. I'd be a hindrance and you are right when you say it would be the end of all you dreamed of . . . and the child must have every chance. You couldn't bring her back here. When you escaped, it was forever.

I thought it might be difficult for you up

there. But apparently you are getting through all the difficulties. I thought, because of the child, you might come back to me, but you say because of the child you must stay. I shall try to understand.

My love as ever,

Ennis

There was another letter.

Meningarth,
near Bodmin

My dearest Daisy,

I am so pleased to hear of your success. You are famous now, my darling. I always knew you would get what you wanted. And the child is happy. She has everything she wants . . . more than she could ever have had here, and you are determined she shall never know the like of what you went through.

You are going on to even greater success. You always got what you wanted in the end.

As always, my love to you and the child,

Ennis

As soon as I had finished reading, Marie-Christine demanded: "What do you think? You are the child he is talking about."

"Yes, I think I must be."

"Why does he write like this? Why is he so interested in you?"

"He is asking her to go back and marry him."

"Noelle, the child he writes about is his."

"He doesn't say so."

"Not in so many words . . . but at the least it's a possibility. We're going to find out, Noelle. We've got to. We're going down there to . . ." She snatched the letters from my hands. "Meningarth," she said. "Near Bodmin. We're going to find Ennis. We've got to. Just suppose . . ."

"That he is my father?"

"And if he is . . ."

"It's too late, Marie-Christine."

"We've got to know. Don't you want to know who your father is?"

"All we have to go on are these letters."

"It's a good start. Meningarth can't be very big, or he wouldn't have to say 'near Bodmin.' And Ennis . . . well, it's not like John or Henry. There can't be a lot of Ennises."

She was excited.

"We are going to find him. We are going to find the truth!"

"It is probing into my mother's past . . . finding out things she clearly didn't want known."

"It's your life. You must know the truth. If she had known what was going to happen, she would have made sure you had the truth. She would want you to know. You'll see that. It's

just the first shock of reading these letters. Noelle, we are going down to Meningarth. We're
going to find Ennis. We are going to know the
truth."

•

Ever since we had decided to go down to Cornwall, Marie-Christine had been in a state of
great excitement, in which I was beginning to
share. The best thing for us both was to have
some project on hand.

Within a few days of the discovery of the
letters, we were on our way to Bodmin.

The train was fairly full all the way to
Taunton. After that people began to get out
and our carriage was empty for some way until
we reached Exeter, when two middle-aged ladies joined us.

Marie-Christine, at the window, could not
stop calling out to me to look at this and that as
we sped past. The glimpse of the sea delighted
her, and she was quick to notice the red fertile
soil of Devon.

The two ladies listened with obvious amusement. Then one of them said: "This must be
your first visit to the West Country."

"Yes, it is," I told them.

"You, as well as the French young lady?"

"The first time for both of us."

"Is it a holiday?" asked the other.

Marie-Christine said: "In a way. We want to explore."

"There's no place like Cornwall, is there, Maria?" said one of the ladies to the other.

Maria said: "It's true. There's something about Cornwall that no other place has. I have always said that, haven't I, Caroline?"

"You have. We've lived here all our lives. We don't leave it much . . . except to see our married sister. She lives in Exeter."

"Do you live near Bodmin?" I asked.

"Yes, we do."

"Do you know a place called Meningarth?" asked Marie-Christine eagerly.

"Meningarth . . ." mused Caroline. "I can't say I've ever heard of that, have you, Maria?"

"Meningarth, did you say? No . . . I don't know it."

"Where are you going to stay?" asked Caroline.

"We haven't decided. We thought it would be easy to get into some hotel for a night . . . and then, if we liked it, stay . . . otherwise we would look round."

"They ought to stay at the Dancing Maidens, oughtn't they, Maria?"

"Oh, the Dancing Maidens . . . yes. They couldn't find anything better than that. That's if they don't mind being a little way from the town."

"We shouldn't mind that at all," I said.

"There's a fly at the station. That could take you out. It's only a few miles from Bodmin. You could walk the distance. They've only a few rooms, but we've heard nothing but good of them. They'd look after you. One or two friends of ours have stayed there. You mention the Misses Tregorran and they'll look after you."

"The Dancing Maidens sounds very jolly," said Marie-Christine.

"It's named after the stones. They're supposed to be like dancing maidens. You can see them from the inn. They've been there for hundreds of years."

"We shall go to the Dancing Maidens as soon as we reach Bodmin," I said. "It is kind of you to be so helpful."

"By the way, we're Tregorran . . . Marie and Caroline."

"I'm Noelle Tremaston, and this is Marie-Christine du Carron."

"Tremaston! That's a good old Cornish name. A good one indeed. You must be related to *the* Tremastons."

"Who are *the* Tremastons?"

"Who are the Tremastons!" Caroline looked at Maria and they laughed. "The family up at the Big House. Sir Nigel and Lady Tremaston. It's half a mile out of the town. The

Tremastons have been here for hundreds of years."

Marie-Christine's look said: I told you we ought to come here. This is getting more exciting every minute.

I could see that she had made up her mind that these were my hitherto unknown relations.

The Tregorrans went on to talk of the Tremastons. The garden fete was held on their lawn. It was in aid of the church. If it were wet, they all went into the house. That was exciting. They almost hoped for rain on fete days. The place was like a palace . . . like a castle.

Talk continued until we arrived at Bodmin. In a flurry of excitement, we alighted. The Misses Tregorran had not finished with us yet.

They took us to where the fly was waiting.

"Oh, there you are, Jemmy," said Miss Caroline Tregorran.

"Have a good visit, miss? And how was Miss Sarah and the children?"

"All well, Jemmy, thank you. Now you are to take these two ladies to the Dancing Maidens."

"Yes, miss."

"They've come all the way from London." She smirked slightly, implying that because of this we might need special care. "If they haven't room at the Dancing Maidens, you must bring them back to Bodmin and try the Bull's Head, or if they can't oblige, go to the

Merry Monarch. They are travelling on their own, and haven't been to Cornwall before."

"I'll be doing that, miss," said Jemmy.

She turned to us as we were getting into the fly. She said: "Mention at the Dancing Maidens that the Misses Tregorran sent you. Then they'll look after you."

"You have been so kind to us," I said. "It was great good luck to meet you on the train."

They went their way, glowing with satisfaction: and we drove out of the station to the Dancing Maidens.

•

The landlord at the Dancing Maidens certainly had a room for friends of the Misses Tregorran. He told us that he had looked after many friends of those ladies and there had been satisfaction on both sides.

The inn was of grey Cornish stone, and over the door hung the sign depicting three stone figures which could, by a stretch of the imagination, be said to be dancing.

I guessed it to have been built in the seventeenth century. The rooms were fairly spacious but low-ceilinged, and the windows were small; there was a general air of antiquity about everything which Marie-Christine and I found interesting.

The landlord took us to our room, in which there were two single beds, a wardrobe, a table on which stood a basin and ewer, another small table and two chairs.

We were agreeably surprised to be settled so soon, thanks to the Misses Tregorran.

The landlord told us that if we could be ready in half an hour there would be a meal awaiting us in the dining room. I said that would be very agreeable.

As we were talking, hot water was brought up, and when he left us we laughed together.

"It is all so exciting," said Marie-Christine. "How glad I am we came!"

She went to the window.

"It's eerie," she said. "The sort of place where strange things could happen."

I joined her. We were looking out over moorland. A slight wind ruffled the grass and here and there boulders jutted out of the earth. Some little way off were the stones which bore enough resemblance to the sign over the inn door to tell us that they were the Dancing Maidens.

I pointed them out to Marie-Christine, who gazed at them in awe.

"What are they supposed to be? Were they turned to stone? Perhaps because they were dancing . . . when they shouldn't have been."

"What a terrible punishment for such a small misdemeanour!"

"People did things like that in the old days. Look at the Greeks. They were always turning people into things . . . flowers and swans and things like that."

We were laughing. It was the laughter of anticipation. Whatever vital facts we discovered, this quest was going to be interesting.

"Come on," I said. "We must dash. That meal will be waiting for us in half an hour."

There was hot soup, cold roast beef with potatoes in the jackets. This was followed by treacle tart.

"We shall certainly not starve here," I commented.

We were served by a plump maid, whom we discovered was Sally. She was inclined to be talkative, which suited us very well.

She regarded me with something like awe. I soon realized why.

"You be Miss Tremaston," she said. "You must belong to the Big House."

I said: "I had never heard of the Big House until today. So I cannot claim that honour."

"Well, everyone do know the Tremastons in these parts, and I never heard tell of any other by that name who wasn't the family like."

"I've always lived in London, apart from when I was in France for some time."

Sally looked at Marie-Christine and nodded.

Marie-Christine said: "Do you know a place called Meningarth?"

"Meningarth?" repeated Sally vaguely. "Now where would that be to?"

"It's near Bodmin," I said.

"This be not far from Bodmin, and I can't say I've ever heard of it."

"Are you sure?" asked Marie-Christine appealingly.

"I can't recall it, miss."

When she left us, Marie-Christine said: "It's odd that the Misses Tregorran hadn't heard of it . . . and now Sally . . ."

We were a little deflated. I was wondering where we could go from here. The point of our visit was to find Ennis, whose surname we did not know, and now no one seemed to have heard of the village where he lived.

Marie-Christine said: "We'll have to think what we are going to do. We'll have to ask everyone. Someone will surely have heard of the place."

After the meal, we went for a little walk. We crossed the moor and made our way to the Dancing Maidens.

Marie-Christine was right. There was a strange eeriness about the moor. We stood beside the maidens. They were the size of humans, and when one stood close, one could imagine their suddenly coming to life.

Marie-Christine shared this feeling.

She said: "I'm sure they could tell us where Meningarth is."

We laughed. We said goodbye to the stone maidens and made our way back to the inn.

"After all," said Marie-Christine, "we can't expect to find everything at once."

•

We had better luck in the morning when we met the landlord's wife.

She greeted us warmly when we came downstairs. A delicious smell of frying bacon and coffee filled the inn.

"Good morning to 'ee," she said. "You be Miss Tremaston and friends of the Misses Tregorran. We are very happy to have 'ee come to the Dancing Maidens."

"We met the Misses Tregorran on the train," I told her. "They were very kind."

"They be nice ladies. I do the breakfasts myself. What would you like to eat?"

We decided on scrambled eggs with crisp bacon, which tasted as good as it smelt.

She was a garrulous woman, and in a short time she was telling us that she had been brought up in the inn, which had belonged to her father. "Jim . . . my husband . . . he took over and it was still my home. All my life I've lived at the Dancing Maidens."

"You will know this place as well as anyone," said Marie-Christine. "Perhaps you can tell us where Meningarth is?"

We were both watching her earnestly, and

our hearts sank at the look of puzzlement in her face. Then she said: "Oh, you'd mean Mr. Masterman's place. You must do. It's Garth. Mind you, it was Meningarth at one time . . . but it hasn't been called that for ten years or more."

Marie-Christine was beaming at her.

"So now it is just called Garth!" she said encouragingly.

"That be so. I remember now. 'Twas in the October gales . . . terrible gales we do get here October month. You should hear the wind sweeping across the moor. It whistles like the devil calling sinners from their graves, they say. It must be all of ten years ago. Terrible they were that year. We had damage at the inn. Meningarth had it worse . . . being more exposed like. It took the roof off of the place . . . tore up the gate and flung it a quarter of a mile away. It took months to put it right. The gate was finished. They had to put up a new one . . . and when it was up, it didn't have Meningarth on it like the old one. They'd made a mistake and put just Garth. Nothing was done about it . . . and people stopped saying Meningarth. It was just plain Garth."

"We used to have friends who knew the people there," said Marie-Christine glibly.

"Oh . . . him . . . he keeps himself to himself. Him and his dog. Fond of music. Plays the violin or something."

"That must be Ennis . . ." began Marie-Christine.

"Ennis Masterman . . . that be he."

"We might call on him," I said. "How do we get there?"

" 'Tis a tidy step from here. A good couple of miles, I'd say. Do you ladies ride a horse?"

"Yes," we said eagerly.

"Well, we get a lot of call from people staying here for a horse. So we have one or two. We hire them out for the day mostly. We could suit you, I reckon. We've got a couple of nice little mares . . . not too frisky. They know the moor, too. It can be quite a tricky place."

"You could direct us to Garth, I'm sure," I said.

"Certainly I could. Well, fancy that. Who'd have thought of Ennis Masterman having young lady visitors, from London!"

We finished breakfast and went immediately to the stables. We saw the mares to which the landlady had referred. We said they would suit us beautifully and, with the landlady's instructions, we were soon on our way.

"What triumph!" said Marie-Christine. "When she told us about the gate's being destroyed, I could have hugged her. It explains why all those people didn't know the place. Noelle, we are on our way."

I was more subdued. Marie-Christine would not feel my emotions, naturally. Suppose our conjecture proved to be correct and I was going to meet the father whom I had never met before? On the other hand . . . suppose we were quite wrong, and were going to crash into someone's private life?

My feelings were in a turmoil.

The landlady's instructions were clear. We passed the little hamlet she had described. It was just a row of houses, a village store and a church. It was necessary to follow the directions very closely. I could see how easily one could lose oneself on the moor.

"If we are on the right track," I said, "Garth should be behind that slight hillock over there."

We had rounded the hillock, and there it was—a long grey stone building, lonely, rather stark and desolate.

We rode over to the gate. "Garth," we both said aloud. "This is it."

We dismounted and tied our horses to a post near the gate. We went through the gate to the piece of land in front of the house. It could hardly be called a garden. There were no flowers, only a few overgrown shrubs.

"Isn't it exciting?" said Marie-Christine with a little shiver.

There was a knocker on the door. I lifted it and let it fall. It sounded very loud in the silence. We waited breathlessly. There was no response.

After a while I tried again.

"There's no one here," I said.

"He's out. He lives here. That's obvious. He'll come sooner or later."

"We'll wait for a while and see if he does," I said.

We walked down the path and out through the gate. There was a stone block nearby and we sat on this.

"Perhaps he's gone away for days . . . for weeks," I suggested.

"Oh no," cried Marie-Christine. "I could not bear that. He's gone to that little village we passed. He'd have to get stores, wouldn't he? We'll find him. This is just making it a little more difficult, that's all."

We waited for an hour, and just as I was going to suggest we must go, he came.

He was driving a pony and trap, and Marie-Christine must have been right when she had guessed that he had gone to the village for stores.

He pulled up in amazement when he saw us sitting on the boulder, and then he leaped out of the trap. He was tall and slim. His face was pleasant rather than handsome. There was a gentleness about him which I noticed even in those first moments.

We went towards him, and I said: "I hope you don't mind our calling. My name is Noelle Tremaston."

The effect on him was instantaneous. His eyes were fixed on me, and he was trying hard to control his features. Then a flush came into his face. He said slowly: "You are Daisy's daughter. I am glad you have come."

"Yes," I said. "I am Daisy's daughter. And this is Mademoiselle du Carron. She has lived with me since she lost her family in the siege of Paris."

He turned to Marie-Christine and said it was a pleasure to meet her.

"We found your address in my mother's bureau," I said.

"Only it was Meningarth," put in Marie-Christine.

"It was called that a long time ago, and then it was changed."

"We thought we would like to talk to you," I said, "when we knew that you had been a friend of my mother."

"Of course. And what am I thinking of? Come in. I'll deal with the trap."

"Can we help you?" I said.

He looked bemused. "That's kind of you. First I must unload."

He unlocked the door, and I thought how strange it was that I should begin my acquaintance with the man who might turn out to be my father by carrying a bag of flour into his kitchen.

I was quickly aware of the primitive nature

of the cottage. I had noticed a well at the back of the overgrown garden. In the stone-floored kitchen, there was just a wooden table, a cupboard, a few chairs and an oil stove on which he presumably cooked.

When the stores had been brought in, he took us into a sort of sitting room which was very simply furnished. There was no attempt at adornment. Everything was for use.

He asked us to sit down and I realized how difficult it was for him to keep his eyes from me.

"I do not know where to begin," I said. "I want to talk to you about my mother. You knew her . . ."

"Yes, I knew her."

"It must have been a long time ago."

He nodded.

"Did she live here?"

"Near here. In the village. You must have passed it. Carrenforth. It's about half a mile from this place."

"I suppose she was very young then."

"She was about fourteen years old when I first saw her. I came here from the university. I did not know what I wanted to do. So I decided to take a walking tour over the moors. My home was some way off . . . on the other side of the Duchy. My inclination was to live the simple life. I love music, but I felt I was not gifted enough to make it a profession. I had a great desire to be a sculptor. I had done a little . . . but I was very uncertain."

Marie-Christine was growing impatient, I sensed. She said: "We found letters in a bureau."

He looked at her blankly.

"They came from you."

"She kept them," he said, smiling.

"Three of them," I said. "I'm sorry. We read them."

"We were clearing out things," said Marie-Christine. "They were in a secret drawer in the bureau."

"So she kept my letters," he repeated.

"These seemed to be rather important ones," I said. "They mentioned a child. I think I may be that child. I want to be sure."

"It is *very* important," said Marie-Christine.

He was thoughtful for a few seconds. Then he said: "Perhaps it would be better if I began at the beginning . . . I mean, I should tell you the whole story."

"Yes. If you would, we should be grateful."

"She had told me so much about Noelle, her daughter. I am a little bemused, I fear. It was so sudden. So unexpected . . . seeing you like this. It is something I always wanted . . . but I think you will understand better if I tell you from the beginning . . . as I remember it."

"Thank you. Do please tell us."

"I was born in Cornwall—some way from here, just over the border in fact, on the Cornish side of the Tamar. I was the minister's son. There were six of us, two boys and four girls. Money was short, but my father firmly believed in getting the best education for his children, and somehow I got to the university. I was a moderately good scholar, but as I grew older, I was a disappointment. I did not know what I wanted to do. I had certain enthusiasms, but they were not the sort which would earn money and repay my family for all the sacrifices they had made for me.

"I loved music. I played the violin tolerably well, but I could not see myself earning a living at that. I was deeply interested in sculpture. I was torn between my duty and inclination.

"So I came on this walking tour. I wanted to be quiet . . . alone. To get right away from everything and everyone and plan. I stayed at the Dancing Maidens, intending to be there for a night or two.

"I wanted to take a look at the stone maidens and I set out one afternoon. It was a strange brooding sort of day. There was not a breath of wind, and the clouds were louring. As I approached the stones, I saw a young girl. I knew something of Cornish folklore, having been brought up in the Duchy. I was perhaps influenced by that, and a little superstitious, but as I came near, I thought one of the stones had come to life and she was dancing. She was so beautiful, so graceful, she seemed to be floating on air. I thought I had never seen anything so enchanting.

"I stood watching in wonder. Suddenly she was aware of me. She turned towards me and began to laugh. It was my first sight of Daisy. Nobody laughs quite like Daisy."

"No," I said. "No one ever did."

"She called out: 'You thought I was one of the maidens come to life, didn't you? Confess.'

" 'For the moment . . . yes,' I replied.

" 'You new here?' she asked.

" 'Yes. On a walking tour,' I told her.

"She asked me if I came there often, and I told her it was my first time and I had only arrived that morning and was trying to make up my mind about something.

" 'What?' she asked.

" 'My career. The work I'm going to do.'

" 'I know what I'm going to do,' she said. 'I'm going to dance. I'm going to be famous. I'm never going to be poor and a nobody. I'm going on the stage.'

"I remember that conversation so well. I stayed on at the Dancing Maidens because I wanted to meet her again. She fascinated me. She was a child one moment and a woman the next. I had never known anyone combine innocence and worldliness as Daisy did. She was fourteen and I some ten years older. She was radiant. I never before knew anyone so beautiful. It was all there . . . in bud, you might say, waiting to spring into its full glory.

"We used to meet by the stones every day. It was not exactly an arranged meeting, but each of us knew the other would be there. She liked to talk to me. I supposed it was because I liked to listen. The theme of the conversations was always Escape. She was going to sing and dance her way to fame. It struck me at the time that she was everything I was not. I wanted to escape from life. She wanted to escape to it. I soon learned from what she wanted to escape. I learned something about the life she lived there. It had been wretched. That was why she was going to get away and never come back. She lived with her grandparents and she hated them. 'They killed my mother,' she said. 'They would kill me if they could.'

"Eventually I learned something of the story. It was not such an unusual one. I could picture the puritanical grandfather . . . stern and unforgiving. Prayers three times a day, no laughter, no love, no tenderness. Daisy and her mother were sinners. Her mother because she had disobeyed the laws of God, and Daisy because the sins of the parents, according to the grandfather, were visited upon the children; and a child born in sin must herself be sinful. I understood her vehemence . . . her determination. She hated them fiercely. She repudiated all her grandfather stood for—the theory that to be miserable was to be good and that to laugh and enjoy life was certain sin.

"She told me that she was waiting; she was preparing all the time. She knew she was too young at that time, but soon she would not be. She must plan very carefully. She must not be rash and foolish. She must await the opportunity and be ready when it came.

"It was an ordinary enough story. Her mother had been seduced and deserted by her lover. The result was Daisy. There was no compassion for the sinner. 'They would have turned her out,' said Daisy, 'but my grandfather realized he could have more fun torturing her while making a show of forgiving the sinner—the old hypocrite. They killed my mother. I hate them. I'll never forgive them.'

"Daisy was five years old when her mother died. She told me about it. 'She could stand it no longer. She was often ill. Her cough frightened me. Then one night, when it was snowing and a gale was blowing, she went out onto the moors, wearing a flimsy blouse and skirt, and she stayed out most of the night. When she came back she was very ill. She died within a few days. She had had more than she could endure.' She was vehement. 'I hate them,' she said. 'I will never be poor. I'll be rich and famous and laugh my way through my life. I will go away and never, never see them again.' "

"She rarely spoke of her childhood to me," I said. "I sensed she did not want to. I understand now. She must have been very unhappy."

"You would have thought a girl in that position would have been. Not Daisy. She radiated the joy of living. Nothing could dampen that. I was fascinated by her. She had decided me. I knew what I must do. Meningarth was for sale. It was very cheap. I could just about afford it. I would set up house here. I should be near her. She used to come often. I would come in and find she had lighted a fire and was curled up by it. I knew I was important to her at that time. It was to me she came when she wanted to talk. I knew of her plans and dreams, and they never varied. They were to escape and never come back to this place. I refused to accept the fact that she would go away. I thought we should go on like that forever and in time she would come to me at Meningarth. I thought she was just a dreamer . . . as I was. But Daisy lived in a world where dreams can come true. She was going to call herself Daisy Ray. She was Daisy Raynor. It was the hated name of her grandparents. Daisy Ray, she said, sounded just right for an actress.

"She used to speculate about her father. She was certain that he was a gentleman . . .

someone wealthy like the Tremastons. 'He was young,' she said, 'and afraid of his family.'

"She built up a picture of him. He had wanted to marry her mother, she said. He had not known that she was going to have a child. The family had sent him away . . . abroad . . . and when he came back it was too late."

"What an unhappy life she must have had," I said.

"Ah, as I told you, Daisy could not be unhappy. It was not in her. She always believed . . . I had never seen such gaiety. She was always dancing. I called her the Dancing Maiden. I said sometimes I believed she was one of those stones who had come to life. She was amused by that. She used to say: 'Here is your dancing maiden.' We would talk about what I was going to do. I was going to be a great musician . . . a sculptor. I made a statue of her. I called it the Dancing Maiden. It is rather beautiful. I will show it to you. It is the best thing I have ever done. I had caught something of her and the mystic quality of the stones. I was offered quite a large sum of money for it. It could have been the start of a career. But I couldn't part with it. It meant so much to me . . . particularly as I realized at that time that she would go away. I felt while I had that I had something of her. It was a symbol in a way. It might have been the start of a career. She said I was a fool. But I couldn't help it. That was the way I was. I could not part with the Dancing Maiden."

"I understand," I said. "I am understanding so much."

"She made me see myself clearly. The more I was with her, the more I saw what I lacked. I did not want to go out into the world and compete. I wanted the simple life I was making for myself here. Daisy knew that.

"She was fifteen years old when she told me she was almost ready. The time had come, she said. She must delay no longer. You can imagine my dismay. In spite of her insistence, I had secretly dismissed her yearnings as dreams. I had judged her by myself . . . which was a great mistake. We had become very close friends. She had confided more in me than in anyone. Our meetings had been important to us both. I could not bear the thought of losing her.

"I asked her to marry me. 'How could I?' she replied. 'I'd be here for the rest of my days. We'd be poor . . . living here . . . and with them close by! I'm going to dance. I'm going on the stage.' At one time I thought I would go with her. She shook her head. She said how much my friendship meant to her, but we were different people, weren't we? I did not believe in things as she did. We didn't really belong together . . . not in that way. I knew she was right. But I argued with her. I said, did she think she was the only country girl who had dreamt of a successful stage career? She said of course not. Did she consider how many thousands ended up in wretched circumstances, worse than those they had left? 'But I'm going to get what I want!' she said. She believed that, and when I looked at her, so did I.

"The day she went away was the most wretched of my life . . . to that time. I said goodbye to her. 'Promise,' I said, 'that if it doesn't work out, you'll come back to me.' But she could not conceive that it would not work out. She said it had been wonderful knowing me, that she loved me, but that we were different. She would be no use to me living here . . . looking after hens . . . driving the trap into the village to get the stores. And I should be no use to her in her career. 'We have to face the truth. We don't fit. But we shall always be good friends.'

"She called herself Daisy Tremaston—after the rich family here—with Daisy Ray her stage name. Then someone advised her to change it to Désirée. Désirée," he repeated. "She did what she had set about doing. She had the fire, the determination and the talent. And she succeeded."

He paused and put a hand to his brow. He had been talking for some time and, I knew, living it all again. I, who had known her so well, could visualize it clearly. I could understand that rebellion the puritanical grandparents had raised in her, that contempt for conventions, the determination to go her own way.

Marie-Christine had listened entranced to all this, but I could see that she was impatient to get to the root of the matter. Was this man my father?

He said suddenly: "I usually take coffee at this time. May I give you some?"

Marie-Christine and I were about to say we would rather talk, but I could see that he needed a pause to recover from the excess of emotion which recalling the past had brought to him.

I said I would go into the kitchen and help him make the coffee. Marie-Christine was about to rise, but I signed to her to stay where she was.

When we were in the kitchen, he said to me: "I have often thought of your coming here."

"With her, you mean?"

He nodded.

"She never talked to me of you," I said.

"No, of course, she would not. She had other plans."

"There is one thing I want to know."

"Yes," he said. Then he paused before he went on. "She would write to me now and then. I knew of her successes. It was wonderful. And

I know why you have come here. You found letters which she had kept, and they have raised a possibility in your mind. Am I right?"

"Yes."

"I kept her letters. She did not write often. They were wonderful days when I received them. I lived her success through them, although I had no part in it. I knew there was no hope of her coming back. Particularly after your birth. I will give you the letters which she wrote to me at that time. Take them back to the inn and read them. They are for your eyes alone. When you have read them, bring them back to me. They are important to me. I could not bear to lose them now. I read them often."

I said: "I will read them and bring them back to you tomorrow."

"I think they will tell you what you want to know."

We took the coffee back to the sitting room, where Marie-Christine was waiting with obvious impatience.

We talked a little about the life he led. He managed to make a living, he said. There was a gallery in Bodmin that took some of his figures. He sold one or two now and then, usually of the Dancing Maidens. Visitors liked a reminder of the places they had seen. He grew some of his food. He had a cow and some hens. It was the way he had chosen to live. He brought out the letters and gave them to me.

I repeated my promise to bring them back tomorrow, which I should do after having read them.

"Then," he said, "we shall be able to talk more easily . . . if you wish to. Perhaps we shall feel we know each other better. This has been a wonderful day for me. Often I have told myself it could never happen. I thought that when she died it was the end. Well, I shall see you tomorrow."

I was eager to get away, for I was feverishly anxious to read those letters.

Marie-Christine said, as we rode back to the inn: "Fancy living there like that! What a strange man! He was interesting about Désirée. Daisy Ray. Clever, wasn't it? What about those letters? I can't wait to see them."

"He wanted no one to see them but me, Marie-Christine. They are my mother's intimate letters."

Her face fell.

"Do understand, Marie-Christine," I begged. "There is something sacred about them. And I have promised."

"But you will let me know what they tell?"

"Of course I shall."

• • •

As soon as we arrived at the Dancing Maidens, I hurried to our room. Marie-Christine said, with admirable tact, that she would go for a walk for an hour or so. I appreciated that, for I knew she was consumed by curiosity.

The letters were undated, but had been placed in chronological order, I realized.

My dear, dear Ennis [ran the first],

How wonderful! So at last you are being brought out of your hiding place. At last you are going to be recognized for the genius you are. So, having seen your Dancing Maiden, some London art dealer is interested in your work. It is a beginning. Aren't you excited? Of course you are. I am. But you will say, "Nothing is certain. We must wait and see." I know you, Ennis. My dear one, you have spent too much of your life waiting and seeing. But this is wonderful! I always thought those models you did of the stones were *very* good. And the one you did of your very own Dancing Maiden, a work of genius!

But the important thing is that you are coming to London. I shall see that you stay in the right hotel . . . and it is going to be near this place. Then we can be together when you are not with your important dealer. I am not rehearsing yet. His lordship, Donald Dollington—Dolly to us—is teetering on the edge of embarkation on a new production. At the moment he is in a state of nerves, appealing to the Almighty not to send him completely mad, and not to allow the continuation of the torture he is receiving from those who are determined to obstruct him. It's a game he always plays at times like this. So if you come next week, rehearsals won't have begun. We can talk and talk. It will be like old times.

I await your arrival with the greatest joy.

Your very own Dancing Maiden,

Daisy

I took up the next letter.

My dear, dear Ennis,

What a wonderful week! I bless that dealer, though he turned out to be such a miserable old thing, and when you wouldn't let him have your Dancing Maiden he wasn't interested. It was sweet of you to insist on keeping it . . . but you shouldn't have. Let it go, Ennis! It might have meant commissions and things. You are an old idiot! It was wonderful to be with you . . . to talk as we used to. Did it bring back the old times? There is no one I can talk to as I do to you. It was like being back in Meningarth . . . only instead of talking about the beginning of the journey, I am now halfway there. Ennis, do try to understand this compulsion to get to the top.

Parting was so sad. But you will come up again. I know what you will say . . . but it wouldn't work. And I know you'd hate it here. You've no idea what it's like leading up to the first nights . . . and there is nothing . . .

nothing but the play. It has to be like that, and you'd hate it. You would really.

I have many good friends here. They understand me. The life suits me. I could never leave it.

So things must stay as they are. But let us remember that wonderful, wonderful week.

Loving you, as always,

Daisy—your Dancing Maiden

The next letter was more revealing.

Ennis, my dear,

I have something to tell you. It happened during that wonderful week. At first I didn't know what to think. Now I am living in a whirl of delight. I know now that it is what I have always wanted. I did not know it until now. It will always be as though part of you is with me.

You know what I am going to say. I think I am going to have a child. I am hoping it is so. I shall write again as soon as I am sure.

My love to you,

Daisy—the D.M.

The fourth letter said:

My dearest Ennis,

No. It is quite out of the question. It simply would not work, as I have told you so many times. It would mean giving up everything I have striven for. I could not do it. Please don't ask for what is impossible. I could not bear our relationship to be spoilt, as it would be. Now I am so happy.

Ennis, let us be content with what we have. Believe me, it is the best for us both.

My love, as always,

Daisy—D.M.

I took up the next letter.

Ennis, dear,

I am singing with joy.

It is true. I am to have a child. I am so happy. Dolly is furious. He's thinking of his new play. What is the use of putting me in the lead? Before long I am going to be prancing round like an elephant. I told him elephants didn't prance; they galumphed. He shouted: "What do you think this is going to do to your career? I suppose it is Charlie Claverham's. Or is it Robert Bouchère's? What a thing to do to me, just when I'm thinking of going into production!" Then there was the usual appeal to God. You can't help laughing at Dolly.

Oh well, nothing . . . just nothing . . . can disturb my bliss.

Loving, as ever,

D.—D.M.

I took up the next letter.

> Dearest Ennis,
>
> All is going well. Yes, I will let you know.
>
> I am going to have everything of the best for him/her . . . I don't care which. I just want *it*. Charlie Claverham is amusing. He thinks it is his. Forgive me, Ennis, he has always been such a very dear friend. He could give a child of his anything, just anything. He is a very good man, Charlie is. One of the best I have ever known. He's honourable and honest . . . and he is very rich. So is Robert Bouchère . . . but he's a foreigner, and I'd rather have Charlie. Oh, I'm running on. I was just thinking, if I were to die suddenly. You never know. It hadn't occurred to me before, but when there is a child to think of, it's different.
>
> I can't think of anything but my baby.
>
> Don't worry, and you certainly mustn't think of sending anything. I can manage perfectly. I am doing very well, and Charlie is, of course, making sure that I have every luxury.
>
> I'm strong and healthy. I'm not old. I've seen the doctor, and he says he reckons I'll be perfectly well after a couple of months . . . able to dance again.
>
> Oh, Ennis, I just can't wait. I know everything is going to be wonderful.
>
> Love to you,
>
> D.M.

The next letter had obviously been written some time later.

Dear Ennis,

She is here. She came on Christmas Day, so I am calling her Noelle. She is adorable . . . everything is in perfect order, and I love her more than anything on earth. I shall never leave her. Dolly fusses and says his hands are tied. He wants me in his next production, but do I think he can wait forever while I go on playing Mother. I told him Mother was the best part I ever played, and I'm going on playing it, to which he replied that I am a sentimental idiot and will I wait until I have had some experience of looking after a squalling brat? Then I was angry. I said: "Don't dare call my little girl a brat!" To which he replied sarcastically: "Oh, she will be different from all the other brats, of course. She'll be singing *Traviata* before she's a year old." Dear Dolly. He is not so bad. And I think he likes her. I do not know who could not love her. She knows me already, of course. Martha pretends she's a nuisance, but I have seen her at the cradle when she thinks I'm not looking. I heard her say the other day: "Didums wants its mummy, then." Didums! Martha! Just imagine! But you don't know Martha. She's the last person you'd think would ever even look at a baby. What use are babies in the theatre? But my Noelle can charm even her. As for the servants, they are overcome with joy and are vying with each other to look after her.

Life is bliss.

Love, D.M.

And the last letter:

Dearest Ennis,

All is well. She grows more adorable every day. The best Christmas present I ever had. I've said it a thousand times, and I'll say it thousands more.

Ennis, you must forgive me for this. I am letting Charlie believe she is his. Don't feel too hurt. It is for the best. We have to think of *her.* She must have everything. I could not be happy if I thought it should ever come that I died and left her. I won't have my child knowing poverty as I did. I won't have her put out . . . as I was . . . into unloving hands. I know you would love her . . . but you couldn't give her what she must have . . . and Charlie could . . . and would. In fact, he has sworn he will. He loves her . . . particularly as he believes she is his. Believe me, Ennis, it is the best. He would look after her if I asked him, but it is better to have the closer bond. Perhaps I'm wrong . . . but right and wrong have always been a bit hazy to me. I want what is best for my child, whether or not some would consider it wrong. It's right for me . . . and for her, which is all that matters to me.

Trust you to think about registering the birth and all that. There may be this new law about putting it in at Somerset House. I'm not doing it, Ennis. I am not putting in writing that she was born out of wedlock. There are some who might sneer at her over that. I'm not having my child sneered at. I know a bit about that from my own experience.

I am going to make sure that she has the best of everything. What could I say? I could not say the truth. That you are her father. But you couldn't look after her, Ennis, not in the way I want her looked after. Charlie's the one to do that . . . if ever it were necessary. She'd have servants . . . nannies . . . everything. So I say there will be no form filling . . . no records. This is my child and I will do it my way.

Perhaps I'm wrong, but I think it's better to do what you can for people, to love them, and there's no one I want the best for more than my baby. I think love is more important than a lot of moral laws. I am not going to try to make some plaster saint out of her. I want her to laugh her way through life . . . to enjoy it . . . above all, I want her to know that she is loved. I know the world would say I'm a right old sinner, but I think that love is the best thing in life . . . love for one another . . . and love of life, too. The preachers would say that is wrong. To be good you have to be miserable, but something tells me that if you are loving and kind that'll be good enough for God when the Day of Judgement comes, and He'll turn a blind eye to the rest of it.

My child is first with me, and I am going to see that above everything she is happy, and I don't care what I have to do to make her so.

It was like hearing her voice. It brought her back so clearly to me. She had cared so much for me. It was an ironic twist of fate that, out of her love for me, she had ruined my life.

I felt the tears on my cheeks. These letters had brought her back so vividly that my loss seemed as fresh as it ever had. This they had done—and something else. They had told me without doubt what I had come here to find out.

•

Marie-Christine had returned. She found me sitting there with the letters in my hand.

She sat down quietly, watching me intently.

"Noelle," she said at length. "They've upset you."

"The letters . . ." I replied. "It was just like hearing her talk. It's all here. There is no doubt that Ennis Masterman is my father."

"So Roderick is not your brother."

I shook my head.

She came to me and put her arms round me.

"It's wonderful. It's what we wanted to hear."

I looked at her blankly. "Marie-Christine," I said slowly. "It doesn't matter now. It's too late."

•

The next day I called on Ennis Masterman.

I had said to Marie-Christine, "I shall go

over to him alone. He is my father, you see. You have been so good. You will understand."

"Yes," she said. "I understand."

He was waiting for me. We stood and looked at each other as though with embarrassment.

Then he said: "You can imagine what this means to me."

"Yes, and to me."

"Ever since you were born, I have been hoping to see you."

"It is strange to be suddenly confronted with a father."

"At least I knew of your existence."

"And then I think I might never have known you. It is just by chance . . ."

"Come in," he said. "I want to talk about her. I want to hear about your life together."

So we talked and doing so, surprisingly, I felt some relief from the wounds which had been reopened when I had read her letters. I told him how she had helped Lisa Fennell, of her sudden death and the wretchedness which followed. I told him about the plays, her enthusiasms, her successes.

"She was right," he said. "She had to do what she did . . . and I should have been no good for her. She was bent on success and she achieved it."

At length I talked about myself. I told him

of my visit to Leverson Manor, of my love for Roderick and what had come of it.

He was deeply shocked.

"My dear child, what a tragedy!" he said. "And it need never have been. You could have been happily married. And all because of what she had done. Her heart would be broken. What she wanted most of all was for you to be happy . . . to have everything she missed."

"It is all too late now. He has married someone else . . . the Lisa Fennell I told you about."

"Life is full of ironies. Why did I not follow her to London? Why did I not at least try to make something of myself? I might have been with her in London. I should have been happy there. But I could not do it. Somehow I couldn't leave this place. I didn't believe in myself. I always doubted. I was weak and she was strong. I was unsure and she was so certain. We loved each other but, as she said, we did not fit. I was daunted by all the difficulties while she confidently danced her way over them."

I told him about my stay in France, about Robert, his sister . . . and Gérard, whom I might have married.

I said: "There were times when I thought I could make something of my life in France, and then memories of Roderick would come back to me. Well, it was decided for me."

He was thoughtful. "Noelle, I shall give you

those letters," he said. "You will need them as proof. Perhaps you will come and see me sometimes."

"I will," I promised. "I will."

"I wish fervently that you had come before, that I could have known you before it was too late."

"Oh . . . so do I. But it was not to be."

"It would have broken her heart if she knew what she had done."

It was late in the afternoon when I rode back to the Dancing Maidens. I was still bemused.

I had found my father and confirmed my suspicions. I need never have lost the man I loved.

KENT

Retrn to Leverson

ent back to London, and I felt saddened
r than elated by the success of our ven-
Marie-Christine was a great comfort. She
med much older than her years and, under-
anding my feelings, tried to comfort me. She
lid to a great extent, and I kept telling myself
ow fortunate I was to have won her affections.

The future looked blank. I wondered what
t held. During that time I often thought I

might have made a good life i[n] Parisian bohemian circles. It would have b[ee]n a substitute;
but knowing Gérard, and cari[ng] for him in a
way, had brought home to me [th]e truth that
there would never be anyone for [me] but Roderick.

Oh, why had we not found th[e] letters at
the time of my mother's death? W[hy had] I not
told her of my growing friendship w[ith] Roderick? How different my life might [have] been.
Marie-Christine threw herself into t[he pro]ject
of changing my mother's room which [had b]een
abandoned when we left for Cornw[all. b]ut
nothing could expunge her memory. It[a]ll
been brought back as vividly as ever by
counter with my father. I was constantly
ing the words she had written. How her
for me came over in those letters! She had
so much defied conventions as ignored th[e]
How often had Dolly cried in exasperati[on]
"You are mad, mad, mad!" But she had blithe[ly]
pursued some course which might seem wild[ly]
preposterous to some, but which was completely logical to her.

It had worked out as she had planned
Charlie had regarded me as his daughter. How
could she have foreseen the consequences tha[t]
would bring?

For several weeks life went on uneventfully
and then Charlie called.

I was delighted to see him. I had been

pondering whether I should tell him what I had discovered. I thought it was only right that he, being so involved, should know. I had wondered what he knew about Robert's death. That was another matter which I should tell him, but I had shrunk from writing to him. And now here he was.

He came into the drawing room and took my hands into his.

"I have just heard what happened," he said. "Someone in the City told me. How dreadful to think of Robert . . . dead. I have been wondering for a long time how you were getting on. I did not know you were in London, and called to see if there was any news here. I was planning to go to Paris to see you, but travel is not easy, as things are still in turmoil in France. How glad I am that you are home and safe."

"Robert was killed with his sister and her son. It was in the Paris house. I, with Robert's great-niece, was in the country at the time."

"Thank God for that! Poor Robert! Such a good fellow. All these years I have known him. But you, Noelle . . ."

I said: "Robert's great-niece is with me. Marie-Christine . . . she lost her family, you see . . . all of them."

"Poor child."

"Charlie," I said. "I have something of great importance to say to you. I have been asking myself whether I ought to write to you

. . . but I wasn't sure. It has only just happened. I've found my father . . . my real father. It is not you, Charlie."

"My dear child, what are you saying? What can you know?"

I told him about the discovery of the letters and my visit to Cornwall.

"I have proof," I told him. "Ennis Masterman has given me letters she wrote, and in them she sets out quite clearly that he is my father."

"Then why . . . ?"

"She did it for me. She was afraid she might die and I should not have all she wanted for me. Ennis Masterman was poor. He lives almost like a hermit in a little cottage on the moors, not far from the village where she used to live, and where she had a miserable childhood. She did not want me to be poor . . . as she had been. It was an obsession with her. She did get obsessions, you know, Charlie. Her determination to succeed . . . her plans for me. She was very fond of you. She trusted you more than anyone. I think I should show you her letters. They are written to another man . . . and I daresay you will find reading them harrowing . . . but you should know the truth. She had so much love to give—to you, to Robert, to my father . . . and for me the greatest love of all. For me she would lie, cheat if need be . . . but it was all for me."

My voice broke and he said: "My dear Noelle, I always knew that. She never disguised it.
Those of us who loved her knew it. We were
grateful for what she could give to us. There
was never anyone like her."

"Can you bear to read those letters?" I said.
"They will prove to you without a doubt."

He said he would read them, so I brought
them to him. His emotion was obvious as he
read.

When he had finished, he composed his features. "It is all clear now then. If only we had
known . . ."

"How is Roderick?" I asked.

"He has changed . . . he lives behind a
mask. I see little of him . . . as we all do. He
is out a great deal . . . round the estate. He
throws himself into work."

"And Lisa?"

He frowned. "Poor girl. She grows worse.
The injury to her spine is permanent, you
know. She will never get better. She is in her
room most of the time now. Sometimes they
carry her down and she lies on the sofa. She is
in some pain quite often. The doctors give her
something to ease it, but it is not always effective."

"How terrible for her."

"They thought it was just a slight injury in
the first place, but she soon discovered that was
not the case. Putting a stop to her career was a

great tragedy for her. She was so despondent
. . . desperate, really. The future must have
looked hopeless to her. But he should never
have married her, Noelle. She could have been
looked after. It was pity, you know. He was
always like that . . . from a child. Easily
touched by other people's misery and ready to
go to great lengths to help. This time he went
far . . . very far indeed. He was shattered
when he lost you. I think he must have acted
on the spur of the moment. There was this girl,
with her dreams of fame and fortune gone forever, facing pain and penury. He had lost you
. . . I suppose he thought he would look after
her . . . at least save her. It was a great mistake. We could have seen that she was cared
for. But marriage . . ."

I could imagine it all so clearly—the silent
melancholy of that household.

"And Lady Constance?"

"She is bitterly disappointed, and she cannot hide her feelings. She avoids Lisa, but there
are occasions when they cannot help coming
into contact. She wanted what she considered
to be the right marriage for Roderick. She is
devoted to him and always has been. And to
me, too . . . though I don't deserve such devotion. She deplores Roderick's marriage . . .
first to a girl whose background she considered
unsuitable and, more important, she wants
grandchildren. It is strange, Noelle, but I be-

lieve she wanted you to marry Roderick. I know when you first came to us she was far from welcoming, but she grew fond of you. It was a blow to her when you had to part."

"It had something to do with that time when we were in great danger together. I think we revealed ourselves to each other."

"Yes, it was after that. It certainly had an effect on her. She has talked of you once or twice. She had an admiration for you. It was a terrible shock to her when she believed you were my daughter . . . in more ways than the obvious one. She had known for a long time of my attachment to your mother."

I thought of the scrapbook I had seen in her room. How her jealousy must have tormented her over the years! And it seemed more miraculous than ever that there could have been that friendship between us.

"Yes," mused Charlie. "She would have been very happy for you to marry Roderick."

What did it matter now? All our feelings went for nothing, all our discoveries were too late.

"You have not thought of marrying?" said Charlie.

I told him about Gérard du Carron.

"The one who was killed?"

"Yes."

"And if he had not been?"

"I don't know. I could not forget Roderick."

"As he cannot forget you. What a tragedy!"

"For others, too. Poor Lisa! I am sorry for her. She was so ambitious, and I knew she loved Roderick."

"We are an unhappy household. One feels it as soon as one enters the place. Roderick is thinking of going away for a time."

"Where?"

"There's a family estate in Scotland. He would not be away all the time, but periodically. I can't help thinking he regards it as an escape . . . an excuse to get out of the house for periods."

"And Lisa?"

"She could not leave Leverson. She is not well enough to travel. I shall have to tell them the news. Roderick must know, and I must tell my wife."

"Do you think it will help?"

He lifted his shoulders. "And you and I, Noelle . . . this makes no difference to my feelings for you. I have always been so fond of you. We must keep in touch. If there is anything you need, I shall always be at hand. Remember that. This makes no difference to my feelings for you."

"Nor mine for you."

"If you need money . . ."

"I don't. Robert has left me this house . . .

and money, too. Marie-Christine, his great-
niece, lives with me. I think it will be permanently. When she lost her family, I was the
only one she could turn to. She, too, is comfortably off. It was fortunate that we were already
good friends."

"I am glad she is with you. As I was saying
. . . if there is anything you need . . . at any
time . . ."

"We do not need that sort of help, Charlie.
But thank you. You have been wonderful . . .
as always."

"It is so good to see you again, Noelle . . .
and here in this house . . ."

"So full of memories," I said.

"Is it good for you to be here?"

"I really don't know what is good for me. I
am hoping that I may discover what I should
do."

"I wish . . . how I wish . . ."

"And I, too, Charlie."

Marie-Christine came in and I introduced
them. She knew who he was and I guessed she
was speculating what the outcome of his visit
would be.

She had a youthful belief that miracles
could happen and, as ever, I was touched by
her determination not to accept the present
state of affairs.

She believed that something wonderful was

going to happen, and to a certain extent for a time she carried me along with her.

•

It was three days later. I was in my room when Jane came to tell me that Mr. Claverham had called and was in the drawing room.

I wondered what had brought Charlie back so soon and hurried down. Roderick was there.

"Noelle!" he cried.

I ran to him. He put his arms round me and held me tightly.

"I had to come," he said. "My father told me."

"Yes."

"It was cruel. What on earth . . . ?"

"Don't blame her, Roderick. She did it out of love and care for me. We discovered by accident. Sometimes I think it would have been better if we had not. It seems so much worse."

"I have missed you," he said.

I could not bear the sadness in his eyes and I turned away.

"What shall we do?" he asked desperately.

"What can we do? You married . . ."

"It is no real marriage. Why did I do it? She was so wretchedly unhappy. Her career gone, her life broken. I feared for her . . . and on impulse . . . I knew as soon as I had spoken that I had made a terrible mistake. I might have helped . . . I could have looked after her, but . . ."

"I understand, Roderick. We had parted. We both saw we had to do that. And all the time those letters were in the bureau. I can't bear to think of what might have been."

He said: "There must be some way."

"We should not see each other," I said.

"I want to be with you. I want to talk to you. It is no longer there . . . that insurmountable barrier. It gives me a sense of freedom. I can't help feeling that, now that is no longer there, there must be hope."

"Lisa," I said. "She is there."

"We might come to some agreement."

"She is very ill. She must be suffering a great deal."

He did not answer for a few moments.

Then he said: "Noelle, we must talk."

"Let us go out," I answered. "Let us sit in the park as we used to. I want to be out, Roderick. At any moment we shall be interrupted. Marie-Christine, who lives here with me, will come in. She will want to meet you. I want to be somewhere where we can be alone."

"I just want to talk . . . anywhere."

"Wait. I will get a coat."

I felt it was safe out of doors. In the drawing room the temptation to be close to each other was too great to be resisted. I had to remember all the time that he was Lisa's husband.

We walked to Green Park, where we had often sat together. I kept thinking of those occasions when Lisa joined us. We sat on the seat where we had been in happier times.

"Tell me what has happened to you, Noelle," he said. "You know what happened to me. I married. If only I had waited. Why did I do such a thing?"

I said: "I went to France with Robert Bouchère. I met his nephew. Marie-Christine is his daughter. Her father, grandmother and Robert were all blown up in their Paris house during the siege. That left Marie-Christine with me, and she has been with me ever since."

"My father has told me something of this. We knew you were in France, and were all terribly worried about you."

"I could have been in the Paris house. Marie-Christine and I happened to be in the country."

He took my hand and pressed it. "I can't bear to think that you could have been in such danger."

"I was thinking of you all the time," I told him.

"You must understand about Lisa."

"I do. You were filled with pity for her. You thought we had lost each other . . . and that you could put things right for her by marrying her."

"I had lost you. I thought it would be the best for her . . . and it would be someone for me to look after . . . to care for."

"We were both trying to make a new life for ourselves. Marie-Christine's father asked me to marry him."

"And you would have done so if he had not been killed?"

"I don't know. I always held back. I couldn't make up my mind. He was an artist . . . a good one. I think if I could have forgotten you, I could have been tolerably happy with Gérard."

"But you could not forget me?"

"No, Roderick, I couldn't . . . and I never shall."

"We must do something."

"What?"

"I shall ask Lisa to release me."

"You married her out of pity. Can you leave her now?"

"She must understand."

"Roderick, I don't think you can ask her."

"She should be made comfortable for the rest of her life."

"She wouldn't do it. She wants you with her."

"But I am rarely with her now. I keep away as much as I can. Before I came up here, I was planning to go to Scotland. At least I should be away for a time."

"How long would you stay there?"

He shrugged his shoulders. "I just have to get away from Leverson now and then. That is what I planned to do. A cousin runs the estate up there. He is in some difficulties. I thought I would go up there to help sort things out. It was an excuse. I had to get away. You cannot imagine what it is like."

"I think I can."

"My mother dislikes Lisa, and makes no secret of it. I think they hate each other. She is convinced that Lisa is an opportunist and schemed to marry me. She knows, of course, that your mother helped her and Lisa acted as her understudy. She thinks she brings disaster, and there is something evil about her. I can tell you, ours is a household of despair. Sometimes I feel the urge to get away, which was what I was planning to do. Now this has come to light, I felt there must be something we can do."

"She will not let you go, Roderick."

"I shall talk to her . . . and to my parents. I will tell her that there is a way out. If only she will let me go. We can divorce. Lisa must see it is best for us all. She can't be happy. In fact, I know she is not. She will see that this is the best way."

I was not sure.

We sat talking for a long time. We could not

help looking to a future which would be ours. There would be difficulties to overcome but we would overcome them.

So we sat and planned. We thrust aside our uncertainties. We needed some comfort, and talking gave that to us. We made ourselves see a future which we had believed was lost to us forever.

•

It was impossible to keep Roderick's return a secret from Marie-Christine. She had heard that Mr. Claverham had visited us . . . *young* Mr. Claverham . . . and she was waiting for me on my return.

She pounced on me. "You look different," she cried. "Something's happened. What? What? Roderick! He's back."

"Yes," I said. "He came here."

"Where is he?"

"He's gone."

"Gone? But why? What did he say? He knows he is not your brother now. Isn't it wonderful? Meningarth and all that. If *I* hadn't found the letters . . ."

"Yes, you were wonderful, Marie-Christine," I said.

"Well, what is going to happen now?"

"He is married, Marie-Christine."

"Well, what are you going to do?"

"I don't know."

"You do. I can see you do. Tell me. I have been in this, haven't I? *I* found the letters."

"You did. And you have been a good friend to me. But you know that we cannot marry now. He is married to Lisa."

"The one who fell down in front of your mother's carriage?"

"Yes."

"She stands in the way. Well, what is he going to do? I can see there are plans."

"He is going to ask her to give him his freedom."

"You mean divorce him? Oh, Noelle, how exciting!"

"I think it will be rather distressing."

"What a pity he did not wait until we had found the letters. Did he say he loved you and will forever? She will say yes, I suppose, and then it will all come right."

"I don't know, Marie-Christine. I don't think it will be as easy as that."

•

I thought about it over the days which followed. In fact, I thought of little else.

It was then that Roderick returned. I could not guess in those first moments what he had to tell, but I was all impatience to hear.

"She was deeply shocked when I explained everything to her," he said. "She was lying on her bed, as she often does, in a certain amount of discomfort. I told her how sorry I was. I explained about us and how it had always been and always would be. She knew, of course, and that at the time when I had asked her to marry me, I had thought marriage was impossible between us two. I told her about the discovery and who your father was, and how you had proof of this.

"She said: 'So now you could marry Noelle if you were not already married to me.' I told her that if she would release me, she would never have to worry about the future again. She should be well looked after. She could have the best possible nursing. She should have complete comfort and lack nothing. She smiled very sadly then and said: 'Except you.' I said perhaps we could all be friends. It could all be easily managed. The formalities could be taken care of. There would be nothing for her to worry about. She listened, and closed her eyes, as though she were in pain.

"After a while she said: 'You have taken me by surprise. I have to think. I need time. Please give me time. You are going to Scotland. Go there . . . and when you come back I will give you an answer. I shall know then whether I can go through with what you suggest.'"

"So she has not refused."

"No. I realize this was a shock to her. It is natural, I suppose, that she cannot bring herself to decide at once. So it is a matter of waiting.

We have to have Lisa's agreement. If we do, it can be done without too much difficulty. I feel sure she will see it is the best way for us all."

"Roderick, you seem so sure."

"I am. Lisa is fond of you. She used to talk of you, always with affection. Many times she has said she will never forget what your mother did for her. She knows she is never going to walk properly again. She knows that she can only get worse. Our marriage has never been a real one. I am sure she will see that there is only one thing for her to do. She won't stand in our way. She is not the evil woman my mother makes her out to be."

"And your parents . . . do they know of this?"

"I have told them. My father thinks it is a solution. All we need is for Lisa to agree."

"And your mother?"

"She is very pleased. You know, when you and I thought we were going to marry, we had her approval . . . in spite of her original attitude towards you. I was amazed, and so was my father. But she had such respect for you. She was eager to welcome you into the family."

"You seem full of hope."

"I must be. Anything else would be unendurable . . . particularly now that we know it need never have happened."

"Then all we can do is wait."

He took my hand and kissed it.

"It is going to be all right, Noelle. I know it. It has to be," he said.

•

I could think of nothing but what was happening at Leverson Manor. Roderick would have left for Scotland. Lisa would be grappling with herself, wondering whether she could do what Roderick asked of her. Lady Constance would be hoping to be rid of her son's wife, whom she hated for a number of reasons. She would perhaps be thinking of me and the time when we were together in Neptune's temple. If Lisa agreed to what Roderick asked, if the divorce could be discreetly arranged, we could settle down to a new life.

To my amazement, I received a letter from Lisa.

My dear Noelle [she wrote],
I do want to see you. I want to talk to you. Roderick has told me everything. It came as a shock to learn that you are not Charlie's daughter and have proof of this, and that there was no impediment to your marriage with Roderick.

I am in a poor state of health. There is perpetual discomfort. I can't stay in one position for long. Roderick has done everything to make me comfortable here, but it is not easy. It is a wonderful place to be. I have found great interest in the Roman remains and Fiona and

510·   Victoria Holt

her husband have been good friends to me.
One of them often comes to see me. I should
have to give up all that if I went away.

Well, there is so much I want to say to you.
I want you to understand. Could you come,
not just for a brief weekend, but to stay a little
while? I want to talk . . . and talk. I remember so much of the old days and everything
that led up to this.

I am in difficulties, Noelle. Do please come.

I was deeply moved when I read the letter. I
wondered what she could have to say to me.
She had to make her decision. I could understand how she had formed an attachment to
Leverson Manor. It was a fine old place, and
she had the friendship of Fiona. I knew she
would have compassion for her and, as she had
acquired an interest in Fiona's own passion for
archaeology, there would have been a bond between them. Lisa must be considering going
away, to some remote place . . . away from
Roderick, whom I believed she had always
loved. It was asking a great deal of her.

But to go to Leverson Manor! The idea both
excited and alarmed me.

I wrote back to her:

Dear Lisa,
Thank you for your letter. I am sorry to
hear of your suffering. I know what Roderick
is asking you, and I do realize you find it hard
to make a quick decision.

I should like to talk to you, but hesitate to come to Leverson Manor without an invitation from Lady Constance. Moreover, I have a young girl living with me, Marie-Christine du Carron. I was with her in France. She is Robert's great-niece and she lost her family in the siege of Paris. I could not leave her.

My love and sympathy,

Noelle

The response was another letter. This was from Lady Constance.

My dear Noelle,

We have thought of you a good deal since you left us. I was very sad to see you go in such circumstances.

Lisa has told me that she wants to talk to you, and that it is important to her that she does so. I think it might be helpful if she did. She says that you need an invitation from me.

My dear, I should be delighted to see you. Neither my husband nor I can see that any harm could come to the position at the moment by your coming here.

It may well be that you can persuade Lisa as to what she should do for all our sakes.

So please come, and bring Marie-Christine with you. You will both be welcome.

Affectionately,

Constance Claverham

• • •

The carriage was waiting for us at the station.

I had never thought to see Leverson again, and how strange it was to be riding through those Kentish lanes.

We had turned into the drive, and went under the gatehouse into the courtyard.

Marie-Christine's eyes were round with amazement.

"What a splendid place!" she cried. "It is like a castle."

I was pleased that she liked it. I felt as though I were part of it. Such had been Roderick's optimism that I could convince myself that it might well be my home one day.

As we passed through the hall, with its pistols and blunderbusses, I remembered the apprehension I had felt when Charlie had first brought me here.

"Lady Constance says that you are to be taken to the drawing room as soon as you arrive," I was told.

We followed the maid, though I knew the way.

In the drawing room she was waiting. Charlie was with her.

"My dear Noelle," he murmured and, taking my hand, kissed my cheek.

Lady Constance came forward. She kissed me, too.

"My dear," she said. "I am glad to see you. And this is Marie-Christine?"

Marie-Christine was a little overawed, which was rare with her, but such was the personality of Lady Constance.

"You will have your old room," said Lady Constance to me. "And Marie-Christine will be next to you. I thought you would like to be close." She turned to Marie-Christine. "This is rather a large house, and people are apt to get lost just at first."

"It is beautiful!" cried Marie-Christine. "And very grand."

Lady Constance smiled graciously.

"I am looking forward to hearing all your news," she said to me. "But now I am sure you are tired after your journey. It is a pity the train arrives so late. But you can change before dinner. Would you like to go to your rooms now?"

I said I thought that would be best.

"I hope you will be comfortable," said Lady Constance.

She rang a bell and a maid appeared.

"Take our guests to their rooms, please, and make sure they have everything they need," said Lady Constance. "And, Noelle, my dear . . . say half an hour? That will give us a little time before dinner is served."

"Thank you very much."

It was all very conventional and normal. No one would have guessed of the drama behind my visit. This was typical of Lady Constance. I felt my spirits rising. Her welcome had been warm in the extreme . . . for her. I was reminded of the reception I had received when I first came to this house.

Marie-Christine was in a state of high excitement. She loved what she called adventure and this was certainly in that category . . . as exciting to her as our trip to Cornwall.

The room looked just as it was when I was last in it. I went to see Marie-Christine in hers. She was delighted with it and all eager anticipation, waiting for what would happen next.

I washed and changed and, with Marie-Christine, went downstairs. Lady Constance was waiting for us. Marie-Christine's presence prevented any intimate conversation, and it was not until after dinner, when Charlie took Marie-Christine off to see the house, that I was alone with Lady Constance.

She said: "I am very happy to have you here. I was sad when you went away. It was a great pity Roderick married. I was very much against it."

"And what about Lisa?" I asked. "Is her trouble incurable? Is there no hope for her?"

"None. She has permanently injured her spine. Roderick has brought in all the leading men in the country. The verdict is always the same. She will remain an invalid, and it is very likely that the condition will grow worse."

"What a terrible prospect for her!"

"And for Roderick. But let us hope there may be a way out."

"It is so tragic for her," I said. "She was so ambitious, and she was getting on well in her profession."

"I do not know about that, but she is here . . . as Roderick's wife. I had hoped . . . you and I could have got along very well together, Noelle."

"I am sure we should."

"I hope I may say I am sure we shall. We've got to make her see reason, Noelle."

"But what is reason for us might not be for her. She is being asked for a great deal."

"She *must* agree. We are going to use all our efforts to persuade her."

"When can I see her?"

"Tomorrow. She has had a bad day today. She does have them. The pain is great then. The doctor has prescribed pills for her. They are quite effective. They are always at hand, but she can't take too many at a time, of course. I think six is the maximum for the whole day. She has to be careful to use them only when she really needs them. When the pain is very bad, she will take two. She had four yesterday, they tell me."

"It sounds dreadful."

"One can be sorry for her."

Charlie returned with Marie-Christine. Her

eyes were round with wonder. "It is the most exciting house!" she cried. "It's very ancient, isn't it, Mr. Claverham?"

"There are older ones in England," said Charlie.

"I don't believe there is one as exciting as this."

Lady Constance's lips twitched with amusement and pleasure. She was always pleased, I remembered, when people appreciated the house. I was glad Marie-Christine was making a good impression.

When it was time for us to retire, I went to Marie-Christine's room to see that she was all right.

"It's nice to be next door to you," she said. "I reckon there are ghosts in this old place."

"Well, if one visits you, all you have to do is knock on the wall and I'll come in to share the company."

She giggled with pleasure. I was so pleased to see her happy and contented.

I went to my room, and it was not very long before there was a gentle tap on my door. I called: "Come in," and, to my pleasure, there was Gertie, the maid who had looked after me when I was last here.

"I've come to see you've got everything you want, miss," she said.

"Gertie! I'm so glad to see you. How are you?"

"Not so bad, miss. How's yourself? And you've brought this young lady with you."

"Yes." I told her: "Marie-Christine lost her family during the war in France and is now living with me."

She looked shocked. "I was ever so sad when you went, miss," she said. "Everybody here was."

"Yes, it was very sad. Do you see much of Mrs. Claverham?"

"Oh yes, miss. I look after her in a way. She . . . er . . . don't seem to fit here . . . her being an actress nobody's ever heard of . . . not like Désirée . . . and being a cripple. Well, she can be a bit touchy at times. It's nothing like it was here."

"And Lady Constance—she is . . . all right with you now?"

"She don't take much notice of me. She don't pick on me. I'll never forget that bust. I reckon I'd have been out of this place in no time if you hadn't took the blame for it. I often think of that and what you done for me."

"It was nothing, Gertie."

"It was to me. We've got a new girl here now. Mabel . . . a sort of tweeny . . . learning and doing all the jobs nobody wants to do. I'd say she was a ha'p'orth short, if you ask me."

"Do you mean she's a little simple?"

"I'd say. And not a little. I'm the one that's

got to keep an eye on her. Will you be staying here long, miss?"

"I don't think so. It's just a short visit. I've really come to see Mrs. Claverham."

"She's ill most of the time. You never know how she's going to be. Well . . . her being crippled like that. Perhaps you'll be able to cheer her up."

"I hope so," I said.

"Well, if there's anything you want, just ring. I'll say good night. Have a good sleep."

I doubted I should. My mind was in too much of a turmoil.

•

The next day I saw Lisa. She was lying in bed, propped up by pillows. She had changed a good deal, and I was shocked by her appearance.

"Oh, Noelle," she said. "I am so glad you have come. What a lot has happened since we last met. You have not changed much. I know I have."

"Poor Lisa! I was horrified when I heard of your accident."

"All my hopes . . . all my dreams of greatness . . . gone, and because of a faulty trapdoor. I fell seven feet onto a concrete floor. I could have broken my neck. It could have finished me altogether . . . instead of finishing my career." Her voice broke. "Perhaps it would have been better if it had."

I had taken a seat by her bed, and put my hand over hers. I said: "You wanted to see me."

"Oh yes. I did. I have for a long time . . . and now this. You are involved in it. In fact, our lives seem to have been involved ever since we met. It's fate. Roderick has told me he always loved you. It was terrible, the way it had to end . . . and all the time it wasn't true. Why did she do that to you?"

"It was all clear in her letters. She wanted to make sure that I was well looked after if anything happened to her. She had suffered during her own childhood, and she was determined that I should not be with people who did not want me. Charlie was rich. My real father was a poor man. She thought he could not give me all she wanted me to have."

"I understand that. She was splendid. She would never let life lead her. She would guide it the way she wanted it to go. But that time it went wrong."

"It was because she died so suddenly. If she had known that Roderick and I were seeing each other . . . if she had seen the possibility . . . she would have explained everything. But she died . . . so suddenly . . ."

"I thought she was the most wonderful person I had ever met."

"You were not the only one who thought that."

"And when she died . . . so unexpectedly . . ." Her face twisted, and her voice shook with emotion. "When I heard what had happened, it was the most horrifying moment of my life. She had done everything for me. No one had ever been so kind to me before."

We were silent for a few moments.

"And now," she went on, "I am asked to give up my husband and my home. Oh, Noelle, I have been happier here than I could be anywhere else. Roderick was so kind to me. I felt safe and secure, for the first time in my life."

"He wanted to help you."

"When it happened, I was completely desolate . . . without hope. I did not know which way to turn. I had saved a little money, but it would not last long. I had no idea what would happen to me. I was finished. I was desperate. I felt there was nothing left for me but to die. I thought of taking my life. He knew this. He is very sensitive. He is a good, kind man. He cares about people. He tried to cheer me up . . . and then suddenly he asked me to marry him. I could not believe it at first. But he meant it."

"He understood what you were going through."

"As no one else did. I could not believe it. It seemed like the greatest good fortune. It was a sudden change from despair to happiness. I think I was a little light-headed. I knew that he was still in love with you. But I thought: They can't marry. Noelle will in time marry someone else. They have to forget each other. I will make him love me. I kept saying to myself: Brother and sister can't marry. It's against the law. It's against nature. There is no reason why I shouldn't marry him. I wouldn't have hurt you for the world, Noelle. I shall never forget what you and your mother did for me. But it made no difference. You couldn't marry him, could you? Or then you couldn't."

"Don't reproach yourself, please."

She lay back on her pillows, her eyes closed.

I said: "You are distressing yourself, Lisa. You must not do that."

"I feel so tired sometimes. Worn out with the pain and not knowing what I must do. You are not leaving yet, are you?"

"No. I shall be here for a little while."

"Come and see me again . . . when I feel better. We'll be able to talk more then. I had a bad day yesterday. It takes me time to recover. I am so tired."

"Rest now," I said. "I will come and see you soon . . . and when you feel better, we'll talk."

•

Marie-Christine was eager to see the site, and in the afternoon I took her there. There was a certain amount of activity in progress. Some excavations were still going on and there were a few visitors.

Fiona greeted us warmly. She introduced us to the young man who was working with her, Jack Blackstock, her husband. He was very pleasant and, I immediately perceived, as earnest about the work they were doing as she was.

"There have been some changes here lately," said Fiona. "The discovery of the temple attracted a great deal of attention."

Marie-Christine asked several questions and there was nothing that delighted Fiona more, as I knew from the past, than other people's interest in the work she was doing. This was a trait she shared with her husband.

Enthusiastically they showed Marie-Christine some of the artifacts, explaining how they were attempting to restore them. And after a while Fiona said we must see the temple.

My memories were stirred as we descended a slight incline. A few steps had been dug out of the earth to make the descent easy, and there we were standing on the stone floor on which I had once sat with Lady Constance, wondering whether our last moments were at hand.

The floor was tessellated in places, and some of the colours were quite beautiful. Fiona said they were in the process of being cleaned and she thought the result would be fantastic. We were confronted by a large figure with enough remaining to indicate that it was Neptune. The distinguishing trident was almost intact, and the bearded face was very little damaged. One of the legs was broken, but Fiona said one could imagine it as it had undoubtedly been.

Marie-Christine was eager to see the baths, and Fiona suggested that Jack take her right away to see them while she and I returned to the cottage to chat over old times while we waited for their return.

I was delighted at the prospect, for I thought Fiona might be able to tell me something about the situation at Leverson Manor.

"I'll give you some coffee when you come back," Fiona promised Jack and Marie-Christine.

Marie-Christine was enjoying this, and I was delighted by her interest in everything.

On the way back to the cottage, I explained to Fiona why Marie-Christine was with me, and I told her a little about my stay in France.

She listened with great interest and expressed her deep sorrow, which I knew was sincere.

I said: "And you, Fiona, how have you been since I left?"

"Well, I married, of course."

"And you are happy?"

"Sublimely so. We are both so wrapped up in all this . . . and for years my grandmother was a great anxiety to me."

"She is still in that nursing home?"

"Yes. She is happy enough there. She lives in a dream world. She is very popular with the others there . . . telling their fortunes, predicting the future. I daresay it makes their lives a little more interesting."

"Does she mind being there?"

"I think she is only just aware of reality. She likes to be surrounded by people whom she can dominate in a way . . . which she has done through what she calls her 'powers.' "

"Does she remember about the warning notice she took away?"

"Oh, what a terrible thing that was! You might have been killed . . . both you and Lady Constance. She forgets all that. She is now immersed in the lives of her fellow companions. Sometimes she seems to have forgotten who I am. It has lifted a great strain from me. And now that Jack and I are together, everything is quite different. I am so lucky. Of course, removing the warning sign was the last straw. That was when I knew she had to be put away. It is strange how something really frightful like that can result in something good."

I thought of Lady Constance and myself down there, and how barriers had been swept away, and we had come to an understanding of each other.

"Discovering the temple," Fiona was saying. "What a wonderful thing that was! And that brought Jack down here and, well . . . it just went on from there."

"I am glad some good came out of it."

"And when I think of what the result might have been!"

"But it disclosed the temple," I said with a smile. "And it brought Jack down here. It also brought home the fact that your grandmother should be under supervision. Fiona, what is it like at Leverson Manor? You go there, don't you?"

"Yes, occasionally I go to see poor Lisa. What a terrible tragedy that is!"

"The accident ruined her career, but because of it she married Roderick."

Fiona shook her head. She looked at me intently and said: "It is a sad household."

"It seems so."

"You went so suddenly. I thought that Roderick and you . . ."

"Have you heard nothing, then?"

"One hears rumours. One never is sure what to believe. Lady Constance never liked me, but she is mildly friendly now. She thought I was after Roderick because he was interested in the site. She did not like that." She smiled. "Well, that little matter is settled now. I go to see Lisa. She came here once or twice before she became so incapacitated. She was always so interested. I take things over to show her sometimes. I think she looks forward to the visits."

"Do you know why I went away so suddenly?"

"Well, I did hear that you were the result of an indiscretion of Charlie Claverham's; you were going to marry Roderick and you found you were brother and sister."

"That was why I went, Fiona."

"So it was true?"

"No. We thought so . . . and that was why I went. But now I have proof that I am not Charlie's daughter."

"And so . . . you have come back . . ."

"Lisa asked me to. I don't know what will happen."

"I see. I know Roderick is not happy. Nor is Lisa. She does not tell me a great deal, but she has mentioned how wonderful Roderick is . . . how sympathetic and how she did not know which way to turn, and it was like the ending to a fairy tale when Roderick asked her to marry him and brought her to the luxury of Leverson Manor."

"I shall not stay here long," I said. "I only came because Lisa asked me to. I was given a very warm welcome."

"Lady Constance has taken to you. That's rare. She likes so few."

"We had that adventure together."

"What is going to happen now, Noelle?"

"I don't know."

"Poor Lisa. She suffers great pain. I often

think of her lying there. She has told me she had dreams . . . of greatness. She talks a lot about your mother. She seems to have an obsession about her. She has said more than once that her ambition was to be another Désirée. She said she could have done it if fate had not been so cruel to her. But at least now she does not have to worry about the future. It is secure, and that means a lot to her."

"Poor . . . poor Lisa."

"And you and Roderick, too."

"I shall have to go away," I said.

"What shall you do?"

"So far I have made no plans."

"You should throw yourself into some work."

"As you do," I said.

"It's the best thing, Noelle. Sometimes we need crutches in our lives."

I heard steps outside the cottage. Jack and Marie-Christine were coming back.

●

Marie-Christine's interest had been captured by the Roman relics, which produced that irrepressible enthusiasm so typical of her.

At the same time, she was anxious about my future.

She needed something to happen all the time. I supposed it took her mind off her loss. It was not that she had been especially close to any of her family, but they had been part of the life from which she had been roughly torn.

I understood and wondered if I had been wise to let her into so many secrets; but at the time it had seemed essential to tell her these things, as she was indeed sharing my life. Young as she was, she had a certain worldliness which was combined with the innocence of the inexperienced, and this showed itself now and then.

She wanted events to move and expected them to. She marvelled that we had solved what we had set out to do in Cornwall. She had been exhilarated by the adventure. Now she was expecting further action.

She said to me: "Is Lisa going to divorce him? I do hope she does. Then we shall come and live here. I love this house. It is so exciting. A bit scary at times, when you think of all those ghosts. But I like that. It makes it interesting. Then there are the Roman bits, and Fiona and Jack. I'd love to live here."

I could see that, characteristically, she was sweeping away all obstacles. She saw Lisa quietly retiring and ourselves coming to live here in this fascinating place which had intrigued her active imagination.

"You are going too fast, Marie-Christine," I said. "We don't know what is going to happen."

"But you've seen her. You've talked to her.

You've told her that we found the letters and you can marry Roderick now."

"It's not as easy as that. You've got to . . ."

"I know," she said roguishly, "wait and see."

"Yes. Please remember that."

"But it is going to be all right. This is such a lovely place. I like Roderick. I like Fiona. I like Jack."

"I'm glad you do," I replied. "But that does not affect the problem."

"So it is back to the old 'wait and see.' Jack has promised to show me an old spoon that was dug up. It is a spoon at one end and a spike at the other. The Romans used it for getting fish out of their shells, which shows they liked this sort of fish which were found off the shore of ancient Britain."

"You are becoming very knowledgeable."

"I think it is all . . . fascinating. I'm going over there now. They said I could. Are you coming?"

"I'll join you later."

Marie-Christine had only just gone when a maid came to my room to tell me that Lady Constance would like to see me.

I went at once to her room.

"Oh, do come in, Noelle," she said. "I did want to have a chat in private. I see the girl has gone off. She is a bright creature, but a very inquisitive one."

"Yes, that is so."

"It is like you to look after her."

"She would not like to hear you say that. She thinks she is looking after me."

"Noelle . . . this state of affairs . . . it cannot go on. You know that I should like to see you here . . . permanently."

"Lady Constance . . ."

"I know, I know. You cannot stay here in the present circumstances. It would be too much. I understand. But you must not go yet."

"As you say, I cannot see how I could stay here . . ."

"Do you remember when we were in that place together?"

"I could never forget it."

"I wasn't thinking so much of the fear of death, but of what we said to each other."

"I think of that, too."

"We became friends. It was rather miraculous. In such a short space of time, we came to know each other."

"It was the circumstances. When people are facing death they may discard barriers."

"That was what I did. I discarded barriers which I had built up over the years. It was good for my soul. It showed me myself . . . my foolish mistakes."

"We all make foolish mistakes."

"I have made so many. I think in a way they cost me my husband. He turned to others."

"You mean my mother. I think you should remember that she was an exceptional woman. Many people were in love with her."

"She could have spoiled your life."

"Unwittingly. How unhappy she would be if she could know what she had done . . . how angry with herself! She wanted everything that was good for me."

"She was a strong woman. To deceive Charlie like that! Of course, he was in a position to be deceived. You know how I was tormented over the years about that."

"I know, and I am sorry."

"It was foolish of me. He is a good man at heart. He wanted to be a good husband, and he was in other respects. When you and I were down there talking . . . things became so clear to me, and I saw that often what happens to us is our own fault. 'Not in our stars, but in ourselves,' as Shakespeare says."

"I think there is truth in that. I hope you will be happier now."

"I could be . . . if I thought Roderick was happy. But he is far from that . . . at this time," she added. "If she were no longer here. If you came back . . . you and I together, Noelle, we could make this into a more contented household than it has ever been."

"If . . ." I said. "A great deal would have to happen before that could be."

"You love him, don't you? You love Roderick?"

"Yes."

"I knew you did . . . before . . . I was putting other things before love, but now I know how stupid I was. As your mother wanted the best for you, I want the best for my son."

"I know you wanted a grand marriage for him. Don't reproach yourself. It was natural."

"Now I want him to have a happy marriage, and because you love him and he loves you, only you can give him that."

"Yes . . . but . . ."

"She will have to go, Noelle. She *must*. She cannot remain here ruining so many people's lives." It was the indomitable Lady Constance speaking. The softness I had glimpsed was gone. She went on: "There is something evil about her. She manipulates. How did she get her chance on the stage? Charlie told me. It was by falling under your mother's carriage. How did she get into this household? By appealing to Roderick's pity."

I said: "She did fall under the carriage. I was there when it happened."

"She must have arranged it, as she arranged to trap Roderick. I am determined that she shall go. She has asked to see you. She said she wanted to talk to you. I thought that was a hopeful sign. Noelle, she must give Roderick up. She will be looked after. A sum of money will be settled on her. She need have no more fear . . . if only she will get out of this house."

"She may refuse."

"She must not be allowed to. Talk to her, Noelle. You talked to me once, did you not? And look what a difference that made!"

"Roderick has talked to her and she has said she will decide soon. It is not a matter about which she can be expected to make a hasty judgement."

"Talk to her. I feel you can make her understand. She must agree."

"I will talk to her. In fact, she asked me to come here because she wanted to talk to *me*."

"I have every confidence in you, Noelle. Oh, how pleased I shall be when this is settled. I cannot tell you how I look forward to the future. I want you to be here. I want a chance to see my son happy. I want grandchildren and I should like you to be their mother. That is what I want more than anything. I want to be happy and at peace in my old age. Noelle, my dear, I shall always be grateful to you for showing me the folly of my ways."

"You endow me with virtues I don't possess."

"My dear, I am fond of you. Nothing will

satisfy me but that I see you here . . . where
you belong."

I was moved. Even now, it was surprising to
hear her talk in such a way.

There were tears in her eyes when she
kissed me.

•

Three days had passed. Marie-Christine went
to the cottage often. I asked them if she was
intruding.

"Far from it," said Fiona. "Jack is most
amused. We're giving her little jobs to do and
she seems to enjoy that."

Lady Constance and I were often together.
We would take walks in the gardens. She took
pleasure in showing me what she had done and
what she planned there for the future—as
though it were already my home. But on all
these occasions, the subject of Lisa was never
far from our minds. Lady Constance was convinced that Lisa would, as she called it, be sensible.

I was uncertain. I saw Lisa each day. She
was in a nervous state. I wondered why she had
been so insistent on seeing me when it seemed
that she had nothing special to say. But that
was not quite so, for there were occasions when
she seemed to be bracing herself, when she
would begin to talk earnestly, and then suddenly come to a halt. I tried to urge her to

continue, but it was no use. However, this did confirm my opinion that she had wanted to see me for a purpose which I should discover in time.

She talked of the place to which she would go if she gave Roderick his freedom. She brought this up several times.

I was with her one afternoon when Lady Constance was resting and Marie-Christine had gone off to the cottage. The house was quiet at this time of the day.

She said suddenly: "I love this house. It is the sort of house I always admired. When I was a child, I would dream of living in such a house. The Big House! I used to stand and stare at the Big House in our village. You could only see the walls and the bell tower, I remember. There was a clock up there. You could hear its chimes all over the village. I used to say: 'When I'm grown up I'll live in a house like that.' And here I am . . . in an even grander one. Who would believe it? And now they all want me to go away. Roderick wants me to go away; Lady Constance always has. She hates me and has from the moment I appeared." She laughed hysterically. "Her son . . . to marry an out-of-work actress!"

"You are distressing yourself, Lisa," I said.

"I'm saying the truth. Why should I leave here so that you can come in my place? You have had everything . . . a wonderful childhood . . . Désirée for a mother. Life isn't fair!"

"It never has been."

"Why do some have all the luck? Why do some of us have to stand aside and grab what we can get? Catching the crumbs which fall from the rich man's table!"

"I don't know, Lisa."

"Oh, dear. I suppose I should live in the sort of place they want to send me to . . . with a lot of people like myself . . . in various stages of decay."

"Don't say that, Lisa. I know you have suffered . . . that you still suffer. But there are times when you feel better."

"What do you know about it? How would you like to be . . . unwanted? To have a chance and, just when you happen to be on the way . . . this has to happen? I could have been another Désirée. I know it. And then this happens."

"I understand, Lisa. It was cruel."

"But I was slapped down . . . cut off . . . just when I had a chance." She was staring ahead of her, and I saw the tears on her cheeks. I longed to comfort her.

"Then your mother . . ." she went on. "Fame and fortune were hers, and then . . . her life was cut off . . . without any warning."

She lay back and closed her eyes.

"Noelle," she whispered. "Pills."

There was a small cupboard by her bed, the top of which was used as a table. On this was a glass and a jug of water.

"Pills in cupboard," she said in a low voice. "Two. They dissolve in water."

I hastily poured out a tumbler of water and took the bottle of pills from the cupboard. I dropped two of them into the water.

She watched me. "They don't take long," she said.

In a few more seconds the pills were invisible. I gave the glass to her and she drank eagerly. Then I took the glass from her and placed it beside the jug.

She smiled at me wanly. "They work . . . fairly quickly," she said. "Very effective. I'll be better soon."

I took her hand and pressed it.

"Shouldn't have said that," she said. "You deserved what you had. She was so wonderful. What a tragedy! I never got over it."

"Don't talk," I said. "Rest."

"Come again soon. I have to talk to you."

"Is the pain better?"

"Getting better. Those pills are very strong."

I saw her features relax a little. She still clung to my hand.

"Sorry, Noelle."

"I understand. I do . . . really."

She smiled.

I stayed with her until she was asleep. Then I crept quietly from the room.

•

At the end of the week Roderick and Charlie returned.

I shall never forget that Friday. It was the beginning of the nightmare weekend.

They did not come back until the evening, and in the afternoon I went to sit with Lisa.

As soon as I saw her I noticed that there was something different about her. There was a spot of colour in her cheeks and her eyes were unnaturally bright. I wondered if she had a fever.

She said: "I'm glad you've come, Noelle. I want to tell you what I have been trying to for a long time. Even now, I am wavering. I don't know whether it's right to tell you. Sometimes I think I should . . . at others that I should be a fool to do so."

"What is it, Lisa, you want to tell me? I know you have been on the point of doing so many times."

"It's your mother. I want to explain something. Take your mind back to that day we met."

"I remember it well."

"I contrived it. I arranged for your carriage to knock me down. I knew how to make it look like an accident. I knew how to fall. I was a dancer. I was agile . . . and I planned it carefully. I wanted to get your mother's attention. You don't seem very surprised."

"Well, I must admit that at times . . . I wondered. I wasn't sure. It could have been an accident . . . or arranged."

"You don't know what it is like . . . never getting a chance . . . seeing others shooting up ahead of you . . . not because they have more talent, but because they have the right friends. I had to get a chance. I knew your mother was generous. I knew she would be understanding. I knew she had a reputation for helping unlucky people. She was wonderful. All that I hoped for . . . and more."

"So it worked," I said. "You got your chance."

"I knew I could do it . . . if only I had the opportunity."

I looked at her steadily and said: "Caper spurge?"

"I . . . I knew something about herbs. You do, in the country . . . if you are interested in that sort of thing. Laburnum, Christmas rose, hellebore . . . there are lots of them. Caper spurge wouldn't cause much harm. There is a milky juice in the fruit . . . well, in all parts. It irritates your skin if it touches you, and it is a drastic purge. People recover quickly from it."

She must have seen the horror in my face,

for she turned away and said quickly: "I was sitting in the garden one day . . . on that wicker seat, and I was thinking that I should never get a chance to lift myself out of the chorus. And I saw it there, near me. I remembered it. And I thought: I want my chance now . . . while I'm young and able to take advantage of it. I thought: It will be now or never."

"You made her ill, so that you could go on in her place and have your chance! *She* had given you your chance . . . and you used her like that!"

"I know. I'm so worried. If only I had known what would happen. The opportunity was there. I thought I'd have it and there would be no harm done. It wouldn't make any difference to her to be off for a night or two. I didn't mean to harm her. I would never have touched it if I had known. It was so easy. I knew how to deal with the juice. When we came in after the show, either Martha or I would get her a drink. I got it that night. It was hot milk. She was always lively after a show. She wouldn't stop talking. She did not notice what she was drinking. She wasn't there. She was on the stage. She and Martha would go on and on about it. Noelle, it was only to make her indisposed . . . just for a night . . . so that I could go on in her place."

"It killed her," I said.

"I didn't kill her. I wouldn't have hurt her

for anything. I loved her. I did, really. Nobody had ever been so good to me as she was. It was only just to give me a chance . . ."

"She died!"

"How did I know she was going to get out of bed and feel dizzy? It was the fall that killed her . . . not what I had given her."

"It was because of what you had given her that she fell."

"I thought you would help to comfort me. I've suffered terribly. I dream about her. I never meant to hurt her."

"I heartily wish you had never come near us," I said.

"You are blaming me for her death."

"Of course I'm blaming you! If she had not brought you into the house, if she had not put you into the chorus, if she had not let you be her understudy . . . she would be alive to-day."

"I'm sorry I told you. I couldn't keep it to myself any longer. It's a great weight on my mind. I hoped that you would understand and help me."

"I understand you and your wretched ambition."

"She was ambitious, too. She lied about Charlie."

I wanted to get away from her. I stood up.

She said: "Wait. I have been through so much. You don't know how I blame myself.

She was good to me . . . no one had been so good before . . . no one ever did for me what she did. I didn't kill her. It has been on my conscience. I dream about it. It's horrible. I thought you'd help me. I thought you would understand."

I could not speak. I could only think of Désirée, and my longing to be with her was so intense that I hated this woman whose action—if indirectly—had taken my mother from me.

I should have tried to understand. I should have realized how desperately she wanted to succeed, and she thought that by merely causing a little discomfort to my mother, she could do so. My mother might have done the same, she would reason with herself. *She* would understand, and perhaps think it rather a joke. I could see Lisa's anguish, and I knew she was telling me the truth when she said how much she had suffered at the tragic turn of events.

Her face hardened. She was trying to suppress her feelings. She said: "I have been through a great deal, and I will no longer. I've paid for what I did to your mother. I was given my chance and I was unable to take advantage of it. It is dangerous to meddle with fate, to try to make life go the way you want it to to succeed. I meddled. It might seem that I had my chance . . . and now, look at me. Your mother did the same . . . and because of that, you lost Roderick. Life is laughing at us. You can understand that, Noelle. I have suffered too much, and I will no more. I shall not leave this house. I shall stay here. I will never, as long as I live, step aside for you. Roderick married me. He chose to do so. He was not forced into it. I shall not give him up. I shall not go and live in some nursing home like poor Mrs. Carling . . . just because I am in the way. This is my home, and I shall stay here."

I could bear no more.

I left her and went to my room.

•

I was terribly shaken by Lisa's revelation, and scarcely slept that night.

The next morning Dr. Doughty paid his periodic visit to Lisa. Lady Constance asked me if I would go up with him, as he liked someone to be there.

Lisa was lying in bed, propped up with pillows. She averted her eyes from me when I entered.

I said: "Dr. Doughty is here."

"Just the usual checkup, Mrs. Claverham," said the doctor. "How are you this morning?"

"Not very good."

"The same old pain in the same old place?"

She nodded, and he spent some time examining her back.

He grunted. "I have some good news," he said, when she was lying back in her pillows, "and I am optimistic . . . very optimistic. There has been a breakthrough in spinal problems. It's an operation, followed by special treatment. I reckon it will be perfected in a few months' time. And then, my dear Mrs. Claverham, I think we could look forward to a change in your condition."

"What would it mean?" asked Lisa eagerly.

"Well, I can't promise you that you will be doing the high kick, or whatever you call it, but you would be able to walk with ease, and there would be a lessening of the accursed pain."

"It sounds wonderful."

"It could be. We'll soldier on, eh? And perhaps in six months' time . . ."

"I can't take it in! I thought this was forever."

"*Nil desperandum,* dear lady. I think you have a very good chance."

Lisa looked at me; her eyes were shining. "Isn't that wonderful news, Noelle?"

"It is indeed."

In that moment she reminded me of the girl I had seen in bed immediately after the carriage accident.

"Perhaps I should have a word with Lady Constance," said Dr. Doughty.

He took Lisa's hand. "Rest assured," he said, "that I shall get more details of what this entails, and when I have them, I shall be along. I am sure this news will be as good as a tonic to

you. By the way, have you plenty of painkill-
ers?"

She looked towards the cupboard, and he
opened the door and took out the bottle, opening it. "You're all right for a few days. Remember, never more than two at a time. I'll send
some along next week. You'll be all right till
then. Effective, aren't they? Well, let's hope before long you won't be needing them."

He said goodbye and I took him to Lady
Constance and left them together.

When he had gone, I went to Lady Constance.

"The doctor has told me," she said. "He
thinks she can be cured, if only partially."

"Yes, he told us so."

"I wonder what this will mean."

"I think it will make her more determined
not to give in. She told me yesterday that she
would never do so."

"We must persuade her."

"I don't think anyone can do that."

"One person should not be allowed to ruin
so many lives."

"She clings to Roderick. She clings to this
place. She cannot visualize a life without
them."

"So much is at stake."

"For her, as well as for us."

"My dear Noelle, think what this means."

"I think of little else."

"She *must* understand."

"She has suffered a great deal," I said. And from that moment, my hatred of her, for what she had done to my mother, began to evaporate. It was swamped by my pity for this unloved, bewildered girl.

•

Later that day, when Roderick returned with Charlie, he immediately went to Lisa. It was clear when he emerged that he was plunged in melancholy. I guessed why. She had given him his answer.

I was with Lady Constance and Charlie when he joined us.

"She insists that she is going to get better," he said. "The doctor has told her that he has every hope of this."

"That is true," said Lady Constance. "He told us that it may be possible in quite a short time . . . perhaps not a complete cure, but it could improve her condition considerably."

"That is good news for Lisa," said Roderick. "I only hope it is true. It would help her a lot. She is naturally elated by the prospect. But at the same time, she is determined not to release me—and I know her well enough to understand that she means what she says. I don't know whether this has made a difference to her decision."

I said: "She told me before the doctor came hat she had made up her mind."

"She must be persuaded to change it," said Lady Constance.

"I am not sure that that is possible," said Roderick.

"I think I should go back to London," I put in.

"Oh no!" cried Roderick.

"I must. I can't stay here. I should not have come."

Yet I had come because she asked me. She had had a compulsion to confess. Poor Lisa! She was as unhappy as the rest of us. And now she was determined to cling to what she had. She was not going to stand aside. She had shown that. I knew in my heart that nothing I could say would deter her.

"What a disaster we have made of things," murmured Charlie. "Is there no way out?"

"We have to see it from her point of view," I said, surprising myself, when I remembered the waves of hatred which had come over me when she had confessed that she was responsible for my mother's death. I understood so well her obsession with her career. Had I not had an example with my mother? She had thought she could pick something out of the ruins and be happy. And then . . . this. I believed she would never relinquish what she had salvaged.

"I must go," I said. "It will be best for ev eryone."

"Where will you go, Noelle?" asked Char- lie.

"Back to London . . . for a while. I shall see what I can do. I have Marie-Christine. We will try to do something together."

"I can't give up hope," said Roderick.

"Nor I," added Lady Constance.

•

That night Marie-Christine came to my room.

She said: "Why is there all this gloom?"

"We are going back to London."

"When?"

"On Monday. We can't go tomorrow be- cause the trains don't run on Sundays, other- wise . . ."

"Go back to London! In such a hurry and all! I can't. Jack is going to show me how to clean some pottery."

"Marie-Christine, we have to go."

"Why?"

"Never mind why. We have to go."

"When are we coming back?"

"I think we shall not come back."

"What do you mean?"

"You know something is going on."

"You mean about you and Roderick and Lisa?"

"Lisa is going to stay here."

"Stay married to Roderick?"

"You are too young to understand these things."

"You know nothing maddens me more than to be told that. Particularly when I understand perfectly."

"But it is true, Marie-Christine. Lisa is Roderick's wife and marriage is binding."

"Not always. Some people part."

"Well, in this case, Lisa is going to stay, and Roderick with her. That means that we must go away. There is no place for us here."

"It can't be! You are going to marry Roderick. We're going to live here. That is what we want."

"People don't always get what they want, Marie-Christine."

"I can't bear to go away. I love it here. I love Jack and Fiona . . . and it's so exciting. I love the Roman things. I want to learn about them. It has been wonderful. I don't want to go away, Noelle."

"I am sorry, Marie-Christine. It isn't going to work out. It may well be that Lisa is going to be cured. She and Roderick are married."

Marie-Christine's face was distorted with misery.

"It mustn't happen," she said vehemently. "It can't. There must be a way to make it come right."

"We can't always make things go the way

we want them to in life. That's what you learn as you get older."

"I don't believe it. We've got to *do* something."

Poor Marie-Christine! She had a great deal to learn.

•

It was afternoon, just after luncheon—a gloomy meal. I was ready to leave the next day, and Marie-Christine and I were preparing to visit Fiona and Jack to tell them of our imminent departure.

I was in my room, putting on my riding jacket, when Lady Constance came in.

She looked bewildered and distraught.

"A terrible thing has happened," she said. "Lisa is dead."

The Verdict

The days that followed had taken on a certain unreality. There were comings and goings, whispering voices everywhere. Dr. Doughty had no doubt what had killed her. It was an overdose of the pills which he had prescribed. He had frequently cautioned Lisa as to the strength of those pills. She had needed such an antidote because the pain she had suffered could be very fierce, but he had told her that she was never to take more than two at a time. She could in dire circumstances take as many as six a day—but he preferred her not to do that often—and if she did, they must be spaced out over a period of twenty-four hours.

The autopsy proved Dr. Doughty right. According to the amount of the drug found in her body, she must have taken at least six at one time—a fatal dose.

We were a silent household. The servants went about as though they were in some conspiracy. How much did they know? I wondered. They would be aware that I had once been engaged to Roderick and that I had gone away suddenly, the engagement broken off. Did they know that Roderick had asked for his freedom so that he might marry me? Did they know that Lisa had refused to give it?

Had anyone asked the question: had Lisa been murdered? When there was sudden death which might be murder, people looked for a motive.

Without doubt the motive was there. Roderick wanted to be rid of his wife. It was one of the commonest motives for murder. He had been in the house at the time of Lisa's death. So had I. And I was as deeply involved as he was.

Those were nightmare days with endless possibilities. I could only try to shut out the terrible thoughts which kept chasing themselves round and round in my mind.

I could not leave the house now. I had been there at the time of Lisa's death and should have to attend the inquest.

I don't know how I lived through that waiting period. I dreaded the inevitable inquest, while I longed for it to be over that I might know the worst. I remembered what had followed my mother's death. There would be no peace until it was over . . . and what would the verdict be?

Marie-Christine had become very aloof. I could not read her thoughts. Lady Constance shut herself in her room and did not want to talk to anyone. Charlie seemed bewildered. I think Roderick felt as I did. We wanted to be alone together, to talk of what was uppermost in our minds. But we were restrained. I sensed that we were being closely watched.

One day the impulse came to me to ride out. I felt I could get everything into a better perspective away from the house.

Roderick must have seen me leave and followed me.

I was sure he was as eager to get away from the house as I was.

I was about a mile away from the house when he caught up with me.

"Noelle," he said. "We have to talk. We've got to say what's in our minds. How did it happen?"

"She must have taken it herself."

"But she thought she was going to get better."

"I know, but she was not happy."

"You don't think that I . . . ?"

"Roderick! Oh . . . no, no!"

"I had asked her to release me and she had refused."

"I know we wanted it to happen, Roderick. But not that way."

"If it were known . . . it would seem . . ."

"It is true that we wanted her to give you your freedom so that we could marry and be together, but not like that."

"What is most important to me is that you do not for a moment think that I . . ."

"I would never believe that. Remember, I wanted this as much as you did. I could have been in her room. You wouldn't think that I . . . ?"

"Never."

"We know each other too well, and that we could never be happy with that between us."

"That is what I think. But the doubt . . ."

"There is no doubt."

"That is what I had to know."

"Then . . . whatever happens . . . that can never be between us."

• • •

I sat in the courtroom with Roderick and Charlie; and Lady Constance and Marie-Christine were on either side of me.

The first witnesses were the experts and a great many questions were asked of them. The analyst explained that there was no doubt that Mrs. Lisa Claverham had died through a massive overdose of the pills prescribed by her doctor.

Dr. Doughty himself gave evidence in detail. He explained that Mrs. Claverham had injured her spine before she came under his care. He gave details of the injury in medical terms and added that it was of a nature to give the sufferer a great deal of pain. For this reason he had provided a powerful painkiller, and had frequently stressed the point that great caution should be taken.

On the afternoon of the first he had arrived at the house to find Mrs. Claverham dead. He had surmised her death had been caused by an overdose of the pills he had prescribed.

Had Mrs. Claverham suffered from depression? he was asked. He replied that there had been times when he had found her depressed. It was when she had suffered a great deal of discomfort and pain. He had thought it natural in the circumstances.

"How was she when you last saw her?"

"She was in good spirits. I had been able to tell her that new facts had come to light about her condition, and there was hope of a partial cure."

There was a deep silence throughout the court.

"And Mrs. Claverham was naturally pleased to hear this?"

"She was delighted."

"And she gave you the impression that she was looking forward to this cure?"

"She did indeed."

At the end of Dr. Doughty's evidence, it seemed unlikely that Lisa could have died by her own hand. The question was, then: how did she die?

Several of the servants were then called to give evidence. Gertie was one of them, because it was she who had gone into Lisa's room and found her dead.

She used to look in at that time, she said, to see if there was anything Mrs. Claverham wanted.

"Did your mistress ever talk to you about herself?" she was asked.

"Oh yes, sir. She was always talking about how she ought to have been a great actress, and would have been but for her accident."

"Did you think she was unhappy?"

"Oh yes, sir."

"Why do you say this?"

"She was always talking about not being a great actress, and if she hadn't hurt her back she *would* have been as great as Désirée . . . only better . . . if she'd had a chance, sir."

"Thank you. You may step down."

Roderick was called.

Had his wife ever threatened suicide?

"Never."

Had he noticed a change in her during the last week?

Roderick said he had been away from home for the last weeks and had returned only the day before his wife's death.

How had she been on his return?

She was elated because she had heard of a possible cure.

"Can you suggest how six tablets came to be dissolved in a glass of water taken by your wife?"

"No."

"Unless someone put them there."

"Obviously someone must have put them there."

"And if your wife put them there and drank the solution, the inference must be that she intended to take her own life?"

"She may have taken a dose and forgotten, and then taken another."

"You mean she put two tablets into the water, took them, and a few moments later took two more, and another two after that?"

"When she took a dose she quickly became

drowsy. It may be that she forgot she had taken them."

That was the end of Roderick's evidence.

The butler and housekeeper were called. They had very little to add and then, to my surprise, Mabel was being questioned.

I had seen her about the house and spoken to her briefly. She was a nervous girl who could not have been more than thirteen years old. She always seemed to me to be half scared. I wondered how she could do the work required of her, and remembered that Gertie said she was simple.

What could she have to tell?

I soon discovered.

"Don't be afraid," she was told. "All you have to do is answer the questions."

"Yes, sir."

"You know that Mrs. Claverham has died?"

"Yes, sir."

"You have told your friend in the house that you know why she died. Would you tell us?"

"He murdered her!"

There was a hushed silence throughout the court.

"Would you please tell us who murdered her?"

"Mr. Roderick."

"How do you know this?"

"I know," she said.

"Did you see him murder her?"

She looked puzzled.

"You must answer the question, you know."

She shook her head.

"Is the answer no, you did not see him?"

"Yes, sir."

"Then how do you know?"

"He wanted to get rid of her."

"How did you know that?"

"I heard . . . didn't I?"

"You heard what?"

"She was shouting. She said: 'I'm not going. This is my home and I'm going to stay here. You can't get rid of me.' "

"When did you hear this?"

"When he came back."

"The day before she died?"

"Yes."

"Did you tell anyone?"

She nodded.

"Whom did you tell?"

"Gertie . . . and some of them."

"That will be all."

I felt sick with fear. It had seemed miraculous that so far nobody had mentioned that Roderick had been engaged to me and now I had returned to Leverson. I should never have come back, I told myself. But what was the use of saying that now? They would discover what had happened, and they would say Roderick had killed her.

Gertie was recalled.

"The last witness has told us she discussed the death of Mrs. Claverham with you. Is that so?"

"She said something about Mr. Claverham. I didn't take much notice of what Mabel said."

"Not when she accused one of the members of the household of murder?"

"No, sir."

"Did it not seem a serious charge to make?"

"With anyone else . . . but not with Mabel. Nothing was serious with Mabel, sir."

"Will you explain?"

"Well, she was a ha'p'orth short."

"What do you mean by that?"

Gertie looked faintly superior at such a profession of ignorance.

"She wasn't all there," she explained patiently. "She fancied this and that."

"You mean that what she said was not to be trusted?"

"Well, you wouldn't believe her, would you? She'd say the maddest things. Nobody took any notice of what she said."

"So when you were told that your master had murdered your mistress, what was your reaction?"

"I think I said: 'Oh, did he?' "

"And you left it at that?"

"Well, you went along with Mabel, didn't you? You didn't take any notice of what she said. She told us she was a lady . . . her father was some lord or other. Next day he was some king who'd been turned off his throne. None of it made sense."

"I see. So you did not believe she had heard Mrs. Claverham say those words?"

"No, sir. I knew she didn't. I'm not barmy. It was only because there was all this chat about Mrs. Claverham taking that dose . . . and she starts dreaming."

"You may go."

I sat there in trepidation. The court was tense. I glanced at Roderick. He was very pale. Lady Constance was clenching and un-clenching her hands in great agitation.

Mabel was brought back.

"Mabel. When did you hear Mrs. Claver-ham say she would not go?"

Mabel wrinkled her brows.

"Try to think. Was it the day she died . . . the day before . . . or sometime during the week?"

Mabel was clearly distressed.

"Was it one day . . . two days . . . three days . . . five days before she died?"

Mabel hesitated and stammered: "It was five days that she said . . ."

"What? Five days?"

"Yes," said Mabel. "That's it."

"She was talking to Mr. Claverham, was she?"

"Yes, he wanted to get rid of her so that . . ."

"But Mr. Claverham was in Scotland five days before she died. So she could not have been talking to him, could she?"

"She was. I heard her."

"Tell us . . . who is your father?"

A smile crossed her face. "He is a prince," she said.

"So you are a princess?"

"Oh yes, sir."

"Your name is Mabel."

"It was given to me when they took me away."

"Who took you away?"

"It was robbers. They kidnapped me."

"And you were a princess . . . from Buckingham Palace?"

There was a faint titter throughout the court. I was breathing more freely. Mabel was proving herself to be deranged.

"Yes," she said. "That's right."

"Would you be Princess Victoria . . . Marie Louise . . . Beatrice?"

"Yes, that's right."

Poor Mabel! And but for Gertie, she might have been taken seriously. Now no one could doubt that Mabel's evidence was worthless.

Lady Constance came next.

Had she noticed any suicidal tendencies in her daughter-in-law?

"When she was in acute pain, I think she might have been tempted to kill herself," said Lady Constance. "I don't think there was anything unusual about that. She suffered intense pain."

"Had she ever talked to you of taking her life?"

"Oh no. She would not talk to me of that."

"She was feeling better at the time. There was hope of a cure."

"Yes. She was feeling hopeful."

"It seems hardly likely that she would have taken her life at such a time."

"Hardly likely," agreed Lady Constance.

"But before she heard this, you think she might have been tempted to do so?"

"She might . . . with years of pain stretching out before her. Anyone might have considered it."

"But in the more hopeful circumstances, most people would be prepared to go on enduring it for a little while longer."

"I think that is so."

"You lived under the same roof. She was your daughter-in-law. You must have known her well."

"I knew her."

"Do you think she was the sort of person to take her own life?"

"Not unless . . ."

"Please go on."

"There was a mistake."

"What sort of mistake?"

"There was an occasion when I was with her. It must have been about three months ago. She was in pain and had taken two pills. She drank the water containing two dissolved pills and put the glass back on the top of the cabinet. Then she lay back. I thought I should stay with her until the pain subsided and she slept, which she usually did after taking the pills. The pain seemed to be particularly acute and the pills took a few minutes to work. She turned to the cabinet and poured out water and had dropped two pills into the glass before I realized she intended to take them. I cried out: 'You have just had two!' If I had not been there she would have taken the others and killed herself then. I think this may have been what she did on the day she died."

It was clear that Lady Constance's evidence was making a profound impression on the court.

"Did you mention this incident to anyone?"

"No. I thought it would worry my son and my husband."

"Did you think it was unsafe to leave the pills there where Mrs. Claverham could reach them so easily?"

"I did consider that, but since she needed

the pills immediately and might not be able to ring the bell for a servant to get them for her . . . and there might not be a servant in the kitchen at that time to hear the bell, I thought it better to leave things as they were."

"So you decided not to do anything about it, and the pills were left in the cabinet, and there was always a glass and jug of water ready for use?"

"I was wrong perhaps. But I understood that it was very necessary for her to take the pills immediately the pain started. I knew that if they were not available, my daughter-in-law would be thrown into a panic . . . which could, of course, bring on the pain."

"Thank you, Lady Constance."

Dr. Doughty was recalled.

"How long did it take for the pills to dissolve?" they wanted to know.

"A matter of seconds."

"How long did it take before they had an effect?"

"It could vary."

"On the pain?"

"On that and other things. The state of the patient's health at the time. The mental state . . ."

"And the effect of the pills could have produced drowsiness . . . forgetfulness?"

"Indeed it could."

"So Mrs. Claverham could possible have

taken two pills, and then another two in, say, five minutes?"

"That is possible."

"And perhaps in her agitation let fall more than two into the water?"

"That is also possible."

"Thank you, Dr. Doughty."

We waited in trepidation. Marie-Christine had taken my hand and was holding it firmly. I knew what was in our minds. What would the verdict be? Murder against some person or persons unknown? Roderick? Myself?

How much attention had been paid to Mabel's account?

She had been discredited, but what impression had her words left behind? Lady Constance's words had had a great effect, and she had spoken in such a precise, authoritative manner—in great contrast to Mabel. I had felt the mood of the court changing as she spoke. I was sickened by the thought of what might be awaiting us. I thought of all the probing questions . . . the answers which could seem damaging. I thought of the danger to Roderick . . . and us all.

I could not help remembering that day when Lisa Fennell had fallen under my mother's carriage, when she had forced her way into our lives. And now she was dead, and still threatening, from the grave.

When the relief came it was overpowering.

Lady Constance's evidence had carried great weight. Mabel's had been dismissed.

The verdict of the coroner's court was Accidental Death.

Confession

It is six years since that day in the courtroom, but it still comes back to me, and I will find myself shuddering with fear. There has been so much happiness in these last years, but it has not been completely unclouded.

Over us all at Leverson has hung the shadow of doubt. There have been times in the night when I have awakened suddenly to find myself back in the past. I will cry out. Roderick comforts me. He does not need to ask what haunts me. He will say: "It is over, my darling. It is finished. We have to forget."

How did it happen? I ask myself. How did she die? Who put those pills into the glass? Was it Lisa herself? I cannot accept that, however much I try.

I cling to Roderick. He is there . . . safe . . . beside me. I am comforted, but I cannot stop my thoughts.

I say to myself: It must have been Lisa . . . not wittingly, of course. It must have been as Lady Constance had suggested in her evidence, which had been a turning point. She had spoken with such conviction.

The verdict had been a blessing to us all, who had been under the cloud of suspicion. It was an end to the matter . . . no, not an end, as we learned. But there would be no more probing, no more awkward questions asked. It was a kind of peace, punctured by our consciences. We had wanted her to go . . . and she had.

We had come out of that courtroom intoxicated with relief. But the doubts remained, and they had been with us these six years.

One year after that verdict, Roderick and I had married. What had happened had had its effect on us all. Marie-Christine had been overjoyed, but she seemed to brood now and then, and there were secrets in her eyes. She could no longer be called a child. There was a shadow over her as with us all.

Roderick and I have a son and a daughter. Roger is four years old, Catherine nearly three. They are beautiful children, and when I watch them playing in the gardens or riding round the paddock on their ponies, I am almost content.

Then I go into the house and pass that room which had been Lisa's. There is no visible trace of her there . . . but somehow she remains.

My father visits us now and then. He is very proud of his grandchildren, and he has often told me what a happy day it was for him when I came looking for him. He gets on very well with Charlie, and I think they often talk of my mother.

I was deeply touched when he gave me the statue of the Dancing Maiden. He wanted me to have it, he told me. It was his dearest possession. I was loth to take it from him, but he insisted. "I used to feel that she was there when I looked at it," he told me. "It has been a great comfort to me. But now I have my daughter . . . and grandchildren. And it is fitting that you should have it."

It stands in my room. I can see my mother when I look at it. He has caught some likeness . . . something which is indefinably her. I fancy when I look at it that she is near, smiling, well pleased because I have come through my troubles to the husband I love . . . and my children.

Lady Constance and I are the best of friends. Her great joy is in her grandchildren. Her nature is not naturally a warm one but occasionally the deep affection she has for me overflows and is apparent; and there is no doubt of her love for the children.

When at length Leverson Manor became our home, Marie-Christine was very contented.

Her interest in archaeology became a passion. At this time she is very friendly with a young archaeologist whom she met through Fiona and Jack. I believe they may soon become engaged.

But the memory of Lisa lingers on, even with Marie-Christine. I wonder if it will always be so. Everyone in the house is aware of it. I know this through Gertie.

A little while ago I had a revealing talk with her. She said: "I was worried when silly Mabel started talking in front of all those people."

Her words sent a tremor of fear through me, but I said calmly: "She was soon proved to be unreliable."

"Well, she could have gone too far. She nearly did."

"Your evidence showed how unbalanced she was, and when she was called back she proved it."

"She must have heard the servants talking."

"Talking about . . . ?"

"Well, they all knew that you was engaged to Mr. Roderick at one time and it was broken off because you thought he was your brother. Then he got married and you found out he wasn't your brother after all, and you ought to have got married."

"How do you know all this?"

"Servants always know everything. They pick up bits here and bits there. Then they put it all together and it adds up. They like you. They was looking forward to you and Mr. Roderick getting married. They couldn't really think much of her. They'd had to put up with Lady Constance all those years, and when I told them you took the blame for that bust, they thought that was really nice. Well, Lady Constance is a great lady . . . but you can have enough of that. But that Mrs. Claverham . . . well, she wasn't enough of a lady. We wanted something in between."

"You mean . . . they knew all that, and they didn't betray it?"

"Well, they answered the questions. They weren't going to say more than they was asked for."

"Except Mabel."

"Well, she wouldn't know much. She'd picked up bits in her batty way, and she'd got it all muddled."

"Gertie," I said, "your evidence made such a difference."

"I meant it to. I didn't want trouble no more than any of them did. We didn't want anything going wrong in the house. Perhaps new people coming . . . and then what would have become of everyone? And . . . I never forgot what you did about that bust. I would have been out then . . . but for you."

I said: "And what did they really think about Mrs. Claverham's death?"

"Oh, they reckon she took it herself. It was a mistake, they think. She'd forgotten she had already had it. That's what they all thought, didn't they?"

I understood. That was how they wanted it to be. What did they really think was the truth? And did they often think about it?

The shadow of doubt lay across the whole household.

•

It was a beautiful spring day. I was sitting in the garden with Lady Constance, as I often did. The children were playing on the lawn and I noticed how her eyes followed them.

"They are beautiful children," she said. "I can see both you and Roderick in them."

"Can you? I have searched for a resemblance in vain."

"It's there. Thank you, my dear. I am so

glad you came. I often think back to that time
we spent together in our deep dark hole. Now
all these people are marvelling at the antiquity
as they cross that floor where once we sat, wondering if it was the end for us. It was a turning
point in my life, I think."

"It was the beginning of our friendship, and
I was grateful for that."

"For me it was a revelation."

Catherine came toddling up to us to show
us a daisy she had picked.

"Is that for me?" asked Lady Constance.

Catherine shook her head and held it out to
me.

"I have found one, Grandmama." That was
from Roger, who had run up to us. "This is for
you."

I was touched to see her pleasure.

I thought then how completely happy we
should be. I glanced over my shoulder at the
window of that room which had been Lisa's. I
could almost imagine I saw her there. It was
often so. It is six years since it happened, I said
to myself. Will it always be like this?

The children had run off.

"It is good that everything turned out as it
did," said Lady Constance.

"We have been happy," I replied.

"As we never could have been if . . . We
have to forget that time, Noelle. It grows far-

ther and farther from us. But I know you can't forget . . . entirely."

"Can you?"

She shook her head. "I remember at times. It comes back and there it stays. I say: Go away. You have caused enough trouble in your lifetime. I am glad . . . glad that she died, Noelle. It was best for her . . . and best for us all."

"She might have been cured."

"She would never have been completely well. I could not bear to have been without these grandchildren. There will be Claverhams here for generations to come. It is the future that is important, but I remember, and shall go on remembering."

She lay back in her chair and did not speak. For some time there was silence, and when I looked, her eyes were closed.

I thought she was sleeping, but after a while I began to grow alarmed.

I spoke to her gently. There was no answer. I laid a hand on her arm. She did not move.

I summoned help. We got her to bed and called the doctor.

•

She had had a heart attack, but she recovered after a few days. She was still very weak and Dr. Doughty said she must rest.

He talked rather seriously to us. "She'll

have to go carefully," he said. "She's doing too much. Make her rest. I know it is not easy to make Lady Constance do anything she doesn't want to, but I think it is necessary, and you will have to be firm."

"Do you think she is going to get well?"

"The heart is a vital organ, you know. She had a big shock at the time of the first Mrs. Claverham's death. I know she appeared to weather the storm, but I noticed it had an effect on her. Make sure she goes very slowly, and let me know at once if there is any sign of trouble."

She had certainly grown frail. She stayed in her room a great deal. I used to take the children to see her each afternoon. That was the highlight of her day.

It was evening. The children had come to say good night to her before their nurse took them off to bed.

She said: "Stay with me, Noelle."

She was lying back in her pillows. The children had exhausted her, though she would not admit it. She looked vulnerable . . . a word I should not have thought to apply to her.

"I want to talk to you," she said. "I want Roderick, too. I want to talk to you both."

"He should be home very soon," I told her.

She smiled and nodded.

I was waiting for Roderick when he came home. We embraced and clung together, as we always do, even after a brief parting. We have not ceased to be grateful for being together. The uncertainty of the past still lingers.

I said: "Something must have happened. Your mother is very anxious to talk to us."

"Is she worse?" he asked in alarm.

"She's different. I think we ought to go to her at once."

Her face lit up as we entered. I sat on one side of the bed, Roderick on the other.

She said: "I want to talk to you both. I have a feeling that there is not much time left and there is something I wish to say."

"Don't tire yourself, Mother," said Roderick.

She smiled at him with faint exasperation. "I am always tired now, Roderick. Now you two are married and are very happy. I knew it was the right thing. I knew it had to be. It is quite a long time now since that happened . . . but everything is not as it should be . . . not quite, is it? Sometimes it is as though she is actually here. I can't forget her. Nor can you. She would never have gone. She was determined to stay. She was a schemer by nature. She was going to ruin life for you . . . for me . . . for everyone . . . as long as she had what she wanted."

I said: "She had a hard time. She had to fight her way. The stage was her life."

" 'All the world's a stage,' " quoted Lady

Constance dreamily, " 'And all the men and women merely players: They have their exits and their entrances; And one man in his time plays many parts.' Ah, we have all played our parts. I have. I wanted the best for you, my son. You were of the greatest importance to me. It was never easy for me to show the depth of my feelings. I could not bring myself to it, although at times I tried. I think I have been a little better since Noelle and I faced death in that dark hole. When I knew that everything was not right between your father and myself, you became everything . . . I would have died for you. I wanted you to make the right marriage. I wanted to see your children growing up. I have been given that blessing and I have you, my dear Noelle, as my daughter. So . . . there is nothing else I could wish for, you might think. All my dreams have come true. But that woman haunts me. Roderick, I said I would have died for you. I would have killed for you."

There was a brief silence. I could see that Roderick was horrified.

She went on: "Yes, I killed her. I went to her on that day. I talked to her. I begged her to let Roderick go. I tried to reason with her. She told me she would never, never release him. She was going to stay here. She shouted. Perhaps that was what the servant girl heard and thought it was you, Roderick, at whom she was shouting. She knew I hated her. Well, she said she hated me, too. Then suddenly, in her anger, she moved sharply. I saw her face distorted with pain. I could see that she was in acute agony. 'Give me . . . my pills,' she gasped. Something within me said: Now is the moment. It's the opportunity. You can change every-thing. There might never be another chance. I poured the water into the glass. I took out the bottle of pills. I tipped them into the water . . . five . . . six . . . it might have been seven. They took a little time to dissolve. She was moaning. I gave them to her . . . and she drank. Then I took the glass and put it back on the top of the cabinet. I watched her for a few seconds. She lay back gasping. I could see she was growing a little quieter. I left her. Then . . . Gertie went in and found her dead."

I could see that Roderick was as shocked as I was.

We were both speechless while Lady Con-stance stared ahead, her eyes fixed in space. I knew she was living it all again.

She gripped our hands.

"I've told you. It is as though a great weight has been lifted from my mind."

"You did it for us," said Roderick.

"And for myself. Oh, how happy these last years could have been if I had not had to kill to reach them."

She lay back in her pillows. The emotion

and effort of talking had exhausted her and she was breathing with difficulty.

"It is all over now," said Roderick. "Nothing can change it. Try to rest." He turned to me. "I think we had better call Dr. Doughty."

"No," she said. "I feel better . . . relieved. I haven't told you everything yet. I have written to the coroner's court. I didn't know if that is the right people to tell, but it will no doubt suffice. It will go to the right hands. It is a long time since it happened. Do you think they will remember? You see, it's here in this house. I have to rid the house of it . . . suspicion . . . uncertainty . . . doubt. There may be some who suspect you, Roderick . . . and you, Noelle. That has worried me a lot. When we left that courtroom I was exultant. I did not think beyond that at the time. We were free. It was over. I had triumphed. And I did . . . to a certain extent. But it was not as simple as I had thought it would be. And then, when I had that attack, I thought I could go at any minute. I knew I had to tell, otherwise the secret would go with me to the grave, and for the rest of your lives this doubt would hang over you. It has to be told. You know the truth. And so must others. It is not good enough to tell just you. In a way I am not sorry for what I did. There was something evil about her. She would never have gone. I could see that in her face. She cared only for her own advantage. I had to do it. Sometimes I say to myself: I have committed murder, but good came out of it."

•

She died three days later. We were very sad. She had been so much a part of our lives.

Roderick said: "We must put the past behind us. We must forget."

"Yes," I answered. "Perhaps we shall, in time."

It was true that Lisa had had an evil effect on our lives. She had been responsible for my mother's death, yet I could not help finding excuses for her. I suppose there are excuses for us all. But she is dead now, and we must obey the command of Lady Constance. We have come to happiness and we must forget by what dark road we had to travel to reach it.